A
SECOND
CHANCE
FOR
YESTERDAY

A

SECOND

CHANCE

FOR

YESTERDAY

R.A. SINN

A
SECOND
CHANCE
FOR
YESTERDAY

R.A. SINN

SOLARIS

First published 2023 by Solaris
an imprint of Rebellion Publishing Ltd,
Riverside House, Osney Mead,
Oxford, OX2 0ES, UK

www.solarisbooks.com

ISBN: 978-1-78618-827-4

10 9 8 7 6 5 4 3 2 1

A CIP catalogue record for this book is available from the
British Library.

Designed & typeset by Rebellion Publishing

Printed in the UK

For our families: we're grateful to be in the same timeline as you.

Table of Contents

QT.19.51.22.22.09.2045

HEAVEN DIDN'T EXIST. Nev Bourne knew better. When she was sixteen years, four months, and three days old, her faith had shattered, like stained glass in a church bombing. Since then, she'd only believed in what she could see and feel. Tonight, on Earth, in San Francisco, on a lovely Friday evening in the late summer of 2045, she was feeling absolutely fucking divine sitting alone in her self-adjusting Memeron chair watching the steam swirl up from her espresso. There was no place Nev would rather be than the Qbito office, after everyone else had vacated the premises, leaving only the faint hum of Tenderloin traffic to remind her of the world below. She could have spent eternity in this very moment: the final sprint before she completed the code for an update that promised to bring the real world a big step closer to paradise.

It was a bit late for caffeine, even by Nev's standards, but sleep wasn't on the agenda tonight. Maybe, if she finished the code in time, she'd grab a power nap on one of the irregularly shaped floor squiggles that the human resource engineers referred to as 'social settees.' She wanted to be in the office at daybreak to begin the weekend of diagnostics before Monday's public rollout. The previous October, Noel Kusuma, Qbito's founder (and according to his business cards, 'Chief TimeLord'), had scheduled the SavePoint 2.0 alpha to be released on the Monday morning after the autumnal equinox, for reasons that neither Nev nor anyone else at Qbito were privy to. But if Noel commanded, his will would be done.

Nev was so close she could taste it—the metallic tang of that final keystroke, the magnetic pull of logic snapping into place, the final lines of code stretching out before her like a book that had already been written. At this point, her brain had already finished, and all that was left was to follow along with her fingers. Her hands flew at lightning speed along her holo-keyboard, eyes tracking the characters hovering in space before her, as she smoothed the wrinkles and the ripples in the code, making it fresh and crisp as a hotel bedsheet. When she got into the groove like this, Nev could spend hours without looking away, locked in perfect symbiosis with the machine, to the point where she could barely tell where she ended and it began.

A buzz behind her ear snapped Nev from her reverie. Jared's avatar—a cheesy 3D selfie in a vintage trucker hat—blinked in the periphery of her viz. Thanks to Qbito's IT department, Nev had the latest EyeVee Pro model, an over-the-ear stereoscopic universal controller with retinal projection, movement tracking, and 12G connection speeds. It was great for manipulating hundreds of lines of code, but not so great when Jared's goofy grin crowded them out in annoyingly high resolution. She blinked and shook her head quickly to clear the pop-up, but before it disappeared completely from her field of vision, the icon was replaced by his brief, unsubtle message:

U up? Coz I am. 👋

Jared was like a snack, good for the occasional late-night indulgence, but lacking nutrition and not worth the extra weight from over-consumption. She tried to limit their encounters to once a week. If the diagnostics went well the next day, maybe she'd ping him afterwards as a treat.

Can't tonight. Nose to the grindstone.

As soon as the message vanished into the ether, Nev set her viz to Do Not Disturb before Jared could respond with a picture of the real deal. *And lead us not into temptation.* The words echoed through her head in her mother's strident voice. That was a visitation she could really do without. If only it was as easy to tune out memories as it was to turn off her messaging app. *Be gone, Satan!* Nev took a deep breath and returned to the task at hand, settling back into the groove, gearing up for the final sprint.

SavePoint 1.0 had been revolutionary. Not in the way that tech companies usually mean it—which is to say incrementally more interesting, useful, and/or lucrative than whatever previous wondertech the product obsolesced—but actual, honest-to-goodness revolutionary. First on the battlefield, then in hospitals and construction zones, and finally in the mass market for the past two years, SavePoint had transformed the way people worked, loved, lived. It was almost shocking how something that had at first seemed like a device from a futuristic game was so quickly absorbed into the ebb and flow of social life and popular culture, as though humanity had been waiting for it all along, had a special place set aside for it in the hollows of their collective eye sockets.

SavePoint's premise was simple; its applications were infinite. A dorsolateral prefrontal cortex implant installed via the orbital cavity behind the right eye constantly tracked your vitals and coordinates in spacetime and transmitted the information back to the cloud. SavePoint was designed to serve as preventative insurance. In case of disaster, simply execute a pre-programmed, custom-designated 'undo' gesture, and the quantum mainframe would restore you to your coordinates five seconds in the past.

The mechanism was based on Rovelli's principle: loop quantum gravity predicted that elementary temporal leaps were small, but finite. Or something to that effect; no matter how often Kusuma explained it, Nev could never quite wrap her head around it. Anissa had tried her best to translate the theoretical physics, but Nev's mind remained stubbornly grounded in pragmatics, which was all she needed for her part of the code. Noel was the Silicon Valley wunderkind who'd made his fortune (and his ridiculous title) for being the first to figure out how to translate Rovelli's theory into a functional product. Nev was just there to wrangle the data.

SavePoint was already raking in profits beyond what any of its earliest angel investors had projected in their rosiest scenarios. From Kusuma's standpoint, SavePoint 1.0 was simply the tip of the proverbial iceberg, and the profits were, well, icing on the cake. The real point of the technology wasn't the benefits reaped by its users, but from them: data, loads of it, about every mistake, made at every point in time and every place on Earth, by millions of paying customers. Those data, fed back into SavePoint's system, could accomplish a lot more than simply change a life or two. They could, Kusuma believed, change Life as we know it.

It was Qbito's Chief Marketing Officer, Madison Barnett, who had realized that SavePoint's predictive potential could also exponentialize the company's profits. Despite the cost—and the cost was steep—customers weren't using SavePoint merely for insurance against devastating accidents. As the Qbito team had known even before the first beta testers had their units extracted, customers were actively *planning* disasters and then using SavePoint to undo the consequences. Since launch, the mechanism had found a boom market on the recovery circuit. SavePoint allowed users, in every sense of the word, to scratch their itches and keep to the straight and narrow, all at the same time. To have their cake and icing, too. Take a drink. Hit undo. Punch out your boss. Hit undo. Make a pass at a random stranger. Hit undo. The casinos ran interference to block the mechanism at the tables and slots, but that didn't stop people with the gambling bug from making side bets at GA meetings on the shirt color of the next loser to walk through the door. There had been rumors on the dark web of far nastier uses. Sex play taken too far, then taken back. Tracheae uncrushed.

Nev didn't judge. After the first month or two, she barely batted an eyelash. She collected the data, crunched the numbers, assessed the deviation between design and usage, and hammered away at the alpha code for SavePoint 2.0, developing algorithms that would suggest to users when they should hit the button. The holy grail, of course, was self-undo, a fully automated global network that would give every SavePoint user—and, by extension, the billions of people around them—the best possible day, every day, all their lives. It would do for human perversion, sin, and plain stupidity what self-driving cars had done for traffic on the perennially congested Bay Bridge.

Along the way, the massive tranches of data Nev collected were already giving Kusuma his best day, every day. Maddy, poached from a job running an online retail giant's home surveillance devices division, had surpassed Qbito's already hefty installation and service revenues by slicing, dicing, and productizing every piece of information users provided unwittingly about their darkest secrets, their deepest desires, their most tragic mistakes. Pharmaceutical companies, financial services, and insurance behemoths all leapt at the data, bidding it up to stratospheric values. With the SavePoint 2.0 launch, both the volume and the value of the data would explode again, leaving the stratosphere behind for the cosmos.

Maddy acted like she could will this vision into existence through sheer brute force. Every couple of hours, her professional headshot avatar would show up, hovering at the edge of Nev's viz, asking question after question about the team's progress on the code, the timeline for completion, the possibilities for new, increasingly specific data insights. She was definitely involved in one of those executive sorority cults, where the women chanted self-actualization mantras while reporting their weekly calorie counts. Nev had been approached several times over the years, but having escaped one sect, she had no plans to ever join another. She preferred to be alone, which might explain the involuntary shudder that passed through her when Nev realized that Maddy was hovering again, this time in the flesh, the harsh track lighting reflecting fractals off her long shiny brown hair.

"Can I help you?" Nev asked, pushing her own springy, brown curls away from her aching eyes. Maddy smiled tightly, her eyes narrowing.

"Just checking in... to see if you need any help finishing up."

Not a chance, Nev thought. Maddy might know coding better than half the new recruits in Qbito's cubicles, but early in her career she'd made the strategic decision to exploit her many talents in the service of marketing rather than product development. Why buck the patriarchy, when you could manipulate it for fun and profit? Maddy had long ago turned a deaf ear to the siren song of source code, and Nev had no interest in letting Qbito's chief marketeer mar her elegant creation with graceless patchwork. Besides, she was nearly at the finish line, all by herself.

She forced herself to smile back, her facial muscles straining slightly at the unusual request.

"Nope, thanks. I'm good. I'll be done in..." she looked up and to the left at the timestamp on her viz; about twenty past. "...maybe fifteen minutes, max." Maddy looked skeptical. "Seriously, Mad, I'm almost there. I just need... Would you please?" Maddy nodded curtly and turned away.

"Ping me the second you're done," she said over her shoulder. "Noel's breathing down my neck." The door clicked shut behind her.

I'll bet he is, Nev thought to herself. *That's an image I didn't need in my head.*

Where was she? Oh, yes. Just a few finishing touches. Nev scanned her viz for code smells. Everything looked tight. No duplication. No dead code. No indecent exposure (unless you counted the trash folder of dick pics that Nev's brogrammer underlings dropped in her viz throughout the day—reason number thirty-one she liked the office best when she had it to herself). The code smelled as fresh as a wheat field after the rain. Nev sighed, drawing the recycled office air deep into her lungs. It didn't taste quite so sweet.

The night sky through the windows was bright from the city lights. Even the double-paned glass couldn't entirely keep out the racket from the encampments. Each year, the number of ceegees—or "climate refugees," as MetaNews called them—living along Market Street seemed to double. Like a Moore's Law for abject misery. Wave after wave came to the city from each newly dehabbed point on the world map. Jakarta. Oklahoma City. Miami. San Salvador. San Francisco had opened its gates, declaring itself a sanctuary city to the world's climate refugees, but of course there wasn't enough space or money to house them, especially with the city locked in battle with the Feds following the 2040 census hack, and every self-respecting startup shielding its taxable revenues in a double Irish crypto sandwich.

Nev supposed living in the camps was better than drowning, but living near them got to be exhausting. When the profits from SavePoint 2.0 started rolling in, just in time for her options to vest, she'd have enough capital to buy a penthouse in one of the eco-towers built at the peak of Mount Sutro, after the 2040 wildfire ripped through the eucalyptus grove. Fifteen minutes from the office, at least until the Bay finally rose up and swamped the Tenderloin too, forcing Qbito to new digs. Whatever future the climate wrought, her Qbito paycheck guaranteed that Nev would have the resources to adapt and survive. She'd learned self-reliance the hard way. Maybe the only way.

This one's for you, Faith, Nev thought, as her fingers tapped out <<run>>.

Series complete. LoopID?QT.43.33.23.22.09.2045

QT.00.30.07.22.09.2045

DIGITAL BIRDSONG GENTLY eased Nev to consciousness, the cheerful chirping soon followed by the sound of boiling water and the scent of coffee emanating from the auto-Chemex station in the small apartment's galley kitchen. *Need coffee,* Nev thought. Her brain was pounding like she had the world's most wicked hangover, and for some reason she was wearing a do-me outfit—slinky top, miniskirt, and... no underwear?

It took longer than she would have liked to collect herself, but she still made it out the door before eight, anxious to return to the office and prep her team for the launch. The previous night was a blur. She'd been on the verge of finishing when Maddy had shown up and ganked her flow. Then... what? Didn't she finish the alpha? For some reason, the harder she tried to picture what came next, the blurrier her memories got. She couldn't remember why she'd decided to head home after all, or how she'd gotten home, or when she'd gone back out again in her decidedly non-work-friendly outfit. Sheer exhaustion must have disrupted her brain's ability to convert short term memories into long term memories. Overwork had pulled a *Memento* on her. Anissa had warned her she was getting too old to pull all-nighters at the office. After all, she'd be turning thirty in a few months. Lately, without Anissa in the office to cajole her out to drinks, Nev's schedule had gone from bad to worse. As soon as the launch was over, she needed to download one of those apps that would send wellness notifications if it detected her working on code sprints for more than twelve hours. Or maybe she should get into kombucha, or ginkgo or something. Her current habits couldn't go on. She had to take better care of herself in the future.

Market Street was still asleep this early in the day. A few city workers carrying pressure-wash tanks strapped to their backs were making half-hearted attempts to spray between the tents and sweep away the previous day's detritus. The city was perpetually on alert against the possibility of another epidemic. Conflicts between Displaced Persons and Public Health made up the meat and potatoes of city reporting. Everyone knew that the DPH was conspiring with the Feds on plans to empty out the camps, and the DDP couldn't do a damned thing about it. The mayor, a photogenic former celebrity chef elected on a Fisc-Con-Soc-Lib platform, fed rhetorical *amuse-bouches* to each side while flying around the world attending ClimateCons with other attractive local leaders, leaving the two agencies behind to figure it out—or, more often, duke it out. Nev had little time for politics and no strong opinions about whether the camps should stay or go, but she did like Jim Bone, the ceegee who had staked a claim to Qbito's front doorstep.

Judging from his lank, graying hair, crow's feet, and hollowing cheeks in what seemed to be a once handsome face, Nev estimated Jim Bone to be somewhere around fifty. It was hard to tell the color of his eyes, they were sunk so far into the sockets. No room for a SavePoint implant back there, Nev thought each time she saw him. Not a potential customer. Maybe that's why she liked him: he didn't need anything from her.

Every time Nev walked through Qbito's front door, Jim Bone was having a conversation with himself. That's how she'd learned his name. "Where'd you put it, Jim Bone? You need to remember, Jim Bone." Sometimes he seemed to lose track of his thoughts mid-sentence, abruptly shifting not only his tone and subject, but even changing his body language so quickly she worried he'd get whiplash. "Head up the hill. That's where she told me to—watch out, Jim Bone. Watch yourself, I said." At least that was a sentiment Nev could endorse whole-heartedly. You had to watch yourself. No one else was going to.

She never saw Jim Bone with anyone. He seemed to have no friends or family in the camps, nobody in town to look after him either. Not even a DDP caseworker, as far as she could tell. Somewhere in the miles of nylon tenting he must have had his own spare lean-to, his sleeping roll, and a few changes of socks, but at almost every hour, day or night, he could be found on Qbito's doorstep, wool hat pulled low on his forehead, deep in dialogue with himself.

Usually, if she was feeling up to it, Nev would nod to Jim Bone on her way in and throw him some loose change, or even croak a terse "good morning"—as though he ever had anything but horrible mornings. And usually, his rheumy eyes would pass over her, hovering for the briefest of milliseconds to acknowledge her greeting, without interrupting his soliloquy. But today, for some reason, as she walked up to the sliding glass doors that opened into the Qbito building's cool, quiet atrium, he spoke. She could see it coming, and had to fight the impulse to turn and run. His eyes focused on her face with an intensity she hadn't thought possible, and his forehead wrinkled into a dozen sine waves as he raised his steel wool eyebrows and took off his cap, running a callused hand through his greasy hair.

"I did what you said. I did it." His voice sounded like it hadn't been used for years. Like a threadbare tractor tire backing up over gravel. "Tell the lady, Jim Bone. I took care of it. I remembered."

"What's that?" Nev didn't want to engage, but she couldn't stop herself.

"I did it." He nodded his head, eyes fixed on hers.

"Um… okay. Thank you?" Nev said. He looked expectant, so

she fished a fiver from her pocket—far more than the handful of coins she sometimes dropped in his cracked palms—and almost threw it at the open cap, which he still held over his heart. He caught it deftly and secreted the cash away somewhere behind him.

A sudden impulse struck her. "Did you see me ... uh, last night? Did I..." She didn't even know what she was asking, really.

Jim Bone pinched his nose and sucked his yellow teeth, replaced his cap, and sat down on the stairs. His eyes trailed away from her, scanning the tops of the tents across the street. Maybe checking to make sure his was still standing.

"Okay. Thanks," she said, not really knowing what else to say. *Why did you do that, Nev? Never engage. Did I touch him?* She blinked at the scanner, passed through the glass doors, took a squirt of anti-bac from the dispenser, and entered the waiting elevator, feeling off-kilter and guilty. As she ascended, her mother's unbidden voice echoed through her mind. *For shame, Nevaeh. There but for the grace of God...*

"Oh, shut the fuck up," Nev said aloud, shaking her head. First thing when she got upstairs, she'd down a hit of espresso. Second thing, she'd check the previous night's logs and see how far she'd gotten before she went home.

A cascade of notifications flooded her viz as she crossed the electronic threshold to the programming pit. Qbito kept a lockdown on out-of-office communications about its technology. The company's human resource engineers claimed this measure was to protect the employees' health and wellness, but everyone knew that Kusuma only cared about protecting SavePoint. Out of office, it was too easy for viz pirates to storm the firewalls and loot every last bit of data, often without leaving a trace. The 2040 elections had been evidence of how one hacked viz could make all the difference in the world. But there wasn't any need for high-tech hijinks, anyway, when old-fashioned corporate espionage worked just as well. A big enough bounty could tempt any employee to hand over the SavePoint source code lock, stock, and barrel. Qbito's employee procedures were microdesigned to guarantee that never happened. No one worked on every aspect of the code. Everything was broken down into discrete units. Communications were auto-surveilled. Personality-profiling AIs sifted through even the most banal messages, looking for evidence of increased negative sentiment, or a propensity for untruth.

It wasn't so bad to have Maddy blocked during off hours, but it sucked to get a dump of notifications from her first thing in the work day. Nev counted over twenty pop-ups from Maddy flash by in fifteen seconds, mixed with the usual mishmash of queries from programmers on her team, alerts from the dozens of in-house apps that she had installed on her viz (including a couple she didn't even recognize), and daily communiqués from Qbito's strategy, public relations, business development, legal, and human resource teams about upcoming deadlines, events, and rollouts. Scrolling through them with a wave of her finger, Nev was struck by the unrelenting sameness of the messages, day after day. "Revised Q4 Targets." "Wellness Training: Know Your Biome." "S3cr3t L0tt3ry H4cks 4U." Even the spam was predictable at this point. On the bright side, she'd be able to breeze through them just as quickly as the day before and get to her real work within minutes. But first, caffeine.

A young man was standing at the commercial-grade La Pavoni espresso machine when Nev stepped into the break pod. She scanned her memory bank for his name. Adrian? Darius? He looked over his shoulder, alert to the feeling of eyes on the back of his head. For a second, Nev felt a feint in his glance, almost like he was expecting her to attack. She had the eerie feeling she sometimes got when people around her had triggered their SavePoints. A millisecond of disorientation. She stumbled back a step.

"Darian," Nev said, his name coming to her lips before her mind had time to catch up. "How's it going so far?"

"Great," Darian said, the fight evaporating so completely

from his eyes that she wondered if it had ever been there at all. "Learning so much. I'm grateful to be part of the SavePoint team." He ended his sentence with a brief toss of the chin, which reminded Nev that his resumé had listed experience as a college cheerleader before injuries forced him off the mat and into the computer lab.

Darian was the brand-new hire on the temporal resolution team, brought in to take Anissa's place at the helm after she'd been escorted from the premises by two burly security guards a few months back. Everyone else was already acting like she'd never existed, but Nev still remembered watching mutely as her closest friend and confidant struggled to retain her laptop and her dignity while being given the bum's rush. Long after the elevator doors had closed on Anissa's livid face, Nev had still been able to hear her beautiful, resonant voice trying to warn them all: "check the code, motherfuckers! You're making a mistake!"

Nev couldn't shake the feeling that she'd made a big mistake by not speaking out. Anissa's only crime was caring enough about the integrity of the product to alert management to a potential fatal flaw. It was minuscule compared to Nev's crime of betrayal—choosing job security over friendship as she watched Maddy tear Anissa to pieces in front of her own team.

At the time, it had felt like the lesser of two evils: If Nev had stood up for Anissa, it wouldn't have accomplished anything except maybe getting them both on Basix, California's latest cashstrapped effort to keep the poorest seventy percent of its residents fed, clothed, and housed. By keeping out of the fray, Nev could stay safely employed at Qbito, and maybe wedge the door open for Anissa's return when things blew over. Another item on her post-launch to-do list.

Nev could just imagine how Anissa would feel now, knowing that a twenty-four-year-old, barely out of school, had stepped into her role. The human resource engineers probably thought they had done well, finding another black programmer for Anissa's slot, but Nev doubted that Anissa would have seen her replacement in that light. It was probably for the best that since her severance, Anissa hadn't spoken to Nev, and wasn't up on office gossip.

Darian lingered while Nev took her turn at the La Pavoni, probably looking to ingratiate himself with one of the company's team leaders.

"How are you doing?" he asked. "Getting close on the SP2 Alpha?"

Nev felt a nauseous wave of defensiveness. Hadn't she closed the final bracket on the alpha the night before? Why was a junior programmer making demands of her? She already had Maddy shadowing her every movement. But when she looked up from tamping her espresso grounds and saw the encouraging expression on Darian's face, she realized he was just trying to cheer her on. Lessons from the mat. HR would have liked that.

"It's all good, Darian. Thanks for asking," she said, and turned back to the machine. Conversation closed. She heard him leave the room behind her. God, she hoped it was all good. No more procrastinating: time to hit the Memeron, check the logs, and find out once and for all where she had left off.

Nev topped her espresso with a dash of cashew milk and strode purposefully to the data team pod. Hazel eyes on the horizon, sharp chin jutting forward, mess of brown curls obscuring her perma-tanned, heart-shaped face from view. When Nev wore that expression—what her father used to call her 'Joan of Arc face'—no one dared talk to her. All her life, Nev had endured people scanning her, trying to categorize her, wanting to know who she was, what she was, where she was 'from.' She had used up her lifetime supply of polite answers before she hit the double digits. Since then, she had perfected the art of withering deflection. It took a person with a rare combination of boundless egotism and total obliviousness to get past Nev's defenses, which probably accounted for Jared's (limited) role in her life. The best she could say was that he came in handy, when she had that itch to scratch.

There was a barely audible whirr of tiny gears making infinitesimal micro-adjustments as Nev sat down. All bullshit, of course: trademarked audio samples like the recorded engine snarls that poured out the vestigial tailpipes of the battery-powered Lambos and Bugattis that the city's tech billionaires drove through the Presidio. But gratifying, nonetheless. Something about it just sounded so... expensive.

She was lowering her fingers to the holo-keyboard, viz 'desktop' materializing before her eyes, when something out of place caught her attention. Something real, and physical, on her *physical* desktop. Waving away the stack of folders floating in her field of vision, Nev looked more closely; there, at the edge of her workspace, was a smooth, flat, round, grey pebble, glinting slightly in the reflection of the overhead LEDs. It was an ordinary rock—nothing strange about it, other than the fact that it didn't belong there. And yet... the stone pulled at her, like a magnet tugging at the iron-rich blood pumping through her heart. She picked it up, and a sharp pang ricocheted through her nervous system, like the echo of a forgotten injury. *What fresh hell is this?* Her first impulse was to toss the stone into the trash, but her fingers wouldn't let go. Instead, she slipped it into her pocket, and brought her viz back online.

Before Nev could get back into the flow, Maddy's avatar popped up, again, its photo background bright red to signal urgency. Nev opened up the message.

ETA on SP2? Promised diagnostic run tomorrow AM. Don't make me a liar.

Tomorrow? Yesterday, Maddy had said she promised the diagnostic for today. That's why Nev had stayed in the office almost until midnight, ironing out the final wrinkles. It wasn't like Maddy to let a deadline slide. She ran according to her own internal clock, which never seemed to flag, and she demanded that everybody else keep pace.

Nev quickly scrolled through the rest of Maddy's morning messages. Half of them were demands for updates. The other half were reminders to Nev about specific data query functions that Maddy insisted should be part of the alpha code. *Did that, did that, did that,* Nev thought, mentally ticking off the work she had already done to satisfy Maddy's demands. They'd been over all this ground the day before. Something weird was going on. Maddy's memory was as shot as hers. Looked like someone else needed to download a self-care app *stat.*

Nev scrolled through the rest of her morning message dump. Everything was eerily familiar. Was there some glitch in the internal message system that was dredging up archived communications? The security team was always patching the IMS to address the most recent attempted hacks. Qbito's antagonists worked just as hard, if not harder, to steal, disrupt, and dismantle the code, as the company's programmers did to construct it. Maybe something had gone wrong with a patch.

Time to check the logs and get to the bottom of the situation. Nev entered the SP2 passkey and her unique ID phrase. So many chokepoints; it reminded Nev of an old TV show she'd seen once in her Stanford days, a comedy where a Cold War spy had to walk through about a dozen differently-shaped heavy iron doors to get to his job. But security was tight for a reason, and so far, the cybersec had held. Each unit of the program had its own passkey, and every programmer had her own ID phrase and biometric profile for building entry, which were refreshed on a weekly basis. Only Kusuma had all the keys to the kingdom.

Nev's logs appeared on her viz. The most recent entry was dated QT.17.22.13.21.09.2045. Lunchtime, the day before yesterday. *Fuck. Fuck, fuck, fuck.* Had the last day and a half of work been wiped out? The only thing worse than trying to meet a deadline was having to rewrite lost code after you'd already gone overtime. Nev's earlier bout of nausea returned with a vertiginous lurch. This was impossible. Even if Qbito's code library was affected by the same glitch that was duping messages, it couldn't have deleted that much; the whole system backed itself up every five minutes or so. *No, no, no. This can't be happening.*

She looked up from her viz, eyes roaming the office to see if anyone else was panicking. The office was definitely buzzing, which was unusual for a Saturday morning, but it was an excited, anticipatory buzz—the normal pre-launch jitters. Same vibe as yesterday. Was it possible that someone had hacked Nev alone? It wasn't like she was storing the SP2 code in some local folder on her personal hard drive, so why would they?

She was about to ping the cybersec team, when she thought better of it. If she called their attention, they'd lock her out of the system straight away. She'd be placed in thirty-day quarantine, and pegged immediately as corporate espionage suspect number one. The SavePoint 2.0 alpha would get finished without her, and she'd have to watch as other, lesser coders took the glory, and, more importantly, got to use the platform, while she stood by on the sidelines.

Thankfully, Maddy had already given her the perfect out: apparently the diagnostics had been pushed back a day, and that was exactly how much time Nev needed to make up the previous day-and-a-half's lost work. She could picture most of what she'd already coded in her mind's eye: perfect little cubes of logic, snapping into place with the force of inevitability. It would actually be easier this time, less buggy, more elegant. She might even finish earlier tonight. Celebrate at a bar with a glass of something top shelf. Or just buy a bottle and bring it home, more likely.

Nev settled deeper into the Memeron, deeper into the groove. Hours flew by as the code reconstructed itself. Lighting changed, the room got louder and then quieter. Aside from the occasional bathroom-coffee-snack circuit, she stayed locked on target, seeing the final bracket drawing ever nearer, every nerve fiber focused on completing this one task. Pings from Maddy went unanswered. Queries from junior coders went unacknowledged.

Come on, Nev, you've got this. She'd done it before, and what could be easier than retracing your own steps? She was just on the home stretch, shoulders aching, eyes stinging, when Jared's icon wiggled into her line of sight.

Hey Nev, sorry I haven't messaged in a couple days. I've needed some time to figure things out. Can we talk?

God, he's getting needy. By her count, he'd last messaged a day ago. Nev shook her head, cleared the alert, and was about to set her viz to Do Not Disturb when another message popped up.

BC I really care about U and I don't know what went wrong. Please don't ignore me.

This was too much. She hadn't pegged Jared for the type to manufacture an imaginary crisis as a plea for attention. He was too confident for that, which was what had attracted her in the first place, when they met at last year's Miller Gahan Lee annual Patriot Day picnic. The law firm routinely invited upper management from its bigger clients, like Qbito. Nev would've skipped it, but Anissa was on the prowl, so she had agreed to be wing-woman. Nev was standing by the buffet spread, strategizing her order of operations, when Jared had bee-lined towards her.

"Can we get some drinks at Table 12? Two Seagram-and-767s and a Pentagon Punch, light on the ice."

"You can get whatever you want, but if I were you I'd be embarrassed to ask for those drinks by name."

Nev was impressed by the speed with which Jared had clocked his mistake and shifted gears, voice dropping from braying demand to interested purr.

"So what would you recommend, then," he asked, "and can I get you something too?"

A man that sure of himself might be up for the kind of no-strings arrangement that Nev preferred. She'd agreed to a drink.

Then she'd agreed to a date. A year later they were still seeing each other, when it was convenient for Nev. Sure, she suspected that in his heart of hearts Jared might have preferred their status to be something more than it was. He might want to be... she cringed even thinking the word... her boyfriend. *But for Chrissakes,* Nev thought, *I don't have time for high school drama club.* She needed to crush his hopes in the cradle with a curt reply.

Sorry busy TTYL

Next thing she knew, he was calling. In spite of herself, she answered. Thankfully, everyone else had gone home, and she was alone in the room.

"Jared, sorry I can't talk, but I have a deadline, and—"

"So that's how you're going to play it? You storm out, you don't talk to me for days, and now you're going to just pretend like nothing happened?"

"Jared," Nev took a deep breath, and let it out as slowly as she could. "I don't know what the fuck you're talking about. And this is really, really not a good time. I mean, we just..." she did some mental math. "We just had a date, like, Sunday night or something. You cooked eggplant. It was nice. Okay? Look, tell you what..."

"No, Nev, I'll tell *you* what. I'm sick of this hot-and-cold routine. I want... no, I need some stability, some intimacy in my life. I deserve to be with someone who appreciates me. And I thought you might be the lucky one. I really did. But if this is how things are—"

With a jolt, Nev realized that Maddy had apparated next to her again—in the flesh—and was looming just beyond the border of her viz. Nev held up a finger—*wait a sec*—and refocused her eyes on Jared's face, hovering in her viz.

"—going to have to take a long, hard look at—"

"Jared, I really don't know what you're so upset about. I have to call you later. I'm sorry, but, like I said, I have a deadline, and I have to take this meeting, so... bye!" Nev hung up, put a temporary block on Jared, and turned to Maddy.

The quick movement of her neck messed with her vision: Two Maddys, kaleidoscoped, not quite in synch. For a moment, she thought she might even faint. *No, Nev, not in front of Maddy,* she thought. *Show no weakness, look what happened to Anissa.* Then everything resolved itself. The world was whole again.

"Can I help you?" Nev asked in a bland tone.

"Time's up, Nev. Whatever you're doing, finish it, or give me your code and I'll finish it for you."

Damn, Nev thought. That was abrupt, even by Maddy's standards. Oh well, if Maddy was going to get all baller about it, Nev wouldn't hold back either.

"Maddy, we had this conversation yesterday. I told you, I don't need you smelling up my code. I'm almost there. I'll have it done in..." Nev looked up and to the left at the timestamp on her viz. About twenty past eleven. Something caught her eye. That couldn't be right. The dizzy feeling returned, this time centered in the pit of her stomach.

Maddy's mouth was still moving. Nev tuned back into her words.

"... what you are talking about, I just hope you're not trying to come up with some excuse for coming in late with the deliverable. I hear that Delhi's on the brink of getting dehabbed. Plenty of programmers out there with your skills, Nev. Rupee a dozen."

"Fifteen minutes, Maddy. I'll get it done in fifteen if you just get out of my hair."

Please Lord, let her leave, Nev thought, the closest she'd come to prayer in thirteen years of avowedly secular living.

"Fine. Ping me the second you're done. Better yet, I'll come down in fifteen and check for myself."

As soon as Nev heard the chime of Maddy crossing the threshold of the programming pit, she expanded the date stamp on her viz to full screen. There was one number wrong. A two where a three should be. How had she missed it all day? It wasn't like her to overlook numbers, but she'd been so consumed with replicating the code that she hadn't been looking. She'd been watching the hours and seconds flash by, but not the date.

No no no no no no no no, Nev silently intoned as she launched her news stream and double-checked the date. She launched her calendar and checked again. She typed in the URL for the Quantum Time clock just to make sure.

She hadn't been hacked. All the dates lined up.

Nev returned to the code screen. Her fingers finished the final lines. She checked the time again. QT.39.33.23.22.09.2045. She watched the seconds tick by.

QT.40.33.23.22.09.2045.

QT.41.33.23.22.09.2045.

QT.42.33.23.22.09.2045.

To execute or not to execute, that was the question.

Series complete. LoopID?QT.43.33.23.22.09.2045

QT.00.30.06.21.09.2045

THE HIGH, SHIMMERY sound of Tibetan meditation chimes woke Nev from her sleep. As her eyelids began to flicker, a soothing voice wove over the bell tones, chanting "ohm shanti shanti shanti ohm shanti shanti shanti." Nev opened her eyes fully, wondering what had happened to the bird song she set as an alarm. "Namaste, Nevaeh," the voice continued. "Today's meditation is to cultivate gratitude to your ancestors. Call your parents and tell them you love them. Ohm shanti shanti shanti ohm shanti shanti shanti."

What the fuck? Nev scissored up in bed, grabbed her viz and clicked it in place above her left ear, thumb and fingers spreading open to access the app menu so she could find the trojan horse and rip out the intruding code. How in the hell had her personal viz been hacked? Never in a million years would Nev have signed herself up to be on the receiving end of such garbage. That being said, she actually felt fresh and rejuvenated, like she'd slept the optimal eight hours instead of staring at floating lines of code for sixteen hours straight and then catching a few desperate REM cycles.

"Got you!" Nev yipped in triumph.

The app was sitting there, smugly, in Nev's personal folder, almost as if she had downloaded it herself. *I don't think so, buddy.* Nev wrapped her fingers around the holographic icon (a pair of bronze chimes engraved in Sanskrit) and made a firm gesture to toss them aside. The icon didn't budge. A red warning scrolled across the bottom of her viz. "Deinstallation requires two-step confirmation. Enter deactivation code."

Now this was getting interesting. Maybe the hacker had just been teasing her by lodging the app so obviously in sight. For shits and giggles, she dug into her passkey folder to see if the deactivation code was there. No dice. Removing the intruder wouldn't be so easy. She might have to trace the trail back to the source. Digging deeper into her viz files, Nev found the initial installation signature. "Motherfucker!" she said, flopping back down onto her mattress. She stared up at her viz, her own digital signature staring back at her. The hacker had spoofed her. If she didn't know better, Nev would have thought she'd installed the app herself. Too bad she hadn't been considerate enough to save the deinstallation code somewhere obvious.

Nev swept away the file tree in disgust and shut her eyes. She chased away thoughts of her parents, took a few deep breaths, and went back into her usual pre-shower routine, thinking through the fresh hell that awaited her when she arrived at work. Or maybe something positive awaited at work for a change. A congratulatory note from Noel for finishing the SavePoint 2.0 code, or at least a cursory acknowledgement from Maddy.

Maddy! Shit. The bed seemed to tilt sideways as memories of the previous night came flooding back to her. Nev had been about to finish the alpha code. For the second day in a row. And then she'd noticed the date. And the time. And then... what? *No. No, no, no. This can't be happening.*

With dots swimming between her eyes and the viz's display, Nev reached up a shaky finger and reluctantly poked her calendar icon. The date enlarged to fill her field of vision. 21.09. The normally solid blue background was now filled with a scrolling "Happy

Equinox" message, and an animation of a spinning Earth. The day before yesterday. A trick! It had to be a trick. Part of the hack. Someone was trying to drive her crazy, play a sick joke. Maybe Anissa somehow used her old access codes to plant a bug. No, that wasn't like her. But what was the alternative? She couldn't—she wouldn't—believe it. It was literally unthinkable.

Nev tore the viz from her ear, heart pounding like a jackhammer, and jumped out of bed. She ran over to the window, looking out over the city streets twenty storeys below. The sun hadn't risen yet, but fingers of purple and orange were already reaching across the brightening sky. About six thirty, by the look of it, just like the viz said. The streetscape offered no information about the date. She needed to find neutral confirmation, something a hacker couldn't possibly have fucked with. Something solid, and permanent, and fixed in place, before she slid right out the window and off the side of the planet. She had a brief impulse to call her grandmother and ask her to check the seed-company wall calendar that always hung above the sink in her kitchen, then remembered with a cold shock that she was a month too late. Another fixture in her life, melted into air. *Shit*. Who else could she call? Normally, she'd consider pinging Jared, but the weird conversation from last night (was it last night?) was too fresh, and she didn't want to get ambushed again. *Think, Nev. Who do you trust?*

Abdul at the 24-hour dot.mart around the corner would be awake. Nev could picture him behind the counter, measuring out the grounds for the giant tureens of coffee he prepared each morning to sell to the commuters who gathered at the corporate bus stop outside his door. No time to shower. She wriggled into a black tee-shirt and a pair of sweats from her workout drawer. Reaching into the shallow bowl where she kept her hair ties, her fingers brushed against something smooth and cool. The mystery stone from her desk. *What? How?* Her heart fluttered, and her hand squeezed shut of its own accord. Its cool weight in her palm felt like the last, missing piece of a puzzle she hadn't known was incomplete. Once again, Nev dropped the stone in her pocket, then she tied back her bed-mussed curls, slipped into her gym shoes, and ran out the door.

It was weird to leave the apartment without her viz. She felt naked, like a neo-Lud living out some half-baked primitive ancestor fantasy. Usually, committed technophile that she was, this would have been her worst nightmare. But right this moment, she needed to get free of it—all of it, if possible—and see what was going on outside the network, beyond the reach of even the most devious hacker. She'd have torn the SavePoint right out of her skull, if she could, and thrown it under the wheels of the oncoming GPlex bus.

A line of sleepy tech workers, bedecked in Hydrepel anoraks and a full spectrum of neon hair dyes, snaked out the dot.mart's door when Nev jogged up to the corner. She heard grumbles as she pushed past the mustachioed dudes blocking the door and beelined for the register.

"Abdul," she said.

A harried looking man in his fifties glanced up from the register, where he was inputting a sale of lattés and lotto tickets. Abdul had a wiry salt-and-pepper beard that covered half his face. His cheeks above them were pitted with scars that Nev assumed he'd gotten in the supermeasles pandemic of 2031-32. She'd never asked, and he'd never told her.

"There's a line," one of the men close to the door said.

"I'm not blind," Nev said. She turned back to the register. "Abdul, what's the date?"

"I'll give you a date," said a guy in a DPH windbreaker, grabbing at his crotch.

"You, out!" Abdul said, pointing at the offender. "You want to know what day it is?" Abdul asked Nev, looking perplexed.

"Yes. Never mind why. Can you just tell me?"

Abdul reached over to the stack of old-fashioned newspapers he kept by the register, and handed her a *SacBee Times Chronicle*. Nev's eyes traveled straight to the top right-hand corner of the page. Seeing the date in plain, smudged black-and-white somehow made it realer than laser-projected nanopixels ever could. September 21, 2045. This wasn't some *Groundhog Day* scenario. She was losing time.

Nev had never been claustrophobic. As a kid, her favorite hidey-hole had been the back seat of an old Buick sedan in her father's junkyard. She'd curl up there, sometimes for the whole day, with her favorite stuffed animal, a good book, and a bag of microwaved popcorn, inhaling the scent of long-expired cigarettes and slowly rotting leather. But now, the walls of the dot.mart seemed to be zooming in at her, the LED fixtures blinking at exactly the wrong interval, the mass of sleepy, cranky tech workers crowding the space with their chatter and shuffling.

She pushed her way out onto the street, walking vaguely towards the Embarcadero, seeing but not seeing the commuters and ceegees she passed, feeling but not feeling the slight chill in the breeze, smelling but not smelling the faint sea spray wafting in the air. She felt like a ghost, a visitor from another dimension, there and not there.

Okay. Clearly, this was more than just a viz hack. Time for Occam's razor. Or, like Sherlock Holmes said, once you rule out the impossible, you're left with the truth, no matter how improbable, or whatever. Nev was either having a total psychotic break, or—she couldn't believe she was even entertaining the idea, but what else could it be—something had gone horribly wrong with SavePoint, and she was somehow moving backwards in time. Not minute-by-minute, or in five-second increments, but day by day, every day. Two days ago, it was today, and yesterday was also today, and today was, or is, yesterday, and tomorrow is going to be two days ago and she was tumbling, like Alice down the rabbit hole, her mind screaming: *Oh God, where does this end? Am I going to just wake up in a never-ending series of yesterdays until I, what, go back to being a kid again?* She couldn't think of anything worse.

It was too much; Nev couldn't even fit it all inside her head. She doubled over, panting, hands on her knees.

"Are you okay, miss?" A police officer, with a square, kind face and a nametag reading Ramirez, was looking at her, sizing her up.

Nev stood up, brushed her hands against each other, and, not knowing what to do with them, put them awkwardly on her hips.

"Yes, I'm fine," she said, making eye contact with the policewoman. "I just, I felt sick for a minute. But I'm okay."

"You sure? Do you need medical assistance?" The cop looked skeptical, one thumb looped in her belt, the other hand fingering her walkie talkie.

"Nope. All good. I'm good. I just... I'm totally fine. Really." Nev gave her a curt wave and a smile, and jogged across the street, then started walking briskly across a park toward the Bay, hoping she looked purposeful and confident, and not at all psychotic. It took all her will not to look back over her shoulder. She strained her ears to hear whether footsteps were following her until she had reached the far side of a playground and was safely out of sight.

Okay. *Okay.* Why was this happening? Nev strolled aimlessly, reflexively dodging self-driving delivery trucks, couriers on bikes, and legions of office zombies, trying to master her panic, slow her breathing, and focus on the details. It must have started when she executed the SavePoint 2.0 alpha code, the night before last. Or tomorrow night. Whenever. There had been some kind of glitch in the code. Or possibly a hardware issue with her own SavePoint device. Nobody else was reporting similar complications (delusions?), so it was, for now at least, a unique, localized phenomenon. *My own private hell.*

So, okay. She executed the code, and woke up the previous morning. And then re-lived the day. Except it wasn't really the same day—not at all. Nev decided to sidebar that issue for the moment. Then, last night, she was about to execute the alpha code again, and then before she could complete the task, she woke up this morning. Today. What had been yesterday. She'd been looking at the quantum clock time right before it happened, and noticed that it was the same time that she had originally executed the code, the first time she lived through the day. *Weird.* So that

36

day—yesterday, or tomorrow—call it Zero Day—seemed to end at exactly the same time on both nights, 11:33 pm and however many seconds. But she woke up at a different time today than she had the previous day. Which means... what? Was this the time she had woken up originally on this day when she first lived through it? *Dammit*, Nev thought, *what were the rules?* Seemed like one step forward, two steps back.

She came to a halt, breathing heavily, a clammy sheen of sweat evaporating from her face in the chilly morning air. Looking up, Nev realized that her feet had taken her back into the Tenderloin, back to the Qbito building. She didn't really want to go upstairs and deal with Maddy again, or re-rewrite the code she'd already finished twice (what was the point?), but she didn't know where else to go, and besides, maybe it wasn't the worst idea to talk to Kusuma. SavePoint was his baby. If anyone could understand what was happening to her—and more importantly, help her make it stop—it was him. Maybe he'd have some brilliant idea, enter a few lines of code into the quantum mainframe, and she'd wake up tomorrow, safe and sound. Real tomorrow, not yesterday tomorrow. As she tried to picture it, the thought sounded outlandish, but then again, so was the prospect of living her life backwards until she devolved into an embryo.

As she walked up the stairs, Jim Bone approached her, mumbling something. He removed his hat and tried to make eye contact. He looked sharper than she'd seen him for a while. Maybe one of the refugee-aid societies had parked a shower truck by the camp and given him a once over.

"Listen, listen, lady—did I—I got to, to talk to you, did I say that already?—"

"Not now, Jim Bone." Nev cut him off, reaching for some cash to throw at him and then realizing with embarrassment that her leggings had no pockets. She really wasn't dressed for the office, even by tech startup standards. "Sorry, I—I'm in a hurry." She hustled through the glass doors and then into the elevator, mashing the button for Qbito's C-suite.

Hong-Mei, the flawlessly beautiful receptionist who sat at a macaroni-shaped marble desk outside of Kusuma's office and played viz games every day from eight til six, tried to stop Nev as she headed in through the brushed aluminum door to his inner sanctum.

"He's in a meeting," she said, half-rising. "Do you want me to make an—"

"Sorry, I just need to—" Nev pulled the heavy door open and stepped inside. As her eyes adjusted to the salt lamps and polarized sunlight, she realized that Kusuma was deep in conversation with Maddy, who was presenting something on the screen that took up most of one wall.

"...open up micro-targeting opportunities in a range of sectors, including pharmaceuticals, financial services, and real estate," Maddy was saying in her crispest voice. The graphic on the screen was titled 'SavePoint 2.0 Revenue Projections '46-'50,' and featured a graph with a lot of differently colored lines, all pointing up and to the right. She stopped talking as both she and Kusuma turned toward the disturbance.

Hong-Mei was behind Nev, apologizing profusely. "I'm sorry, Noel, she just—"

Kusuma, looking perfectly at ease in his customary form-fitting black tee-shirt, tan canvas pants, and knotted hemp thongs, examined the intruders.

Nev almost felt bad when she saw the terror creasing the receptionist's smooth face. You wouldn't think to look at Kusuma's benign brown visage that he would inspire that level of fear in his employees. His face perpetually bore the serene expression of an ancient Buddha statue, like the ones at Borobudur—not too far from the village where Kusuma was born—photos of which decorated Qbito's main lobby. Kusuma oozed the serene peace-of-mind of an enlightened being, saved by technology from the burden of any missteps. Whatever the receptionist was scared might happen, Kusuma barely reacted.

"It's okay. Thanks, Hong-Mei," he said, waving his hand

dismissively, as though swatting a fly away from his impeccably shaven head. He turned back to Nev. "Nevaeh. I was expecting you." Judging by the look on her face, though, Maddy neither expected nor welcomed Nev's intrusion.

Nev's need to spill her guts to Kusuma competed with her equally strong need to show no weakness in front of Maddy. What if she *was* having a psychotic break? Maddy wouldn't think twice about using Nev's breakdown to force her out of the company. Everything she had been working for since she was sixteen would be lost. As Nev hesitated, uncertain what to do next, Kusuma signaled for the presentation to continue. Maddy looked reluctant, but, ever the rule follower, she picked up where she had left off.

"So, as I was saying, when Nev's team *finally* completes the SavePoint 2.0 alpha, we'll be able to use the new data for micro-targeting opportunities that our brand clients have never dreamed possible. We'll know exactly when our users are most, um, targetable for calls to action. Just imagine how much better the metrics for Cannabiz's 'Real Slim Lady' product-line would have been, with aggregate user data showing when females ages 18-35 were most likely to hit undo following a cannabis-related provocation. Now, imagine A/B testing pegged to actual individualized SP trigger points. Cannabiz could screen a viz ad in a user's maximum receptivity window. My initial projections show the effectiveness of SavePoint-assisted micro-targeting improving view-to-revenue ratios by a factor of two thousand percent, and I think that might be conservative."

Nev had never heard Maddy lay out the case for SavePoint 2.0's data mining potential so clearly before. She realized that Qbito's chief marketeer had never bothered to tell her *why* she wanted the query functions she asked for, and, to be fair, Nev had never bothered to ask her. All Nev had cared about was the challenge of writing the code. The vision thing was far above her pay grade. Listening to Maddy pitch the new product platform to Kusuma, Nev finally got it. How much had Maddy promised her potential buyers? No wonder she was constantly hounding Nev to finish the alpha.

"Are there any limits to the query options we'll be selling?" Nev asked, an unfamiliar sense of discomfort squeezing her chest. Kusuma and Maddy stared at her as though she'd sprouted an extra eye in the middle of her forehead. "I'm just wondering about the implications for my team."

"Really, Nev? *Now* you want to know?" Maddy wasn't even trying to hide her dislike. "It's a little late. Maybe if you'd bothered to communicate more regularly, we could have gone over your questions prior to rollout-minus-four."

Nev was floored. She and Maddy had never exactly gotten along, but they weren't sworn enemies or anything. As a rule, Maddy was too focused on achieving her own ambitions to waste time picking fights with programmers. Besides, Nev had been pulling virtual all-nighters in the office for weeks, working against the limits of her own parasympathetic nervous system just to get the alpha ready for launch. Maddy knew this. She'd been all too present throughout the process.

"Sorry, did I do something to make you angry?" Nev asked, her hand unconsciously fluttering to her heart.

Maddy opened her lacquered lips to say something snide but apparently thought better of it, turning back to Kusuma as though Nev had already gone. Nev recognized the abrupt change in emotional energy: Maddy had almost definitely said something, then triggered her SavePoint to undo and save face. It must have been a doozy.

"Do you want me to finish the presentation?" Maddy asked.

Kusuma steepled his fingers beneath his chin, in a gesture that he might have picked up from a handbook for being a tech-genius, and gazed contemplatively at the two women.

"I think, Madison, it might be best to continue this conversation tomorrow morning. Tell Hong-Mei to schedule us an hour before lunch."

Maddy stared daggers at Nev, turned on her heel, and stalked from the room. Nev wasn't looking forward to the next time they crossed paths. Maddy could get nasty, and she wielded a lot of power. Nev had seen her reduce junior staff to quivering blobs with a well-chosen sentence or two. Then it hit her: As things now stood, she would never have to face Maddy's wrath moving forward, because Nev *wasn't* moving forward. If she didn't see Maddy again today (and Nev was going to do her best to avoid it) then the next time she saw her was likely to be yesterday. Or the day before, even. That's why she was here in Kusuma's office, after all, not to argue over some stupid product rollout.

"Mr. Kusuma," Nev said, taking a shaky breath, "there's something I need to tell you."

He gestured to a dark wooden stool, carved with what appeared to be a dolphin Poseidon, replete with trident. Nev sat down.

"Please, Nevaeh, call me Noel."

Kusuma was the only person in Nev's new life, her post-sixteen life, who called her by her full first name. She had discarded that name along with everything else from her childhood when she left eastern Washington for Stanford. But it was a point of connection with Kusuma. They had both come from ultra-fundamentalist families, and both bore the traces on their IDs. Noel and Nev—Christmas and Heaven—in the same room together: Christ, what a joke. The difference between Kusuma and Nev was that he seemed to take pride in remembering where he came from, and what he'd left behind, while she would have much rather forgotten the past for good.

"Noel," Nev said, her words rushing over one another before she could form them into coherent sentences, "something's happening to me. I don't know what to do. I can't control it. I don't, I can't—I know it sounds crazy, but I think—I think something happened with the SavePoint 2.0 rollout. I mean, it already happened. I know it's not for four days, but I think when I executed the program on Friday, something went wrong, and ever since then, I've been moving backwards in time. Yesterday, I woke up, and I'd been restored to the morning of the same day

I just finished. And then today, I woke up and I've been restored to the day before that, which is four days before the launch, if you're following. The dates keep going backwards. I thought it was a viz hack, but the newspapers don't lie—at least, not about what day it is. I'm so scared, Mr. Ku—Noel. Have you ever heard of something like this? Do you know how to stop it?"

Kusuma remained absolutely still as the words spilled out of her. She thought maybe he was practicing some yogic form of single nostril breathing. She stopped and stared at him anxiously, trying to read his face to see whether he believed her, or thought she was nuts, or both.

"Thanks for sharing your concerns, Nevaeh. I value the trust you've placed in me."

He paused, weightily.

"It's only natural to feel anxious before a large product rollout. Being scared is normal. You should know that I have absolute trust in you to handle whatever challenges SavePoint 2.0 creates for you. You are the key to SavePoint's future, Nevaeh. The key to everything. That's why I put you in charge of this project, because I know that you have the tools to accomplish it. Remember Rovelli, 2018, chapter five, page ninety-one: 'the difference between past and future does not exist in the elementary equations of the world; its orientation is merely a contingent aspect that appears when we look at things and neglect the details.' Don't neglect the details, Nevaeh, and you'll sort this out."

Kusuma finished speaking and took a sip from a copper cup on his obsidian desk. Nev was still trying to figure out whether he believed her or not when he spoke again.

"Please ask Hong-Mei to come in on your way out."

QT.44.51.21.21.09.2045

"No, no, no. This is important. Pay attention. Watch." The guy with the stubbly lips—what was his name, again? Mason? Conner?—threw a roasted corn kernel in the air and caught it in his mouth, coughed a little, licked his lips, and then smiled victoriously at Nev, his eyes swimming.

"I don't—"

"That's the thing, right? I can do math, even in my mind, even when I'm—"

"That's not math!" Nev was laughing. "That's, I dunno, acrobatics. Math is, like, um, it's like, you know, linear functions, and, like—" *what was the word? Something about a duck.*

"No, that's the point I'm trying to—"

"Quadratic equations." *Quack, quack.* "And, like, and calculus, and shit." She slammed her beer bottle on the bar for emphasis and chased it with a shot of Cuervo.

Mason-Conner was eyeing her like a cartoon wolf, pouring corn nuts into his mouth and chomping them noisily, a tough feat with the bar's speakers blaring '20s trap hits at top volume.

"Hold on, just a wee little moment, I have to go wee." Even drunk, Nev still loved a pun.

"I see what you did there. I'm gonna wait right here."

"Yeah, okay. Whatever." Nev slid off the stool and lurched towards the back of the bar, past the retro pool tables, towards the can. Where was she? Some bar in the Tenderloin. Frankie's? Paulie's? Something like that. Not her usual kind of spot, but she'd gotten a viz ad offering three-for-one kamikazes, and after the day she'd had, the offer was too good to pass up. She could remember being a kid in Washington, when there were still men's rooms and ladies' rooms; at least you had a 50/50 shot at a clean seat. Now, there was just piss. Everywhere. She hovered above the bowl, skirt hiked up, checking the feed on her viz. Jared and his fucking homemade pasta. It looked like squiggled brains swimming in blood sauce. *Yuck. Who wants to see that?* The bile rose in Nev's throat, and she forced it back down. *I'm not gonna puke. Not gonna puke.* She turned around, bent over the bowl, almost puked, and then, thinking better of it, swung herself upright. The toilet flushed itself. Jimmy's was all class. *That was it. Jimmy's. Chimmies. Chimichangas. No, chimales. Maybe it's time to get some chimales.* "Chi-maaaaaa-les." The word sounded so silly out loud.

Nev teetered over to the sink, placed her palms firmly on the cigarette-pocked Formica, and stared through the etched graffiti and spattered goo at her own reflection. *Wow.* She looked old. Which was kind of funny, because she was getting younger. Everyone else was aging, sagging, wrinkling, dying. And she was just going to keep getting younger and younger. Like Benjamin fucking Button. *Suck it, normies.* Tequila sure helped you see the humor in things.

The music had switched to '30s algo by the time she sidled back up to the bar. Stubbly guy was nowhere to be seen; maybe he'd found another Little Red Riding Hood to wolf his wolfy face at. She downed another shot, then slid over to the little dance floor and did the only move she knew, an old BTS routine she and her friends had learned from the internet, until her Mama had discovered she was listening to devil music and shut it down.

She never even saw Elissa outside of school again. *Elissa. Anissa.* Anissa didn't ping her any more, didn't talk to her any more. With a pang, Nev realized she missed Anissa, who was maybe her only real friend. The only person who at least kind of got her, didn't want anything from her. Didn't want anything more to do with her, more like it. *Elissa. Anissa. Miss ya, miss ya. Wouldn't wanna kiss ya.*

Nev opened her eyes and scanned the bar for someone worth sleeping with.

She'd made a half-hearted attempt to return to her Memeron chair and log into the system after meeting with Kusuma that morning, wondering if there was some evidence she could bring back to his office to prove that she was telling the truth. But her mind kept drifting, her hands dropping from the virtual keyboard down to her pockets, to fidget with her mystery stone. She felt the same pang every time she touched its smooth surface. Eventually, the ache became familiar, in an oddly comforting way. Frustrated with her lack of progress, she finally dropped the stone on the desk and immersed herself in Qbito's server logs. But that didn't help. There was no use looking for evidence in the SavePoint system, Nev soon realized, since she didn't really understand its temporal protocols. That was Anissa's (now Darian's) unit. And besides, she didn't think she had the oomph to rewrite the same damned code a third time in a row, especially knowing that it probably wouldn't stick. So she'd logged out and left the office, wandered home in a daze, took a couple of REMaidz, pulled up the covers and passed out, happy for the sweet relief from the vertigo of her brain racing circles around itself. Slept all day, pretty much. Ate some toast. Ate some chocolate. Tried to do a sudoku. Went back to bed, tossed and turned until dark, considered streaming some porn, and then remembered that the world was now her oyster, without the risk of norovirus. Why watch other people have all the fun? If there's no tomorrow, Nev had realized, there's no consequences. Forget the five-second undo window: she could knock over a bank and still wake up innocent the previous day, no need to pay the price. No need to pay for anything, in fact.

She had searched through her closet for a suitably vampy dome outfit. The obvious choice was the tube top and miniskirt she'd woken up in yestermorrow morning, but as she reached towards it, her scientific mind edged out her libido for a moment. *What if I don't wear this outfit? What would that do to the timeline?* Instead, she grabbed a Spice Girls VReunion Tour crop-top, wondering whether it would still look as good on her as it did back in Stanford days. But as she brought the shirt towards her, she felt something snap in her belly, with an almost audible creak like the first board in a wooden dyke giving way before a devastating flood. She swooned slightly. Maybe it was just the last of the REMaidz coursing through her system, but Nev had a feeling that if she tried leaving her house in the Spice Girls shirt, she'd end up regretting it. She'd dropped the crop-top back in her drawer, and instead put on the tube top and miniskirt, instantly feeling the wave of nausea ebb. No deluge tonight, thank you very much. *Shut up, science brain. Let Ms. Libido do her thang for a while.*

Tonight was just about tonight. No past. No future. No risk. No consequences. No credit card bills. She skipped over to the bar, feeling the alien bass of the AI-generated dance track buzzing inside her solar plexus. Slapped her platinum card down ostentatiously on the soggy wood, stood on her tiptoes, cupped her hands around her mouth, and shouted "Drinks on me! Nothing fucking matters!" A surprisingly loud cheer went up around the room, and several people raised their glasses at her, though one person nursing a beer over in the corner just shook her—his?—head, as though she'd done something personally disappointing to them.

On second look, Nev thought maybe she did know that person. Or knew who they were, at least. Dark purple hair, kind of a pointy face, arched eyebrows, long, iridescent nails on the narrow fingers curled around the bottle. The name was on the tip of her brain... It was someone maybe she'd known at Stanford. *Oh. My. God.* Somewhere deep in Nev's sozzled skull, the pieces clicked into place: Airin!

Airin Myx (or Minskoff, as Nev remembered from the first day of Data Structures & Algorithms) had dropped out of the comp sci program after year two, and reappeared as a star of the Bay Area hacker underground before Nev had finished her BA. They (gloriously nonbinary, even in their college days) had made a name for themself, and probably a fortune in cryptocurrency, finding and fixing bugs and other vulnerabilities before the black hats could exploit them. People spoke of Airin in hushed whispers; their prowess at finding the one exploit in an otherwise invulnerable data system was so legendary that some coders seemed almost afraid to say their name aloud, lest their servers explode on the spot. Every major tech startup in the area had hired Airin at some point, along with God knew who else. But Nev hadn't laid eyes on them for at least a decade; the hacker was notoriously private, reclusive even. Definitely not someone you'd just run into at some shitty Tenderloin joint like this. *So why are you here?*

Maybe it was just the booze doing its devilry, but suspicion flared in Nev's mind like a Molotov cocktail. Why *was* Airin here? Staring at her across the room, tracking her coolly with their catlike eyes? As far as Nev knew, Qbito had never hired them, but that didn't mean they wouldn't be interested in the SavePoint code. Despite Nev's best efforts to develop something airtight and elegant, there was clearly a major flaw in the new alpha—she was living proof, backwards—and maybe it was more than just a coincidence that a notorious hacker showed up right before, or right after, whatever, everything went haywire.

Nev was just steeling herself to confront Airin head on when a big, brown blur occluded her vision. Looking up, she saw that a tall, well-built man in a tight-fitting flannel was standing next to her, or over her, a sly but friendly smile on his face.

"Thanks for the drink. The name's Levi, by the way," he said.

"What did you mean, just now, when you said nothing matters?"

"Oh, it's just, um—" Nev tried to crane her neck around his broad torso, to see whether Airin was still watching. "It's nothing, just, y'know, something I say when I'm buying drinks."

"For everybody."

"Yeah, for everybody. Listen, do you mind, I, uh…"

"I don't mean to be forward, but isn't it about time that you and I got out of here? I know a really good tapas place not far away. I'd love to hear more about whatever it is you're trying to forget." *Tapas. Chimales. Chimaaaaaaleeeees.*

"I don't know, I have a lot of work, and I…" Nev managed to steer herself around Levi and get a clear view of the table in the corner. Airin was gone, their beer bottle balanced upside-down in the center of the table. Nev wondered whether she'd seen a mirage, or maybe Airin was just a ghost like her.

"Come on," Levi was saying. "I'm perfectly harmless, I promise."

Nev took a closer look. Muscular shoulders, powerful chin. An intelligent, laughing smile behind his eyes. Not her usual type, but, hey, no consequences, right? Harmless, harmful, what's the difference? She put a hand on his chest. It felt like a refrigerator door.

"You know what, Levi? I think maybe it's your lucky night. Let's go get some chimales together. Chimaaaales." She rolled the word around in her mouth, tasting it. No skipping dessert tonight.

QT.00.30.07.20.09.2045

MEDITATION CHIMES, AGAIN.

"Motherfucker," Nev cursed aloud, jerking up in bed and reflexively wincing, in anticipation of the mother of all hangovers.

"Ohm shanti shanti shanti Ohm shanti shanti shanti. Today's meditation term is clarity. Imagine the sound of ..."

Nev selected snooze to stop the alarm. She was feeling ... fine. No. More than fine. She was feeling, in fact, a perfect sense of clarity, as if she hadn't had a drop to drink the night before. Her lungs were a little scratchy, but she certainly didn't feel as if she had spent hours alternating shots and beers, then gone out for late night chimales, and fucked a stranger in the restaurant bathroom, screaming at the top of her lungs because who cared what the other customers thought when she wouldn't be sticking around to suffer the consequences. She didn't even remember anyone looking at her funny, once they were done. Come to think of it, she didn't remember anything after the bathroom. And, for that matter, why was she wearing a plush velvet bathrobe? She couldn't remember ever having seen it before, let alone going to bed in it.

Oh shit. The penny dropped, as her grandmother used to say. That explained the hangover she'd woken up with two days earlier, the day after tomorrow. She grabbed her viz and clicked it into place to confirm. QT.15.33.07.20.09.2045. *This is happening. This is really happening.* She wished she could tell her future self, her 22.09.2045 self, to go for an STI screening. Too bad her today self didn't know what her earlier self was going to do yet, though clearly it came with a free bathrobe. Judging by the lack of hangover, she was going to lay off the booze tomorrow, er, yesterday night. Ugh, she had to start developing some new language to make sense of this one-step-forward-two-steps-back situation she'd landed in. Or maybe, just maybe, she should give up and ride it out. Maybe now was the moment when she made the decision to stay in bed for the rest of time. What did she have to lose?

Nev was just drifting back to sleep, half dreaming of the ocean as she'd first seen it, on a frosh week field trip to Big Sur—amazing to have grown up in a coastal state without ever visiting the coast—when the goddamn alarm went off again.

"Ohm shanti shanti shanti ohm shanti shanti shanti. The Earth is your mother. She holds you safely in her womb. Give thanks and praise—" This time, Nev turned off the alarm for good. She rested her head back on the pillow, trying to recapture the sound of the surf in her mind's ear.

Give thanks and praise. God, if that stupid app only knew what her actual mother was like, it wouldn't be talking about safety and wombs. Christina Bourne was about the furthest thing from an Earth Mother. She was cold and distant, more like Mars. Before she'd gone prematurely gray, she even had the red coloring to match.

And the temper. Mars might have been the God of War, but he wouldn't have stood a chance against Christina on one of her crusades. Once that woman believed herself to be in the right—in God's graces, in other words—there was no stopping her, no opposing her. Nev had seen her face off against the entire damned county when it came to issues of public morality, or public education, or *Oh, God,* public health, and win every time. She'd never met anyone with the stones to withstand one of Christina's onslaughts. Even Kusuma would probably curl into a ball and roll away if he had to face her. The image appeared unbidden in Nev's mind, making her laugh out loud—something she wouldn't have dared to do in her mother's presence.

The last time was the worst. Daddy just stood there in his Sunday suit, watching limply while Nev and her mother faced off like superheroes over her grandmother's casket.

"How dare you show your face here? In this sacred place?" her mother had said, not shouting yet, but the knife-sharp edge glinting in her voice. "Where were you when your grandmother, God rest her, who took you in when you were a lost soul, who gave you shelter and comfort and more love than she had to spare, was dying in her bed?"

Nev had considered triggering her SavePoint, but it wouldn't have been enough, and it couldn't have stopped what came next. "We don't need you here. We don't want you here! Go back to Babylon, where you belong!"

Only a month ago, and her mother's voice—no less powerful than she remembered it, though maybe a little rougher around the edges—was still ringing in her ears. And now, *Oh, God, please no*—now, she was hurtling back towards that day.

The weight of it landed on Nev's lap, like an anvil dropped by a delivery drone. She was going to have to go back. Experience her grandmother's funeral again. In the near future. Past. Whatever. And then... and then, if she couldn't stop it, couldn't find a way out of this mother of all glitches, she was going to have to go back all the way. Back to Washington. Back to the junkyard. Back to the church. Every single day of her childhood, each one uniquely miserable, each one the same, each one safely behind her, or so she had believed, had moved from her rearview mirror to her dashboard cam. Nev was on a collision course with her past.

The thought was almost too much to fit inside her skull. For some reason, Nev found it even harder to handle than the bigger stuff, the violation of entropy, the power of a quantum processor doing exactly what it wasn't supposed to do. She was going to keep waking up each yesterday, until she woke up in her old bed, in her old house, with her young parents, every day, until…

Out. She had to get out. Up and out. She didn't know what to do, where to go. The blood rushing to her head sounded like the crash of surf.

The beach. She'd take the day off work and go to the beach. She never played hooky. No matter how hard she'd tried to shake off her childhood, she couldn't seem to shake the old Protestant work ethic. The Devil finds work for idle hands, Christina liked to say. Usually right before tasking her with a few hours of mindless drudgery. Then again, maybe her mother was right this one time. Nev was on her own in this world. If she fell down, no one was going to pick her up. If she couldn't work, who was going to pay her way? Time off could wait until she had stowed away enough to plan for every future contingency. A dragon-sized nest egg. But it turned out the future had been canceled. So fuck it, why not go to the beach.

Nev didn't bother to call in sick. She took a long shower, enjoying the steaming hot spray on her skin, not worrying about paying the astronomical water bills that came with living through year ten of a super drought. She tossed a water bottle, a blanket, and a Luisa Rey mystery novel that had been sitting for months on her night table, into her backpack. Looked at the bottle of SPF-30 on her bathroom counter and left it behind. The dark complexion Nev inherited from her father had always protected her against sunburn. The only reason she used sunscreen was vanity; she didn't want her skin getting leathery and old-looking. But there was no danger of that now.

She was about to hail a Dryverless when she thought better of it and headed out to the street. Twenty minutes later, Nev walked away from the kiosk at the nearby Luxurental with the passcode to the newest Tesseract EZ5 on the lot: a cherry red two-seat convertible with a streamlined body that made Nev want to shout and holler. *Oh, Daddy, if you could see me now*, she thought, remembering the hours, days, years her father devoted to refurbishing the wrecks in his junk yard. He couldn't get the refined gas to fill up their old combustion engines, but that didn't stop him from lavishing love on their exteriors. An ancient Mulsanne Blue Corvette Stingray was one of the only things Nev had ever seen Matthew Bourne lavish with love. He'd always been better with things than with people, a predisposition Nev had inherited.

Then she was out on the road, heading down Turk Street, through the Fillmore, past the green hilltop campus of USF, and out along Fulton, the tent cities of Golden Gate Park unfurling to her left, until finally the slate blue of the Pacific appeared on the horizon. The car directed itself into an empty spot in front of the Park Chalet, a two storey Spanish Colonial restaurant with a pillared portico outside and amazing old murals painted on the walls within. She'd been there once before on a date with a young engineer who'd gotten in on the ground floor of an AI security company that was acquired by Lothlórien Partners. Unfortunately, he had more money than personality, and had spent the evening talking about how the city should tear down the Chalet and let Lothlórien build their newest black cube office stack on its site. Nev had spent the evening staring out the restaurant's floor-to-ceiling windows at the beach, wishing she were alone.

It was five degrees colder than it had been in SoMa, where she lived. A strong, autumnal wind was blowing off the water. She decided to nip inside for a hot chocolate before her walk. Maybe the weather would warm up while she ate. And why not throw in a shot of Jamesons and a dollop of whipped cream? There was a line that stuck with her from *Paradise Lost*, which she'd read an excerpt from in "Poetry for Engineers," the only lit class she'd taken at Stanford. Something about making a heaven of hell. Good advice. Thanks, Milton. Maybe she'd get a plate of beignets while she was at it. She could imagine the smell of the hot donuts, dusted in powdered sugar, and the greasy marks they'd leave behind on her fingertips. Future Nev could pay the price, if there was a future Nev. Who even knew.

She strode up the mural-lined carved staircase to the top floor where breakfast was served. A waitress came and directed Nev to a table by the window. The dining room was half-empty, with groups of tourists and retirees clustered at the square tables. Nev's life didn't usually intersect with the leisured classes. Must be nice to have nothing better to do on a weekday morning than sit in a beautiful room and look out at the beach, she thought. *Why yes it is*, she answered herself, in an upper-crusty inner voice, lifting an imaginary teacup with little finger raised.

One elderly couple was sitting side-by-side, rather than across from each other, at their little table. Did they just like to be close? Or were they waiting for friends? And what was the story with the old guy and the middle-aged man sitting together? Father and son? They didn't look that similar. Or were they lovers? You never knew in San Francisco, that's one of the things Nev loved about the city. And how about that person with the purple hair sitting alone in the corner, the only one looking into the room rather than out through the windows. It was a weird choice. Nev was still coming up with explanations when she realized with a jolt who she was looking at.

It couldn't be a coincidence. No way in hell that after not seeing Airin Myx for close to a decade, she had seen them twice in two days. Airin must be following her. But how could they be following, when they had gotten to the restaurant first? It made no sense. Nothing about this scenario made sense, and that made Nev uncomfortable. She was used to working on equations that could be solved. It's why math was so much better than religion: It was ruled by logic, not ambiguities. There were right answers. But right now, right here, there were only wrong answers. Well, there was *one* right answer. Nev was getting the fuck out of there. *Sorry, beignets... another time.*

If there is another time...

She stood up abruptly, her chair leg squeaking against the floor. Had Airin noticed? Nev couldn't tell. The hacker wasn't making eye contact, hadn't budged an inch. It was possible they were lost in thought. Possible, but highly unlikely.

Nev thought about looking for her waitress to cancel her order, realized what's the point, and flew back down the stairs. Suddenly, the idea of a walk on Ocean Beach didn't sound so appealing. Instead, she got back in the car and set the nav for Big Sur, opting for the coastal route. Why not? She wasn't in a hurry. Airin didn't seem to be following. And, besides, no matter how quickly she moved, the only way Nev could go was backward.

By the time she hit Pescadero, Nev could breathe again. The sun was almost directly overhead, warming her skin faster than the rushing sea breezes could cool it. Why didn't she do this more often, she asked herself. The EZ5's control systems were top of the line, leaving Nev with nothing more to do than watch the scenery scroll by, high bluffs on her left, blue ocean to the right. Stands of cattails every now and then. Brief barricades of windblown, dark green bushes blocking sight of the ocean for a few rotations of the axels, before giving away again to the vastness of the Pacific Ocean. Time lost its coherency as the car chewed through the road. Forwards and backwards all looked the same. Traffic got busy as she passed through Santa Cruz. Nev directed the EZ5 to a drive-through espresso shack, ordered an 'eight ball'—four shots of espresso with a glug of cashew milk and two pumps of CBD syrup to take the edge off—plus a fat slice of huckleberry cake, then pulled back onto the highway. She breathed in the good air of the woodlands, south of Santa Cruz, then it was out into the flatlands and farm fields of Watson, the Pacific Ocean a mirage on the far horizon. The sun was high in the sky when Nev reached the breathtaking cliffs of Big Sur and pulled onto the small turn off the highway that led into Esalen.

Esalen. The susurration promised peace of mind. She had first heard its name whispered at Stanford by her professors. Later, when she moved to San Francisco, she heard it from the mouths of her bosses. It was a place that the powerful visited to 'detox.' Vizzes were discouraged in all communal areas. SavePoint too, as of last year. They impeded 'honest communication,' threw up barriers to 'self-work.' Guests paid a high price for the privilege of unplugging, thousands of dollars for a weekend of workshops on connecting to your inner-net, tens of thousands for a whole week. Two hundred dollars just to visit the hot springs at night. Nev had never been; the nest egg mattered more than self-indulgence. But no point saving for tomorrow when there was no tomorrow. At the front desk, she gave optical scan approval to open a limitless tab, and registered for the holistic package.

QT.00.30.07.19.09.2045

AGAIN, THE CHIMES. Nev was almost starting to expect them. To like them, even.

"Ohm shanti shanti shanti Ohm shanti shanti shanti. Today's meditation is about space, and place. Locate yourself within the world, and the world within yourself. Ohm shanti shanti shanti…"

Nev stopped the alarm, checked the date (the 19th, as expected), and then closed her eyes, trying to regain… what, exactly? She'd been getting a hydrolyzed bentonite clay rub in her Esalen suite, listening to a biofeedback binaural loop on her viz, augmented by the sound of the surf through the open French doors. She hadn't realized how much stress she was keeping in her lower back, it felt awesome to have healing hands work out all the kinks. But nothing good can stay, especially when you're falling backwards towards the moment of your birth, and now it was like the massage had never happened, which she supposed it hadn't.

Just goes to show you should set your affection on things above, not on things of the Earth, as her mother would have said. Yeah, well, she'd tried at Esalen. She really had. She'd gone to the afternoon meditation walk through the zen rock garden. She'd bitten her tongue through the Soul Motion workshop, eaten dinner at a communal table, passing colorful serving bowls of fermented garden vegetables and whole grain pilaus, then gathered at the yurt for a Consciousness Hacking session before retiring to her room for a bodywork nightcap. She'd tried hard to connect. And all that effort had just made her feel how deep the absence of connection was in her life, and made her realize that Esalen couldn't possibly supply what was missing, no matter how much time or money she spent there. She took a deep breath to clear her mind, but started coughing and wheezing instead, her body apparently intent on clearing her lungs. What had futurepast Nev gotten up to? Maybe some steam would help.

She stood up, heading for the shower to add another twenty bucks to the water bill she'd never have to pay, but when her feet hit the poured concrete floor, it felt like she'd stepped into quicksand. Try as she might, she could not move her legs from their fixed positions. The air around her thickened, trapping her torso and arms in the same immovable sludge. She strained against the atmospheric resistance, battling to break free. Then something snapped around her with the force of a rubber band, and she found herself hurtling towards the bathroom door like a turbo-charged Junichi Jones, the ninjato-wielding protagonist of *WhisperWorld*, her all-time favorite RPG. It was almost exactly like a game lag, when the server crunched too many stats at once, and the action froze, then zipped ahead in double time to catch up.

Half an hour later, freshly scrubbed and glowing beneath a full body sheen of shea butter, Nev was curled up on the couch in sweats and a tee-shirt, her Grandma's macramé blanket across her knees, a supersized mug of coffee and cashew milk on the coffee table, and her viz projection set to surround. She took a long pull from the vape pen that had been sitting neglected in a kitchen drawer for months. She was surprised to discover the battery still charged after all that time, and even better, she'd held onto those sample cartridges of TikTokToke she'd been given by a Cannabiz rep who'd stopped by the offices a few weeks back (although there were a few gaps in a case meant to hold ten—cheap bastards).

"It's been a long time, Junichi," Nev murmured, as she logged onto the game.

"Moshi, moshi, Nev. Today, we will avenge my grandfather's killers. His sacrifice shall not be in vain!" The holographic avatar bowed.

Nev giggled a little. "I hear you, little buddy. I recently lost my grandmother, too." A sob rose unexpectedly in her throat, cutting the giggle short, and she tamped it down with another pull on the vape. Junichi wobbled before her, then pulsed a bit, his colors glowing more vividly than she remembered. Wow, this stuff was effective. Shit had gotten stronger over the past few years. Or she'd become a total lightweight. Both, probably.

Nev realized she was stuck on the same puzzle that had driven her to quit the game three years earlier. Junichi returns to his small hometown at the outskirts of Yuzu City, where he must discover the Ring of Truth buried beneath O-jiichan's dojo. She'd searched every goddamned corner of that virtual town, and never found the way in. The game had prompted her a zillion times to check the boards for hints and walkthroughs, but Nev was too proud to get help from some punkass Weeb casting from his mom's couch, so she'd just decided that *WhisperWorld* was more trouble than it was worth.

Kind of like her own hometown, come to think of it. But while Junichi's halcyon days were spent under a pellucid blue sky teeming with seabirds and colorful blimps, Albion was just dinky, all golds and browns, and so dirty. Country dirty, not dirty like the ceegee camps across the street. A whole different palate of eye-watering smells, different shades of earth tones, different noises to keep you up at night. Why her parents had moved there was hard to grasp; why they'd stayed was a mystery for the ages.

"You had it lucky, Junichi," she murmured around the mouthpiece of the vape, feeling the fragrant plumes tickle her sinuses as she exhaled through her nose. This stuff was really too good.

Her dad had been living in Chicago, on the South Side, with his mother, who was still cleaning houses back then. Janey Bourne, may she rest in peace, was a woman Nev and her sister Faith had never met in person, only spoken with over grainy tablet video each year on Christmas and Easter, and on their birthdays sometimes. Then she must have died or something, because she just evaporated from their lives. Nev's mother had originally gone out there for some reason—a wedding?—and met Nev's father Matthew, who was just finishing up his studies in automotive tech. They'd fallen in love real quick, and he'd returned with her to her childhood home in Union, Oregon, happy to join the sort of family he'd lacked growing up. Then Christina's father had died and the bank took the house to cover his debts, and the three of them—Nev's mother, father, and Grandma—had picked up stakes and moved over the border to Washington, to Albion. Land of religious freedom and no real estate tax.

Matthew had gotten a line on a junkyard for sale, dirt cheap. He never truly fit in with the townsfolk of Albion, who treated him as a city slicker. He didn't look like them either, with his dark complexion and tightly-curled hair, which he wore shaved close to his head. The parents of Nev's friends used to ask her whether her father was Italian, seeing as he came from Chicago, but Nev couldn't satisfy their curiosity. Her grandma Janey wasn't Italian, as far as she knew, and she'd never met her grandpa. She didn't think that Daddy had ever met him either. Any time she asked questions about this mysterious progenitor, Matthew deflected. He seemed uncomfortable with the idea that Nev might feel as out of place as he did in Albion. So she stopped pushing for answers. When she made it to college and began meeting more people who looked like her, Nev began to suspect that the man who had knocked up Janey Bourne was Black. But she wasn't about to take a DNAmazing test and find out. Nev knew from working in the industry not to trust any slippery assurances about privacy protections. Her genetic sequence would be sliced, diced, and priced out to half the silicon state before the results appeared in her viz. Anyway, by that time she had made her peace with not fitting in back in Albion. She was proud not to be one of them. What more did she need to know?

Mama, on the other hand... Christina Bourne didn't just fit in to Albion, she became the town's most celebrated resident. After they moved to town, Mama built an 'anchorage' out of the front room of their rancher. Christina's adherence to Pauline doctrine wouldn't allow her to claim the name of minister for herself; instead she'd stretched the definition of anchorite to its fullest. She decorated the front room with pictures of the fourteenth-century anchorite Julian of Norwich, seated at a narrow table, writing her *Revelations of Divine Love*. She launched an account on Believers Only, calling herself Christina of Albion, and sharing her revelations with a growing flock of international believers.

Soon they'd had Nev, then seven years later (a Biblical number, her mother had probably planned it that way), they'd had Faith. And, for a while, it had been okay. Nev's father had his cars. Christina had a pretty large following for her weekly teachings and daily micro-insights. Nev and Faith had each other, and they both had their grandmother, who was—as Nev later discovered, when she got the chance to catch up on all the TV shows she'd missed as a child—right out of central casting. Always baking, knitting, hugging. The furthest thing from a pushover, but someone you just wanted to please. She took pride in her girls, gave them pride in themselves.

Then came the Fall. Literally. In November of '31, the supermeasles outbreak finally made it all the way to Whitman County, where it tore through the town like a tornado. Only one hospital in a fifty-mile radius, not enough beds to go around, and Christina too high and mighty to vaccinate, bragging to her followers that the Lord's protection was worth a thousand needles. They were washed in Jesus's blood, they didn't need Satan's apothecary. The virus was supposed to be the most dangerous for the oldest people, but for some inexplicable reason, it was Faith—beautiful, angelic Faith, the youngest in the household—who got it the worst. She fainted in the yard, and by the time Daddy took her upstairs to bed, she was sweating and shivering, thin, red pin pricks on her arms and chest. Over the next few days, they grew into blisters, and she was either asleep or delirious or moaning in pain, and nothing made the fever go down—not prayer, not ibuprofen, not a single one of Grandma's homespun remedies. They gave her ice baths, which helped a little but made the shivering worse, and Nev read to her and told her stupid jokes, and tried to feed her, but she still got sicker and sicker, until she fell asleep one night, and in the morning, she was dead.

They tried to tear Nev away, told her she'd get sick too, and not to worry because her little sister was already with Jesus in His kingdom, but she held on to Faith like a life preserver, refusing to let go until the men from the morgue came in their full body protective gear and peeled her off, gripping her arm so tight she had a bruise for weeks.

Nev blinked away a tear and looked at the virtual Japanese landscape around her. Without realizing it, she'd parked Junichi at his family shrine, and at some point, he'd settled himself into the lotus position, eyes half closed, hands on his knees. He looked infinitely less silly than those nimrods at Esalen, all racing each other to enlightenment. With a low, grumbling whine, a boulder in the middle of the yard slid aside, revealing a staircase down into the Earth. There it was: the secret entrance to O-jiichan's subterranean dojo.

The Ring of Truth was within Nev's grasp. Hope bloomed in her chest like a lotus unfurling. Tears gathered at the corners of her eyes. Junichi had found his path forward from confusion and pain. Maybe she could, too.

Junichi descended the granite staircase into darkness, accumulating brightly colored karma points along the way. Nev guessed there might be a demon guarding the ring, a nemesis dangerous enough that she would need those points to survive the battle and take the prize. The sooner Junichi unsheathed his ninjato, the better. Nev checked her inventory, making sure she had enough elixir to heal the injuries from any necromancy weapons that the demon might throw at Junichi. She made him do a tricky flip-roll-parry move as he jumped down the final stair and ricocheted around a blind corner. But there was no demon awaiting. The room was empty, except for an iron scrollwork pedestal at its center, with a multifaceted glowing hunk of jade perched on top.

Junichi approached slowly. The room remained empty. It couldn't be that easy, Nev thought. But, facing no impediment, she extended Junichi's hand to grasp the ring. As soon as his fingers made contact, the room melted, swirled, and disappeared. The viz went dark. Then Junichi reappeared, standing in an empty void next to the spectral figure of O-jiichan.

"Yokoso, Junichi," the phantom O-jiichan said. "Welcome."

"Arigato, O-jiichan," Junichi said, making a deep bow.

"I've been waiting for you."

"Sorry, I've been busy at work, I haven't had any time."

"Time is an illusion, Junichi."

The familiar gong of declining Karma points followed O-jiichan's response. What were the rules here, Nev wondered? What was this place?

"Where are we?" she murmured, watching her words dance and fade like vapor around the virtual dojo.

"You are exactly where you need to be."

"But what am I supposed to be doing here?"

"Doing nothing is better than being busy doing nothing." Gong.

Hmm, Nev thought, maybe this Ring of Truth wasn't worth acquiring after all, if she was going to lose points every time she said the wrong thing. The game was making no sense. O-jiichan's dialog was about as coherent as the 'ohm shanti shantis' from Nev's alarm app. She looked around the void for an exit, but there was nothing but darkness in her periphery.

"Is there a way out of here, O-jiichan?"

"Follow the path of least resistance."

"Where is the path of least resistance?"

"All paths are the same path." Another gong. Junichi's karma points took a nosedive.

"Whatever, O-jiichan, how about I just turn this fucking game off?"

"Body and mind dropped off."

Nev hit escape and the game went to black. *Body and mind dropped off.* Maybe O-jiichan had a point, and it was time to unplug. She took her viz off and rubbed her eyes, watching the lights pop in the blackness, feeling the calluses at the bases of her palms where she rested them while typing, tasting the fumes of the vape, and something even more toxic beneath it, wafting up from her esophagus.

The game was worse than the real world. Puzzles within puzzles, no code book. And O-jiichan was about as helpful as Kusuma. Nev giggled again, imagining Noel's bald, muscular avatar inside the virtual dojo.

Okay, Nev. Enough dicking around. She was actually really good at solving puzzles, and if that's what it took, that's what it took. No magical ancestor figure was going to give her the secret key to unlocking this time glitch she'd gotten caught in, so she'd have to work it out herself. There did seem to be rules. And if she could figure out what the rules were, maybe she could figure out how to break them. Or, at least, turn them to her advantage. She took a deep breath, and closed her eyes again.

Rule number one: Each night seemed to end at exactly the same time, 11:33pm and however many seconds. She thought back to her second time through Zero Day, when she watched in disbelief as the final moments of the day ticked by on her viz.

Forty-three seconds. Maybe. Probably. Easy enough to check. *Good.*

Rule number two: She woke up each morning a day earlier than the one she'd just finished. She seemed to wake up at the same time that she'd woken up that day the first time through. But maybe that was just because her alarm had already been set, rather than some immutable rule of the Glitch. Which was a good segue to...

Rule number three: The days weren't the same. Not only was she living them differently than she had originally, but her past seemed to be different. Like, someone had changed the alarm on her viz to that stupid inspirational meditation app. And the mystery stone. She'd never seen it before she got stuck in the Glitch, and now it seemed to appear nearly every day. Like this morning, she'd found the stone in bed beside her, then put it for safe-keeping in her hair-tie basket. Which meant that the past that lay before her could influence the future that lay behind her. And she could influence the past, which meant...

A wave of seasickness washed over her, and she had to brace herself to keep from toppling headfirst off the couch. *Ouch. Maybe I shouldn't have taken that last toke. Focus, Nev. You got this.*

She opened her eyes again, ready to face reality.

Okay. So, three rules. Let's call them Time Limit, Two Steps Back, and Past Primacy. That's helpful. But wait, there's more. Nev could also imagine some additional hypotheses. Nothing she could prove at this point, but threads at the edge of the knot.

Hypothesis number one: Even if Nev didn't experience the future consequences of her actions, other people did. So, if she went on a killing spree, even though she'd never be arrested for the crime, her victims' lives would still end in the future she couldn't experience herself. There would be funerals. Crying. Lives ruined.

This was getting real thorny, real quick. So, what happened to the future that she'd already experienced? The one where the victims wouldn't be dead? The one where her alarm hadn't been hacked. The one where Jared had texted her an eggplant emoji instead of flipping out on her. Was it still out there somewhere, untouched by her current predicament, or had it been overwritten by recent events?

Qbito had invited a quantum physicist from CalTech to give a lunchtime talk a few months before, who'd explained the mathematical and mechanical bases for the 'many worlds interpretation' of quantum loop theory. Any time something happens, he said, there's a parallel universe in which it didn't happen. Toss a coin, it comes up heads. *Boom,* in another, separate world it comes up tails. All these universes, sprouting like new branches on a massive tree, each of them inaccessible to the others, invisible to the others. Maybe each alteration Nev made, each time she played hooky instead of heading to work, was a new branch in the tree. If so, it was growing quickly.

Question: Did Nev continue to exist in those universes, even if she—Backwards Nev—never got to experience those futures? Is there a Nev who finished fucking broad-chested Levi in the restaurant bathroom, and then, what, gave him her number? Told him thanks and see you around? At the very least, if that future Nev existed, she hoped she was getting tested for STIs.

And also… let's say that Nev did eventually find a way out of this. Fixed the Glitch, started living in forward gear again. Which of those futures would she live in? Would she return magically to Zero Day as if nothing had ever happened? Would she be stuck in the Levi-fucking future, maybe with a case of herpes? Would she live all of them at once, or one after another? Or would her final trip forward overwrite all the others? Not enough data to formulate an answer. But something to keep in the back of her mind.

Hypothesis number two: This wasn't a mere glitch, but a hack. Someone had gained access to the SavePoint 2.0 alpha code, and messed with it. Maybe it was malicious, and Nev's situation was an intentional assault by someone with a grudge. Or maybe it was opportunistic, the result of corporate espionage gone wrong (or right). Or maybe it was just a curious hacker who poked around in the code to see what it did, neither intending to send Nev spinning backwards, nor even necessarily aware of it.

The Why question couldn't be answered yet. But the Who question had some tantalizing data points. *Who* had been giving her the stinkeye across the crowded bar the other night? *Who* had mysteriously been waiting down at Ocean Beach the previous day, even though Nev herself had only shown up on a whim? If this were a video game, the obvious villain would be Airin Myx. Maybe time to move this one to front-of-mind.

Suddenly, an idea struck her.

"Do u have contact info for Airin Myx?" Nev selected Anissa's avatar, still first on her Favorites list, and hit send. Then, instantly regretting it, she brought her left thumb and pinky fingers together, to trigger her SavePoint. Her hand froze, fingertips millimeters from meeting. Contacting Anissa had been a colossally bad idea, but using her SavePoint might be even stupider. What would happen if she triggered it inside of the Glitch? Would it work as usual? Would she zoom five seconds into the future, since she was already moving backwards through time? Or would it glitch out the system even worse, sending her back to the Renaissance, or the Jurassic, for that matter? If she was going to test SavePoint, she'd have to do it in a more controlled environment.

Come to think of it, Nev realized, testing her rules and hypotheses wasn't the worst idea. She was a scientist, damn it. This might be the first time a human being had experienced quantum weirdness at such a scale (although, she realized with a shudder, it might not be). But weird though it was, it was still rooted in the fundamental principles of physics, not the arbitrary magical thinking of a game designer or comic book author or religious fanatic. She could figure this out. Bit by bit, piece by piece. Assemble data. Test theories. Come to a conclusion. Fix the problem.

Begin by changing one variable.

QT.21.33.15.19.09.2045

ONE HUNDRED AND thirty miles south-southeast of San Francisco, in a patch of desert between nowhere and nowhere, buried deep beneath the ground, a network of vacuum tubes encased in graphene-carbon nanotube aerogel, protected by an outer layer of titanium plating, performed the cascade of calculations that were required each microsecond to run SavePoint's operations. Nev had visited the quantum mainframe once, soon after she was hired, on a leadership retreat conducted by Kusuma himself. "This is where the magic happens," he'd said, waving his hands in front of the rows upon rows of shiny metal cases visible behind the viewing window of the reception room where the tour had ended. Afterwards, Kusuma had taken the leadership team to a nearby hot springs that appeared on the horizon like an oasis. Nothing but dust, rocks, and brown hills as far as the eye could see, then suddenly, a patch of green scrub and a hand-painted sign pointing to a dirt road trailing off the cracked roadway.

Anissa, a city girl through and through, had been terrified of getting bitten by a scorpion or rattlesnake. Nev, hardened by a childhood of junkyard injuries and encounters with desert critters, hadn't been scared in the least, just annoyed to find herself back in the dirt she'd hoped to have left behind for good. That was the weekend they became friends, Anissa clinging tightly to Nev as they walked at night from the soaking tubs to the 'rustic' cabin which, as Qbito's only two female unit leaders on the retreat, they'd been designated to share to promote 'team building.' The two of them moaning and groaning from their bunks, passing a bottle of Remy that Anissa had picked up from the resort's small commissary. Both women counting the minutes until morning came and they would be free to return to the city, where they could breathe free.

Nev had no intention of ever returning to SavePoint's buried mainframe. Today she wanted to get as far away from it as possible.

It was two-thirty in the afternoon by the time Nev had picked up her Tesseract EZ5 (even fewer miles on it than last time, whoopee!) and programmed the nav to take the fastest road out of the city at the fastest velocity the car's safety system would allow. An hour later, Sacramento was in the rearview mirror, and I-80 was unrolling before her like a ribbon of grey smoke.

Variable one: proximity.

Did the rules of the Glitch include spooky action at a distance? Qbito's technology relied on quantum entanglement, meaning that, theoretically, you could travel across the entire universe and still trigger your SavePoint. The devices certainly worked all over planet Earth; to date, the company had sold something like one-hundred and fifty million of them, on every inhabited continent, in every nation that hadn't banned the technology.

But what Nev was experiencing wasn't necessarily bounded by the same rules. To generate something this messed up took a tremendous amount of energy, which might, if she was remembering her undergrad course on mechanics correctly, diminish exponentially with distance. So, theoretically, if she got far enough away from the behemoth lurking beneath the desert dirt of Llanada, California, she could break free of the Glitch's grasp and start living for the future again. The thought sounded a bit hollow inside her head, an underbaked bit of wishful thinking. A Hail Mary, as her grandmother used to call it. But what the hell, it was worth testing, at least. If only to eliminate the variable.

So here she was, zooming east at ninety miles per hour with nothing to do but contemplate her own gradual implosion. She considered firing up *WhisperWorld* again, but her brain already hurt too much from playing all morning, and she'd left the vape in her apartment, so instead she just stared out the window at the endless stream of outlet malls, beauty strips, and digital billboards, blurring into a brown slurry that somehow reminded her of the Palouse River after it rained, when the mist was rising in the hills. The scrolling landscape stilled her busy mind. Her eyelids grew weighty.

The mist cleared, to reveal a figure standing in a clearing: O-jiichan, his robes rippling in a nonexistent breeze. His hand was extended before him, and in the middle of his wrinkled palm was a SavePoint implant, glowing and pulsing slightly, casting a greenish light on the old man's face, bringing the bags beneath his eyes into sharp relief. Except it wasn't an implant, was it? It was a scintillating green ring, cut from jade.

Junichi approached cautiously, took the ring from his grandfather, and lifted it to his eye socket. For a moment, the scene was dark, as his hand covered Nev's field of vision.

"No!" She shouted. "Don't do it! I'd rip mine out if I could."

Too late. Junichi's eyes blinked, two parallel ovals hiding and revealing the image of his grandfather, still rippling before him. "Ahhh. Now I see. The truth is, there is no truth. Thank you, O-jiisan."

"Do not thank me." The old man's voice was everywhere, like thunder. "Thank Nev. For she has revealed to you the meaning of the emptiness within. There is no depth when there is no height. No silence without sound. No darkness without light." The ground beneath O-jiichan shimmered, and he began to sink into it. He stood, placid as a statue, as the Earth swallowed his legs, then his torso. Just before his head went under, he opened his mouth, and the air rumbled around her. "Konnichiwa, Nev. Remember: No I without you."

Then he was gone, and Junichi was alone on the desert plain. Nev could feel the mainframe throbbing far below her like a calliope, grinding in time to the Earth's rotation. It hummed a tune, which echoed like a chorus through her bones. It was a song she recognized, something she remembered her grandmother singing along with the satellite radio receiver on her kitchen counter.

Hey, la, baby hello-ah
Hey, la, baby hello-ah
Hey, la, baby hello-ah
Hey, who farted?

Nev woke with a start. The stench was overpowering, a sulfurous reek that dominated her senses. *I'm dead. I've died and gone to hell. My mother was right.* Then higher functioning kicked in, and she realized the car was still gliding along I-80. It was dark out; she'd slept through the remains of the day. Out the window to her right, low, rocky hills slid by. To the left, she saw only flatness, and maybe a shininess. Dark, still water. Then it clicked: The Great Salt Lake. She'd never seen it—let alone smelled it—in person, but this had to be it. Man, she must have been out for a long time. Wisps of dream returned to her. Quicksand. Music.

She checked the nav: Tooele, Utah. Never heard of it. But Salt Lake City was just a couple miles ahead. She saw no sign of it through her dashboard other than some light pollution, a grayness in the sky over the ridge to her right.

"How long until I reach Salt Lake City?" she asked out loud.

"You will arrive in twelve minutes, at eleven forty-two p.m.," the Nav responded in the voice of D'Arcy Simmonds, a slap singer whose hit 'Fire n Bone' had been nauseatingly ubiquitous for most of the summer. Nev made a mental note to change the voice next time she rented the car.

Wait.

Something tugged at Nev's mind. Something important. She looked at the clock. 11:31pm. *Holy shit. Okay.* She had a quick decision to make. If she blipped out and disappeared from the car in two minutes, in a puff of smoke, what would happen? Would it just keep driving east forever? Would it sense that she'd left the car, and drive itself to a rental lot? Would it stall out on the highway when the battery finally ran down? Best not to risk people's lives.

"Pull over," Nev told the car. It rolled onto a shoulder near a watery ditch. She checked her viz: 11:32:12. Okay, this was it. About a minute to go. Nev watched the seconds tick by, trying to pay attention to every microsecond, straining to feel the moment when her consciousness departed this day and reappeared in the previous one.

11:33:36. The moment was coming soon. Nev couldn't exactly recall, but she thought the accident had happened around the 43-second mark. She breathed deeply, trying to slow her heart.

11:33:41
11:33:42
11:33:43
11:33:44
Could it be?
11:33:45
11:33:46
Yes, I think…
11:33:47
11:33:48
Yes. Definitely.
11:33:49
11:33:50

Nev waited until 11:34 and 11:35 had passed, just to be sure. Then she had to get out of the car and dance around, whooping and hollering at the top of her lungs. She'd done it. She must have done it. She'd escaped. It didn't really make a lot of sense, but getting away from the event horizon or whatever of the quantum mainframe must have ejected her from the Glitch. A wave of relief and exhaustion washed over her, and she had to sit down in the dirt. She gathered her knees up in front of her, rested her head on them, and let herself sob until she didn't have anything left.

A few minutes passed, still without a reset. *So,* Nev wondered, still reveling in her newfound freedom. *What next?* Would she wake up tomorrow, and live September 20th, 2045 for the third time in a row? Could she accidentally run into herself, like in one of those sci-fi games where you have to sneak around your earlier self without getting caught? Or would she overwrite the day again, the way she had the second time through it? And what would happen once she got back to California? Would she be recaptured in the time trap if she got within a certain proximity of the mainframe? So many new possibilities.

Okay, well, worst case scenario, if she started heading backwards in time again, she could always repeat this process, head out east until she was out of the mainframe's grasp. Maybe get a new job in Chicago, or New York. Or London. Hong Kong. Anywhere, really. The world was her oyster. Sometimes you didn't understand how amazing life was until you'd almost lost it.

She'd just slept half the day away, but God, she could use a good night's sleep. Okay, new plan: Nev would rent a hotel room in Salt Lake City, and in the morning she could reassess her options, form new hypotheses, and develop new strategies.

Half an hour later, she'd sent the EZ5 to the local Tesseract depot and checked into the Presidential Suite at the Grand America. Okay, maybe now Nev would have to start paying her bills again, but, damn it, she deserved this. Just this one night, she could luxuriate and celebrate. There was not a drop of alcohol at the hotel, unfortunately. Too bad she hadn't brought that vape.

Nev turned on the vid screen across from the bed and ordered hot chicken and waffles followed by chocolate volcano cake. She stripped her clothes off, washed away the traces of the road, ensconced herself in the plush, velvet bathrobe hanging by the tub, padded back to the master bedroom in her complimentary memory foam slippers, and flopped onto the massive, pillow-packed king-plus bed, to wait for her food. She checked the time on her viz: about twelve-thirty. It was tomorrow.

"Congratulations, Nev" she said to herself, clinking an invisible glass of champagne. "You—"

Series complete. LoopID?QT.43.33.23.19.09.2045

QT.47.00.07.18.09.2045

"WHAT THE FUCK are you doing here?"

Nev's eyes flew open. Jared was staring down at her, face close enough that his morning breath warmed her cheeks. Nev shrank back into her pillow. She glanced from right to left. Not her pillow. Not the hotel's pillow. Jared's pillow. Jared's Marina District apartment.

"How'd you even get back in here, Nev? How'd you get past security?"

Black stubble was poking through the blue-white skin of Jared's square jawline. His dark, wavy hair was flattened down along side of his head and poking out in unruly shocks along the other. His eyes were pink and puffy. To all appearances, he had just woken up. As had Nev.

Rule number two confirmed: *Two Steps Back*. Nev was going to wake up each morning in the same place and time that she'd woken up the first time through, regardless of where she had spent the night before, because there were no longer any nights before, only nights after.

It just didn't make sense, though. She'd been free! She'd defeated the Glitch! She'd already made it to tomorrow, for

Chrissakes. *What's the last thing I remember?* Nev thought back. She'd checked into the Grand America. Washed up. Ordered room service. Checked the time on the TV. It had been well past glitch o'clock, about an hour past—*Oh. Oh, no. No, no, no. Stupid Nev. Stupid, stupid, wishful thinking.* Nev closed her eyes, if only to get Jared's red-rimmed stare out of her field of vision. She'd gone to Salt Lake City. Which is in Utah. Which is in another time zone. *No, no, no.*

Yes.

Rule number one confirmed: *Time Limit.*

"Well?!" Nev opened her eyes. Jared was still poised above her, looking incredulous. "Answer me! Why are you here? In my apartment? In my fucking bed, Nev. Don't tell me you used your programming voodoo to get in here. That's not cool, Nev. You know that's not cool." His voice quavered.

The bed bounced as Jared threw himself back down onto his own pillow, sniffing loudly. Was he crying? And, more importantly, why *was* she here? Nev stared at the rustic timber slats on the ceiling, trying to remember. She recalled having woken up in Jared's bed on her first time through this day (the 18th, was it?), after a night of reliably good food and sex. But Jared hadn't been freaked out or pissed off. In fact, he'd tried to get her to stick around for Spanish omelettes and wanted to talk about getting a dog or something. This wasn't right. Something must have happened the previous night, something horrible that Nev hadn't experienced yet. Something to look forward to.

Rule number three confirmed: *Past Primacy.* Whatever had happened futurepast night to lead to this shitty morning, she'd soon find out. But this only led to more questions. What if, when the time came, she tried to avoid fighting with Jared? Avoided seeing him altogether? Being here, now, like this, meant she mustn't have done that. But why not? And, if she disappeared each night at 11:33 pm (or 12:33 am Mountain Time), exactly when on the timeline did she reappear? Just before she woke up? If so, was she getting any sleep? God, it didn't feel like it.

Nev scooched to the edge of the bed, preparing for an awkward, naked dash to the bathroom. Jared had seen her in the buff plenty of times before. She didn't know why it should feel different now. It just did. But to her surprise, she was already dressed, in a less tawdry version of the outfit she'd worn to Jimmy's on the night before her hangover. Her clothes and hair reeked of cigarettes and beer. Still, she reflected, a small price to pay for her privacy.

Hmm. Time to add a fourth rule, Nev thought: *Physical Persistence.* SavePoint had been engineered to recognize clothing and implants—that way, you wouldn't end up naked or minus a pacemaker when you jumped five seconds through time. Whatever was happening to her, the SavePoint server seemed to be applying the same rules: whatever she'd been wearing the night before was still there when she woke up the next morning. And, in this case, clearly she'd been somewhere funky.

Definitely time for a shower. Nev hopped from the bed. As she beelined for the bathroom, she had the unpleasant sensation, familiar from dreams and cheesy movies, of the room telescoping out before her, the door getting further from her with every step towards it. Then, all of a sudden, she was in the bathroom.

As she slammed the door behind her, heart pounding, she heard Jared's plaintive voice, muffled by the overhead extraction fan.

"Nev? Where are you going? What's going on? We're not done talking. Okay?"

Nev stared at her face in the bathroom mirror. She should be looking worse after all she'd been through the past few days. But she looked fine. Perfectly fine. Her hazel eyes were clear. Her skin had good color, lightly browned like she'd been out in the sun all her life. Her curly hair was crossing the tipping point to frizzy, but when she wet her hands and ran them through her locks, her mop returned to its normal, messy tangle. If she wasn't getting sleep, it didn't show. Maybe she didn't need sleep, because she had it banked from the first time through the timeline? Nev quickly brushed her teeth with the toothbrush that she kept at Jared's, then took a two-minute rinse in his ultralux Swiss spa shower (he still had to pay his bills, and each minute in that bastard used up five gallons of water). She put her clothes on and stepped back out of the bathroom. She couldn't hear Jared crying any more. Good.

"Jared," Nev said in as gentle a tone as possible, "what time did we go to bed last night?" What she really wanted to ask was, what time had he last seen her? When did the switch happen? But she couldn't figure out how to make the question make sense, even to herself. And if she was going to share her secret with anyone but Kusuma, it sure as hell wasn't going to be this guy.

"What the fuck are you talking about, Nev? We didn't go to bed last night."

He jumped out of bed. Nev averted her eyes, but not before she got an eyeful of his gym-toned body and other assets. Oh, yes. There was a reason she made it a point to spend the night with Jared at least once a week.

"Nev, Nev, what are you doing to me?" Jared asked in a strangled voice, spreading his arms wide. "Last night you tell me you never want to see me again and storm out of here, and now you're back, and you'll look at my junk, but you can't even meet my eyes. Fuck, Nev. I can't take it. What do you want? Tell me, please! You want to get married? Is that what this is about? Is this like that book my sister keeps talking about, the one with the rules for how to get a guy to marry you? If that's it, Nev, you can stop now. I'll do anything you want. Anything."

He looked down, and she did too, against her best intentions. If his tone was reticent, his body was anything but. He put his hand around his cock, and waggled it at her puckishly. "You can touch it, if you want."

"What? *No*, Jared. No." Nev grabbed a towel (plush, Turkish, top of the line) off a nearby chair and tossed it at him. "I don't want to get married, Jared. Jesus fucking Christ. I, just, I'm going through some stuff right now. It's hard to explain."

"Yeah, well, how will you know if you don't even try? If you tried, maybe I could help. You know, that's the problem with you, Nev. You never let anyone help you. Your parents should have named you Never instead of Nev. 'Cause who's ever heard of the name Nev, anyway?" Jared's voice broke. A heavy tear rolled down his cheek.

Nev strode to the door and yanked it open. "I've got to go. I'm sorry. I'll explain later," she promised. She owed him at least some honesty. Then she remembered: no, she really wouldn't have the chance to explain. Then again, next time she saw him—futurepast night, by the looks of it—he wouldn't remember either her promise or anything else about this fucked up morning. She didn't look back as Jared's door swung shut behind her.

This was all too much to handle. Usually, Nev looked forward to mornings at Jared's because his absurdly fancy, old-fashioned copper espresso machine, locally roasted Ethiopian beans, and immuno-infused cashew milk made just about the perfect macchiato, which she'd enjoy, privately, if possible, on the little balcony leading off of his dining room. But now, here she was, rushing down the street without a molecule of caffeine in her system, and something needed to change quickly or this day was going to be unbearable.

Who did Jared think he was, psychoanalyzing her like that? They'd been sleeping together for about a year, but she'd made it clear she didn't want anything more from him than she was getting. And he seemed fine with it. More than fine. Nev couldn't ever remember him saying no to a hookup with her, or being anything less than totally satisfied at the end of one of their nights together. He was handsome enough. And he had a sweet apartment, which his parents had probably bought him even though he pulled down beaucoup bucks at Miller Gahan Lee, the big tech law firm that represented Qbito and about a dozen other companies in their office building alone. He wasn't exactly bad in bed, and his gracious endowments didn't hurt. But, God, he was so needy. Had he actually woken her up this morning by screaming in her face, and then *proposed to her* before she could get out the door? How could she possibly even consider getting close to someone like that?

Nev was out of breath. She realized she'd been climbing Fillmore for the past few minutes. The sky was absolutely gorgeous, wisps of horsetails wafting in the blue, and the mixture of Victorian and neocubist architecture around her was so pretty it looked like a cutesy viz game version of the city. Her mother would have approved; Nev was finally "setting her affection on things above" instead of getting her kicks from more...sublunary pleasures.

Without planning to, Nev had walked to one of her favorite cafés—Sankofa Roasters. She and Anissa used to hang out there sometimes and work in parallel when they got overwhelmed by the testosterone levels at Qbito, taking regular breaks to duel in their favorite tabletop AR game, MicroMangaz.

Nev pushed open the bright green-painted door and walked straight up to the counter, looking around as her eyes adjusted to the relative darkness and serenity of the café. Not too crowded, just your typical gaggle of students, writers, and coders, typing away at virtual keyboards, wireless keyboards, and a handful of ancient laptops and tablets. No Airin Myx, thankfully. But before Nev could take comfort in that fact, she spotted Anissa.

It was hard to miss her, truth be told. She was wearing a bright, multicolored top in a geometrical motif, and bracelets up and down both arms from wrists to elbows. Her curls popped out from her head at every angle, in a big beautiful afro. And she was singing to herself under her breath as she worked, just the way Nev remembered from SavePoint 1.0 days. The sight of Anissa filled Nev with joy. Her mother would have called it providence. "Let there be lights in the firmament of the heaven to divide the day from the night; and let them be for signs." Anissa was as close to a light in the firmament as anyone Nev had met since she'd moved to San Francisco, and maybe this was a sign. Too bad that when Anissa looked up from her programming and caught sight of Nev lingering in the café doorway, her eyes darkened into black holes. But now was no time for pride. Impulsively, Nev slipped into the seat across from Anissa.

"I need your help, 'Niss. I'm in trouble."

Anissa waved away the code floating before her with a quick gesture. For a moment, Nev got her hopes up, but Anissa dashed them with brutal efficiency.

"What do you want, Nev? Looking to peep my code? Running out of your own ideas?"

"What? No! I'm not here to steal your code."

"Why not? Not good enough for you now that I'm a lowly contractor?"

"Your code is great, Anissa. Always has been. Better than mine."

"Funny you didn't say that when it counted. Why are you here, Nev? Actually, you know what? Don't bother answering that. I've got work to do. You best be on your way." She waved her hand dismissively towards Nev's face, the recessed lights reflecting in her lacquered nails like tiny stars.

"Wait, 'Niss—" The look in Anissa's eyes when Nev called her by her nickname stopped her cold. "Just give me a second to explain. You were right, Anissa. About the code, I mean."

"Yeah, what's your point? I know I was right. You knew I was right, too. You just didn't have the guts to say so when Maddy was in the room."

"I know, I know, I'm sorry. But... Anissa... I'm in serious trouble, and I think you might be the only one who can help me. The temporal function on SavePoint 2.0 has glitched, or maybe it's been hacked. I'm not sure yet. Anyway, I ran the alpha, and now," Nev lowered her voice to a whisper, "I'm going backwards through time."

Anissa stared at her.

"Did you just say *I'm sorry*?"

"Um, yeah? But the point is—"

"I heard you. Saying sorry doesn't make everything okay,

Nev-ayyy-uh," Anissa said, dragging out each syllable of Nev's full name. "It doesn't come with a salary so I don't have to do this shitty-ass freelance work to pay my rent. It definitely doesn't come with health insurance so that I can get tested and immunized when the next super-virus hits town. It doesn't undo what you did. But you know what, if you're going back in time, seems like you'll have the chance to make shit right soon enough. How about next time around, you stand up for me when I expose SavePoint 2.0's potential for temporal anomalies, and you don't let Maddy get my ass fired?"

Nev bit her tongue to hold back the flood tide of sorries trying to pour from her mouth.

"I will. I will. I promise. But I need your help now, Anissa. I'm scared of what's happening, of where I'm going to end up."

"I'm sure you are. You should be. But if I help you now, you're not going to be back at that meeting again to help me, are you?"

"I—" Nev realized with a queasy feeling that Anissa was right, and shut her mouth again with an audible snap.

"You know," Anissa said, "if you'd been a decent friend to me when *I* needed it, I wouldn't have thought twice about helping you now—no matter what kind of crazy shit you've gotten into. But you weren't, Nev. You're a user, and you've used me up."

Damn, Nev thought. The truth knocked the wind out of her. She couldn't breathe. Her heart throbbed against the inside of her rib cage. *What kind of a monster did you have to be if your best friend wouldn't even lift a finger to save your life? Okay, technically ex-best friend. But still...*

Anissa stood up to leave, sweeping her gear off the table and opening her bag to stow it away amid the chaos of data boxes, chargers, and tech accessories that she toted around as a coder for hire. Nev could see a couple of the pocket-sized classic sci-fi novels that Anissa was always reading bobbing alongside all the technology. And flashes of beads and silver, from her endless collection of bracelets that she was always compulsively putting on and taking off. And, what was that?

"A lotto ticket, Anissa? Really?" Nev couldn't believe that her math-genius former bestie would be suckered by those odds.

Anissa broke into loud laughter.

"What?" Nev asked.

"To see the look on your face. Man, you got more of your mother in you than you know. I don't need to explain jack to you. But I don't want you gossiping about how far the mighty have fallen. None of your business, but I ran into that poor ceegee, Jim Bone, this morning on my way here. He gave it to me. He wouldn't leave me alone until I took it. Just my luck the numbers will come in and I'll have to track the crazy bastard down to split the proceeds. Serves me right for giving a damn about other people."

Anissa closed her bag, slung it over her shoulder, and headed for the door.

Well, shit, Nev thought. That was a disaster. She stifled her impulse to undo. Even if her SavePoint worked perfectly inside the Glitch, five seconds wasn't nearly enough time to heal the miles of scorched earth between them.

The door chimed as Anissa pulled it open. Then, looking over her shoulder, she called back to Nev, "Has it occurred to you what's going to happen when they roll out the beta? Might be time to start thinking about someone other than yourself, sister."

QT.56.19.10.18.09.2045

"PACK OF SPIRITS, Abdul."

He looked at her inquiringly, but said nothing as he took the cigarettes from the rack behind him and placed them on the counter, along with a book of matches advertising a DNA date-matching app.

Nev eyed the row of cannabis and alcohol products next to the smokes. So many ways to absorb a few simple molecules: vaporizers, pills, transdermal patches. And, of course, good, old fashioned liquid and smoke. The packages beckoned to her with lurid colors, holographic labels promising sex, power, fun, forgetfulness. All of that sounded pretty good right about now. After the shit-show with Anissa, Nev felt like she was stuck on a sinking island, having burned her final bridge. Nowhere to go but down. Nothing left to do but drown.

Yes. She could stock up on brain-numbing chemicals, go home, play *WhisperWorld* until she passed out, wake up the previous day, and repeat the exercise until… Until what? Until she started waking up at home again, in her childhood bed, to the sound of her father and his power tools, her mother recording her homilies. Or until she decided to end it, more likely. Snuff herself, jump off the Golden Gate Bridge, overdose on Obliteryl or something. But, God, she'd probably just wake up the previous day, fit as a fiddle and no worse for her efforts. *No escape.*

No. What she needed now wasn't oblivion. What she needed was focus. There was a way out of this ridiculous situation, and with or without Anissa or Kusuma or anyone else's help, she would find the way. Had to find the way. She'd already confirmed the four rules, and tested one hypothesis. Time to expand the model, collect new data. *Knowledge, keep my lamp burning; reason turns my darkness into light.*

Cigarettes would help. Back in Stanford days, when all the other kids were popping prescription amphetamines and buying 'smart drugs' on the dark web, Nev had discovered that plain old nicotine gave her just the edge she needed to cram for tests, ace her papers, and code her way through the increasingly challenging puzzles posed by her professors. It was purely utilitarian rather than recreational; she'd steered clear of smoking habitually, because she didn't want to become dependent on anything, ever. And, besides, lung cancer seemed like a shitty way to die. But now there was no danger of dying in the future. And she needed all the help she could get.

"Are you okay, Nev? Do you need anything else?" How long had she been staring at the vice rack behind Abdul's head? His brows were knitted together with genuine concern. Apparently, he hadn't gotten the memo that she was a shitty person and a bad friend.

"Yeah. No, thanks, Abdul. I'm... fine. I just..." Nev looked around, embarrassed at having let herself slip. On the screen by the door, a line of dancing ping-pong balls with fishnet stockings was advertising the day's winning numbers. Her grandmother's fifth birthday. A prime followed by its square. And that verse from Proverbs about strength and honor that her mother was always quoting. Nev couldn't help it; any random string of numbers instantly became a series of associations in her mind, weaving together into a story she told herself. There was a word for it: Apophenia. The misperception that the universe had some order lurking beneath all the chaos. The illusion that anything mattered. Sometimes, she reminded herself, a random number is just a random number.

Something tugged at her. Anissa had had a lottery ticket in her bag. She said Jim Bone gave it to her. *Jim Bone. Oh my God. Of course.*

Nev told herself the story of the numbers one more time to make sure she remembered it, then thanked Abdul again, and went home to smoke her way through the pack of Spirits, turning the mystery stone slowly in her hands, past over future, future over past.

QT.00.00.09.17.09.2045

A PEAL OF church bells, deep and melodic, roused Nev from deep slumber. With her eyes still closed, Nev could imagine herself lying out on a grassy hillside, somewhere in rural England, listening to an old church steeple call the parishioners to prayer. But when her eyes opened, she was lying in her own bed, in her small SoMa apartment, a mile from the nearest church. Nev grabbed her viz from the night table, and shook it hard enough to make the bells stop ringing. She let her lids fall and tried to sink back into the oblivion that had enveloped her before the reverberations dragged her into consciousness. But it was no use.

Her mind strayed to thoughts of England and how, thanks to the Glitch, she'd probably never have a chance to visit there, or anywhere else that took longer than half a day to reach. Her Grandma had had a passion for all things merrie-olde-England. She was always reading English mystery novels and streaming BBC crime dramas. Of course, nobody in the family had ever had the money to visit. Nobody until Nev. She should have taken her grandmother while she still had the chance. Put in for actual vacation time—a week, or even ten whole days—and brought her on the sightseeing trip of her dreams. Double decker buses and Beefeaters and everything. Too late now, for Grandma, and for Nev.

With a low groan, she groped on the side table for her viz and snapped it into place above her ear. A red beacon signaled a waiting message from Christina Bourne. It was shaping up to be a very rough morning. May as well get this over with, Nev thought, and opened up the text.

> Sunday Blessings, Nevaeh. You are in my prayers today. I hope things are going better than last week. May the Lord bless you and keep you, my daughter. Much love, Mama.

Much love, Mama? Much love, Mama?? What the hell had happened? They hadn't spoken to each other for a month, and the last words her mother had screamed at Nev were some crazy lady vitriol about going back to 'Babylon.' What alternate timeline was she living in where she had a mother who loved her? And what had futurepast Nev told her mother to make her behave this way? Just how weird were things going to get as she kept going backwards?

Nev didn't intend to find out. She was putting an end to this. Today. The solution was obvious. She couldn't imagine why it hadn't come to her sooner. But before she fixed it, she had something else to take care of.

"You work too much, Nev," Abdul scolded gently, as she stood at the dot.mart register half an hour later, placing her usual order for a double-shot espresso with cashew milk. Hold the CBD this morning. She had business to take care of.

"I'm just going in for a couple hours," Nev said.

Abdul made a snorting noise in the back of his throat.

"Anyway, you're one to talk. You never go home, you're always here!" Nev said. As soon as the words slipped from her mouth she wanted to claw them back. She wasn't sure exactly where Abdul had come from before he moved to the Bay Area, but wherever it was, he was probably sick to death of Firsters and other racist idiots telling him to 'go home'—especially when home was probably a tiny room behind the shop. Who knew what, or who, he had lost in coming to the U.S. What he'd been forced to leave behind.

Nev's words had barely registered for Abdul; his eyes were just beginning to flash with the grief that always lingered just beneath their placid surface, when instinct took over and Nev clapped her left pinky and forefinger together. She had no time for reflection or regrets before she felt the familiar zero gravity sensation of her SavePoint activating. Then she was standing there, five seconds in the past, listening to Abdul snort his disapproval again. She released the breath she didn't know she was holding, but it froze in her lungs as the air turned to concrete around her, and relief turned to panic. She strained against the alien thickness, but it would not budge. She was trapped. Frozen in amber. *No, no, no,* her brain protested. Not when she had just figured out the key to save herself.

A whooshing noise filled her ears as the atmosphere melted back to its gaseous state. Nev shook her head to clear away the last crusts of concrete trapping her in place. Well, another question answered and rule revealed. SavePoint worked the same way in the Glitch as it had before, but if using it came with the risk of lodging her permanently in a single point in spacetime, Nev wouldn't be trying that again. The issue would soon be moot anyway. But this unintentional experiment she was performing on herself would prove useful once she was back in her Memeron chair, moving in the right direction, fixing the problems in the SavePoint 2.0 code. She couldn't wait to talk it all over with future Anissa, which reminded her...

"Abdul, I'll take a lotto ticket too. Let me give you the numbers." He nodded, showing no sign that he'd noticed her trigger her SavePoint, let alone seen her struggle against the glitch that followed.

"Okie, dokie, Nev. Have a good one."

It was an unseasonably warm day. Still late summer, Nev

reminded herself. But she'd get back to autumn soon enough. By the time she reached the Qbito building, she was covered in a film of sweat, and wishing she'd had the sense to check (or remember) the weather, and wear something lighter. She probably had some serious B.O., and if everything went according to plan, she'd be in a small room with a biotech for an hour or more. Oh, well. Too late now.

Thankfully, some things were predictable, whichever direction you were heading through time. Jim Bone was sitting in the same place as always, looking particularly grimy, even by his usual ceegee standards. The holes in the knees of his pants revealed pachydermal skin caked with soot, or worse. His greasy hat looked like it had been thrown in a sewer and left to dry in the sun. Nev wondered whether she had any of the knit caps her grandmother used to make for her tucked away in the hall closet of her apartment. Maybe she could fish one out for Jim Bone as a replacement. As Nev approached, he took off his cap, and stared at her with the same rheumy, pleading eyes that had gotten her to dig into her bag for money the first time she'd seen him, and most of the workdays since then.

Today, for a change, Nev took two things from her bag. The first was a crisp fifty, fresh out of the ATM in Abdul's shop. The second was an envelope, with 'Anissa' written on it, in red capital letters.

"Jim Bone, I've got a favor to ask you," Nev told him. Typically, she'd be dubious about his ability to deliver, but considering that she'd seen the ticket in Anissa's bag yestermorrow, she felt pretty confident today. She watched his eyes tracking the fifty. "Are you listening to me, Jim Bone?"

"Ain't we already been—Listen to the lady, Jim Bone. I'm listening."

"Good. Do you know Anissa Reynolds, who used to work here? Black woman with an Afro? Lots of bracelets?" She mimed Anissa's jewelry, sweeping each hand down the opposing arm, and shaking them briefly.

Jim Bone nodded.

"Great. Okay. I'm going to give you this fifty…" She extended it, and Jim Bone snatched it, tucking it away with surprising grace and dexterity. "…and I want you to give this…" she placed the envelope in his callused hand. "…to Anissa."

He looked around, as though the former Qbito employee would be walking up any moment.

"She doesn't work here anymore. She got, uh, you know that, right?" Best not to get into details right now.

Jim Bone nodded uncertainly.

"She usually works up at Sankofa on Fillmore. Right up the hill? The café with the green door." He nodded again. "Super. So, can you please go and find her, as soon as you can? All you have to do is give her this envelope. And if you do… if you do, I will be very grateful, and, well, there's more money for you after that. Got it?"

"I got it." Jim Bone plopped his hat back on his head and started gathering his handful of belongings.

"Thanks so much, Jim Bone. There's no one else I would trust with this important message." Nev smiled in what she hoped was an encouraging way, and then half frowned, realizing that she had told Jim Bone the God's honest truth. He rushed down the steps, nodding his head, and headed up Ellis Street in the direction of Fillmore. She watched him until he'd crossed the street, then she headed into the Qbito building.

First mission accomplished. Next up: Finish the Glitch, once and for all. Seize destiny by the horns. Onwards and upwards. And other words to that effect.

Nev ordinarily steered clear of the Phys Unit. The floor creeped her out. She'd toured the labs when she was first hired. Kusuma believed that each new employee should acquire a 'holistic' view of the Qbito operations before they embedded in their own unit. He'd designed the protocols with the input of a Systems Theory guru, Eugene Zhang, a man small of stature but large of ego who was on the board of half the companies in the Bay Area tech corridor. But the only lesson Nev had learned from touring Phys was that she was grateful not to be working there.

In her memory, the biotechs all shared a faded colorlessness, like characters in a game where the designers had turned the chromatic saturation dial all the way down. There were large rooms with cages full of white mice, rats, and rabbits. Some cephalopods in tanks. Nev tried not to think about the experiments conducted on these poor creatures. Another lab room was filled with models (at least Nev hoped they were models) of orbital sockets, eyes, and brain regions, many of them stuck through with microfilaments leading to circuit boards. Multiple projections of brain activity crowded the live screen walls of the lab. Phys also hosted the human subject pods, where the poor and willing signed up to be guinea pigs for new attachments, configurations, and integrations of the suborbital hardware that connected clients to the quantum mainframe. The pods were tastefully decorated in ersatz optometrist's office décor, replete with paper magazines and punny meme posters on the walls. Zukunft and Vergang, the interior design firm that Kusuma had hired to outfit Qbito's office, had also hung huge, old fashioned vision tests in each pod. The gradually shrinking tiers of letters gave subjects something to focus on as the biotechs operated the harmonic scalpels to make the incisions through which the device was installed.

Nev had sat in one of the pods herself, after she was hired, to have her older model implant upgraded with the newest hardware. She knew that Qbito's biotechs were the best at what they did. She'd use them any day over one of the licensed hacks that operated out of the city's strip malls. But she had fervently hoped, after the procedure was done, never again to step back into one of the pods. You could put lipstick on a pig, but no eye chart could turn Qbito's creepy Phys Unit floor into anything but a Boschian nightmare.

And, like all of Nev's worst nightmares, it was recurring. She had no choice. Here she was, back in Phys, and it was every bit as creepy as the last time. Even on a Sunday, Nev knew she could count on there being a skeleton crew of biotechs hard at work, pale faces poking out above the white necklines of their Qbito monogrammed lab coats. Nev stifled a shiver as she crossed the threshold of the reception area.

She watched the tech behind the front desk check her credentials on his viz before he addressed her personally.

"Good morning, uh, Nevaeh." He pronounced it KNEE-vee-yah, something that typically brought down her wrath. Today, this scrawny eel of a man was going to be her salvation, so she held her tongue. "I don't see an appointment for you on the calendar. What can we do for you? Everything okay?"

Nev hadn't thought past this point. How much should she tell him? The minimum viable amount to qualify for device removal, not a sentence more. She didn't want to end up being referred to a psych ward.

"Hi, sorry about that, I didn't... I think I'm having some trouble with my unit, and I'd like to have it taken out. Now."

"You want it removed altogether? I'm sure whatever the problem is, we can address it through a code scan. It's much less, er, invasive. Besides, all kappa six employees are required to maintain installation, barring medical referrals."

Nev had forgotten about this detail, one of about a million she was supposed to retain from her week of managerial onboarding. She had to say something that would convince the tech to remove the damn implant. Once it was gone, problem solved. No SavePoint implant, no SavePoint 2.0 regression in time. She'd be free to figure out how to prevent the Glitch from ever happening again. Maybe stop it from happening in the first place. But now was the time to suck it up and play the part of the helpless girl.

"Look, I, uh, I'm in pain, okay? And I think the unit might be, I don't know. I think it might be, like, touching a nerve, or something like that. I promise, I'll get a reinstallation as soon as it's fixed. But please, can't you help me?" She rubbed her right temple in slow circles with the heel of her palm, searching the tech's watery, gray eyes for some sign of sympathy, or, better yet, empathy. They gazed blankly back, fixing on her for a moment longer than she could handle.

"Please?" she allowed just a touch of desperation to enter her voice.

"No problem." He spoke the moment she had. Weird mind game, or just terrible social skills? Or maybe he was just waiting for validation on his viz. "Let's just get you into an installation pod." He led her back, past the desk, through a door, and down a hallway she remembered from her last visit, then sat her in a reclining tan microsuede chair in the middle of a small, well lit room. "I'll need you to remove your vizcom device."

Nev dutifully removed her viz, stowing it in her bag, and looked up into his pale face. He pulled an industrial-looking holoscope over his eyes, and peered down at her through it, waving a small plastic wand around the bridge of her nose. It buzzed hypersonically—a wheedling, insistent tone she could feel rather than hear. Nev could sense her implant responding at the same frequency. All at once, her eyes went blurry, and the biotech split into three, no, five, no, an indeterminate number of biotechs. Each lagged microtemporally behind the other, like reflections in a hair salon mirror. A line of eels, waving their electric tails in her face. *Get it together, Nev. Focus. This will all be over soon. Just hold on til then.*

With deliberate effort, she collapsed the cascade of biotechs back into one body, operating on one time scale. If the eel man had noticed anything amiss, he didn't show it. He certainly didn't act like someone who had just been split into a million refractions of himself, then suddenly reunited.

"Hmm."

That didn't sound good.

"What?"

"Shhh, don't speak until I'm done."

Nev bit her tongue, focusing on her breath as he continued to poke and prod at her, waving his wand first before one eye, then the other, adjusting some invisible dials in his field of vision, and repeating the process. She could feel the hypersonic whine changing pitch, and her implant humming in ticklish harmony. After what seemed like an hour, but was probably closer to five or ten minutes, he stowed the wand in his lab coat pocket, and looked at her with a new intensity.

"What? What is it?" Part of her didn't want to know.

"Ms., uh, Bourne. Has anything unusual happened to you recently? Have you experienced any head trauma, for instance? Or noticed any psycho-cognitive impairment? Forgetfulness? Dizziness, nausea? Hallucinations?" His deadpan delivery was worse than a leer somehow. Nev felt like he was accusing her of something.

"What? No. Nothing like that. I just, like I said, I'm feeling a bit of discomfort, and I'd really like to get this thing out of me for a while. Can you please take it out?"

He sighed. *Oh, no.* "Ms. Bourne, believe me, I would like to. Of course. And that's your right as a Qbito user. But, even if I could—even, that is to say, if I had the proper authorization and documentation, well, the fact is... I couldn't."

"I—I'm sorry?"

"I've never seen anything like this before. Here, I'll show you. You can replace your vizcom device now."

Nev hooked her viz back over her ear, and he flicked his hand toward her. A digital image appeared in her home folder, which she enlarged. It looked like a green spider clutching a circuit board, but she knew exactly what it was without his telling her.

"As you can see, that's your right orbital cavity, this is your frontal bone, your cranial two, you know all of this anatomy, correct?"

"Yeah. Yes. Correct."

"Okay. And that, obviously, is the SavePoint implant. Which is right where it should be. And this, right here..." the green spider thing lit up in her viz display, "well, to be honest, I'm not sure what this is. It looks to me like a ganglion of some sort. Those are definitely nerve fibers over here. But, as you can see…" He rotated the image in her display, showing her the same scene from a lower angle. "They seem to have gone completely hyperplasial for some reason."

"What?" Nev's stomach lurched in a sudden rush of dread, like she was spiraling into a black hole. She grabbed the chair's armrests, instinctively reaching for something solid.

"Well, I don't know why, or how, but basically, your nervous system seems to have grown into the device, or at least grown around it somehow. I… I've never seen anything like this." He met her eyes again, through both vizzes. "You must be very uncomfortable."

"I *am* uncomfortable." She took a long, slow breath to stop her voice from shaking. "That's what I've been trying to tell you. So, can you take it out?"

"Well, that's the thing. As I was saying, even if I wanted to, I don't know how I could. I certainly wouldn't want to cut my way through those nerve fibers, at least not without knowing what the medical consequences might be. It could cause a hematoma. A coma. Even death. If it's alright with you, I'd like you to stay here overnight. We can bring in some senior members of our neurological faculty tomorrow, and do a full workup."

Nev jumped up, out of the chair and was through the door of the pod before the biotech could blink.

"Actually, I forgot something! A meeting. I've got to run. It doesn't really hurt that much. I'm sure it'll be fine. I, I …"

Out of excuses, Nev turned and fled in silent terror.

QT.29.21.11.17.09.2045

"Nev?"

Maddy Barnett was waiting in the elevator when the gleaming steel doors opened.

"Everything alright?"

Nev froze, heart pounding after her frantic escape from the Phys Unit. She tried to slow her gulping breath as she stepped into the elevator. Maddy wrinkled her pert nose at the stench of fear filling the confined space. Nev had to use all her will power to resist looking over her shoulder for the biotech. The doors closed, the elevator lurched downwards, and she felt something unclench in her abdomen. Just a little.

"Oh. Hey, Maddy. Yes, I'm fine. Great, actually. How's it going?"

"Everything on our end is going well. I hope you'll be ready for the alpha launch next week. It's been a little while since we've gotten an update."

I've been here seven goddamn days a week, burning the midnight oil for months, Nev's brain shouted at Maddy. Except, Nev realized, maybe she hadn't. Not in this timeline. Whatever she was going to do in the days, weeks, months to come as she kept sliding backwards in time, it sure as hell wasn't going to be business as usual. Now that her Hail Mary had fallen on deaf ears, she had to come up with a new plan. A fresh exit.

"Nev?"

"Oh, yeah, sorry about that. My team has been working hard on rollout. I think we're still on target."

"You *think?*" Two perfect vertical lines appeared between Maddy's immaculately threaded eyebrows. Who did this woman think she was? Nev reported to Kusuma, not to marketing.

"I'm confident," Nev said. "I guess we've just been so busy, I haven't had the chance to file a status report. I'll have that in your folder by close of business, promise." Wow, she'd never lied about business deadlines before, but then again, she'd never been free of the consequences before.

"See that you do," Maddy said, as the doors opened onto the eighth floor, where Qbito's Biz Units were clustered. "And, for God's sake, Nev, stop dressing like a teenager. You're a unit leader. Act like one!" The elevator doors had already shut again before Nev could think of a halfway decent retort. A whiff of expensive perfume lingered behind. The elevator hummed back into motion and Nev noticed that the button for the sixth floor, programming and product development, was helpfully illuminated. Thanks, Maddy.

Maybe Maddy had a point. Kusuma had given her the brush-off. So had Anissa. Deinstallation was a bust. Nev was on her own. She hadn't really applied herself to ironing out whatever monster bug in the code was responsible for the Glitch. Once she had realized the issue was in the temporal code, she'd begun to doubt her own ability to fix it. But she'd never been one to shy from a challenge before. How many rusted out old machines had her dad dredged up from the junkyard and set her to work on when she was a kid? She'd brought old vacuum tube amps, cathode ray televisions, and 3D printers back to life, without instructions, or even formal schooling, all on her own, because her father threatened her with a whupping if she didn't. If she could make it work as an eleven-year-old, when all she had was a screwdriver, a soldering gun, and fear to run on, surely she could tackle this problem with the powerful combination of supercharged espresso, a masters from Stanford, and existential terror?

Plus, she missed her Memeron chair.

But first, caffeine. The sixth floor was mostly empty, as expected. Late morning on a Sunday was probably the quietest moment of the week. Everybody was drone racing in Mission Dolores Park or eating their way around the globe at the ceegee street food market nearby. Or they were home sleeping, catching up on all the hours of REM they'd missed pulling late nights during the week. Or most likely, they were playing the newest game release, Patriot Day, downloading the freshest skins. Whatever, Nev was glad to have the place to herself. Except—

"Darian?"

Anissa's replacement was standing at the La Pavoni again, head tilted to one side, seemingly perplexed by the vast array of buttons along its front. He jumped an inch in the air at the sound of his name, turning to face Nev with a petrified look in his eyes.

"Sorry," Nev said in as gentle a tone as she could muster, remembering their previous encounter at the La Pavoni when she'd terrified him into triggering his SavePoint. She didn't want to see what would happen to her if he used it again while he was standing mere inches away; another battle against invisible concrete was more than she could handle. Nev gave Darian a small smile and watched with relief as the fear in his eyes dropped by several gradients.

"Can I help you with that? It's kind of confusing."

"You wouldn't mind?"

"Not a problem," Nev said, stepping up to the machine.

Darian's shoulders went slack. He laughed with evident relief.

"To be honest, this is the first time I've been brave enough to go near that beast. I thought I'd wait until the weekend when no one was around before I tried to figure it out."

Nev was about to make some joke about their previous run-in at the La Pavoni before she remembered that it hadn't happened yet. *Huh*, she thought, as she gave Darian a quick tutorial on the machine's workings. She'd attributed his excessive friendliness last time they met to his cheerleading background, but maybe it was more than that. Maybe they had established some sort of bond today that bore fruit in the future. And maybe it would be helpful to have Darian on her team, after all. He knew something about temporal engineering, even if he'd only been at Qbito for a couple of weeks. Then again, whatever rapport she established now wouldn't exist the next time she saw him. If Nev was going to get help from Darian, now was the time.

"So, how's Qbito treating you? How are you finding the Temporal Unit?"

"It's great, really great. I feel blessed to have been hired."

Nev nodded in response as she contemplated the fork in the road ahead. Should she gain Darian's friendship by following his lead, putting her years of maternal bible instruction to service, and mirroring his positivity? Or say something cynical, cut through the bullshit, and bond through shared skepticism? If she made the wrong choice, she might have to risk undoing it with her SavePoint again.

Nev didn't like either option. Thankfully, there was a third way. Buy Darian's trust, or at least his undying gratitude.

Anissa had helped her hack her account a few months back, disabling the 24-hour control limit that normally prevented users from looping. SavePoint 1.0 beta testers had figured out quickly that, if they triggered the device at just the right interval, they could relive the same five seconds over and over again. For a few of them, it became a tunnel to madness, a way to chase and catch their dragon of choice, whether pleasure, pain, or simply pharmacological oblivion. Excessive loopers were prone to developing cerebral aneurysms, which ended up costing the company a few million slush fund dollars to hush up.

Then again, in more responsible hands, it was a nice trick to have up your sleeve. And, bible thumper though he might be, Nev was certain Darian would be grateful for the opportunity to catch whatever dragons he'd been chasing. Bottle the Holy Spirit. Worth a try, anyway.

"Cool, cool. So... anyone showed you yet how to hack the looper control on your account?"

Darian's eyes bugged out of his skull.

"Wait, I can do that?"

Bingo.

"Well... *you* can't. At least, not on your own, because you can't access the user account scripts. But if we work together, if I supply the user account password and you supply the temporal engineering passwords, then yes, *we* can."

Darian looked around the kitchen, as if checking for hidden cameras or microphones.

"Don't worry, Darian. No one's watching us." (Nev wasn't sure that was true, but she was pretty sure that if anyone was watching, they weren't too worried about a little in-house self-hacking.)

"Come on, let me show you my pod."

The SavePoint 2.0 alpha data team pod was entirely empty. Nice as it was to have the place to themselves, Nev felt a wave of annoyance at the slackers she'd hired. With the boss distracted, apparently they weren't putting in the hours. If she remembered correctly, when she'd lived through this day the first time, she'd definitely spent the afternoon with at least one or two junior coders. Once Nev finally got herself moving forward in time again, the whole team would be getting a talking to. She'd channel Christina's most righteous fire and brimstone sermonizing style. But for the moment, she had to play the role of Cool Nev, and get Darian on board.

"Excellent, we've got the place to ourselves. Pull up Andy's Memeron," Nev said brightly, gesturing beside her as she sat down to a glorious whirring of gears.

Darian dutifully sat down, awaiting further instructions like a robotic pet.

Nev pulled out two old-fashioned keyboards, placing one before each of them. She then used her viz to log into the SavePoint codebase, while tapping a dummy password into the keyboard in front of her. Darian made a point of looking in the other direction while she typed, but best not to take any chances.

"Now it's your turn," she said. "Log into the temporal processing server, then I'll be able to run the hack." She turned away to give Darian some presumptive privacy, opening a little home-brewed viz app designed to record the sound of keystrokes and extract inputted text. She watched the probabilistic model reveal the most likely keystrokes as Darian typed next to her. By the time his fingers had stopped, his password floated before her in acid green lettering: "T4rryT0wn-L3V1T1CU\$-gW3nd0L1nE-&bDsM". *Interesting.* You could learn a lot about someone from their passwords. She blinked, closing and saving the app's output to her password database, then turned back to face him.

"Okay," she said. "We're in. Now all you have to do is run this code…" she found LoopSkip.app in her viz library, and flicked it at him, enabling a single-use permission, "…and I'll get a prompt to validate on my end. Then you should be good to go."

She watched as Darian ran the app on his viz, then validated his access to the codebase. He smiled—a handsome, confident smile that momentarily dispelled the aura of awkwardness and repression that normally surrounded him like a raincloud—and reached a hand up to touch his nose. At the last moment, Nev realized what he was doing, and darted her own hand out to grab his finger.

"Ow! Wha-what was that for?" He sounded hurt and confused. The cloud was back.

"I'm sorry, Darian, I just—it's best not to try looping inside of Qbito's offices, okay?" She was riffing, but Darian was too close for comfort, and she'd say or do whatever was necessary to prevent another microglitch from happening. "Kusuma looks the other way when we hack on our own time, but the company doesn't need the liability if its own coders can't follow basic safety protocols in the office." *Wow, that sounded pretty legit.*

Darian nodded gravely. "Yes, I understand. I'm so sorry, Nev, I'm just excited... this is maybe the coolest thing that's ever happened to me."

I'll bet. "Heh, believe me. I can relate. But save it for the really fun stuff. You know." She looked at him frankly. "The safety protocols are there for a good reason. You can blow a capillary, put yourself into a vegetative state if you loop too much."

He nodded again, sweat beading his brow.

"I'm serious. The chances are pretty low if you take it easy, but don't overdo it, okay? You don't want to incur some damage you can't undo."

He nodded, putting on a serious face. "Yes, I understand. Thanks, Nev." Then he smiled, seemingly in spite of himself. The raincloud receded again, for a moment. "This is the greatest day of my life!"

Maybe mine, too, Nev thought. If the password she'd just swiped would give her access to fix whatever was causing the Glitch, she might actually be able to start living her life again, in the right direction. Seeing the smile on Darian's face also made her feel a little less guilty about abusing his trust. "You're a user," Anissa had told her. "You created this situation." Well, maybe she had, but she was doing her goddamned best to find her way out of it. And if young Darian could manage to use his newfound powers in moderation, not only was Nev doing no real harm, she was actually helping him. When used correctly, looping could be an interesting path to self-actualization.

"Well," Darian said. He seemed to have returned to his base state of awkward shyness. "I should, uh, probably be getting back to..." He half stood up, and the Memeron clicked and whirred, seemingly undecided about whether he was staying or going.

"No," Nev said, surprising herself. "No, I mean, you don't need to go yet. Tell me something about yourself. I know you were a cheerleader, right?" He sat back down, and she felt the guilty burn in her chest subside a bit more.

He grimaced. "Yeah. USC. Trojan for life." He did something with his fingers—presumably a team gesture. "I was actually captain junior year. Then…" he sighed, letting the air out slowly through puffed cheeks. "Well, I took a bad fall, spent half of my senior year in traction and PT."

Nev furrowed her brow sympathetically.

"But, you know. It's all good. That semester in bed was when I got really serious about physics. Read everything I could about loop quantum gravity, spatial-temporal dynamics, all the stuff we use here. It's kind of amazing, what we do. Especially once SP2 launches, right?" He smiled at her encouragingly, but she didn't take the bait.

"Well, tell me more. Like, where are you from? What got you into cheerleading? And applied physics?"

"Oh. Well, I dunno. The usual, I guess. I was the smart kid in my class, never much good at sports, though I always loved gymnastics. Grew up in Westchester." Nev shrugged and shook her head. "New York suburbs. Really nice place. My parents are both doctors. My dad works at a hospital in the city, my mom's got a family practice."

"Wow, two doctors. You must have been really healthy." *And really rich.*

"Heh, heh. Yeah. I mean, I guess I was. Am. Like I said, I wasn't really into sports or anything. Actually… the reason I got into cheerleading was for a girl."

"Ohhhh… Do tell. Was she, is she the Love Of Your Life?"

"Heh. No, no, no, no. It's not like that. I mean, I liked her a lot, but Gwen didn't really like me that way. But, anyway, I'm over that now. I've got, um, other stuff in my life, other people. And she did introduce me to cheering, so." Darian looked around him, then stood up decisively. "Well, Nev, it's been really great. Thanks for, uh, showing me how to use the coffee maker, and for, well, for everything. You've changed my life. Really."

"Hey, Darian. It was my pleasure. Glad to help out however you need it. If there's anything I can do for you, let me know.

Seriously, any time."

"Thank you so much." Darian extended his hand awkwardly, and Nev shook it. Then he pirouetted with surprising grace, and walked out of the room. He might not cheer any more, but Nev had to admit, he was still in very good shape.

Nev turned back to her desk, stowing the dummy keyboards back in a drawer, then pulling up the SavePoint 2.0 alpha code in one viz window, and the temporal processing code in another, unlocking it with Darian's password. But before she could get into her flow, something odd happened. She suddenly realized that the code was unintelligible to her. The closer she looked at it, the harder it was to read. It was as though each character on the page was simultaneously itself, and a superposition of every other possible character, a blur of probabilities that obstinately refused to settle down in its syntactical bed. And she wasn't so much sitting any more as floating, looking down through the viz at a bubbling cauldron of code soup.

For a moment, Nev even worried she might puke all over her desk. Then, with every synapse she could muster, she focused, directing all of her mental energy at a single character on a single line of code. She squinted through the viz, willing the character to resolve itself into anything definite. An ê or an 8, or a {—it didn't matter which, as long as it was *something*. After what seemed like an eon, she felt something move, just slightly, like an enormous cube balanced on a single corner, pivoting by a single degree. Then, all at once, it was as if she could feel the entire wave function collapsing, and she came crashing down to Earth, through an ocean of code, landing with a springy thump back in her Memeron chair. She focused on the character again. It was an i.

Another microglitch, despite her her assault on poor Darian's finger in her efforts to prevent one. They were getting more frequent, Nev thought. And more severe, maybe.

She sat there, breathing in the silence, for ten or fifteen minutes, eyes closed, feeling tiny electrical twinges all up and down her nervous system. *Come on, Nev. Now or never. Do or die.*

Nev opened her eyes. The alpha code and temporal code were still hovering in her field of vision. Each window was clearly legible, ready and waiting for her. The alpha code was substantially close to completion; she could probably get it into executable shape by the end of the day again. But the deeper she dug into it, the more she noticed changes from the original version she'd already completed. Strange syntax. Stems from other codebases. It was alright, she could work with it. Work around it.

There was something so peaceful about being alone in the room with the alpha. It hadn't even been a week, as Nev reckoned it, since the last time she'd had the chance to get elbows deep into pure code, but she realized very quickly how much she'd missed it—how much she needed it to maintain her emotional equilibrium. In the years after Faith had died and before she'd escaped to California, Nev's laptop had been the one place where she felt safe, and in control. In fact, it was the one thing in life that had made any sense at all. Now the Glitch had taken even that small comfort away.

Nev's fingers flew over her virtual keyboard, and the hours flew by beneath them. It was late afternoon, and her third coffee was beginning to wear off, when she reached the point where she had picked up the code on Zero Day. She was at the home stretch. Primed to finish the SavePoint 2.0 alpha code. *Congrats, hot stuff,* she toasted herself.

But Nev's feeling of victory was short lived. Almost at once, two hideous thoughts descended on her, bringing back with a rush the queasy feeling she'd experienced after she'd hacked Darian for his password this morning.

First, *what the fuck was she doing?* What was the point of completing the SavePoint 2.0 alpha again, when there were so many good reasons not to? For one thing, she knew from experience that she'd wake up again yesterday, with all of her hard work undone, like it had never happened to begin with. For another, this thing was dangerous. Executing the SavePoint 2.0 alpha code was the reason she'd gotten stuck in the Glitch to begin with. This time around, the code was different, somehow, but God knew what would happen if she tried to execute it. Could she get stuck inside of a second Glitch inside of the first Glitch? What would that even mean? *Jesus, Nev. Sisyphus much? You've just spent the entire afternoon repeating your own worst mistake. Figure it out, already.* She had to learn to start thinking about consequences.

Second—and, if anything, this was even more unnerving— Nev realized why the code seemed different. It was hard to pin down, because whoever did it had done a great job of covering their tracks, but the entire program was riddled with hooks into another code base. It was almost like finding out that there was a trap door in the basement of your house, leading to a whole other house that you could see into but couldn't enter for some reason. This was Kusuma-level code, foundational Qbito stuff. Gospel. *That bald bastard.* Nev realized he definitely knew more than he'd let on when she tried to tell him about the Glitch.

She was halfway to the door of the office, heading back up to the C-suite pod to confront him, when she realized he wasn't here. He'd spent most of the month before launch at some kind of ashram, an Esalen on steroids (or ayahuasca, more likely) in an undisclosed location. No vizzes, no phones. No SavePoints, even. *How convenient.*

As Nev stood in the dim, polarized afternoon light, wondering what to do next, Jared's dorky selfie wiggled itself into her periphery, interrupting her thoughts, such as they were. She glanced at it in spite of herself, opening the message in her viz. A picture appeared in her sightline, an oversaturated snapshot of eggplant slices coated in panko crumbs on a hardwood cutting board, next to a laser-engraved Japanese nakiri and a bottle of '42 Sonoma Zinfandel with a handwritten label. The accompanying text read,

Looking forward to tonight ;-)

Nev's stomach growled.

QT.07.51.22.17.09.2045

THE ONLY REASON she hadn't woken up at Jared's on Monday morning with a hangover, Nev realized as she slid her ass onto the barstool at Jimmy's, was going to be lack of time. She had approximately forty minutes to blot out the memory of the disastrous dinner with her once and future ex, before the Qbito quantum mainframe blotted her out.

"Boilermaker," she told the burly bartender.

He gave her a familiar cheeky grin.

"Good to see you back. Let me know if you need anything else."

Was the bartender flirting with her? His face rang a bell. Not his face, she realized as he turned his back to grab a pint glass from the shelf behind the bar. His shoulders, muscles bulging beneath his tight-fitting flannel. Hadn't she dug her nails into them in the bathroom of a pop-up chimales restaurant around the corner? He must have been off shift when she met him here the first time. Nev's face flushed as (Levi?) served her pint on a paper coaster, a shot glass of well whiskey on the side.

Blurry memories of their drunken encounter rushed back. He probably thought she was a total skank. At least he had

113

the grace to play it cool. Beyond a bit of heavy eye contact, he showed no sign of knowing her in the Biblical sense. Rare to meet a gentleman these days.

No, Nev. He's not playing it cool. It just hasn't fucking happened yet.

"Another," she said, putting down the empty shot glass. "Make it a Johnnie Walker, Black."

Jared had a membership in a whiskey club in the Marina, where they brought in exclusive labels. Nothing commercially available. Membership fees just paid for tasting access. Drinks began at $25 an ounce. Nev had no idea of the upper limits. He was always trying to persuade her of the superiority of Glen Gloyne Goine Morange McFiddich, or whatever. If life were fair, she'd never have to feign interest in his opinions again. Too bad they'd be back together again by yestermorrow morning.

Nev groaned loudly, sinking her head into her hands.

"I don't mean to be forward," Levi the bartender said, "but if you want to talk about it, I'm a good listener."

"You've already tried that line on me, Levi," Nev said.

"Oh yeah?" He smiled unapologetically, the same sly but friendly look in his eyes that had lured Nev in before. "I thought we hadn't made it past eye contact yet. So, did my line work?"

"Sure did. Odds of it working again would be decent, but I don't have time tonight."

"Hard to believe I could forget something happening between us, but if you say so..." Levi looked momentarily disconcerted, but his features soon slipped back into their habitual easy confidence. "I promise I won't next time." He gave her a wink and moved down the bar to another customer.

No matter what direction time moved, Nev seemed destined to repeat herself. Whatever her intentions. She'd gone to Jared's tonight meaning to do things differently. She didn't like him anymore, and maybe she never really had, but she figured she owed him the decency of ending things properly. She felt bad about their argument Monday morning. She was hoping that she could avoid that future for him by parting on amicable terms and forestalling what sounded like a doozy of a fight. But once she'd gotten to the apartment she didn't know what to say. She'd never been good at breaking up with guys. Typically she just ghosted them when the relationship stopped working.

It had taken her until after (an admittedly delicious) dinner to find the right words. She told him that she'd never meant the relationship to get serious. She had just been looking to have fun together, but she could see he wanted something deeper, so she thought it was only fair to break it off. Then it turned out those weren't the right words. He started saying something about how she'd been using him. She got angry and told him that she honestly didn't need this shit, she had enough on her plate already. He made a pointed remark about how her plate looked pretty empty to him. Maybe waiting until after dinner was a mistake. She said the argument was pointless anyhow because he wouldn't even remember it the next day. He asked her what the fuck she was talking about. Then she stormed out to avoid having to explain.

Next time they broke up, she wouldn't even get to eat first.

"This seat taken?"

Nev turned, prepared to tell the dude sidling up to her to fuck off, since what did she have to lose—she'd be blinking out in a minute anyhow. But it wasn't a dude. Or, at least, she wasn't certain if they thought of themself as a dude or not.

"Airin?"

"Nev." It was just a single word, and yet somehow the way that Airin said her name sounded like a poem a thousand lines long.

"I don't understand. What are you doing here?"

"I don't have time to explain now. Meet me futurepast morning. The Park Chalet."

"Huh? Why? Wait, what time?"

Series complete. LoopID?QT.43.33.23.17.09.2045

115

QT.51.32.09.16.09.2045

As NEV'S TESSERACT EZ5 backed itself into a parking space at the Park Chalet, a tangerine orange 1973 Porsche 911 Carrera RS electrofit pulled in alongside, its glossy paint job refracting the rays of the bright morning sun to blinding effect. Nev had to squint to see the figure emerging from the car. She expected some fat cat brogrammer wearing steroidal kicks and smart shades to tumble from the driver's-side door, but instead, a pair of long, shapely, black-clad legs slid out, followed by a lean and muscular torso, topped with radiant purple hair, waving in the ocean breeze.

Nev jumped out of her seat, slamming the EZ5's car door as she stalked over to the hacker, who stood beaming next to the gleaming orange carapace, like a sci-fi hero gloating over a vanquished space bug.

"9:33:23" Airin said, catching Nev off guard.

"What?"

"Tomorrow night you're going to ask me what time we meet this morning. That's the answer. 9:33:23."

"What the fuck, Airin? Were you following me?"

Airin turned around and stared pointedly at the tangerine Porsche.

"Did you see me following you?"

"No…"

"Don't you think you would have noticed?"

Airin had a point. There was no way Nev could have overlooked this beast in her rearview mirror. For one thing, the '73 Porsche 911 was one of Nev's top five favorite cars of all time. Her dad had kept a stack of old Porsche calendars in the trailer he used for his office at the junkyard, and Nev had spent many happy hours memorizing their contents when she was little. For another thing, it was *bright fucking orange*.

"What then? Are you geotracking my phone?"

"No, Nev. I'm not tracking you. You told me what time to get here."

"I don't remember that."

Airin looked at Nev expectantly, waiting a beat for the logic to set in.

"From your perspective it hasn't happened yet," they said finally.

Nev knit her eyebrows together. "So you say, but why should I believe you?"

Airin gestured at the car again.

"Do you think it's a coincidence that I pulled in here driving one of your childhood dream cars? How many of these do you think are out there? You're the one who bought it for me."

"I did what?"

Nev's knees went wobbly, and for a second she thought she might collapse, but then Airin was by her side, their left hand supporting Nev's elbow, grip surprisingly strong.

"Come on, let's go inside. I'll buy you a hot chocolate and I can explain."

Ten minutes later, Nev was seated across from Airin at a corner table against the window, shivering a bit despite the warm sun and the aromatic steam curling up from her mug. Airin, who hadn't touched the blondie on their plate or taken a sip of their gen mai cha, was watching her silently, eyebrows slightly raised, like two inverted breves over their deep brown, almost black eyes.

"Okay," Nev said, after a deep, shaky breath. "First things first:

we haven't spoken since Stanford. Frankly, I'm shocked you even remember me. But here you are," she gestured abstractly, "buying me hot chocolate, driving my favorite car, acting like... like... we're friends or something. Like you *know* me. So, you know, pardon me if I find this all a little hard to swallow."

Airin laughed to themself, purple bouffant bobbing as they shook their head, giving Nev a glimpse of dark roots beneath.

"I get it, Nev. Believe me, I understand. But you know how this works. Your past is my future. And your future, well, I've been a part of it. For a while. I *do* know you. We *are* friends. At least, we were. We will be."

A plume of suspicion erupted in Nev's chest, spreading its acid warmth through her limbs. The first thing Qbito taught its engineers in its obligatory tactical cybersec workshop was that the human heart is the weakest link in any sociotechnical system. Trust needs to be earned. Verified. More precisely, if a notorious hacker suddenly appears in your life, acting like an old buddy, assume the worst until they've proven themselves.

"How do I know this isn't social engineering? How do I know that you're not the one who... who got me into this mess to begin with?" Best not to tip her hand too far; who knew what Airin did and didn't know about the Glitch.

"You're right." Airin put their hands on the table, long fingers splayed. "You don't know me from Adam... any more. I know I've got to earn your trust. Well, for starters, you once told me that nothing matters to you more than Faith."

Nev could hear the capital F in Airin's voice. If the hacker was engaged in some kind of long con, invoking her dead sister was a pretty low blow. Then again, it did sound like the kind of thing Nev would tell a close friend who would need a shortcut through her defenses. She took a sip of hot chocolate, just to hide her face until she could compose herself. Then she put the mug back down on the table between them, like a chess piece.

"Sorry, not good enough. If you really know me, you know what I've been going through, right?"

Airin smiled, almost ruefully, and dropped their voice to little more than a whisper. "Yes, I know about the Glitch. I've been working with you on it for weeks. In fact, I know a lot more than you do, right this moment. Though, of course, that will change, too."

"So you've been helping me fix it?"

"After a fashion, yes."

"Yeah, sorry, that doesn't compute. First of all, as far as I can tell, nothing has changed. If you've spent the past few weeks 'helping me', why am I still stuck going," Nev lowered her own voice to match Airin's, "backwards in time? And, second of all, why am I only hearing from you now? Where have you been for the past week, while I've been dealing with this fucked up situation on my own?"

"Nev." Airin sighed. "I don't know what I'm going to do between now and Zero Day—that's the future for me. But I do know that we finished our coding work together yesterday, and today is the first time we're actually having a conversation, at least from your point of view. Wow, I guess this is almost the end for me ..." they trailed off. Airin turned away for a moment, like they'd seen a friend out the window. Then they turned back with a small smile and sighed. "I wouldn't change a thing, though."

Feeling awkward, Nev reached in her pocket for the mystery stone and flipped it back and forth in her hands.

"I wish I had one of those," Airin said. "It always seems to bring you comfort."

Nev looked at her hands with a start. "What do you know about my stone?"

"Remember: your future, my past; my past, your future. I've seen you do this before."

Nev tried to reorient herself to the proper flow of time. After a week in the Glitch, it was a struggle to remember that Zero Day was actually ahead of Airin, not behind them. It was exhausting, trying to live in two directions at once.

They both sipped their drinks, an almost companionable silence settling between them. Nev studied Airin's profile, illuminated in the morning sun. Somewhere outside, a dog barked.

"Well, actually, tomorrow isn't really the last time."

"What?" Airin turned back towards her. There was a quiet intensity about them.

"It's not really goodbye for you. Not yet, I mean. Technically."

"You mean, we see each other again after tomorrow night?" Something in Airin's voice made Nev trust them even more. Genuine eagerness, but also a sadness, deep enough that she couldn't hear the bottom of it.

"Yes, twice more, this past week. And then, after that, who knows? The first time, or, I guess, the last time, from your perspective, was the night before Zero Day, at Jimmy's. We didn't talk or anything, but I saw you there, watching me. I thought... I thought maybe you had something to do with the Glitch."

"Well, you were right. I did. Technically."

Now it was Nev's turn to smile. She didn't remember Airin being this warm and clever back in Stanford days. They'd always been so cool and distant, like the light from an ancient supernova that's traveled halfway across the galaxy before trickling into your eyes.

Now, the heat in their eyes was almost incendiary.

"And you said there was a second time?"

"Yeah. Sorry. I saw you the next day. The day before. Wednesday morning. Here. At the Park Chalet. I came here on a whim and you were already sitting here. Right over there, at that table. I wondered if you were watching me and how you knew where to find me when I had no idea where I was going to be five minutes earlier," Airin looked over, clearly making another mental note. Something dawned on Nev. "But I guess it was because... because I just told you that."

The force of the realization hit Nev like a punch in the gut. Airin knew her. More than that, Airin knew what Nev was going through. She didn't have to try to find the words to explain it, because apparently she'd already found those words. And

Airin wanted to help. No, Airin already was helping. Nev felt an unfamiliar wetness in the corners of her eyes and before she could wipe it away, a horrible sob wracked her body. She cried ugly tears, mortified by the snot running from her nose but unable to stem the outpouring. Airin watched with a pained expression. Nev had the distinct impression that they wanted to reach out and stroke her hair, or hold her by the hand, but resisted for Nev's sake, uncertain whether the touch would be welcome. Instead, they extended a handful of napkins for Nev to wipe her face.

"I, I'm sorry," Nev gasped. "This is so embarrassing. I never cry like this. I just—" she hesitated, uncertain how to finish the sentence.

"You've just been bottling it up inside since Zero Day and have had no one to talk to about the fucking crazy situation you're in. Honestly, Nev, I can't believe you've held it together as well as you have. I would have lost my shit a long time ago."

The kindness of Airin's words sent Nev into a new cascade of tears. She could feel the stares of the restaurant's other customers, and was dimly aware of Airin gesturing the waiter away, making space for Nev to regain her composure. When she finally caught her breath, words took the place of sobs and Nev was pouring out the story to Airin of everything that had happened since the Glitch. By the time she finished, her drink had gone cold.

"So what do we do now?" Nev asked, pushing the cup away from her.

"Order you a fresh hot chocolate?"

Nev actually laughed. It felt good.

"No, you know what I mean. Although, a hot hot chocolate does sound good."

Airin waved over the waiter and placed the order, adding on a cheese plate ("we're going to be here for a while").

"The first thing we have to do," they said, "is work out our protocols. How we're going to work together when you're moving backwards and I'm moving forwards. It's not so easy, as I've learned. Especially since you can't write anything down one day and have it to read the next futurepast day. Good thing you never forget numbers."

Nev blushed a little at the praise, then scolded herself. No time for vanity. No need to clothe herself in scarlet and deck herself with ornaments of gold. Better just to focus on the situation at hand.

"So, how do we handle it?" Nev asked. "I guess you already know the answer?"

"The basic principle is straightforward. We take each day on its own. We don't share a future, we don't share a past, we only have the present. Each day, each of us has to tell the other where our next meeting will be. I'll tell you where we met the day before, you tell me where we meet the next day. Since the code has to be built from the foundation up, I have to run the project. You have to trust me and follow my instructions."

Nev felt a tiny tongue of suspicion flare up again in her chest, and Airin nodded slightly, as if they could see it.

"For now. In the past it was the other way around, you'll see what I mean," Airin said reassuringly. "There are two key constraints: I can't go to Qbito, and you can't go past 23:33:43. If I'm going to give you instructions for a day's coding package, it has to be in the morning before you go to work. You need to get to Qbito with enough time to get through the package before 11:33pm."

"Wait, wait," Nev said. "Slow down. I'm trying to follow, but I don't understand—how can I code on foundations that I haven't yet built?"

"You have built them already. You're the one who designed the program."

"Well, can you tell me what we've built, so I understand what I'm doing each day?"

A mournful look passed over Airin's face. They shook their head, schooling their features into bland neutrality.

"I can't do that."

"Why not?"

"You have to have the idea yourself."

"Why? Who cares whose idea it is? Or was?"

"Sorry, babe."

Babe? Not in a million years would Nev have imagined that the infamous Airin Myx would be calling her by endearments. But that mystery paled in comparison to the bigger questions swarming through her head.

"Come on. You have to tell me more. What the fuck are we working on?"

The expression on Airin's face softened a bit under Nev's importunate gaze.

"You know I wouldn't have expected it, but I'm really going to miss that angry face you make. I bet it's a spitting image of your mama."

Nev tried to protest but Airin waved away her objections with a practiced hand. "Keep that angry feeling for the next time you see me, when I show you the code we've been working on. You're going to need that fire in your belly. Now let's get down to business. This Humboldt Fog isn't going to eat itself."

QT.38.24.09.15.09.2045

NEV'S VIZ READ "9:24am 15 Sep" when the blue line she'd followed from her doorstep terminated at the loading bay of a Dogpatch factory whose address Airin had sent over sometime before the chimes woke her that morning. After a backwards week of yestermorrows and futurepasts, it was refreshingly simple to think of each day in terms of its fixed date, not its relationship to other days—a protocol that Airin had put in place on the 16th before they parted ways at the Park Chalet. Or maybe it was Nev's idea and she just hadn't had it yet. Who knew?

Nev hoisted herself up to the dock and stood in front of the mottled iron door reading "Sino-Tronic Ltd" before entering the 12-digit number Airin had given her into the keypad mounted on the jamb and smiling awkwardly into the cam above it. An almost inaudible click alerted her that the door was unlocked, and she pushed it open on its heavy hinges, entering a dusty, gray hallway terminating in an old-fashioned freight elevator with an accordion-style iron gate.

After getting in and closing the gate behind her, she pulled the lever to the right, enjoying the simple thrill of operating the lift herself—a first, as far as she remembered—and stopped at the fifth floor. As soon as she arrived, the door rolled open on its casters, and Nev's senses were bombarded with a dazzling cascade of sunlight, the funky croon of Stevie Wonder, and the enticing smell of fresh coffee.

Nev stumbled blinking into Airin's apartment, a high-ceilinged loft space whose dimensions seemed to defy physics, stretching at least twice the length of the building as seen from the outside. But before her eyes or brain could adjust to its homey grandeur, a small polar bear rushed towards her and leapt for her jugular.

"Ava! Down!" Airin's laughing contralto chided the dog as they came over and took Nev by the hand, guiding her to sit on a surprisingly comfortable 3D printed faux wooden loveseat. "Here," they said, handing Nev something that looked like an oatmeal cookie. "She loves these." The Great Pyrenees gobbled it up in one bite from Nev's shaking palm, then proceeded to lick between her fingers, up her arm, and all over her face and neck, for good measure. "She loves you, too," Airin said, laughing even harder. "Don't worry, you love her back. Can I get you some coffee?"

"Yes, please, with—"

"Cane sugar and cashew milk, right? No need for an 8-ball today, I think."

"Thanks. Yes. Right." Of course Airin knew. "How long—?"

"Have we been working together on this? Oh, not long. Not long at all. Only about three weeks. We met on August 29th. Though I think I might have seen you the night before, at Jimmy's. I don't know, it's been... it seems like much longer." They sighed, placing a steaming mug on the elaborate, polished mahogany table in front of Nev. It looked strangely out of place in the hacker's loft; Nev thought it would have worked better as set dressing in one of the BBC costume dramas her grandmother loved. "Careful, it's hot. And Ada Lovesnacks here has a bad habit of knocking things over."

Airin watched thirstily as Nev took her first sip of coffee.

"Aren't you going to have some too?"

"Oh, no. I don't like coffee. I'm more of a tea sort of person." Airin laughed, a little self-consciously.

"Oh, okay," Nev said uncertainly, taking another drink from her mug under Airin's watchful gaze. "It's not drugged or something, is it?"

"What? No! NO! I'm sorry, am I being a little weird? Right, right. Straight to work." Airin's facial expression settled into the studied nonchalance that Nev remembered from their classes together. Picking up a black Moleskine and pen from the mahogany table, they flipped to a ribbon-marked page.

"First order of business: where and when do we meet on September 16th?"

A twinge of hurt passed through Nev at the realization that Airin did not remember—could not remember—their hours-long conversation at the Park Chalet. She did her best to hide her feelings, attempting to work her own features into the same bland neutrality that Airin had assumed.

"9:33:23 in the parking lot of the Park Chalet."

Airin studiously took note in the Moleskine. Was that a little smile at the corner of their mouth?

"Oh, and the next night, the 17th, I guess, you meet me at Jimmy's, around 11:30, shortly before, uh…"

"Before your reset? Okay, thanks. Now it's my turn. Remember this, Nev. We met on September 14th here at my place, 9:17:52."

Nev made a mental note.

"What now?"

"Now, we get to work."

Airin stood up abruptly and walked behind the loveseat towards one of the loft's cinderblock walls, which were hung with realistic oil portraits of thoroughbreds standing in front of trees, next to or underneath country esquires in English riding gear. Nev watched in astonishment as Airin placed their hands on the wall, causing a double row of blocks to give way beneath their touch, falling in and then sliding aside, revealing a narrow, dark hallway beyond. Airin sidled through and disappeared from view. Ada Lovesnacks, who had been sitting next to Nev, drooly chin propped on one of her knees, looked up with her soft doggie eyes and whined.

"You expect me to go in there?"

Ada didn't answer.

"I sure hope this isn't a Bluebeard's Castle situation," Nev said to the dog. She sighed and stood up. "Even if it is, I guess I won't be trapped back there for long." She glanced at the time stamp on her viz. "Just another thirteen hours, give or take."

Nev stepped cautiously through the gap in the wall. She was in a narrow passage lit by dim runner lights attached to the floor. They pulsed in a slow green wave, gesturing forward like an arrow. Nev followed the lights to a sharp corner, and turned a hard left into a second short hallway that ended abruptly in a steel door, open on its hinges. Nev stopped at the threshold but Ada, who had been following on her heels, nudged her forward in her eagerness to reach Airin. Nev tumbled through the door, half persuaded she was about to enter a torture chamber, but instead of iron maidens and wooden racks, the room was packed with tables and shelves hosting all manners of tech, from the archaic to the modern to the futuristic and completely unrecognizable.

"Oh. My. God. Airin. What is this place? Where did you get all this stuff?" If it weren't for her pride, she would have squealed with delight. If her father could see this place, he would have thought he'd died and gone to heaven.

Then she noticed the translucent projection screen, filled with lines of code that Nev recognized all too well, Airin's face dimly visible through the characters.

"The SavePoint 2.0 alpha! How did you get that?" Nev demanded, the icy tentacles of suspicion compressing her heart once more.

"You gave it to me, Nev. How else? Take a seat. I'll show you."

Nev sat down on a chair opposite to Airin, so that the projection hung between them. A keyboard illuminated beneath her fingers. From Nev's perspective, the code appeared in the correct orientation. By some trick, Airin's perspective must have appeared in the correct orientation as well. Either that, or Airin could read and type backwards, since as soon as Nev sat down they started typing, picking up where they must have left off the previous day. Nev watched for a couple of minutes as the lines accreted, recognizing the foundations of the code that she had seen during her last visit to the Qbito offices, after she'd escaped from the human subjects pod and wiggled her way out of the confrontation with Maddy.

"Wait, wait … what is *that*?" Nev said, her own fingers flying over her keyboard as she isolated a bracketed sequence within the new lines.

"That," Airin said, picking up the line from where Nev's cursor hovered, "is the uh … fix you've designed." Characters spilled forward as Airin worked.

"But that's not Qbito code," Nev said.

"No," Airin agreed, "it's not."

"I thought Qbito's security protocols were impossible to hack. How did you get onto the server?" Nev asked in wonderment.

"We're not on the server. This is a mock-up that we've built. A Potemkin Qbito. Every night I work on the problem of how to insert the fix code you've designed into the Qbito code. You come here in the morning and I walk you through the implementation. Then you go to work and make the insertions. We're almost finished."

"But if we're almost finished and the plan is so good, why am I still going back in time? Doesn't that mean the fix isn't working? Isn't going to work?"

"I'm sorry Nev, I really am. But I can't answer that question. The only thing I can tell you is that the fix is your design. I'm here to help you figure out how to get it into the Qbito code, the rest is your handiwork. Look here."

Nev's eyes followed Airin's cursor as they opened a cascading function stack. She watched, mesmerized as the code peeled back to a line harboring a numerical sequence inset at its base, 56110817112031. *Dear God.* The date and time of Faith's death was a numerical sequence Nev would always remember, and no one else—not even the Bay Area's greatest hacker—could possibly guess. There was no doubt about it now, Nev herself had built the Potemkin. Ava nosed her hand, and Nev stroked the dog's silky head absently, scratching behind her ears.

"OK. I'm convinced. Let's do this."

QT.52.17.09.14.09.2045

ADA LOVESNACKS GREETED Nev at the elevator bay, pushing her wet nose into Nev's hands.

"Hold on a moment, I'll get you a treat to feed her," Airin said, tugging Ada by the collar to make room for Nev to get off the elevator.

"No need, I've got it covered," Nev said, allowing Ada to burrow between her fingers and find the nacho cheez flavored Milkbone she'd been concealing. Nev had discovered a box of them, three-quarters full, on the table by her front door that morning. She didn't know Airin well enough to assess how the hacker would feel about their beloved beast dining on fast food, but Ada sure seemed to appreciate it, crunching the biscuit loudly between her incisors.

"You're going to miss those orange MSG-bombs when this is over, aren't you Ada," Airin asked, eyes fixed down on the dog, long fingers scratching its broad white forehead. "Thought this might be the day, but you got lucky."

"Sounds like this isn't the first time Ada's gotten a nacho Milkbone from me, but it's the first time I've given her one," Nev said, trying not to trip up on the weirdness of the situation. Her prior self must have bought the MSG-sticks at some point recently, and since the box hadn't been in her apartment yestermorrow that must mean she would get rid of it later tonight, presumably since she now knew this was the last opportunity she had to dispense them to their intended recipient. Add that to the to-do list

"Yestermorrow—I mean September 15th—was the first time I met her. I got here at 9:24 a.m. You sent me the coordinates on my cell phone."

"Oh, right," Airin said evenly. "OK. Let me make a note."

Airin pulled their black Moleskine from a pocket of their pants and scribbled briefly with a thin silver pen.

"We met here yesterday, I mean futurepast—September 13th—a little earlier than today. Closer to 9."

"Cool."

An awkward pause floated between them, before it was mercifully interrupted by the loud click of an electric kettle shutting off.

"That's the water for your coffee. Give me a minute, I'll be right back," Airin said, retreating hastily to the loft's kitchen corner.

Nev wandered over to the loveseat, thought about taking a seat on its hard surface, reconsidered, and walked over to the painted cinderblock wall that concealed Airin's code dungeon. She searched the cement grouting between the horse portraits for some sign of fracture, but the rough surface betrayed nothing. Raising her hands to the wall, she gave a tentative push in the area where she remembered the door manifesting itself. There was no give or movement. She was running her fingertips along a vertical groove when Airin walked up, holding two steaming mugs, wreathed in the mingled scents of fresh-brewed coffee and genmai cha.

"You should put some cream on that," Airin said, gesturing towards a faded red welt on her left hand that Nev hadn't noticed.

"Oh," Nev said. "Thanks, I will." *Wonder where that came from. Guess I'll find out.*

"Are you okay? What are you waiting for?" Airin asked.

"I don't know how it works."

"But ..." Airin looked surprised, if only briefly. "Right. I guess this is when I teach you. Hold these."

Nev took the hot drinks, sipping from the coffee that Airin had considerately placed in her left hand.

"The mechanism is heat-triggered. Certain areas are painted with ThermoSensor latex. You have to make contact with five distinct target areas at the same time for the unlock sequence to activate. Watch carefully."

Airin stepped up to the wall and arranged their hands in carefully splayed positions so that their fingertips made contact with five different sections of cinderblock. The door magically sank inwards beneath their touch.

"It helps to have long fingers," Nev observed.

"Yeah, they come in handy," Airin said with a mischievous look.

Nev raised her eyebrows, surprised.

"That's not what I meant!" Airin blushed furiously. "I was just making a pun. Long fingers... Handy. Get it? Jeez, Airin, stop talking, you're just digging in deeper."

Nev took another sip of coffee, watching over the rim of her mug as the hacker stammered. They were kind of cute when they were embarrassing themself.

"Just close the door already and give me a chance," Nev said, putting Airin out of their misery.

It took a few attempts, but eventually Nev managed to get her fingers into the awkward arrangement that triggered each of the heat sensors. The feel of the wall giving way beneath her touch was even more satisfying than the sound of the Memeron's gears whirring when she sat down at Qbito. Even better, this mechanism was the real thing.

She followed Airin's lead into the dimly lit hallway that led to the steel door. Again, she found herself dazzled as they entered the space, lined with racks of arcane technology, like a cross between a museum and a speakeasy dreamt by the world's nerdiest sleeper.

Nev wondered where Airin had gotten hold of half the things on the tables and shelves. It wasn't the kind of stuff you could buy online—even at most of the darkweb warez merchants she'd patronized in her Stanford days. It also bore little resemblance to Qbito's gleaming R&D labs, chock full of snazzy prototypes and clean as a baby android's bottom. It was somehow both immaculate and messy, futuristic and atavistic, all at the same time. And, to top things off, she noticed an old 1980s-era arcade game in the corner that had somehow escaped her attention yestermorrow, illustrated with comic book-style space battles and laser blasts. Something called Defender. The perfect icing on the cake. This room was the stuff Nev's own skunk works dreams were made of.

It was overwhelming. Nev had stumbled into an all-you-can-eat gourmet buffet after a long fast. Every place her eyes landed offered up new treats, new promises for adventure. But her joy and excitement were tinged with unease. She felt like an impostor who had gained entry to the promised land under false pretenses. Yestermorrow morning, the idea that Airin would blithely hand over the keys to their kingdom would have seemed insane. They hadn't been friends at Stanford. She doubted Airin even remembered her from then. That was probably for the best. Nev had never been great at making friends, or even being one, as Anissa had made so abundantly clear. Yet here she was, standing in a goddamn wonderland, at the invitation of the most notoriously secretive red-hat hacker in the Bay Area. Nev had no idea what she would possibly say or do in the futurepast to earn Airin's trust, or how many times she'd be invited back before the two of them were strangers again.

QT.58.39.12.13.09.2045

"ANOTHER CUP?"

"Mmm. Yes, please."

Nev stroked Ada's velvety, white forehead and passed her empty mug to Airin. It was a glorious, warm day. The windows were wide open, bringing the sounds of gulls cresting through the room on gentle gusts of a salty breeze undercut by the oily tang of biodiesel. After spending the past three and a half hours cooped up in Airin's windowless code dungeon, Nev could almost feel her skin cells sucking in the fresh air and full-spectrum light.

Airin came over and placed her mug in the center of the little mahogany table, handle perfectly positioned to accommodate Nev's left-handedness. For all their studied coolness, Nev was beginning to sense an obsessive-compulsive strain in Airin's personality matrix, a dislike of disorder, a love of symmetry and balance, a need to keep everything just so. The loft was brimming with knick-knacks, but everything had its place, like the fabbed composite shelf along the wall, stacked with vintage glass electrical insulators, each one a different color of the rainbow, and each one perfectly spaced a hand's width apart from one another and gleaming as though they'd been dusted that very morning.

It was kind of reassuring, considering that Nev's life probably depended on Airin's fastidious attention to detail. But it was also a stark contrast to her own spartan sloppiness. As wonderful as it was to visit Airin's loft, Nev found herself wondering how long she'd last trying to live there. She owned few possessions—maybe a reaction to her own upbringing in the midst of a ten-acre lot littered with industrial detritus—but she still tended to leave them in a jumble.

"Nev." Airin was standing in front of her, a steaming mug of tea in their own right hand, half smiling. They looked almost angelic, backlit by the midday sun, their purple hair shining like a halo. Or an aura, if you believed in that kind of thing. Which Nev definitely didn't.

"What. Yeah. Sorry. I was just, uh… I guess I'm kind of wiped out. That coding session was pretty intense." *Keep it together. Focus on the task at hand.*

"For sure. But I think we're getting close to finished."

"Yup. Two more days. We wrapped it all up on the 15th."

Airin's smile faltered a bit, but they seemed to catch themselves, lips twitching before settling into a School Photo Day simulacrum of cheer. "So. Right on schedule, then. Great. Do you want to stay for lunch? You should still have plenty of time to implement today's batch before reset if you get to Qbito by 1:30 or so… But, hey, no worries either way, I've still got a metric fuck-ton of work to do on the Scotland project, so, whatever."

Nev felt a slight pang of guilt. Maddy had been dropping hints about her absenteeism, and Nev's Memeron logs, showing unprecedented hours of empty seat time, were probably setting off flashing red lights in HR. If she slacked off this afternoon, Maddy would break out the tungsten nailfile and start sharpening her talons for the kill. But that was a problem for yestermorrow Nev.

"No. No, I'd love to hang out for a while. Clear my head before I get back into this stuff. Hold on a sec, I need to go to the baaaaaaaaaaa…"

Airin's face was suddenly at the end of a long hallway. Or maybe the wrong end of a telescope. And it was below her, and she was falling towards it, faster than sixteen feet per second squared, more like the accelerating gravitational yank of a black hole. She could see her own nose and hair spaghettied out in front of her, miles-long tendrils of Nev toppling into a bottomless well with purple hair and a worried look, and somehow above and behind a polar bear like a crescent moon arcing through the daylit night, the rippling echo of a growl and a bark battering her nanometer-thin spaghetti legs like the first song plucked on the superstrings of nothingness at the instant of creation, and then she was on the floor in a heap, broken shards of ceramic mug around her face and the fresh, wet bite of scalded skin all along her fingers and wrist.

Now Airin was the one looking down at her, and the crescent moon was licking her face, and all Nev could do was close her eyes and try to catch her breath, which was still erupting in ragged, painful coughs and sobs.

"Nev! Nev! It happened again. A megaglitch! But not as bad. They seem to be getting better. Hold on, I'm going to get you a pillow and an ice pack. Don't move."

"Getting better?" Nev croaked. Her head was splitting.

Airin came back with the pillow, which was down-filled in a linen pillowcase. They must have snatched it off their bed, since the living room furniture was all angular and decidedly un-puffy. Nev hadn't been inside Airin's bedroom, which was at the opposite end of the loft from the hacking lair. As Airin gently tucked the pillow behind Nev's head, she was soothed by the smell of their shampoo and something else behind it. The smell of Airin.

"You should be prepared," Airin said, laying a cold gel pack on her hand. "From your perspective, they are going to get worse."

"How much worse?"

"It won't be good," Airin said, in a tone that dissuaded Nev from pushing any further. "I'll fetch you a painkiller, too." They disappeared again.

Nev closed her eyes and took a series of slow, deep breaths, trying to regain her composure. What was it her alarm had said this morning? That old Ronald Niebuhr prayer her mother had stitched onto a sampler and hung in the living room: *God, give me Grace to accept with serenity the things that cannot be changed, Courage to change the things which should be changed, and the Wisdom to distinguish the one from the other*. Whoever had hacked Nev's viz and installed the app had an uncanny sense of timing.

Airin came back in the room with an aerosolized NSAID ampule. Nev took a quick sniff and immediately felt the medication work its way along her neural pathways, dampening the flares of pain in her cerebral cortex and on the burned flesh of her hand. She lay back for another minute until the pain in her skull had retreated enough that she could see clearly, then she gingerly began to sit up.

"Whoa," Airin said, placing a hand on Nev's shoulder to keep her down. "Don't you think you ought to take it easy for a while? That might not have been as bad as your worst megaglitches, but it was still pretty scary."

"Airin, I'm fine, really." She placed her hand over Airin's to give them a reassuring pat, but an unexpected tingle of electricity passed between them as bare skin brushed bare skin. Both snatched their hands back suddenly and the warm flush of mutual embarrassment heated the air between them.

"I'll go get the dustpan," Airin said, rushing from the room.

Nev took another deep breath, stood up and put on her light jean jacket, and had crossed to the elevator door by the time Airin returned.

"You're leaving already?" Airin asked.

"I have to. Lots to do. Time to change the things which should be changed, etc. etc."

"Of course! Of course."

"Well, see you tomorrow, September 14th, here at your place, 9:17."

"Right, saw you yesterday, September 12th, my place, same timeish."

QT.41.07.13.12.09.2045

"SOMEONE'S GETTING A late start," Madison chirped as Nev walked through the ground floor lobby at Qbito a little after 1:00 p.m.

Nev had taken up Airin on their offer of lunch today, to make up for her hasty departure the day before (or tomorrow, from Airin's perspective). The weather was hot and dry: wildfire weather. For a welcome change, though, there was no smell of smoke lingering in the September air. Airin had suggested a pizza place around the corner for a quick bite. Nothing fancy, but it had a nice patio, perfect for soaking up the UV rays and storing some vitamin D before the city's monsoon season set in. *If I ever see the other side of Zero Day.*

Nev wondered when was the last time Maddy had eaten pizza. Judging from her rail thin body and hollowed-out cheeks, she guessed it had been a while. *What will it profit a woman if she gains the whole pie, and loses the ability to eat a slice?*

"Yeah, I'm shifting to more of an afternoon-through-late-night schedule, Mads. Finding the quiet hours at Qbito are really upping my productivity," Nev said, trying to mirror Maddy's passive-aggressive cheerfulness, as she breezed past the CMO into the waiting elevator.

139

She knew Maddy hated being called Mads. Some ex-boyfriend she'd caught cheating used to call her that, according to Anissa. Goddamn, Nev really missed Anissa sometimes. She felt a flood of regret that she hadn't stood up for her truest friend when it counted the most. Nev could hardly identify anymore with the hard-ass careerist who had left Anissa dangling in the wind just to keep the peace with a snake like Madison Barnett. Nobody could have seen the Glitch coming, but at least Anissa had been smart enough not to rule it out. Asking the mainframe to not merely restore users to their previous spacetime coordinates but also to predict their multiple possible futures for the benefit of corporate marketing stressed the calculation capabilities of the quantum mainframe to the point of temporal destabilization. Unfortunately, the one potentiality Anissa hadn't been prepared for was that she'd get fired for even raising the issue. And Nev had watched mutely as Maddy had laid into her closest friend, questioning her 'loyalties' as though she was a suspected Antifa at the Carlson hearings in '38. It hurt to contemplate.

For so many years, Nev had lived by the axiom 'no regrets,' but maybe allowing yourself a few regrets was important. How else could you change, grow, learn to do better? Learn to *be* better? If she could just get her timeline turned back in the right direction, Nev was going to fix some of the things she'd gotten wrong. She was almost ... hopeful? The unfamiliar feeling made her giddy, and then, like a reflex, her mother's voice echoed through her mind: *Don't put the cart before the horse, Nevaeh.* She shook off the unwelcome intrusion. For now, Nev would focus on achievable redemption. Her mother might be a lost cause, but there was still hope to make things right with Anissa.

Nev wondered if future Anissa had redeemed the Lotto ticket yet, and, if so, what she was doing with her newfound wealth. She imagined the big reveal: Guess what, Anissa—that mystery envelope from Jim Bone was really a gift from me! I was stuck in a time vortex, and I took advantage of it to make up for my shitty failures as a friend.

Would it be enough? Could Nev play any role in Anissa's future timeline? Was it happening simultaneously—whatever that meant—somewhere in possibility space, in synch with the timeline she was experiencing here and now? Even though she was well versed in the principles of both relativistic and quantum spacetime, not to mention the fact that she was spiraling backwards towards the moment of her own birth, these sort of questions still boggled Nev's mind. Anissa was usually the person she went to when she needed an explainer, some kind of visualization her brain could hold onto.

As Nev caught sight of the La Pavoni through the open door of the snack room, her mind wandered from Anissa to Darian. Maybe he had mastered enough temporal logic during Qbito training to answer her question. But they'd be strangers again, from his perspective, so she could hardly walk up and ask him, even if she wanted to. He was so jumpy, he'd probably run screaming from the room before she was even finished.

After a quick check-in with the doodz (had to keep up managerial appearances, if only for Maddy's sake), Nev sank into the blissful comfort of her Memeron and logged into the system. The Qbito code assembled before her eyes. She was struck with admiration for the mock-up that Airin had constructed back in their code dungeon. The resemblance was really fine. This process of cross-timeline collaboration, trying to stitch today's batch together from bits of Nev's tomorrow and Airin's yesterday, was kind of beautiful in its own, extremely messed-up way.

Even in the handful of days Nev had worked on the project with Airin, it had begun to assume a logic of its own. It wasn't that different from disassembling an engine, something she had done a thousand times at the junkyard. The more you took it apart, the clearer the grand design became. And the further back in her own code that Nev traveled, the clearer her plans became. She felt the answers to her questions hovering just out of grasp: What was she trying to achieve by the alien bits of hackery she was inserting with Airin's help into SavePoint? Where would it end? And when? And how?

Now that she was back in the groove, brain-deep in code, the hours seemed to melt away. Nev remembered a Qbito lecture a year or two back by a physics professor who moonlighted as a rabbi (or maybe vice versa)—something called the 'Talmud of Temporality.' At the time, it seemed like a stretch: A ham-fisted attempt to find some kind of spiritual underpinnings to the cold, arbitrary truths of the natural multiverse. The kind of thing her mother would have linked to on her blog. The kind of thing Nev usually hated.

But the one cool thing she'd picked up from the lecture was that, unlike the literalist devotion to the Word that her mother taught, Talmudic tradition treated the Bible as open to interpretation, and reinterpretation. It was a living document, and rabbis literally wrote new scripture in the margins of old scripture. As the lecturer spoke, it had struck Nev how much the process sounded like coding: forkings and comments, kludges and ports, a Gordian knot of logic just beneath the surface of the page, giving rise to the illusion of continuity for the end user.

Working on the umpteenth parallel-universe version of what was still officially demarcated as SavePoint 2.0 alpha, Nev felt kind of like a rabbi herself. She was marking up her own code, revising what hadn't been written yet, rewiring the logic according to some plan she didn't even understand, but had to believe in completely and totally, because her life depended on it. A plan she'd helped to create, but didn't yet remember. If the universe was random, it was pretty fucking weird. And if it wasn't, God had a sick sense of humor.

It was about 10:30 when Nev inputted the final line of code they'd mocked up that morning in Airin's dungeon. She massaged the base of her neck and took what felt like the first breath she'd had in hours. When she stood up, the Memeron played its patented readjustment soundbites, a satisfying set of clicks and whirrs that somehow perfectly communicated the idea of a robot saying "Aaaaaaahhhhhh" after a long day's work. *What now?*

Nev had about an hour to kill before reset, and at the very least, she needed some fresh air. She considered messaging Airin for a quick nightcap, but that felt excessive and maybe a little creepy. Who knew what kind of plans Airin had for the evening? But a drink didn't sound like a bad idea; she could be at Jimmy's in about fifteen minutes, quick enough to down a few shots and a pint of beer before yesterday hit her. She grabbed her bag and headed out at a brisk trot—every minute counted at this point.

Nev went down the elevator, blessedly empty at this time of night (the doodz had filtered out by 8:00 or so), across the LED-lit lobby, out the door, and onto the front steps, where Jim Bone sat on a dirty picnic blanket, knees sticking out through the holes in his greasy jeans. A misty, gray rain was falling, making Nev shiver with the damp. She hadn't dressed for this weather, and neither had he. Then again, he never did.

"Hey, Jim Bone," she said. "Don't you have a place to go? A tent, maybe? Or, like…" Nev had always assumed Jim Bone lived in the ceegee camps half a mile away. She'd never been clear on where he had come from originally, but the city was so filled with climate refugees over the past few years, it was a safe bet that his hometown was either under water or a dustbowl.

"Nope, nope, nope. No place but now. No time but here." His watery eyes hovered over her face, searching for something. It almost seemed like he was looking out through his own pupils, from somewhere else altogether. Another planet. Another universe, maybe.

No place but now?

It had taken a moment for Jim Bone's words to filter their way through Nev's sense-making mechanism. Usually, he mumbled in monosyllables, or soliloquized under his breath in what she thought was just garbled crazy-talk. "That's right, Jim Bone, you've sure got yourself in a spot, Jim Bone." But something about his last comment felt… familiar.

No time but here?

A shudder of recognition shook Nev like a tiny earthquake, and she found herself sitting down on Jim Bone's blanket because she could no longer trust her legs to hold her.

No. It can't be.

What if... What if Jim Bone wasn't merely homeless, but timeless? Maybe he wasn't a ceegee after all, as Nev had always assumed. Maybe he was a time refugee—like her. Maybe he'd been stuck in his own personal glitch, for who knew how long? Nev shuddered again, looking at Jim Bone, who had retreated into the shadowy corner of the doorway and closed his eyes.

There wasn't much evidence either way, but it stood to reason that if the Glitch could happen to her in 2045, it could happen to him—or to anyone else—especially in the future, once tech like SavePoint was more ubiquitous, more sophisticated. More powerful.

Nev tried to imagine a cleaner-cut version of the ghost next to her, sitting in an office like hers, maybe in this very same building, sometime in the not-so-distant future. Or maybe he'd always been like this. Maybe he was a ceegee after all, just a random human subject pulled off the street to test SavePoint 5.0 or whatever game-changing sci-fi tech came after it. It was tough to tell his age beneath the layers of accreted grime, sometimes he seemed older, sometimes younger, sometimes more with it, sometimes more lost.

"Jim Bone," she said, unsure of how, or whether, to pose the question. He opened his crusty eyes just a crack and looked at her under weather-worn lashes. "Jim Bone, where did you come from? And how did you get here?"

His mouth contorted into a grimace of pain, as he reached up and slid his greasy hat around his head. Nev felt a wave of pity for him wash over her. Whatever his story was, it wasn't a good one. He seemed to be having even more trouble than usual connecting his scrambled thoughts to spoken language.

"I did it," he said at last, his voice husky and low. "They said it couldn't, I couldn't..." He began to quiver, as if with barely contained rage, or maybe just fear. "They tried to tell Jim Bone it was impossible, and I said okay, but I knew. No point, no point in telling them..."

"Telling them what? What was impossible, Jim Bone?" Nev saw the scene as if from the outside—a privileged young woman, toying with a deranged vagrant on a grimy blanket, in the middle of the night. Goading him on. Or maybe just sharing in his insanity. But in her heart, she felt neither cruelty nor confusion, and the distance between them had never seemed so small.

"They told me, they said I..."

"What did they say?"

"I tried to fix it. I tried, I did, but no time. No time."

Nev felt like she was losing the thread. "No time for what? For who?"

"No time to stop it. No time to stop the—"

Series complete. LoopID?QT.43.33.23.12.09.2045

QT.00.30.08.11.09.2045

EVERYONE WHO WAS alive back then always said they remembered exactly where they had been on September 11, 2001. Grandpa was working on a homily, and watching the early morning headlines scroll across the bottom of the TV on mute, so he wouldn't wake up Nev's mom, or Grandma, who were both still asleep down the hall, when the first plane hit the World Trade Center. He was watching live when the second plane hit. So was Nev's mom, who had woken up and padded out to find her father just in time to see the north tower collapse.

Christina Bourne had only just turned seven. As an adult, she often said that watching the tower come down was her first real memory. No doubt, the images had been scorched into her limbic system by their endless replay on the television in the days that followed. When Grandpa was still alive, she used to say, the TV was always on at their house.

Nev wasn't born until fourteen years after the attack, so naturally she had no firsthand memory of it. But she could recall perfectly how she'd spent September 11, 2045, her first time through. The Carlson Administration loved its military pageantry, and had decreed a national holiday by executive order four years earlier, fulfilling one of its least repugnant (and costly) campaign promises. Qbito and all other 'non-essential' businesses were required to close up shop.

Lockheed Martin SR-72s from Travis Air Force base had sliced through the airspace over the Presidio, where Nev had joined Jared at the Miller Gahan Lee company picnic. Cater waiters (essential workers) wearing stars-and-stripes vests, white polo shirts, and tomato red Bermuda shorts passed around canapés of halved mini blue potatoes with a dollop of crème fraiche and red salmon roe, cold shots of tomato gazpacho with floating white cubes of cucumber and flecks of blue crab, and mini-tarts sporting rows of raspberries, blueberries, and meringues in loose approximations of the American flag. Nev had struggled to make small talk, repeatedly resorting to her SavePoint to extricate herself from failed stabs at conversation.

Eventually, she'd gotten railroaded into a lengthy conversation with Neela Lee, a gorgeous Afro-Vietnamese woman who must have been snatched right off the runway in Milan by Kip Lee, the firm's youngest and most flamboyant senior partner. Over the course of three champagne cocktails, Neela had provided Nev with the unsolicited details of her many extramarital adventures, starting with Kip's best friend and groomsman Brandt and eventually working her way down the line to Pablo Blum, a hulky associate who had hovered not far from the two women, nursing a beer, throughout the entire monologue.

When the final drop of champagne had disappeared down Neela's swanlike throat, she dropped the plastic flute at her feet, looking over Nev's shoulder at Pablo distractedly.

"But you know how it is," she had said, signaling that the conversation was coming to a close. "Sisters got to look out for themselves. Amirite?"

Without waiting for an answer, Neela had walked off towards the visitors center, a low building housing some bathrooms and vending machines. Nev had watched Pablo look around for a minute, then follow her. Kip, meanwhile, appeared to be deep in conversation with a gaggle of younger attorneys. Nev hadn't been able to hear him, but he was miming a bird flapping its wings, and they were all laughing.

Sisters got to look out for themselves. Truer words had never been spoken. Or maybe it was "sistas." Nev could never be sure how people interpreted her racially ambiguous features until they told her what they saw. Usually, they just seemed to see what they wanted to see. Nev wondered whether Neela would have been as forthcoming if she hadn't tagged her as a sista.

"Hey gorgeous!"

Somehow, Jared had sidled up to her while she wasn't looking. He handed her a plate with a small black-and-white cookie on it—a pleasant break from the jingoistic fare that covered most of the tables. She nibbled it hungrily.

"Saw you talking to Neela. You two seemed to hit it off. She's really something, isn't she?"

"Yes, Jared. She is really something."

He had patted her shoulder proudly then rested his hand on the small of her back, looking around to make sure people saw what a handsome couple they made.

"Well, something tells me you'll be seeing a lot more of each other. You know, Kip is kind of like a mentor to me. I mean, someday not so far from now, we could have what they have. I could make partner by forty, Nev. I don't want to tell you how to do your thing, but let's just say you could learn a lot from someone like Neela. She's a good friend for you to have."

Nev must have thrown her drink in Jared's face and SavePointed at least a dozen times in a row. "Undo therapy," she and Anissa used to call it.

This time around, her SavePoint was useless, but she could redo the whole day from start to finish. Nev reached over to the nightstand and grabbed her buzzing viz (today's wake-up mantra: 'Carpe Diem, Namaste'), slipping it over her ear and selecting Jared's trucker-capped icon, which was already flashing to signal unread messages.

J: Off for a 10k to burn some cals before the air show. You
might want to do the same.
Hear the appies finna be lish.
J: What time are we meeting up? Don't want to get there
too late. Can't miss the partnerz.
J: What are you wearing? Nothing too punky for the wives,
K?
N: Sorry, Jared. I think I'm going to have to bail. Feeling
sick 😔

Nev minimized Jared's avatar and closed her eyes to return
to sleep. She was certain that would be enough to get him off
her back, he was a total germaphobe. But before she could
return to the excellent dream she'd been having (something
about swimming with giant turtles?), the viz buzzed her back to
wakefulness. Nev opened her eyes to find Jared's avatar dancing
in her field of vision.

J: Still? I was hoping you'd be better since you bailed on
Friday.
J: Are you nervous about the wives? They'll love you.
J: Maybe you should wear a dress? How about that white
one I picked out for you when we went sailing with mom
and dad? Pair it with the blue jean jacket?
J: And your red lace panties 😺

I'm not fucking wearing red lace panties for you, dipshit.

N: My nose is running. Think I might have a fever.
N: Did you get the alert about that new virus detected in
the ceegee camp in Houston? Do you think there's any
chance it's made it past the quarantine controls?
J: ……..

Nev watched the blinking dots for a minute as Jared wavered.

It was time to seal the deal.

> N: Why don't you pick up some Tamiflu and bring it to my place? I guess if I'm careful not to cough on the wives it should be okay.
> J: ......
> J: NVM. I'll go solo 🤘 Hope none of those wives take a liking to me.
> N: Fingers crossed!

Jared's avatar shrank out of sight. No 'feel better' or 'get well soon.' No loss. Nev hoped that was the end of it. She closed her eyes, willing sleep to return, but the sea turtle had escaped her.

She was sitting on the couch in her sweats and a ratty old Stanford tee, taking the first sip of morning coffee and debating whether to log on to *WhisperWorld* or try *Patriot Day*—a new RPG her team had spent all yestermorrow messaging about—when she realized that Airin had forgotten to tell her where and when they were meeting today. They'd been just about to exchange dates when a burly white guy with blonde dreads sat down next to them on the pizzeria patio, along with his dog, a white Komondor with nearly identical hair. Airin and Nev had locked eyes, and without a word, they both started giggling. Every time Nev got a hold of herself, Airin would laugh again, and then by the time Airin got a hold of themself, Nev was laughing again. It went back and forth for five minutes, Nev guiltily hoping that the man didn't think they were laughing at him and his dog, but he hardly seemed to notice the two of them at all. By the time it was over, they'd forgotten all about the date exchange.

What was the proper protocol, Nev wondered? Should she message Airin and ask? Was it too early? Nev had no idea what Airin's ordinary schedule was like. They had never complained about being awake for the morning coding sessions, but maybe they were a night owl and were sleeping in, happy to finally get a break from Nev, who, after all, was little more than an annoying stranger who had intruded on their life. Or, maybe Airin was at home right now, waiting for Nev to show up.

It was already after nine. Maybe Airin had forgotten that they hadn't told Nev where to meet up. *No stupid, they haven't lived that day yet.* Airin would have no idea that they hadn't told Nev yestermorrow what time to come over today, and so they would have no way to know why Nev wasn't there, if, indeed, Nev was supposed to go there today, which she didn't know whether she was or wasn't, because it hadn't yet happened. *AIGHHHHH!!!* She magnified Airin's avatar and hit the voice call icon—anything, even an awkward conversation, was better than a free fall down the temporal logic rabbit hole.

"Hello? Nev?"

"Airin? Did I wake you?"

"What? No. Why? Where are you? Is something wrong?"

"Shit, I was wondering whether I should be there already. You forgot to tell me yestermorrow when we were meeting today. Just give me half an hour, I'll be right over."

Nev was about to hang up, when Airin's voice stopped her.

"Wait, wait. I've got a better idea. Your gift arrived yesterday. It's beautiful. Nev, no one has ever given me something so nice. How about I drive over and pick you up and we can take a road trip? Have a day off. Go wherever you want. Just as long as I can get back by tomorrow morning, since it sounds like we'll be meeting up."

"Yes!" Nev was too excited to worry about sounding excited. She'd never needed a day off more than she needed one today. "Do you know where I live?"

There was a long pause on Airin's end.

"Yeah, don't worry about it. I've been there before."

Twenty minutes later, as Nev was standing vizless in a yellow sun dress and sandals on the sidewalk outside her condo, Airin pulled up in their gleaming orange Porsche 911, blasting some kind of heavy orchestral music from its tricked out 24D audio system. They leaned out the passenger side window, massive smile shining almost as brightly as the morning sun. "Hey, lady, need a ride?"

"Sure thing. Seems like beach weather to me." Airin flung open the door and Nev climbed in, sinking into the bucket seat with a sigh that would have made her Memeron jealous. The air conditioning was exactly the right temperature, evaporating the light sheen of sweat that Nev could feel along her upper lip, without making her shiver or dig in her bag for a scarf. The car smelled pleasantly of old cigar smoke, but also deliciously like Airin's loft. Ada poked her massive white head between the seats, demanding scritches, and Nev happily obliged.

"I was thinking the same thing. How about Baker? I'm kind of jonesing for Lupe Taco, which is right on the way."

"Ack! No!" Nev sputtered. She didn't want to imagine the Glitch that would come if Jared and Airin collided in orbit around her.

Airin turned to her, a puzzled frown on their face.

"Sorry, I mean, I don't want to go anywhere near the Presidio today. They've got that air show, and it's... a bit much. How about Ocean Beach? It's one of the places we first met. For me, at least."

"Sure, we could grab a bite first at that cool old-fashioned restaurant with the windows. I've always wanted to check that place out. Sorry, Ada—you'll have to stay in the car while the grownups are talking."

"The Park Chalet? Sounds great. Happy Patriot Day, citizen."

"Happy Patriot Day, comrade."

They drove companionably through the Haight, listening to Berlioz, according to the home-brew viz monitor Airin had suction cupped to the dash. It looked more like a weekend than a Monday; the streets were full of families and young couples, mixed in with the standard swarms of ceegees. People crowded the tables at sidewalk restaurants and cafes. Here and there, a car, tee-shirt, or office window was decorated with the American flag or #NeverForget memes, but this was San Francisco, so the overall level of jingoism was a lot milder than things would be back home in Washington.

"You know, Nev, I... I can't believe you bought me this car. It's so absofuckinlutely amazing. I mean, wow," Airin said, still grinning like a kid on Christmas morning. "I mean, what... why...?"

"Honestly, Airin, I don't know," Nev replied, grinning too, for what felt like the first time since long before the Glitch. "From my perspective, I haven't even bought you the car yet. For all I know, maybe the reason I'll buy it for you is because of this. Because you picked me up in it today, and told me I did." *And because you look so cute when you smile,* Nev didn't add.

Airin nodded. "Yeah. Right. Forgot about that. Hmm."

"Don't get me wrong, though. I definitely appreciate all you're doing for me, helping me escape from this insanity. And I'm sure that, however much I'll pay for this car, it's a drop in the bucket compared to your usual consulting fees."

Airin nodded, still smiling but no longer beaming. "True, true."

"And..." Nev already knew she'd tell Airin, but still felt apprehensive. "To be honest, this is more than just a snazzy gift. It has kind of a deep personal meaning for me."

"Don't tell me—you lost your virginity in the back of a Porsche."

"What? Hah. No. Though you're actually not all that far off. But, no, it means a lot to me because it reminds me of my dad. He ran—runs—a junk yard, up in Washington, and I kind of fell in love with classic sports cars because of him."

"Does he fix them up and sell them or something?"

"No, nothing like that. He's pretty low end, generally. Fridges and ovens and boilers and stuff like that, though lots of cars too, obviously. But, when I was growing up, a classic 911 Carrera RS was, like, I don't know, a symbol of everything that *could* be, know what I mean?"

"I think so." Airin nodded gravely, looking quickly at her, then turning back to the road. They were almost at the Park Chalet. The Pacific loomed before them, scintillating in the sunlight.

"Like, I never even saw the ocean before I came to Stanford. Even though I lived in a coastal state, or whatever. So this car—I know it sounds kind of corny, I don't know—I was like, if I could have a Porsche, anything is possible."

"Yeah. Yeah, I get it." Airin pulled into a parking space, and the car's electric motor shut off with a click. Instead of getting out, they turned to face Nev, looking into her eyes. Something rumbled deep inside of her, like an old gas engine revving up.

"And then, when I finally got here, and started making money, and something like this was in reach, well, I don't know, it seemed silly in retrospect. Like, more of a fantasy, or a symbol, than something I'd actually want in my life. I mean, it's funny…" Nev realized she'd never even acknowledged this to herself before. "But I haven't really splurged on anything. Ever. Like, I got so used to having nothing that I never actually got myself something."

"That's sad. You should treat yourself once in a while."

"Yeah, it is. I should. And, I guess, that's what this is. Maybe the way I'm going to treat myself is by treating you. Or something like that."

Airin nodded. "Well, whatever your reasons were, or will be, I fucking love it. Thank you, Nev. Now, can I buy you some breakfast? I was about to eat when you called me, and now I'm starving to death."

The Park Chalet was running a Patriot Day brunch special. Nev opted for the 'All American,' two eggs, bacon, potatoes and white bread—the sort of platter that would have set you back no more than ten dollars where she came from, with a bottomless cup of coffee included. The Chalet was offering it for thirty, coffee an extra five on top, but Nev got the feeling that Airin wanted to splurge, so she bit her tongue. They opted for the 'Red, White, and Blue,' a double stack of buttermilk pancakes topped with whipped cream, blueberries, and strawberry compote. It was the

Miller Gahan Lee picnic all over again, Nev thought. *But better company.*

The plates came out quickly, the Chalet running at maximum efficiency to turn the tables on a busy day. Nev watched with amusement as Airin dug into their pancakes with gusto, abandoning their usual precision as they shoveled down heaping forkfuls of carbs. Finally they pushed the empty plate a few inches away and collapsed back in their chair.

"Oh my god," Airin said. "I can't believe I ate the whole thing."

"I don't see what God has to do with it," Nev said.

"You're right, it's all on me. I make bad choices when I get too hungry." An anxious look passed over Airin's face, "I didn't offend you, did I?"

"Big nope. Believe me, you can't offend me where God is concerned. He and I parted ways a long time ago."

"Sounds like a bad breakup. Want to talk about it?"

"Definitely not," Nev laughed.

She drank the dregs from her coffee mug, wishing that the Chalet offered refills. Airin was watching her, quietly. Nev did not like to talk about the past, ever. She had never told Jared much about where she came from. She couldn't stand the thought of how condescending he would be. Jared, raised in a beautiful Queen Anne in Pacific Heights, the son of an intellectual property lawyer and a lifestyle coach, would have regarded Nev's family history the way he saw his vintage trucker cap collection: as some colorful bit of gritty authentic Americana to be put on display. He'd tell all his work bros about Nev's hard luck story, to up his own cred by virtue of dating her. Just thinking about it made Nev want to smack him. So she was surprised by the temptation she felt, under Airin's gaze, to open up.

Nev didn't know Airin well enough to know how they would react. She didn't know much about Airin's background, although she had a vague sense they came from the east coast, and weren't on the best terms with their own family. Nev hoped, for Airin's sake, that they were on better terms with their folks than she was with hers. Maybe the reason she was willing to risk intimacy with Airin today was because she wouldn't have to experience the consequences. Next time she showed up at Airin's loft, they wouldn't remember a word Nev had told them, wouldn't yet have heard anything to remember. They would start fresh, at least from Airin's point of view. Nev would still remember, but then Nev always remembered. No matter how hard she tried not to think about the past.

"Did you ever have faith?" Nev asked.

Airin knit their eyebrows together, then shook their head. "That wasn't exactly our thing."

"I did. That's how I was raised. There wasn't any room for questioning when I was a kid. My mother ran a ministry out of our living room. Any time of day or night, I never knew when there'd be strangers in the house, Mama laying on hands, healing their spiritual and bodily afflictions. Her own Daddy, my Grandpa, he was a minister too. And his Daddy before him. They all had the calling. It seemed to skip me. I was always more comfortable in my father's junkyard than in my mother's prayer circles. But Faith, she inherited it. Mama said she could see Jesus's light shining in Faith's eyes from the moment she was born.

"There was never any doubting that Mama loved her best. But I didn't resent it. I swear. I loved Faith the best too. There were seven years between us, not for want of trying on Mama and Daddy's part. The longer God withheld his blessing, the harder my mother prayed. By the time Faith arrived, Mama had entered into an agreement with God to follow all of His commandments to the letter. No mixing of flax and linen. No letting your hair be unkempt. Daddy couldn't trim his beard. It was hard to follow all the rules. It seemed like I was always getting in trouble with her, and running away to hide in the junkyard.

"But when Faith came finally, it was all worth it. Mama prayed, and God delivered. We felt like, I don't know, like we'd unlocked the secrets to the universe or something. Like we had cracked the code. And then… Oh my God, I'm talking too much. Am I talking too much?"

She looked across the table at Airin, whose eyes were fixed on her with such intensity she could feel it warming her face. Somehow, the table had emptied, and her mug had been refilled.

"Not at all," said Airin. "So what changed? How did you lose faith?" This time, Nev couldn't tell whether they were capitalizing the F.

"Well, of course, you remember the supermeasles epidemic. The first one, the real bad one. I was sixteen, and, um…"

"Yeah, so was I. Tough year. For all kinds of reasons."

Nev wiped her nose on the back of her wrist, and brought the coffee shakily to her lips.

"Yeah." She took another sip, using two hands to put the mug back on the table in front of them. Airin reached across and held her left hand in their right. It felt cool and dry, and surprisingly comforting. She took a deep, raggedy breath and looked up. "Well, long story short, she died. We maybe could have saved her, if Mama hadn't been so obstinate about vaccinations and hospitalizations and all the rest of it. And, for me, that was it. I just didn't, couldn't believe any more. In God, in Mama, in anything, really. Except logic, of course. It's the one thing that'll never let you down. You might not like where it leads you, but at least it won't lie along the way."

They raised their perfectly arched eyebrows at this, but said nothing.

"So, yeah, that's my tragic tale. I might not have been called, but I believed with all my heart. And then I didn't." She finished her second cup. "Actually, God's pretty lucky he doesn't exist, because if he did, I'd hate him so bad he'd wish he didn't. That fucker took away everyone I ever loved."

Airin smiled a sad smile. "Everyone?"

The waiter arrived with a tablet on a silver tray, which he set down before Airin. "Will that be all?"

QT.00.00.09.10.09.2045

"IS EVERYBODY HAPPY?"

The little boy's voice called out, waking Nev from wherever she existed between conscious intervals. Her eyes sprang open, staring blindly in front of her as Donny and Jimmy Osmond's warbling voices burst into the familiar refrain of 'Me and My Shadow'...

Nev grabbed her viz and threw it at the floor. The music stopped. She wasn't sure if she had broken the headset, and in that moment she really didn't fucking care. After all, it would be magically returned to its former unbroken state the next morning.

It was no use. The alarm stopped but the Osmonds continued singing away mercilessly in Nev's sonic memory. She had told her troubles to some soul, and it had been like pulling the cork loose from a bottle. Memories of Faith had come pouring out, taking over her mind—and apparently, somehow, her viz alarm as well.

She and Faith used to sing the song as a duet at the family piano. The Osmonds were one of the few pop music acts that Christina Bourne allowed her daughters to listen to. She and

Nev's father had seen Donny and Marie perform in Las Vegas on their honeymoon, making a special trip to sin city for the show, back when Christina was still willing to bend a little. There was no more bending by the time Faith was born, but the Osmonds were still permitted. At age fourteen, Nev would rather have pierced her eardrums than listen to their saccharine bubblegum pop. But for the sake of Faith, who listened to the Osmonds without complaint, like she followed all their mother's dictates, Nev was willing to make a sacrifice. She would do anything to make her sister happy, even subject herself to voluntary musical torture. In the years since she'd lost Faith, she couldn't hear the Osmonds without collapsing into tears, but thankfully that wasn't that much of a problem, because no one but her mother listened to them anymore.

Nev wondered if her mother still did, or if even she had stopped playing the Osmonds by this point. Nev wouldn't know. She had run away from home after Faith's funeral, sleeping in the bushes by the river that ran through town before Grandma was brave enough to take her in, against her daughter's express wishes. For the first time, Nev had gone to public school, busing to Pullman High in the nearest big town. She got an after school job in Pullman too, working the front desk at the Holiday Inn Express, which was slow enough that she had plenty of time to study and make up for lost years. Her hard work paid off. She got a full scholarship to Stanford, and left Washington behind her, literally never looking back. Christina would have said something about Lot's Wife, but then again, from her perspective, Nev had run towards Sodom, not away from it.

Ever since the Glitch, though, Nev seemed to be looking back more and more. It was hard not to, when, despite all her and Airin's hard work, she was hurtling towards the past with seemingly unstoppable velocity. If the hack didn't work, she'd be seeing Mama soon enough whether she wanted to or not. One day, a little more than two weeks from now, she'd wake up in Albion again, on the morning of Grandma's funeral.

A rattling sound drifted up from the floor. Nev leaned over the edge of the bed and grabbed her viz, clicking the vibrating device into place above her ear. An avatar of her mother's face flashed. *Weird.* She'd never programmed her mother into the contacts. More hackery? Nev thought about rejecting the call. Then she thought about her sister. Her little shadow. Nev knew what Faith would want her to do. Besides, if she was going to come face-to-face with Christina again, the more prepared she was, the better. Based on those recent messages, it seemed like maybe she'd be able to make some headway in bridging the Great Divide.

"Hello? Mama?"

"Sunday blessings, Nevaeh. Your father and I are just calling to see how things are going." *What the ever-loving fuck?* "We thought you might appreciate some kindness and inspiration."

Christina's icon blinked, and was replaced by a live video window of Nev's parents at their kitchen table, clearly crowding around the same old tablet they'd kept there for the past 20 years. How was that thing even running, Nev wondered. The OS had to be at least a decade old. She stared at her parents through a film of evaporated cooking grease, which created kind of an old-school Hollywood halo effect around them.

At her grandmother's funeral, Nev had been surprised by how kind the years had been to Christina, and how cruel they'd been to Matthew. Her father looked like a bona-fide old man now, kind of like that Black actor who played the president in those action films when she was at Stanford—Jeffrey Winters? Jeffrey Wright? For a second, she'd felt her old curiosity bubbling up again. She was almost tempted to ask her father point blank, not let him get away with deflections this time. But she'd missed her chance. It didn't matter anyway. She knew all she ever wanted to know about her family, thank you very much.

But they really didn't know her. She hadn't given them the opportunity.

"I'm not doing so good. To be honest."

"What's troubling you?"

Where to begin, Nev thought.

"I've been thinking a lot recently... about Faith," Nev said, reluctant to speak her sister's name in her mother's hearing. However raw her own grief still was, however angry she was at the choices they had made, some part of her could not ignore that her parents' grief must be like an ocean to her puddle. Well, maybe more like an ocean to her sea.

"I pray to her every day. I know she's watching us from Heaven. All of us. One day soon we'll all be together again."

It was amazing to Nev that her mom could be so wrong, and yet at the same time, so right. What if she was onto something, though, in her own over-the-top, doctrinaire way? Maybe the Glitch was just a foretaste of the Afterlife. What if we all spend eternity reliving our tiny, finite lives, viewing them from every angle, at every scale? Maybe heaven is in our finest moments, and hell is all the things we wish we could have fixed, but didn't. If that's the case, Nev reflected, she was getting a rare chance to reclaim pieces of her own life, to turn them into something worth savoring forever.

"That would be nice, Mama. I'd love to see Faith again. And Grandma. And you and Daddy, too. Maybe I'll get a chance to visit you soon."

"I would like that, Peaches." Matthew's voice sounded gravelly, like he hadn't used it very much recently.

"You are always welcome in our home, my daughter. Your father and I have been very concerned about you since our call last Sunday. Are you still having trouble? Is there anyone there who can help you? Or are you still a stranger in that strange land?"

'Stranger in a Strange Land' had been a massive algo hit about five years ago—a fact about which Christina was probably blissfully unaware—and now, Nev couldn't help but hear its earwormy bass line looping in her mind. She'd have to listen to it on her viz en route to Airin's this morning, just to get the damn thing out of her head. She smiled in spite of herself, and was shocked to see her parents smile back at her.

"Actually, Mama, I'm not such a stranger these days. I have a... a new friend, and, um, they're helping me get through my troubles."

"Oh, how wonderful. I've always told you, Nev, you can't make it alone. Nobody can. Not in this world. Certainly not in San Francisco. The Lord watches over the lonely and afflicted, but it's also important to have someone you can count on, here on this Earth."

Maybe Nev really was going crazy, after all. Either that, or her mother was making a lot more sense than usual.

"Yeah, that's true, Mama. I've been pretty lonely since.... Well, for a long time, really. And it's nice to have someone I can turn to. Someone I can count on."

"Well, that young man is very lucky, Nevaeh. And so are you, by the sound of it. I don't know how much my advice means to you these days, but I counsel you to keep him dear. When you find someone who's willing to be a true friend in your darkest hour, you can expect to reap much joy when the daylight returns."

If the daylight returns. Still, despite Christina's weird scripturey tone, and the sing-songy voice she always slipped into when doling out life advice, Nev had to admit she was right again.

"Thanks, Mama. Actually, I need to go now, they're waiting for me."

"Well, don't let us get in the way of True Love. We have to go down to services, anyway. We love you, Nevaeh."

"Love you, Peaches."

"Love you too." The video window closed, leaving Christina's icon in its wake. Nev considered adding it to her favorites' list, then realized it wouldn't make a difference, and started getting ready to head to Airin's.

QT.51.27.08.09.09.2045

EYES OPEN. CEILING coming into focus. Wood slats. Not her apartment. The sound of snoring.

Nev turned her head as carefully as she could. Jared was curled up at the edge of the mattress, hugging the blankets, with his back to her. She inched away, attempting not to shake the mattress or disturb him.

Had she spent futurepast night with Jared? Or if he woke up and found her there, would he be shocked, like the last time she'd woken up in his bed? Either way, she didn't want to find out. She couldn't deal with his sloppy affection or his sloppy anger. Better to sneak out before he woke up and, if necessary, make excuses later.

Nev slid out from the ultra-high thread count sheets, one socked foot hitting the floor, then the next. Interesting. She appeared to be fully dressed. But she didn't feel her viz nested into its place above her left ear. So wherever she had reset, she'd probably still been awake, but making herself comfortable.

Jared snored loudly and rolled over, throwing one arm and leg heavily in Nev's direction. She dropped down to the floor and held her breath.

Was that a pile of magazines under his bed? Nev squinted to read the spines. Of course, Jared would think it was cool to have a collection of original hard copies of turn-of-the-century porn mags. A snort of derision escaped her before she could clamp her lips shut.

The mattress squeaked loudly, and Nev held her breath. She sensed movement overhead and rolled under the bed just before a hairy foot hit the ground, soon followed by another. A loud rumbling had Nev reaching up to pinch her nose before the smell wafted down to find her. The bed sank down, then sprang up again as Jared plodded to the bathroom. More farts and a long, loud stream of piss hitting the toilet.

He hadn't yet called for her, which meant he probably wasn't expecting her to be there. Nev felt a surge of gratitude that she wasn't going to spend her next night in Jared's company. All she had to do was be patient and wait for Jared to take a shower, so she could make her escape. *Come on, come on.* She waited for the sound of the tap to turn on. Instead, heavy footsteps thudded back her way, topped by the naked smack of flat soles on polyurethane. *Dirty bastard, you didn't even wash your hands. I can't believe I ever let them touch me.* Nev held her breath, trying not to move a single muscle, praying that he wouldn't catch sight of her under the bed. The mattress crunched down overhead, Jared's feet disappearing from view.

Hand down, rooting around under the bed.

"Where are you?" Jared's voice asked.

He had seen her! Humiliation burned Nev's cheeks as she wondered how to explain herself. She was just about to slide out from her hiding place when Jared's fingers hit the stack of dirty magazines, grabbing the issue at the top.

"Got you."

Fuck me, Nev thought, as she heard glossy pages flipping and the beginning of a slow but all too-familiar thwapping. In fact, she supposed he *had* fucked her the first time she lived through this day. Jared could always be counted on for a morning tune-up when she stayed over the night before. It was one of his best qualities. Perhaps his very best quality. Nev ricocheted between mortification and resentment as the page flipping came to an end and the thwapping began to pick up speed. It had been close to two weeks since her encounter with Levi. And since then, nada. No tune-ups from Jared. She hadn't even taken any time to tune herself up. She'd been a little busy worrying about the existential threat she was facing. *Nev, Nev. Only you could land in a magical, consequence-free temporal vortex, and still be more stressed than ever.* Why wasn't she living free and easy, hooking up in a hotel suite with a different guy each night?

The bed was creaking above her, panting sounds mixed in with the increasingly rapid thwapping. From the sound of it, he was about to close the deal. Good thing, because Nev wasn't sure how much longer she could wait it out. She was starting to feel a little hot and bothered herself. She tried to picture Jared's snot-streaked face during their last breakup to cool herself down, but instead, unbidden, Airin's face took shape before her eyes. Airin's long fingers. She wondered how they'd feel touching… *Stop it, Nev.* The bed was shaking vigorously now. How much longer could this go on? Quite a bit longer, she knew. Jared did have his good qualities.

"Unnnnhhhh!"

Thank the Heavens, as Mama would say.

Minutes later, her footsteps masked by the white noise of Jared's high-pressure shower nozzle and his enthusiastic but painfully arhythmic rendition of the *OBAMA!* musical soundtrack, Nev crept out from her hiding place, stole a pair of Under Armour slides from the shoe rack, and made her escape into the crisp San Francisco morning.

Hiding herself in a crowd of tourists, Nev jumped on the back of the Powell Street cablecar, heading south. She counted the blocks as the campily retro ticket collector (black peaked cap and hot pants held up by suspenders) struggled through the thick bodies, jammed in shoulder-to-shoulder for the short trip to Market. The last thing she needed was to get arrested for fare evasion, but, 'no viz/no dollaz,' as the MC CG lyrics went. Nev jumped out at Geary, making eye contact with the collector as she stepped off the car, which had stopped for cross traffic.

Access to her own apartment was thankfully biometrics-activated—no viz required. Nev checked all her usual spots for the device. Not on the bedside table—which wasn't a surprise, since she'd still been dressed when she reset. Not on the coffee table by the couch. Not in the bathroom. Not in the bowl by the front door. She gave her apartment a suspicious sniff. No traces of dinner smell lingered behind. She was getting the suspicion that she hadn't been at home when the clock turned 11:33:43 futurepast night. Where, then? Where else would she have been comfortable enough to take off her shoes and viz?

Unfortunately, the answer to that question would have to wait. According to the clock on the auto-Chemex, it was 9:30 already, and Airin had told her yestermorrow that she arrived at their place today at 10:04. She had barely enough time to change her clothes, slip on her boots, and hail a Dryverless on her gamestation, if she wanted to make it there on time. And what if she didn't? How would that change what came next, the days that she had already lived through but Airin hadn't? It was something to talk about with them, but Nev certainly wasn't going to risk disrupting the timeline that she herself had apparently designed.

QT.40.04.10.09.09.2045

"ADA! DOWN!" AIRIN said, struggling to pull the great white beast back from the door to the freight elevator when Nev stepped off.

"What's the matter, Ada?" Nev said, rubbing the dog's ears affectionately as it strained to lick her face.

"I don't know what's wrong with her. This is excessive, even by Lovesnack standards."

Nev gave up under the assault and knelt down to the floor, letting Ada cover her in tongue wash for a couple of minutes.

"Sorry about that," Airin said in an embarrassed tone. "I think maybe she's worried about you."

"Worried about me? Why?"

"I'm not sure," Airin said, "but it might have to do with this." They reached out a closed hand, and opened their fingers to reveal Nev's viz tucked within.

"Oh! I left it here!" Nev said, taking back her viz and snapping it into place. She ignored the pile-up of notifications from Jared cluttering her field of vision. "What happened?"

"That's the weird thing. I don't really remember."

Airin led the way into the kitchen, where Nev smelled the familiar aroma of her coffee brewing. They poured her a cup and topped it up with cashew milk, handing it over with the handle facing outward.

"You came by yesterday evening, late, after work. I remember letting you in, and sitting on the couch talking."

"And then?" Nev asked.

"That's it. That's all I remember. Us sitting on the couch. I don't remember when you left, or going to bed, or anything else. I woke up this morning and saw your viz on the coffee table and your shoes by the loveseat."

"Huh," Nev said. Was it possible that something had happened between her and Airin, and Airin was just too polite to mention it? Maybe Airin didn't want to put Nev in an awkward position by telling her that something was going to happen between them before it did, thus depriving her of the free will to make that choice. Did Nev even want something to happen between them? She took a long look at Airin, who blushed and looked down.

"I woke up this morning at Jared's," Nev said.

Airin looked back up, sharply. *Interesting.*

"Have I told you about Jared yet? I don't know."

"You've mentioned him," Airin said in a neutral tone.

"I was in bed with him. Fully dressed. I guess I must have spent Friday night with him the first time through. But I don't think I am going to make it there next futurepast night. He didn't seem to expect me, to say the least."

"Really?" Airin asked, smiling now.

"Really," Nev said, telling Airin the story of what had happened earlier that morning.

By the time she got to the punchline, both Nev and Airin were gasping for breath at the circular table in their kitchen nook, Ada Lovesnacks jumping and yawping along, clearly wishing to be part of the fun.

"Magazines?" Airin asked. "Like, paper ones? With still images in them?" Their eyes were streaming tears of laughter.

"Yeah, they all have names like *Jugz* and *Cum Again*. And, oh my God, they smelled like old cheese."

"Yaggghhh!" Airin shook their arms and torso in exaggerated disgust, like Ada drying herself off after a walk in the rain. "That is an image I did not need. Thanks a million, Nev."

"To be fair though," Nev said, taking a sip of her coffee, "he is not too shabby in the sack. I mean, he's got the right stuff, and he knows how to use it."

Airin winced a bit.

"I mean," Nev continued, "of course it depends on what you're into. Like, I don't know, do you, are you... do you like dudes, or...?"

Airin half-smiled, then raised their mug to cover their mouth. "Yeah. I like 'dudes,' Nev. I also like women. And everyone else." They raised their perfect eyebrows. "I'm less interested in a person's gender identity, and more interested in the person themself. Of course, the chemistry's got to be there, too. But why should I restrict myself based on some arbitrary identity marker? The world's shitty enough as it is, without making it needlessly worse. Anyway... what about you, Nev?"

She felt herself flush, a pleasant prickling at the edges of her scalp. "What about me, what?"

"Well, I know you like men, but, I mean... is that it? Are you, like, open to other possibilities? Other experiences?"

Airin stood up and edged around the table as they spoke. They were standing very close to Nev, close enough that she could smell their hair, a whiff of essential oils, the toasty rice of genmai cha on their breath. God, their eyes were beautiful, Nev thought. It was like staring into twin galaxies.

Airin's hand was on her shoulder, long, delicate fingers touching the back of Nev's neck, the pleasant prickle spreading like wildfire down her spine. As they leaned in towards her, Nev could feel their breath mingling in her mouth, every nerve ending aflame in anticipation of something so Right, so Inevitable, so utterly Beautiful that her mind and body melted into a singularity and she spun straight into those twin galaxies, twisting in both directions at once, an impossible superposition of spin and anti-spin, balanced on the brink between universes, spliced between two, then four, then eight, then an infinity of parallel timelines, and it was too much, too many to reconcile. Nev could feel her mind scattering like a flock of geese, like the grease on the surface of a pan in the sink, like the blink of the eye of God and oh God what where when was she was she was she even even steven reason no reason no season no believing no relief no reliving no forgiving no forgetting no four no eight no infinity no no no no no no Nev

"Nev! Noooooo!"

Eyes open. Ceiling coming into focus. Painted concrete. Too far away. Not her apartment. The sound of screaming.

Nev reached up her arm and awkwardly patted Airin's face and shoulder.

"'Sokay. 'Mokay. Stop. I'm okay. It's alright. Just... please. Stop shouting. My head..."

"Oh, thank fuck. Nev! That was terrifying. You... what the hell is going on?"

"I dunno, it just happens sometimes, since the Glitch. Seems to be getting worse. It's like, hard to say. It feels like I'm being torn apart, particle by particle. But also like I'm simultaneously in different, um, realities? Like, there are shards of mirror in my brain or something." She tried to sit up, winced, and lay back down. "And now, I feel kind of hungover. Like I just woke up from a blackout drunk. Why? What did it look like out here? To you?"

"Well, we were, you know, about to, I think. And you got this faraway look in your eyes, and then kind of flickered, almost. And then you just dropped to the floor like a stone. You were out for about a minute. I didn't know whether you were, you know..."

Ada pushed her nose into Nev's neck, and she heaved herself up, grunting, to give the dog cuddles.

"Ow. Have I ever—have you seen that happen to me before?"

"Not exactly this. Last week, you kind of passed out, but I didn't really know you as well yet, didn't really understand exactly what you were going through. Damn, Nev, this is awful. Have you ever been diagnosed with epilepsy, or anything like that?"

"No." Nev crawled over to a large, silvery bean bag near the loveseat and flopped onto it. "Like I said, this started with the Glitch. At first, it was just little things. Skips and starts. You know, like buffer lags. But lately, I don't know. It feels like the whole world is toxic to me. Or vice versa. Oof." She leaned back, eyes closed, and rubbed her hands slowly over her belly and down her legs, just making sure everything was still in the right place. *If not in the right time.*

"Hmm." Airin sat on the loveseat, staring out the window.

"Hmm what? I know that hmm. What are you thinking, Airin?"

They took a deep breath, letting it out very slowly without looking away from the window. "Well, I'm no physicist, Nev, and maybe the folks at Qbito can help you better than I can…"

"Believe me, that's not an option."

Now Airin looked like they were going to be sick, too. "Oh. Okay. Wow." They turned and fixed their eyes on Nev. *Twin galaxies.* "I don't know how else to say this, Nev, but I think something really bad might be going on. And I guess it's up to us to deal with it."

Nev sat up as well as she could on the bean bag and took a deep breath. "It's okay. I'm a big girl. Give it to me straight."

"Well, obviously, you're familiar with the 'many worlds interpretation,' parallel realities, et cetera, et cetera?"

"Yeah, of course."

"So, you haven't been living your days the same way in the Glitch that you did the first time through, right? Like, you weren't here at my loft the first time you experienced September 9th."

"Right… So…"

"So, did you ever wonder what happened to those other days? The days you lived the first time through? Like, have they been erased, or what? And what do you think happens in the future, like, past the point where the Glitch started, a couple weeks from now? Does the world continue as is, or as was?"

"Yeah, of course, I've been wondering the same things. And what happens when I reset at night? Like, have you ever watched me blink out? Do I disappear, or do I just fall asleep, or what?"

"Hmm. I don't think I've ever seen you reset, but now that you mention it, I'm not completely sure. We should test that. So, yeah. Anyway, here's what I think is happening. If the many worlds interpretation is true, then we're constantly spawning parallel universes. Like, every time you flip a coin, there's one universe where it comes up heads, and another where it comes up tails, right? Just, gazillions of new universes every millisecond. But those universes are completely inaccessible to us, so it kind of doesn't matter to our physics."

"Right, it's irrelevant to our calculations whether they exist or not."

"Right, except, thanks to the Glitch, all of a sudden, it *is* relevant. Not to our calculations per se, but to the Qbito mainframe's. It has to keep track of the original timeline, plus every new timeline you generate when you do something differently as you go back. Every single thing you do now that you didn't do the first time adds to the processing load exponentially, creates new forks to keep track of. And the mainframe is doing its best to hold it all together, to reconcile the expanding number of parallel, slightly differentiated universes. And the further back you go, the more of them there are, and the more different they become, so…"

Nev felt the weight of it hit her like an anvil dropped from the top of a skyscraper. "Oh. Fuck. Right. So basically, these microglitches I'm experiencing are, like, a stack overflow of epic proportions. Which explains why they get triggered if I use my SavePoint."

"Right." Nev had never seen Airin look so miserable. "And if we do nothing, your glitches will keep getting more frequent and severe, and eventually, you'll, I don't know, blink out of existence altogether, or worse."

"Worse?"

"Imagine being stuck in a glitch like you just had, but forever, in all timelines."

Nev shuddered involuntarily, and Airin came over and wrapped a light knit blanket around her. She leaned into their embrace, and the two of them sat together on the bean bag for a few minutes. It felt so good, Nev could almost make herself believe everything was going to be okay. Almost.

"Okay. So this is basically a code problem, right? And who's better at fixing shitty code than us? I mean, we're already working to fix the Glitch, right? So let's switch gears and focus on debugging the microglitches first.

Airin turned to look at her, and Nev knew what they were going to say before they opened their mouth.

"We can't debug the code, Nev. The bug isn't in the code. The bug is you."

"Alright, so I'm the bug. So... so how do we take me out of the equation, without... without, um, taking me out of the equation altogether? Oh! I know. I could just try to re-live these days exactly as I lived them the first time through, to lighten the load on the mainframe."

Airin shook their head. "What did you do today, the last time through?"

"I had a date. With Jared." She winced involuntarily.

"And did you work at all on fixing the Glitch with me?"

"No. Obviously not. Okay. I see your point. Well, if we can't take me out of the machine, maybe we can take the machine out of me. I already tried to get the Qbito techs to remove my SavePoint unit, and apparently it's fused into my temporal lobe or something. But, hey, if it's a choice between a mild lobotomy and blipping out of existence altogether, that's a no-brainer, right?"

Airin laughed in spite of themself. "I dunno, Nev. I don't think it's so simple."

"What?" Nev stared at them. "Not as simple as *slicing my brain open*? What are you talking about, Airin?"

Airin cleared their throat. "Please. Don't blame the messenger. I mean, I can't possibly imagine what it must be like for you."

"Let's hope you never have to."

"Well, that's my point, Nev. You're not the only one who's at risk, here. You might be the only one caught in this particular Glitch, but that doesn't mean you're the only one who could be. Or who ever has been."

Jim Bone. Another wave of chills, and Nev pulled the blanket tighter around herself. "Actually, I think I might have met another one. I'm not sure. He might just be schizophrenic or something. Then again, maybe I'm just schizophrenic, and this is all a delusion."

"If it were, I promise I would tell you, Nev."

"Gee, thanks. That's reassuring. So, what, then? Are you saying that SavePoint is a risk to everyone? To the world?"

"Well, we can't know for sure, but yeah. Clearly, the architecture of SavePoint 2.0 creates the possibility for stuff like this to happen. How many users do you currently have?"

"That's proprietary information, Airin. I could get investigated for telling you. Investigated!"

They both laughed. It didn't change anything, but it made Nev feel a whole lot better, if only for the moment.

She did her best Maddy Barnett impression: "Qbito currently has over one hundred and fifty-five million satisfied customers in seventy-two nations and territories around the globe, growing year-over-year at thirty-eight point two percent as of this fiscal year's second quarter. And we anticipate a significant uptick in onboarding as we clear further regulatory hurdles and extend into exciting and dynamic new market categories, including the second-generation revamp of SavePoint, our anchor service, which serves as the linchpin of the Qbito product ecology." It was shocking how much Nev had osmosed over the years, despite her best efforts to the contrary.

"Right, so imagine what happens to those one hundred and fifty-five million satisfied customers when they flip the switch on the SavePoint 2.0 rollout."

"Ohhhhh God. Oh no. No no no no no."

"So if you take yourself out of the equation, Nev, there's nothing we can do about it."

"Sorry, Airin, this is horrible to contemplate, but I don't know what we can do about it, even if I don't get lobotomized. I mean, I can't exactly go back to the future at this rate, and I've already tried talking to Kusuma, who just blew me off with some cosmic mumbo jumbo. And Anissa... Oh, wow, she saw this coming. She tried to warn us. She saw the risks for everyone, but I was such an idiot, I thought it was all about me. Now it's too late. I lost her trust and there's no time to get it back. Though I've tried to make things right, in a way."

"Right, Nev. But *I'm* still headed forward into the future. Towards the launch date. And if we work together..."

The chills were back, along with a creeping, crawling sensation up Nev's spine. "Airin... how well do you understand the architecture of the hack we're already working on?"

"Not that well. You told me you'd handle the structural stuff. I'm just working on implementing code at the day-to-day scale."

The floor tilted beneath Nev's feet, as the light of understanding exploded through her mind like an atom bomb. "You told me the same thing. I've just been trusting the vision thing to you, and working on a siloed, daily basis."

"So then, up to this point, *neither of us* has had a clue what we've been building? Nev, are you saying what I think you're saying?" Airin's voice sank to a whisper.

"I think so... Airin, what if... What if the hack we've been working on *is the solution*? What if we're not engineering me out of this mess? What if we're engineering me *into it*? What if we're sabotaging SavePoint 2.0 so that it implodes when I execute the alpha code? Something so totally devastating that I'm the only victim of the Glitch?" Nev's legs collapsed beneath her as the floor gave way entirely.

Airin looked horrified. "Oh, Nev," they said in a low voice, crouching down beside her. They put an arm around Nev's shaking shoulders. "So... going forward," they said cautiously, "and backward. I guess we don't explain this to each other? Like, I was in the dark about our real strategy until today. And I guess you were too."

"Yeah. I don't think I could have handled it. I can barely handle it now," Nev said, her voice dropping to a whisper as well.

"Me neither. Definitely too weird to get involved in."

Silence enveloped the two of them, as if they both had run out of words.

Nev was the first to speak. "Wow," was all she could muster.

"Yeah, wow," Airin said.

"What happens to me after Zero Day, then? Does my body disappear from the timeline? Do I die? Do I keep living, not this me... but some other me?" Nev asked, her voice regaining some strength as her mind grabbed onto this new puzzle like a life raft.

"I don't know, and I guess I won't know until I get there. By which time..." Airin paused, unwilling to speak the thought aloud.

"By which time, either I'll know too... if I'm even me... or I won't."

Nev looked into Airin's eyes, finding strength in their starry depths. Airin gazed back at her in equal wonder and sorrow.

"But..." Airin said after a moment, "what's to stop Qbito from just building it again, if we do? It's not like we can fry the quantum mainframe itself."

"Probably not, but it'll buy some time. Because you can go public, explain what happened to me. Put pressure on Kusuma and the board to discontinue the project. Maybe even push a broader moratorium on temporal manipulation, at least until our species has worked through its shit a little better."

"So, forever, then."

"Ha, ha."

"Seriously, Nev, so what you're saying is that we're sacrificing you, intentionally, to save everyone else from suffering the same fate? That's pretty fucking epic."

"I know, right? It doesn't sound like me."

"It does to me." Airin held her tightly, and they swayed gently a bit.

QT.00.30.07.08.09.2045

"'HOPE' IS THE thing with feathers — That perches in the soul — And sings the tune without the words — And never stops — "

The sonorous lines of poetry split Nev's skull like a jackhammer. She cracked her eyelids open half an inch to search for the viz on her nightstand and instantly recoiled from the blinding white light streaming in through her bedroom window. Her stomach lurched vertiginously. Something was wrong. Deeply wrong. Another glitch? She blindly patted the bedside table until she found the viz and shook it, silencing the poem on the word "extremity," which looped through her mind like a synthglitch hook. As sick as she felt, the fluidity of her movement through space and time suggested that the problem was not a glitch but something far more base and corporeal: hangover. Nev was filled with loathing for her futurepast self, who would drink her into this state with abandon, having already lived through it. *Fuck you, Nev.*

Hope was the thing with feathers. Nev remembered those lines from her mandatory Poetry for Engineers course at Stanford. The other comp-sci students were always petitioning to be exempted from the course. Nev, just grateful to be admitted with a full scholarship, hadn't risked pushing her luck by asking for special treatment. The TA who led their discussion section was always encouraging the surly STEM students around the seminar table to acknowledge the universal truths of great literature as being on par with the universal truths to be found in the field of pure mathematics. Naturally, no one took her seriously. This morning, Nev doubted that Emily Dickinson would recognize the truth if it walked up and bit her on the ass. The scribbling spinster had clearly never contemplated the possibility of toppling backwards through time towards your own disappearance from the universe. It didn't leave much room for 'hope.'

A wave of nausea lapped up Nev's throat. She hurled herself from bed and raced to the bathroom, barely making it to the toilet in time to heave the contents of her stomach into the porcelain bowl. She shut her eyes tight and flushed, not wanting to see whatever it was she was going to eat for dinner the night before, a sight which would surely make the meal as unpleasant going down as it had been coming up. Nev rocked back on her heels, propping her head against the bathroom wall, and fell back asleep.

She was awakened minutes later by a buzzing notification. Her eyes flickered open to find Jared's avatar blinking fuzzily against the tiled wall.

J: We on for tonight? I got rezzies at that new submolecular gastrobar near Tel Hill.

Memories of eating a bowl of quark, whipped into a non-Newtonian solid and topped with compressed cytochrome filaments tasting vaguely of sea buckthorn, came back to Nev, prompting a new wave of nausea to sweep through her body, sending cascading ripples of toxicity out to the tips of her fingers. Her viz buzzed again.

J: You there?

She had to respond to Jared quick if she wanted to nip the conversation in the bud before it escalated to dick pics. She was not up to dick pics this morning. How was it possible that she had ever been up to dick pics?

N: Sorry, J. Not feeling too good this AM
J: ...
N: rain check?
J: Rain check? Do you know how hard those reservations were to get? I had to ask my dad to pull strings with one of the investors to even get our name on the waitlist.
N: ...
J: Fuck, Nev. Come on. Rezzies aren't til 9. Maybe you'll feel better by then?

Nev took a selfie, and her magnified face, weirdly pallid and beaded with minute sweat droplets, filled her vision before vanishing into the ether.

J: Fine. But you better be recovered by Sunday. I RSVP'd for you at the MG picnic.
Don't make me look like an asshole.

Nev refrained from responding that he didn't need any help with that, and shut her eyes again. The viz had gone silent.

An hour later she woke up, feeling marginally more human—at least, human enough to pop some painkillers, take off the clothes she had blinked out in the night before, and step into the shower to wash the grime away. After ten irresponsible minutes under the hot water (not as high-pressure as Jared's top-of-the-line Swedish fixture, but a decent enough Chinese manufacture), Nev toweled off and got dressed. One benefit of going back in time was that she didn't have to do the laundry. Things she'd worn the day before reappeared clean and folded, tucked back neatly into her dresser drawers. That was something she could get used to.

Not that I'll have the chance.

According to Airin, Nev didn't come over today until after work, when they had some mysterious interaction that Airin couldn't recall and which ended with Nev waking up the next morning at Jared's, fully dressed but without her viz or shoes. Seeing that it was already past eleven in the morning, Nev could guess why there was no time for the coding dungeon this morning. It was fine. She and Airin had worked through quite a lot together on Saturday, when Nev had only felt compelled to put in a few short hours at Qbito. She had lots more to do today, though, to bring the code to the point where she had picked up yestermorrow.

Why she hadn't yet stepped off this bullet train to non-existence was hard to explain. The only good thing about the ride was that it stopped at Airin's each day along the way. At least she had that to look forward to later in the evening.

Jim Bone was in his usual spot on the sidewalk outside Qbito's front door. It appeared to be one of his good days. Maybe her futurepast self had been giving him more money to help him out. His pants were discernibly blue and his knit cap looked like it had been washed. Nev reached into her wallet and pulled out a twenty to give him when she passed by. She certainly wouldn't be needing it. He took it from her, his rough fingers briefly coming into contact with her palm. He looked into her eyes and she thought he was going to say something, but before he got the chance, a familiar voice came from behind.

"You shouldn't do that."

Nev blinked her eyes for the biometric entry scan, resisting the urge to look over her shoulder and tell Maddy to fuck off.

"Security's been trying to move him from that spot forever. Every time you give him money you just make their job harder."

The door opened, admitting Nev and Maddy in rapid succession.

"Why does Security care? Jim Bone's not hurting anyone."

"It's hurting our appearance, Nev," Maddy explained in a patronizing tone.

The elevator doors opened and the two women stepped on together.

"You may not care about *appearances*," Maddy stressed the word, as if to imply that Nev thought such things were beneath her, "but it's my job to make us look good. I've got potential opportunities coming here every day. They don't want to walk past some scuzzy, mentally ill ceegee just to get through the front door."

"What do you have against Jim Bone, Maddy? People've got to live somewhere. You want DPH to just round everyone up and bus them to the flyover camps?"

Truth was, when DPH started the round-ups, Maddy would be the first one out there with a broom to sweep up after them. Nev cursed her bad luck to be stuck once again in a confined space with Madison Barnett. Why, she wondered, hadn't her futurepast self prepared a schedule of Maddy's comings and goings so that Nev could just avoid her?

"If you really want to know, Nev, it's not just about appearances. Security's been noting some unusual activity. They're being extra careful until the SavePoint 2.0 alpha rollout. If you don't care about revenue, at least you should care about saboteurs threatening your code. Or is that beneath you, too?"

"Jim Bone's not a saboteur, Maddy," Nev said. The elevator doors opened at her floor, and Nev stepped out. "He's just a harmless refugee."

Maddy stared at Nev as the elevator doors drew back closed.

Quick trip to the La Pavoni, then down to the pod to input the latest tranche of Airin-infused SavePoint alpha code. Nev waved at the doodz, eased into her Memeron, put her viz on surround mode, and tried to settle down into her favorite programming groove.

First, a quick game of Slavatar.

Too quick, just one more game.

Might need another cup of coffee. The hangover was still lingering behind her eyes and at the base of her skull.

Ok, back with a fresh mug. Time to code.

Had Andy been using her chair again? It felt a little too high off the floor, the lumbar support a little too supportive. Quick adjustment.

Any messages from Jared about his stupid reservations? If he had the sense to choose a restaurant that actually served things like meats, carbs, and veggies, she might even have considered spending an hour or two across the table from him tonight. No, no messages. Nothing from Airin, either. They must be working on the Scotland project. The Silicon Highlands were flush these days, on the heels of the Trans-European Data Thingummy.

The Memeron still wasn't right. Just a few more tweaks. Get up. Sit down hard.

Whatever. It wasn't like she'd have to spend much more time in its customized embrace. She wouldn't be spending much more time at Qbito, period. Weeks, probably. Days, maybe. Wouldn't be spending much more time at home, either. How many nights did Nev have left in her own bed? Not that she remembered her nights anymore, anyway. And even fewer days and nights at Airin's. How soon before they didn't really know her? How soon before they met for the first and last time since Stanford? How soon before...

C'mon, woman. Back to coding. Nev used to marvel at people who talked about 'the grind,' celebrated 'hump day,' said they were 'living for the weekend.' What could possibly be better than getting paid an absurd amount of money to do your favorite thing in the service of a magical and amazing product? Nev's favorite moments in life had probably been spent in her Memeron, working on the SavePoint code. Not that they had a lot of competition, but still, it was like dancing through rippling curtains of pure light, coasting on unpolluted waves of logic, exploring virgin territories. Unlocking the map. But now...

Now that Nev had no future, and precious little past left to live; now that SavePoint itself was doomed by Nev's own hand; now that she was working to destroy, and not to create, well, shit, all the color had drained out of it. For the first time since she'd left Albion, Nev felt like work was just a slog. Something tough and flavorless to chew through, necessary nourishment but utterly without charm or pleasure. "Work is a four-letter word," Grandma used to say, when Nev was still scraping together grocery money at the motel reception desk. She would give anything to call her grandmother now, to see her sympathetic eyes twinkle like rhinestones, and then to pour out her troubles in a flood of tears.

Somehow, minutes stretched to hours, and hours stretched past sundown, and finally Nev had inputted the last of the SavePoint alpha code for the day. She closed the terminal window, bid farewell to the last remaining doodz, and rushed into the elevator, thankfully devoid of Barnetts.

QT.49.06.21.08.09.2045

NEV GAVE ADA Lovesnacks a few listless pats as she stepped off the elevator, then straightened up and looked gloomily around the warehouse apartment. It was as pretty at night as she might have imagined, with the uncurtained floor-to-ceiling windows looking out over the twinkling lights of the city. Too bad she hadn't gotten close to Airin back when there was still time to enjoy it all.

"Are you okay? You seem off. Did something happen at Qbito?" Airin looked thoughtfully at Nev, scrutinizing her like a puzzle.

Nev bit her tongue. *Oh, no big thing. Just coming to grips with my own imminent self-destruction to save the universe. Otherwise, everything's fine.* As much as she wanted to say the words, she figured that if Airin had managed to hold their tongue during the past week of close collaboration then she could repay the favor for the next however-many-days until Nev set the groundwork for the hack and their time together ended. There was no use for both of them to feel miserable from now to the beginning. Although, Nev wondered, how bad would Airin feel about what fate had in store for her as their time together unraveled? The shorter they had known Nev, the less they would care. *And who said things couldn't get worse?* Nev sighed loudly.

"Was there a problem with the code?" Airin asked. "I was a little worried when you told me yesterday that you wouldn't be checking in this morning."

"There's nothing wrong with the code, Airin." *Nothing wrong except that Nev was coding her own destruction.* "It's working exactly as it's supposed to."

A flash of interest in Airin's eyes. In a studied, casual tone they repeated Nev's words: "it's doing what it's supposed to do ..." their voice lifting in tone as their words trailed off, hinting at a question without directly asking anything. Plausible deniability. It was a level of canniness that Nev didn't expect from Airin, who was usually, remarkably, on the level.

"Yes, Airin. It's doing what it's supposed to. Don't worry, you'll know soon enough what that means." *Sooner than you'll like.*

"Sorry, Nev. I didn't mean to pry."

They sounded genuinely apologetic. And Nev felt genuinely sorry for snapping. The day had been too much for her. She should have gone home to get some 'rest.' She wasn't in any shape to spend time with another person. She'd come because she was supposed to. She'd come because yestermorrow her shoes, her viz, and Airin's memory had all said she would. But what sort of reason was that?

"No, I'm sorry. Maybe I shouldn't have come. I've had a shitty day."

"Sounds like you could use some company," Airin said. "And something to drink. Let me see what I have. Take a seat."

Nev made her way to the loveseat, took off her shoes, and tucked her feet up beneath her. Then she slipped off her viz from behind her ear and shook out her hair. Why fight destiny?

A few minutes later Airin came out of the kitchen carrying a silver tray with an elegant green glass bottle and a couple of matching glasses.

"Those are pretty," Nev said, watching as Airin poured a syrupy golden liquid into the green glasses. Airin's contradictions never ceased to surprise her. Half cyber-techno-geek with a dungeon full of hardware, half antiques-enthusiast, with a collection of Art Nouveau glass to rival a Nob Hill hostess.

"Thanks. I hope you like plum brandy. I made it myself with a recipe from Alice B. Toklas. She was from San Francisco, originally. She lived through the 1906 earthquake."

"I didn't know you were interested in history," Nev said, taking a sip from the glass. It tasted sweet and mellow.

"There's a lot you don't know about me. We haven't known each other for very long. Have we?"

"No. No we haven't." Nev watched as Airin took a drink from their glass. A verse from 'Song of Solomon' came unbidden to mind: *Let him kiss me with the kisses of his mouth: for thy love is better than wine.* Her mother tried to forbid the girls from reading that book of the Bible when they were little. She said it was only for 'after they were married.' Good thing Nev hadn't listened, since she now knew for certain that she was never going to get married. And she was never going to kiss Airin and taste the sweetness of their mouth.

But she could still get to know Airin. There was time enough left for that.

"So, tell me something," Nev said. "What should I know about you that I don't know already?"

"What do you want to know?"

Nev put down her glass on the coffee table and looked directly into Airin's eyes.

"Everything."

Airin flushed and darted their eyes down to their glass. They cleared their throat. "Um, well ... I don't know where to begin."

"Tell me what you were like as a kid."

"Why would you want to hear that tale of woe?"

"I told you about my miserable childhood. It's only fair."

"No you haven't. Oh. Wait. Never mind. I guess I have that conversation to look forward to? Okay. Me as a kid..." Airin paused to refill their glasses, more as a delaying tactic than because either had made a serious dent in their brandy. "The weird thing about my childhood is that I was just the same as a kid as I am today. I've always been exactly the same person inside. I loved computers when I was little. My parents understood that part. I also loved animals, classical music, and antiques, which they didn't get. I have two older brothers, Noah and Jacob, who were more into the classic boy things, and everyone kind of expected me to follow suit. But when we went to my grandparents' house for holiday dinners, I was more interested in polishing the silver with Grandma than playing touch football with my brothers and my cousins."

A memory came to Nev. The first time she and Airin sat down to talk, after the Glitch. At the Park Chalet. When Airin first gave Nev a reason to trust them.

"There's something you said to me—I mean, you're going to say to me. Look, I don't mean to pry, but I think maybe it's something I'll need to know. Later, when you don't remember me anymore. You can tell me to mind my own business, but, when you were little, were you named Adam?"

Airin flinched a little, making Nev regret that she'd asked.

"Don't apologize," Airin said, predicting Nev's next move as accurately as if it had already happened. "You're right. We had a conversation about my name when you first asked for my help. It was part of how you persuaded me to trust you. Adam was the name my parents called me, but I never thought of it as *my* name. When I was little I came up with new names for myself all the time. When I first learned about silent letters, I decided the *m* in my name would be silent, so for a while I was Ada."

The dog lifted her head from the floor and looked inquiringly at Airin, but seeing that there was no food on offer, she lowered it again and resumed snoring.

"I've never told that story to anyone but you before."

Nev felt honored, as though she'd been entrusted with something precious and fragile, like the chrysalis of a rare butterfly.

"Thanks for sharing your secret with me," she said. "I'll keep it safe and use it wisely."

"It hardly even feels like a choice whether or not to trust you. When you first reached out to me, I learned that I already trusted you, even though I hadn't lived it yet. I've known since day one that I was going to tell you the story about the time I named myself Ada, I just didn't know when I was going to tell you. And now I know. Which is reassuring, but also, kind of sad, because it means I don't have that moment to wonder about any longer. If there's one thing I can say about this experience, it's given me so many things to wonder about, which is doubly strange, since I've never had such access to information about what comes next."

"It's a world of wonders, my Mama used to say."

"That sounds like it's from the Bible. Your mom's really religious, right?"

"You could say that," Nev answered. "I'll tell you all about it some time. I promise." She checked the wall clock. "But I don't have time to get into it now."

"Oh," said Airin, looking stricken. "You have to go?"

"In a manner of speaking."

"Reset?"

"Mm-hmm."

Airin swallowed their drink, then seeming to gather courage, said, "Can I ask you something?"

"Sure. Anything. What do you want to know?"

"It's more... something I've been wondering about. I want to know what happens when you reset. Do you mind if I sit here with you while it happens?"

"No, Airin. I don't mind at all." Of course Nev would agree. Had agreed. The answer was as inevitable as everything else about this exceptional evening. And then, the next day, when Nev showed up here for their appointment, Airin wasn't going to remember it. The end of the evening would vanish from their memory, as Nev's extraction from this timeline stole a portion of Airin's along with it. Who knew what might happen in those lost hours, what secrets lingered in the forgotten night? Nev never would.

"But you should know…" Nev bit off the end of the sentence without finishing it. Airin had to figure out how the Glitch worked for themself. Plus, Nev didn't want to wreck this moment, because this delicious moment was all there was. They had no future together. No past. Only the present.

"What?" Airin looked at her so sharply, it felt like a needle.

"Nothing. It's nothing." Nev sipped her brandy. It felt warm inside her, a little bit like love. "So, tell me something else about yourself. Something secret. Something juicy. I promise not to tell."

QT.50.57.12.07.09.2045

NEV WAS SWEATING, and it wasn't just from the brisk walk over to Qbito. She'd overclocked her brain running the numbers at quantum mainframe speed, without the benefit of a heat sink to cool her down. She'd calculated every permutation of words that might persuade Hong-Mei to let her past the front desk into Kusuma's inner sanctum. Each iteration yielded a nil answer. No variation of please... I forgot... Mr. Kusuma asked me... it's an emergency... produced anything but negative results.

What then? More computations. Should she fall to the floor? Pretend to have a seizure? Hong-Mei would call in help. Race for the door and lock it behind her? Hong-Mei would call in Security. Then Nev would be banned from the building, which meant she wouldn't be able to install the hack that she had been working on over the yestermorrow week with Airin, which meant that there must be some other solution to this problem, because otherwise she wouldn't have the memories she had. Somehow she was going to get Hong-Mei to step aside and let her poke around in Kusuma's office.

Nev needed to find Kusuma's passcode, because otherwise she wouldn't be able to lay the foundation stone for the hack in the futurepast week, and she wouldn't be standing here today. The certainty made the task seem futile, a proposition she once brought up with Airin. Why should Nev make the effort to find the passcode when it was clear she (her future: would get it) (Airin's past: had gotten it). Because, Airin had reminded her, back when they still knew the Plan, if you don't make the effort and you (your future: don't get it) (my past: didn't get it) then your timeline will be so fucked, who knows what will happen to you, and meanwhile Qbito will just promote one of the doodz on your team to finish the SavePoint 2.0 alpha, and soon enough all one hundred and fifty-five million users will be just as fucked as you. *Damned if you do, damned if you don't.*

She and Airin were making great progress on the hack. Even though they were moving closer and closer to the start date, now that Nev knew what the Plan was, the code they'd written and the code they had yet to write made a lot more sense to her. It was not only a more elegant version of the alpha she'd written the first time through, it was a brilliant hack in its own right, using the stems into the Qbito code base to trigger a kind of autoimmune response in SavePoint, a cascading series of self-corrections that would not only destroy the program from inside but restrict its effects solely to Nev's own device.

The problem was, they still needed access to the foundational code—the stuff only Kusuma could edit. Without that, Nev and Airin could probably trigger the Glitch, but they had no hope of eliminating the root cause, which would mean leaving hundreds of millions of people potentially exposed to the same ratfucked outcome. So today, Nev's task wasn't merely to enter the latest batch of doctored alpha code, but also to spend some time in Kusuma's office, looking for any clue to his password.

Unfortunately, she had no idea what she was looking for. It wasn't like he'd have a piece of paper in a drawer somewhere, saying 'secret root code password.' The other problem was that Security was going to be on her like a swarm of surveillance drones. According to Maddy, they were already on elevated alert, probably triggered by her own unsanctioned hacks and erratic behavior. Entering Kusuma's office was like waving a red flag saying "hey, check me out, I'm a corporate spy." If she weren't so irreplaceable at this point, Nev had little doubt that Maddy would have lobbied successfully to have her taken out of the picture the minute after Kusuma left on his vision quest.

As Nev approached the building, Jim Bone came down the landing to meet her on the sidewalk. She'd never seen him so animated, or so relatively coherent. He was almost making eye contact, and speaking intelligibly. He must have spent the night in a shelter, because his normally eye-watering stench was barely noticeable.

"Has it happened?" he asked, adjusting his hat on his relatively unfilthy hair.

"Afternoon, Jim Bone," Nev replied, reaching in her bag for a bill. She fished out a twenty and handed it to him, then tried to step past him to enter the building. He moved into her path, not exactly blocking her, but making it difficult to pass him without an awkward shuffle.

"Has it happened yet?" he asked again. "You gotta know…"

Nev didn't have time for this shit. "Jim Bone," she said, trying her best to look him squarely in the eyes, and finding it oddly difficult now that he was able to return her stare. "Listen, I need to go inside now, and you need to stop harassing me"—urgency amplified her voice, making it sound harsh to her own ears— "because they already want to call DPH on you and have you sent…"

Jim Bone laughed—a wheezing snortle that sounded like air being squeezed through a broken bellows. Nev had never heard it before, and never hoped to hear it again.

"They can send me, they can send me," he said, more to himself than to her. "They already sent me, heh heh, more than once, it's true. They can send me all they like, but I'll still be here tomorrow, still be here yesterday. Jim Bone ain't goin' nowhere." He nodded grimly, no longer laughing. "Nowhere, no time."

For a brief moment, curiosity and concern distracted Nev from her own grim situation. The deeper she fell into the Glitch, the more convinced she became that Jim Bone was a fellow traveler. Or a fellow prisoner, more like. But what could she do for him? She couldn't even help herself without engineering her own erasure from the timeline.

"Jim Bone, sorry, 'scuse me—I've gotta go. I'll see you tomorrow, okay?" Nev stepped around him, blinking her eyes at the door scanner and entering the lobby. Technically, she was telling the truth. She had seen Jim Bone tomorrow, when she defended him from Maddy. But who knew whether she'd actually see him again on *her* tomorrow? Or on his?

"Tomorrow and tomorrow and tomorrow," she could still hear him wheezing to himself on the steps as the elevator doors closed.

She bypassed her own floor and went straight to the C-suite, striding with purpose to Hong-Mei's marble desk.

"Good afternoon, Ms…"

"Nevaeh. Nevaeh Bourne." *You know my name.*

"Yes, of course. Ms. Bourne. It's nice to see you. Mr. Kusuma is away on business. Can I help you with something?" *Unlikely, but I'm about to help you.*

All her overclocked computations had finally yielded one positive result: bribery. Money was the only possible answer.

Qbito rhymed with cash flow. That's why they were all here. Hong-Mei, Kusuma, Madison, Darian, Nev's team of brogrammers, the techs in the human subject labs, Nev herself. They could bullshit themselves about making products for a better world. *Doing the right thing.* But each of them were here for the money. Only, some of them were making a lot more dosh than others. C-Suite at top. Programmers near the top. On an average week, Nev fielded ten to twenty contacts from headhunters. Whenever a hyper-leveraged new startup appeared on the scene, she might get twice that number. Demand drove salaries. Biotechs were further down the ladder. Installers only needed a med-tech cert to get hired. The diploma mills out by Modesto kept Qbito and the rest of the industry supplied with a steady flow of workers. Security were near the bottom of the Qbito pay ladder. Admins were only a notch above cleaners. Hong-Mei probably earned more than most. Her sort of looks and cool didn't come cheap, but they weren't cheap to maintain either. Add the cost of living in San Francisco. Well, everyone in this city needed more money, and Nev was going to have to hope that, despite her air of aloofness, Hong-Mei was one of everyone.

"Don't say anything. Just listen to me. I'll give you fifty grand on Trackless if you let me look around Kusuma's office for five minutes. Ten grand a minute. Ten if you let me walk in the door now. Forty delivered to you five minutes after I walk back out, as long as security isn't here to greet me. I'll leave everything as I find it and wipe the waiting room footage when I get back to my floor."

Nev watched a thousand computations flicker past in Hong-Mei's eyes, the expression on her face unchanging, until with a single arching eyebrow, she raised a perfectly manicured finger to her viz. A Trackless request strobed yellow in Nev's sightline. She approved the transfer and crossed the room to Kusuma's office, hearing the gentle click of his door unlocking as she reached its threshold.

The salt lamps had been dimmed to a light pink glow during Kusuma's absence. The office felt inert without his powerful presence at its center, like a vacant spider web. She paused for a moment, almost hating to disturb the stillness, but there was no time for hesitation. She couldn't use her SavePoint to buy more time. She had to find whatever she was looking for quickly.

Nev started with a quick scan of the room. Two huge photographs, each one two feet high by four feet long, stretched across one wall. The first showed a massive wave approaching a shoreline densely packed with red roofed buildings. The second showed a small group of people in swimsuits racing through ankle-deep water towards shore as a tall wave approached from the sea, a white sailboat buried up to its mast in the oncoming water. Nev gripped the first of the photos, lifting the picture wire carefully off the hooks that held it in place and setting it down on Kusuma's vast empty desk. Nothing on the wall behind it. No slips of paper tucked into the back of the frame. She ran her fingers along its seams and felt... nothing. She replaced the photograph and repeated the procedure with the second picture. Still, nothing.

Besides the two terrifying photos, Kusuma's office was decorated with zen-like minimalism. Nev turned the salt lamps upside down. She prodded through the pebbles filling the three potted succulents perched on a low carved teak table. Discovering nothing, she turned finally to Kusuma's obsidian desk. Made of three unornamented panels, the desk had no drawers or cavities to secret things away. She dropped to her hands and knees to climb under the desk, staring up in the dim light for scratchings in the stone, but the desk was as smooth on its underside as it was on its surface. Qbito was a paperless office, and Kusuma's desk was uncluttered by in- or out-boxes. Surely there had to be somewhere that Kusuma dumped his physical junk. Or maybe Hong-Mei took care of all that for him.

In a last, desperate attempt to deliver on her fifty-grand gambit, Nev flicked on her viz and scanned the room's digital surfaces, looking for beacons, hot spots, code keys, anything at all that could be used to store or retrieve information. But the info-ether was as clean as the desktop, a mute surface almost painstakingly featureless. Blank as Kusuma's face, smooth as the dome of his skull.

There was nothing there to find.

Shit. Shit. Shit.

Nev walked out the door just as Hong-Mei was rising from her seat to retrieve her. They locked eyes for a moment, Nev resisting the assistant's inquiring stare, trying to achieve Kusuma-grade levels of impassivity.

"Thanks. Give me five minutes, and the rest is yours. And don't worry about the footage."

Hong-Mei sat down again, and Nev saw the corners of her mouth twitch upwards just slightly as she resumed whatever viz game she had been playing when Nev had first stepped off the elevator ten minutes before. *Don't spend it all in one place,* she managed to avoid saying out loud.

Nev rode back down to her floor, but instead of heading to the open plan area where her Memeron awaited, she went straight to one of the 'privacy pods,' small rooms with actual doors and a range of data-blocking options reserved for sensitive meetings and personal affairs, as well as the occasional late-night hookup. Nev saw a few raised eyebrows as she closed the door behind her, but she knew for a fact that she wasn't going to be discovered until she'd successfully completed her grand act of sabotage. Hell, in a couple days' time, even she wouldn't know what she was really up to.

Once the door was closed and the full-spectrum LED lights had blinked on, Nev sat at the room's tiny desk, dropped the rest of the bribe money into Hong-Mei's account, and opened a window to Qbito's Security core. She had picked up a 24-digit access code almost accidentally more than a year ago, half-watching and half-listening as a coked-up EVP had pulled up surveillance footage at a holiday party, showing a dozen drunken partygoers a hilarious video of one of Anissa's team picking his nose and eating it with gusto. She'd stowed the code in the back of her mind, hoping she'd never have occasion to use it. Now, she hoped she still remembered it, and that it was still valid.

Let's see... the year of the Gold Rush, Caden Jenson's football jersey number, a section of her own Social, a four-digit prime she knew for some reason, *what was it, what was it,* a verse and chapter that her mother was far too fond of, her age and her father's age the year Faith was born, and two consecutive counting numbers. *That should do it. Please please please...*

It worked! *Thank you, brain.* The main Qbito Security interface opened in front of her eyes—a dead simple menu-based affair that was clearly QA'd on Neanderthals. First things first: Cut five minutes of video footage from Kusuma's office cams and paste them over the footage from her fruitless visit a few minutes ago. Easy enough.

Next up: Poke around the Human Subjects files. Nev found the search interface and entered 'Jim Bone.' No such luck. 'James Bone.' Nothing. She tried 'James B*' and got a list of five subjects who shared the same first name and last name initial. James Bakhtiari. James Berenstein. James Bonfoco. James Bonilla-Mendez. James Burris. *Hmm.* Two possible hits.

She opened James Bonfoco's file. A poorly-lit photo of a white man with a few days' worth of dark stubble. Rounder face than Jim Bone's. Closer-set eyes. He had been a test subject for an early, external prototype of SavePoint—a booth that sent inhabitants backwards a few microseconds. Nothing they'd notice personally, but the single-ion clocks they wore on lanyards attested to the success of the technology and impressed investors enough to back Kusuma's vision of a device in every eye socket. Last test: June 28th, 2039. Successful trial, no complications. Fee paid upon completion. Unlikely candidate.

Next, Bonilla-Mendez. This file was marked with a secure extension—accessible to users with a kappa clearance rating of seven or higher—but thankfully the password she'd lifted was for a kappa eight account. A face hovered before her, strange and familiar. 3D-scanned, not just a flat photo. Sixtyish. Heavy brow, thin face, prominent cheekbones, clean shaven. Knowing, intelligent eyes. Handsome, in an avuncular way. *Oh my god. It might be...* Heart pounding, Nev ran through the file. He'd been tested for a device she hadn't heard of—maybe a prototype. A subcortical implant, smaller than a grain of rice. Pretty far afield from anything she'd been briefed on. She checked the date, and felt the hairs on her arms and neck stand up before her mind had even absorbed its import: February 9th, 2057.

Nev was certain: This was Jim Bone's origin story. It all made sense, except that it made no sense at all. Bonilla-Mendez had entered a clinical trial for SavePoint version five or six or seven, more than a decade from now, and something must have gone horribly awry. A Glitch, on par with what Nev was experiencing. Or worse, maybe. Who knew? She had no way of understanding what his experience of it was, and he barely seemed to know himself, let alone have the ability to tell her.

A wave of pity washed over Nev, threatening to drag her out to sea. The pastfuture weeks had been so miserable for her, so confusing. So lonely. At least she had her scientific training and Airin to keep her company. Without those, she would have gone mad already. But twelve years of it was too much to comprehend. Twelve years alone, spent as a hobo on a stairwell, watching your future tormenters pass you on their way to work each day. Twelve years with nobody to talk to, except yourself... and Nev. When had he realized? How had he known?

And, even more to the point, how did Qbito know? Why did the company even have a file on a human subject who wouldn't officially enroll in a trial until 2057? Who knew that Jim Bone was stuck in his Glitch, and what, if anything, were they doing about it? There were no innocent answers, only shades of evil.

As Nev closed her eyes and shook her head, trying to clear the plaintive, not-yet-wild-eyed face from her visual memory, a glimmer of hope appeared in her mind's periphery. *Rule Number Three: Past Primacy*. If Nev prevented Jim Bone from joining the trial, maybe she could erase his twelve years of temporal slavery as though it had never happened. Although there was probably nothing she could do to prevent him from enlisting; even if he'd already made it to the Bay Area in 2045 from whatever desiccated wasteland he originally hailed from, she couldn't exactly walk up to him and say, "Oh, by the way, please don't sell access to your subcortex for a quick buck in 2057." He'd be the one calling the asylum to come and get her.

No. She couldn't stop Jim Bone from doing the wrong thing. But could she stop Qbito? It was, after all, part of the Plan for Airin to publicize the Glitch (and Nev's resulting erasure) as a way to put pressure on Qbito and the entire industry to adopt more ethical practices. Not for Nev's sake, but for the 150 million SavePoint users today, and who knew how many more in the years to come. On the other hand, Nev had been around tech long enough to know that the industry suffered from a short memory for failure and a long view of profitability. She might save millions from falling into their own personal temporal hellscapes this year, or next year. But a decade from now? The very fact that Jim Bone was still here, she realized with a queasy, sinking-into-quicksand feeling, was probably proof positive that she couldn't, or at least wouldn't, be able to help him out of his jam.

Sorry, James Bonilla-Mendez. Looks like we're equally fucked.

Nev left the pod, closing its bay doors behind her, and returned to her Memeron. The rest of the afternoon felt like a waste of her increasingly finite moments left on Earth before, as Airin put it, she glitched out for good. When would the final glitch happen? Would she see it coming? Would it strike her down like an assassin's bullet, or would it happen by her own hand?

Inputting the tainted code into the SavePoint alpha had become a matter of pure rote. Without something to look forward to, a big launch, an unknown and exciting future, accolades and promotions, new and exciting discoveries, it was worse than anticlimactic. Now that Nev had resigned herself to the literal inevitable, she didn't even feel like she had free will. Her job was basically being a data relay from Airin's code dungeon to the Qbito workpods, little more than a semi-skilled cut-and-paste monkey.

After the hours had crawled by and Nev had finally inputted the last line of the day's code dump, she was ready for a drink. Hell, ten drinks. She'd already paid the price with yestermorrow's hangover, so why not reap the rewards and lose herself at the bottom of a bottle somewhere? And as much as she missed that fifty grand she'd pointlessly contributed to Hong-Mei's clothing budget, she could at least take comfort in the certainty that the money would appear in her account again as soon as she woke up the previous day. There were benefits, it turned out, to living life backwards.

Standing at the elevator bay in the polarized sunset, Nev could almost taste the tequila waiting for her at Jimmy's. Ten minutes. Fifteen, tops, before she had a line of shots in front of her like tiny undo buttons.

The doors slid open with a bing, and there was Maddy, looking sleek, ruthless, and hungry as a great white shark. Thankfully, she didn't try to talk to Nev this time, just looked at her through slightly narrowed eyes, as though from a great and lofty height. Nev looked back at her and nodded, but Maddy didn't acknowledge her greeting, except maybe by narrowing her eyes a little further. *God, what a bitch.*

Nev had to give it to Maddy, though. The woman knew who she was, and what she was about, and didn't spend a dollar or a minute on anyone or anything that didn't benefit her directly in some way. Nev realized with a slight shudder that she could say more or less the same of herself, at least until she'd fallen into the Glitch. She missed the purity of focus, the simple self-interest of a normal life spent in forward motion, towards a series of goals, with reliable rewards along the way. *My life. Mine, and mine alone.*

Alone.

She had to admit that, simple and pleasurable as it may have been, her life before the Glitch was even lonelier in some ways than the past few weeks had been. Now, at least she had Airin's company. A sense of shared destiny with Jim Bone. And a sense of purpose, with consequences for someone besides herself. With consequences for everybody, really.

All the way to Jimmy's she pondered it: which was worse? A perfect life, spent utterly and entirely without love or intimacy? Or a doomed and fucked up life, destined to end soon in a blaze of data, but with good company, and true purpose? As painful as her situation was, she wouldn't trade it with Maddy's for anything. *There but for the grace of Glitch go I.*

Levi was there behind the bar, his winning smile spread wide across his face. "Nice to see you again. What can I get you?"

Two weeks ago (in either direction?) she might have said 'you.' But at this moment, it was Airin or nothing.

"Shot of Patrón. Then another."

QT.00.30.07.06.09.2045

"APPLICATION FAILURE CODE 591. Application failure code 591. Application failure—"

The motherfucking rogue alarm app installed on Nev's viz was really outdoing itself this morning, stuttering out an error code instead of dispensing its usual daily dose of banal deep thoughts. She closed out the app and stared up at the ceiling. She'd been lying there awake since dawn, free from hangover, but riddled with anxiety.

In Nev's first semester at Stanford, her professor for Mathematical Foundations of Computing had opened the class by posting a slide with a quotation from Thomas Edison: "I have not failed. I've just found ten thousand ways that won't work." The rosy warmth of good feeling that spread throughout the lecture auditorium lasted for all of ten seconds before the professor posted the next slide, a bar graph tracking the failure rate in the class over the previous twenty years.

"Unfortunately, none of you are Thomas Edison. Going on the evidence of the previous two decades, thirty percent of you will drop out of Computer Systems Engineering by the end of the quarter." Basically the message was if you had any doubts about being a CSE major, you should go ahead and drop the class right away. It wasn't going to get any easier moving forward.

One student had literally run from the classroom in tears before the professor switched to the next slide, and Nev remembered feeling... happy. One less person to compete with. She had decided to take *failure is not an option* as her mantra from then on. Wrote it in sharpie on her laptop lid. Thomas Edison had been too easy on himself. She wouldn't put up with ten thousand wrong answers to find her way to the solution.

That was then. And now?

Let's see. So far this morning she was way past ten thousand wrong answers to her problem, and still counting. Maybe that was a slight exaggeration. But only slight. She hadn't found Kusuma's passcode in any of the numerous places she'd searched, and she hadn't yet come up with a single good answer to where to search next. But as anxious as that cascade of wrong answers made her feel, she couldn't go running from the classroom. Failure, it turned out, might actually be an option. Who knew how many times she'd failed already, how many more times she might still fail. Five hundred and ninety-one. Ten thousand. Infinity. At least she had someone more sympathetic to turn to than Professor Dreamkiller.

"How about you go back to Hong-Mei and try again?" Airin asked an hour and a half later, as they drank their tea and coffee at the kitchen table. Airin didn't have any cashew milk that morning, so Nev had to settle for cow juice instead. It didn't taste as good, but caffeine was caffeine, and caffeine was badly needed.

"Can't go back to Hong-Mei. She didn't expect me yestermorrow, which must mean that I don't ask her today."

"So?" Airin asked, a confused look on their face.

"Well, if I deviate from the timeline..." Nev left the words hanging, expecting Airin to jump in and finish the sentence. But they didn't.

"Aw, fuck," Nev muttered.

"What? What's the matter? What happens if you deviate from the timeline?"

"I, uh, I can't tell you." *BECAUSE IT DEVIATES FROM THE TIMELINE. And the further I deviate from the timeline, and the more days I live backwards, the worse the glitches become and the sooner I glitch out for good.*

Airin quirked their beautiful eyebrows. For a moment, Nev lost herself in Airin's twin galaxy eyes. She felt a rush of yearning, as deep as any she'd felt in her life. And then she very carefully and conscientiously returned her gaze to her coffee cup.

"OK, so assuming, as you say, that you can't go to Hong-Mei until tomorrow, that must be a wrong answer. What's the next solution?"

"Oh my God, you know what I was thinking about this morning?" Nev asked. "Remember the first day of MFoC? Weren't you in the same class as me? Remember how on the first day of class the professor showed us a graph of previous years' failure rates and told the class that anyone who wasn't up to the work should drop out? And someone went running from the classroom?"

"That didn't happen, Nev."

"Sure it did. I remember. She opened up with that Thomas Edison quotation about never failing, then told us we weren't Edison and if we had any doubts we should get the fuck out of class."

"No, Nev. That might be what you heard, but I'm telling you— that is not what Professor Hoffnung said. She's the best. She was the faculty advisor for the Women and Sexual Minority Student Engineering Society. She cared more about students than any of the other crusty bastards who taught our first-year classes. She used to organize extra tutoring sessions for the students who were struggling. She got me to TA for her second year, before I dropped out. She always started the semester with straight talk about failure rates, but her goal wasn't to chase students from class—it was to prepare students to deal with failure and keep going."

"Wow."

Nev let Airin's words sink in. She trusted them implicitly, trusted them with her life. And she knew that Airin hated to lie, considered it a form of self-abuse, even. So if Airin said that Professor Hoffnung was a kind and supportive mentor, and that Nev's memory of her was fundamentally flawed, either corrupted by time or founded on a deep misunderstanding, then it must be true.

But she remembered the scene so well. It had been a turning point in Nev's own narrative of herself, a story she'd returned to over the years, held in her hands and examined like a keepsake from a life-changing vacation, or a gift from a long-dead lover. It was an important part of her, and it was... false.

Maybe she hadn't started living in an alternate timeline when the Glitch hit—maybe she'd been living in one all along. Mama had her world, with Jesus and the angels watching over every move. And Maddy had hers, a corporate ladder leading to wealth and power. Anissa had hers, too—a world in which you're supposed to Do The Right Thing, not because some deity was watching over you, but just because that's what life was about. Jared lived in a world of accessible luxury, plain vanilla hedonism, and, above all else, comfort. Airin's world felt most familiar to Nev, but it was still a strange place, a timeless bubble populated with sparkling antiques and futuristic junk. And a very sweet dog. As much as Nev wished she could live there with them, she knew it was just a way station, a portal from the world they'd undone to the one they were coding together. One with no place for Nev. One in which she had neither future nor past.

But this new, Nevless world would have something the old one lacked: Hope. Without the Glitch, the future would have a future again. Mama could look forward to the rewards of heaven, and Jared could make partner by forty with a pretty and adoring wife at his side, and Anissa could spend her lottery winnings on a startup, or a school, or whatever her sweet, virtuous soul most desired. And Airin... well, Airin would move on.

It wasn't like they were a couple. They hadn't even kissed and now they never would. Never had. The term 'star-crossed lovers' reverberated in Nev's ears, strobing in time with the light in Airin's eyes, watching her patiently as she sorted through the confusing morass of feelings that had been set loose by their unexpected revision to her memories. What else didn't she remember quite right? What world had she been living in all these years?

"Look, uh, we should probably..." Airin's patience was wearing thin. Of course, Nev realized, they had other work—paying work—to get to, and at this point, they probably weren't all that invested in what seemed like Nev's problem. An interesting one, to be sure, but nothing worth losing a lucrative consulting contract over.

"Yeah, sorry, you kind of threw me for a loop there. I'm starting to realize that, no matter how many times I experience my life, I might never actually understand it."

"Ha. Join the club, kiddo. C'mon, I think you know the way to my office. You can leave your coffee cup over by the sink."

"Yes, I—thanks. See you back there in a minute."

Without another word, Airin opened the secret door in the wall, and walked through the dimly lit hallway behind it, then disappeared around the corner.

QT.19.42.09.05.09.2045

"DON'T WORRY, SHE'S always like this when she meets people for the first time."

Ada Lovesnacks was barking at Nev with all the ferocity of Cerberus's three heads in one.

"Down, Ada, down." Airin pulled at the dog's collar, backing up as Nev stepped out of the freight elevator.

Nev reached into her pocket, feeling woeful now that Airin had confirmed that this was the last day she would have a chance to feed Ada one of her beloved nacho Milkbones. She'd suspected as much earlier that morning, when she'd noticed that the familiar red box with the happy black lab on its front wasn't waiting in its customary spot on her hallway table. She'd had to make a quick trip to Abdul's to buy the treats before heading off to Airin's half an hour later than usual. The 24-hour dot. mart turned out to be low on supplies, since it was the Tuesday following Labor Day weekend and the Amazon-One World delivery fleet operators were just coming back online after a three-day sickout. The dog treat shelf was nearly bare, all the nutritious options having been scooped up by the health-minded pet owners of SoMa, leaving Nev with a choice between Nacho cheez flavor and CBD-boost Milkbones. Not sure whether Airin would approve of spiking Ada's diet with cannabinoids, Nev had opted for Nacho, although it wasn't much of a 'choice' when she made it knowing that she already had. At least she could feel good about the clear evidence of Ada's appreciation for her selection.

"Here you go, pups," Nev said, bending at the knees and extending an open palm containing the bright orange biscuit.

Ada immediately switched from barking to sniffing, straining forward to the waiting treat. Airin looked dubious but relaxed their hold on the dog's collar, and soon Nev's empty palm was coated in a slick sheath of drool.

"Don't worry, you and I are going to become great friends." Nev scratched Ada behind her ears, and the dog panted happily.

Rising to her feet, Nev couldn't miss the tug of disapproval at the corners of Airin's finely shaped lips. Airin would probably be even more unhappy if they knew that there were two more Milkbones still lodged in her pocket, and Nev did intend to deliver them before the morning work was over.

"Trust me. It was the best choice I had," Nev said.

"I'm trying to trust you, it's just… not easy."

Nev tried to keep her face blank, but the words still stung. How long had Airin been working with her? How many more days did they have together?

An awkward pause bloomed between them. Nev resisted the urge to count the seconds.

"So… should we get to work?" Airin asked.

"No coffee first?"

"Oh! I hadn't thought of that. I figured you would have had breakfast before you came here. I'm more of a tea-drinker myself. I don't even know if I have any coffee in the cabinets. Can I offer you some genmai cha?"

No cashew milk yestermorrow. No coffee today. *Oh, shit.*

"Um, that's okay. I'll do without. You're probably right, we should get to it."

Nev walked over to the cinderblock wall which hid the door to the coding dungeon. Ada trailed behind her, sniffing at the pocket of Nev's pants containing the remaining biscuits, but Airin remained fixed in place, a look of astonishment replacing their earlier skepticism. Nev lifted her hands to the wall, carefully arranging her fingers to touch the five thermosensors that unlocked the entryway.

"How do you—? No one knows—what..." the words came out in a stutter of unfinished thoughts.

"You showed me."

"*I* showed you? I've never shown anyone. Ever. There are things behind that door that could get me sent away to the black cells for decades, Nev. There are things that could get me killed?"

"You will show me. Just, just trust me."

"I guess I will," Airin said, unable to scrape the doubt from their voice.

But you're not there yet.

Nev let Airin lead the way through the passage to the steel door, hanging back to give them space. She was in unknown territory. She didn't know just how tenuous her connection to Airin was at this point. If she made the wrong move, if it felt to Airin like she was pushing, Airin might end the collaboration prematurely. No collaboration, no hack. No spiking the SavePoint 2.0 alpha. No rescuing SavePoint's user base from getting trapped in a Macro-glitch for eternity—one hundred and fifty-five million souls, each drowning in their own bottomless wells. Nev's insides lurched, and she reached out her hand to touch the solid wall, willing it to hold her up.

"Be careful," Airin said, "it's a little dark in here. I've built it to avoid detection by thermal imaging cameras. DPH likes to fly drones overhead."

"I'll be careful."

Airin opened the inner door, and they stepped into the familiar warmth of the coding dungeon. Nev looked around the room intently, trying to memorize each beloved detail. The old Defender arcade game in the corner, which she still hadn't played, the shelves of vintage and not-yet-invented hardware, the crowded desktops. She wasn't sure she would ever see them again.

Airin looked embarrassed. "Oh God, it's really cluttered. I've never had someone back here before, so I don't tend to think about it. I swear it's safe! You don't have to worry—"

"No! I'm not judging. It's perfect. I love it," Nev said.

"You do?"

For the first time that morning, Nev saw the trace of a real smile on Airin's lips.

"Okay. Well, just, clear yourself a space? I guess you've been here before. Where do you usually work?"

Nev pulled a chair from the corner and took her customary spot at the aft side of the two-way projection. Airin sat down opposite and illuminated the shared screen.

"So I've been thinking," they said. "We need to work on finding a way for you to access Kusuma's founder's code that we're building the hack on top of."

"Good point. It's kind of the final frontier, at least from my perspective. We've more or less inputted the entire hack into the SavePoint code, but I—we, I guess—still don't know Kusuma's passcode. I even looked around his office for it, a few days from now."

"Yeah, he's too smart to keep anything there."

"*Now* you tell me."

Airin smiled again, a little more warmly. Nev would do anything to keep them smiling like that. But seconds later, it vanished, replaced by an expression Nev knew all too well as Airin's back-to-business face.

"First things first, Nev. Get the code. Otherwise all this," they waved their arms around the dungeon, "is pointless."

"Agreed."

The rest of the morning slid by, almost like normal. Airin kept stopping to explain or ask things, and Nev would have to patiently walk through issues they'd worked on seamlessly in pastfuture sessions. But, she reflected, it came with the territory. She'd already reaped the rewards of the groundwork she was laying now. It was kind of the flip side of getting the hangover before the high. Speaking of which, her head was pounding slightly—probably the early stages of caffeine withdrawal. She'd have to hit the La Pavoni as soon as she got to Qbito this afternoon.

Finally, they reached a point Nev recognized from the beginning of their previous session. "Okay, I think we end just about here," she told Airin.

They shook their head, purple bouffant waving in the dim light. "I can't get used to this," they said. "It's just so weird."

"What?"

"Just the fact that, you know, our future is dictated by your past. Like, we stop coding not because we reach some natural break point in the process, but because that's where you *remember* starting it again tomorrow."

"Believe me, it's just as weird on my end. Weirder, even. Like, I've had to code this whole thing in reverse. And for most of that time, I—" Nev bit the sentence off and clamped her mouth shut. *For most of that time, I didn't even know I was coding my own doom.*

Airin looked at her, hard. A penetrating stare, like they were analyzing a malfunctioning program, looking for the flaw in the logic.

"Yeah. Yeah, I can see that. C'mon, let's get you on your way."

Airin led Nev back out of the code dungeon, then walked her over to the loft's sliding door. Before she stepped into the elevator, Nev snuck the last Milkbone to Ada, who rewarded her with some extra licks and a cautious nuzzle against her hip.

"Oh! I almost forgot. I guess today's the, um, first day we worked together here. Where and when do we meet on the morning September 4th? We met here on the 6th at 9:09am."

Airin's lovely brows knitted together. "We didn't meet

yesterday morning." Nev felt a quick surge of panic in her gut. *This can't be the last time. This can't be the last time we meet.* "We met at that bar in the Tenderloin, Jimmy's, around 9:00 pm. You know it, right?"

Yes. I know it. Not trusting herself to speak, Nev kept her mouth shut and quickly nodded her head as she closed the elevator door. She could hear Ada's muffled yipping from the other side. The ride down to the ground floor felt longer than the rest of the morning combined.

QT.00.30.08.04.09.2045

"No gods, no masters."

Nev awakened to the sounds of raucous voices chanting. No pretty poetry or mystic deep thoughts from her hacked viz alarm this morning. Instead, the throaty sounds of a crowd united in proclamation of a universal aspiration: "No gods, no masters. No gods, no masters".

She slipped the viz into place above her left ear and checked the date, as she always did when she woke up—just in case something had changed and she was no longer in retrograde. September 4th, 2045. Still on track, then.

As Nev shut off the alarm, the app flashed a reminder that it was Labor Day. Qbito was closed, its front door locked fast against misguided employees who might defy dictates and try to sneak in a few hours of work.

The whole day stretched out empty before her. She wasn't meeting Airin at Jimmy's until evening. Jared was out of town, as she recalled from the first go-round, on a three-day surfing vacay in Cabo with his frat brothers from USC. Soon enough, he'd be messaging her a shirtless chest pic, all rippled pecs and abs, poised to appear effortless despite the hours of labor he put in at the gym to look that good. Anissa was out of the picture for now, and Nev had no idea whether she'd survive the back slog through her timeline long enough to reach a point where her dearest friend would reenter it. If she did, she'd set things right. Really right this time. Have Anissa's back when she tried to warn Maddy and Kusuma about the potential dangers of SavePoint 2.0. Repair the friendship, stop the Glitch in its tracks.

But, no. Anissa was still angry at her, and the Glitch wasn't showing any signs of stopping, so if past primacy was still correct—and of course it was—that meant she'd either blip out of existence before she reached the point in the timeline where they'd parted ways, or she'd fail Anissa just as badly the second time through. *Which was worse?*

No gods, no masters. No friends, no family. No future, no past. Only twelve hours to kill until she could be with Airin again. How the hell was she going to pass the time?

Sex was out. If it couldn't be with Airin, Nev wasn't interested. Dulling the pain with chemical stimulants was also a non-starter, for a related reason: Nev didn't want to miss out on being fully present when the time came for their date at Jimmy's. Video games felt pointless. If she logged onto *WhisperWorld*, she'd no longer have the Ring of Truth. All of Nev's usual go-to dopamine catalyzers were failing her when she needed them most. What else remained? The pitiful truth was, all Nev really wanted to do was work. But she couldn't make any progress on the doctored alpha without Airin's help at this "early" stage in the process.

The next big step would be heading out to the Qbito mainframe and opening up the root system to finalize the hack. But first, she needed to figure out Kusuma's access code, and she'd had shit luck with that so far. It wasn't like she could just confront him face-to-face and shake the damn numbers out of him, could she?

Could she?

Nev reached back in her memory: Kusuma had just returned from his monthlong retreat when she'd last seen him in the office, about two and a half weeks from now. Which meant that right this moment, he was somewhere, maybe even in Northern California, doing something... spiritual? Inspirational? Hedonistic? An image of Kusuma wearing a Guy Fawkes mask and nothing else, dancing in a circle around a bonfire with other masked billionaires, appeared unbidden in her mind's eye, making Nev laugh in spite of her loneliness and frustration.

Maybe it wasn't such a bad idea, after all. If he was anywhere closer than Salt Lake City, she could hop into 'her' EZ5, drive out to Camp Creepshow, and threaten, cajole, or beg the code from him. For a second, Nev toyed with the idea of printing a gun at Qbito's fab lab and threatening her boss and mentor with it, but it felt ridiculous, too out-of-character. And he'd probably just laugh and knock it out of her hands, anyway. Kusuma was probably an ultra-blackbelt in something or other. But maybe, just maybe, she could get him to listen to reason this time. Explain that it wasn't just her, but the whole company—the whole world, really—that was at stake. He'd have to be insane not to listen to her.

Kusuma's personal data security was top-notch, because he was an Airin-level coder and every bit as obsessive-compulsive. Even if she could somehow get a location on his devices and implants, he'd probably left them behind for his vision quest, so there was no point in wasting the day trying to pinpoint their GPS coordinates. But, Nev realized, the same probably wasn't true of Hong-Mei. His assistant might be good at giving unwelcome visitors the cold shoulder, but she spent all day, every day, playing viz games downloaded from who-knows-where and built by who-knows-whom, and when Nev had bribed her, she'd been greedy enough to use her Qbito address to send the anonymous Trackless request. Shockingly bad data hygiene, come to think of it.

Nev spent the morning on her couch, setting up a basic spear phishing trap for Hong-Mei. Nothing fancy. Script kiddy stuff, really. It didn't need to do anything but capture her Qbito login credentials, so Nev could use them to check Kusuma's office calendar and maybe the recent history on his expense account. The back-end was the easy part—just setting up a reasonably legit-seeming entry form on some rented server space. The tough piece would be crafting a perfect message to lure the fly into the web.

Ultimately, Nev decided to make the most of the little she knew about Hong-Mei, and write something so audacious and personal that she wouldn't dare to ignore it. By the early afternoon, it was ready to go.

From: noel@qbito-inc.com
To: hongm@qbito-inc.com
Re: Social play alpha
Hong-Mei,

Greetings from a place of peace. Whilst cleansing my mind and body, I have been working with some fellow developers and entrepreneurs on what I think is a fun, and potentially transformative, new model for social gaming. It's a simple token-collection scavenger hunt at this point, but the really innovative part is full integration with the SavePoint service, for shared temporal challenges. We will be launching an alpha with a $10,000 prize once I return, but in the meantime, we need to pre-populate the service with early adopters. Please sign up via this link at your earliest convenience using your Qbito credentials, and let me know if you run into any snags along the way. Happy hunting. I have a good feeling that you'll end up winning the first prize. ;-)

Namaste,
N

Nev read it through one final time to check for spelling and to make sure the embedded link was accurate, and sent it off. Then, mostly just to keep herself from obsessively checking the server logs for her prey, she programmed a double Guatemalan drip on her auto-Chemex and headed off to the kitchen to make sure she had enough cashew milk in the fridge.

Forty minutes later, belly full with some pan-Asian leftovers that had magically appeared in her fridge (dinner tomorrow night, she assumed) and nerves tingling from the mug of coffee and three squares of dark chocolate she'd chased it down with, she plopped back onto the couch, flicked on her display, and checked the logs.

There it was, waiting like a juicy little fly in the middle of the web she'd woven: Hong-Mei's Qbito login credentials. Her password was *n0elT1mel0rd123*, because of course it was. Poor girl, she was probably smitten. Had Kusuma…? Would he even…? Nev shook her head to clear the suspicions out of her mind before she could finish thinking them. She had bigger fish to fry right this moment. *Eyes on the prize, Nev.* Maybe she'd grill him about his relationship with Hong-Mei eventually, but not until she'd gotten what she needed first.

Nev pulled up Qbito's administrative app (accessible outside the office because they outsourced much of the work to New Korea), entered Hong-Mei's credentials with a small shudder, and checked Kusuma's calendar. The entire month was taken up by a block entry, simply reading 'Prequinox.' No location data, no logistics. *Shit.* She tried checking a few search engines for 'prequinox' but the results seemed to consist entirely of cannabis ads, DIY crafters with metaphysical motifs, and social media witch covens. Nothing that looked like a sleepaway camp for absurdly wealthy techbros.

After a little bit of digging, Nev managed to find the records for Kusuma's personal expense account. Scrolling through the entries, she didn't see anything marked 'prequinox,' 'retreat,' 'vision quest,' or anything close to it. Although, she noted, it was kind of shocking how many of his personal and household expenses were covered by the company. A monthly $229 fee for 'water freshening' at his nine-bedroom Cow Hollow bungalow? A weekly $650 'chakrosacral alignment session' with his Ukrainian Levkoy? *Focus, Nev.*

About four months back in the records, something caught her eye. Nev wasn't even sure why she looked at it twice. It seemed innocuous enough. Sure, the price was fairly steep, but after all, that was the rule, not the exception: 'Temporoharmine Ind. Full Package... $68,500.'

Following her itch, Nev did some more digging. A search engine query for 'temporoharmine' came up empty. Zero hits. But a search in the state real estate records for 'Temporoharmine Industries' showed a single listing. It was the owner of a one hundred and twenty-acre parcel of land in the Central California desert. Doing a little more digging, Nev found the name of another business located at the same address: Thyme Springs Enterprises.

Thyme Springs. Thyme Springs.

Something about the name felt very familiar, but Nev couldn't put her finger on it. She went to the kitchen to make some more coffee. As she was nibbling another square of dark chocolate, the answer popped into her mind, fully assembled, and tied up in a sparkly little bow. *Thyme Springs!* It was the name of the retreat she'd gone to when she first joined Qbito. Right near the site where the mainframe was buried. The place where she and Anissa had become best friends, literally overnight. *Happier times.*

QT.12.10.21.04.09.2045

"So why did you want to meet up tonight?"

Nev tried not to choke on her beer.

Jimmy's was surprisingly empty tonight. Even so, Nev had taken possession of a booth near the back of the bar to wait for Airin, not wanting to chance being overheard by the small handful of hardbitten regulars who occupied the stools lining the deeply gouged and heavily varnished wooden bar.

"You told me we met here," Nev said, "I'm just following orders."

She didn't think that answering more truthfully—*I can't imagine going a whole day without seeing you*—would be well received. Airin looked exhausted. Nev wondered who they'd been spending the weekend with, then had to tamp down a bilious surge of jealousy. She had no right. As Airin told her at the beginning of their collaboration, they had no shared past and no shared future. There was only now, and she had to wring as much pleasure and joy from it as she could.

Airin nodded capitulation. Their eyes darted around the room, maybe already planning their escape. They didn't look eager to settle in. *Say something,* Nev thought, *something that will get their attention. Don't let them walk away.*

"Actually, I do have some progress to report. I think I've figured out where Kusuma is and how to get his passcode."

Airin raised their eyebrows. "Huh? I thought you already got it."

"I did? That's good to hear. So maybe I'm on the right track."

"Wait a moment. SavePoint it back a sec. This is so confusing."

"I can't use my SavePoint, Airin. And neither should you, when you're with me. We can't add any more stress to the timeline integration."

"Okay, okay. I was speaking figuratively. Just, start from the beginning."

"Do you want a drink? This might take a little while."

Airin glanced toward the bar with a certain amount of trepidation. Levi was on shift, chatting up a crusty, bearded fat man in a studded leather vest. It was hard to tell whether he was a leather Daddy or an aggro Cult of Carlson biker type. Airin was probably debating their odds of being verbally assaulted before they finished their drink order.

"Drink's on me. What do you want?" Nev said, standing up from the booth.

"Calvados?"

"I'll do my best, but you might have to make do with apple schnapps. Back in a sec."

Five minutes later, a fresh beer in her hands and a Crown Royal Regal Apple on ice sweating on a coaster in front of Airin, Nev launched into the story.

"So, um, I don't know what you consider to be the beginning. From what you've told me, shortly after we meet for the first time I am going to use the founder's code key to authorize the"—her eyes darted around, checking for eavesdroppers, and she dropped her voice to *sotto voce*—"fix we're making to the SP2 alpha, but at this point, I don't know how I'm going to do that. I don't have Kusuma's code and I don't know where to find it. You need to urge me to work on this in the days to come, since it hasn't been simple, so far. I don't want to screw with the timeline by giving you any details about what's to come, and you should probably hold back from telling me too much about what's already happened.

"But I'll tell you about today, because it was awesome. I've been thinking, maybe I need to track Kusuma down and make him cough up the digits—but he's been away on this retreat, unplugged, etc. etc. I'm guessing he's even had his SavePoint implant disabled or extracted. No way to track him, right? That's when I had the idea to get in touch with Hong-Mei."

"Hong-Mei?"

"His personal assistant. I'm, um, gonna find her helpful in your future. I have a sense of her weak spots, right? So I put together this spear phishing message, inviting her to take part in testing a new SavePoint integrated game, temporal challenges, cash prizes, yadda yadda, and she bit! Delivered up her employee ID and password. Holy fuck, all those hours of corporate security training go in one ear and out the other, all you gotta do is dangle some cash..."

"Should you have done that?" Airin asked. "Isn't it unfair to Hong-Mei?"

Nev nearly choked on her beer for the second time in the evening.

"Unfair? What choice do I have?"

"I don't know, Nev. I understand that something really bad has happened to you, but is it right to risk someone else's life and career to fix it?"

Nev stared at Airin, not comprehending, until finally it dawned on her that Airin still thought the Glitch was *her* problem, and her problem alone. If she told them otherwise now, what would happen? How would that change the days to come for Airin? The days Nev had already relived? Nev was still staring, slack-jawed, when Airin started again.

"Honestly, Nev, I dunno know if I want to be part of this. I don't want to fuck up some stranger's life—someone who's done nothing to me."

"You've got to help me, Airin," Nev said, frantic. What would happen if they walked away now? What would that mean for the timeline? What would that do to her poor heart? She'd lost everything else, she couldn't lose the last two weeks to boot.

"I guess I do. I mean, you claim I already have, and you've brought the receipts. But I don't like it. I don't like feeling hedged in by things I haven't done yet, but according to you I'm going to do. It makes me feel like, like a piece of code. Like, I don't have any free will."

"Ha!" Nev laughed without meaning to, the last gulp of beer snarfing out of her nostrils in a way that was probably very unflattering. She wiped her lip with the back of her hand. Airin was staring at her like she was insane. "No. No, you're right. You're totally right. It's just, I've kind of been living without the illusion of free will for a while, now? And I'd almost forgotten what it's like to believe I'm in control of anything."

Airin shook their head, purple hair flopping. "Wait, but... Aren't you trying to get me to participate in this big"—they waved their long fingers around, distributing invisible confetti—"grand act of sabotage? But that would be an act of free will on my part, wouldn't it?" Airin looked justifiably skeptical on every count.

Nev tipped her beer bottle back into her mouth, to give herself a second to think, but also kind of hoping something more would come out. No such luck. She really did need another drink, but wasn't certain that Airin would still be here if she went to the bar for a second round. So she placed the empty bottle in the middle of the table, upside down. Airin had done the same thing, once upon a time. Maybe it had a special meaning for them. Again, no such luck. They didn't bat an eyelash, just glanced at the vintage Cortébert watch on their left wrist and took another small, disappointed sip of the Crown Royal.

"Well," Nev responded, not sure where she was going with this. "I mean, yes and no, right? I was the Queen of free will until all this happened. I grew up in this religious family. I know you didn't really..."

"Depends on your definition. We were Passover religious, but not Purim religious."

"I don't know what that means. Anyway, my mom was—is—a very devoted Christian, you know, like, 'the very hairs on your head are all numbered' type of stuff. And after, well, I kind of left the Church before I left home, and we used to get into some really serious arguments about exactly this question. Pretty much from the time I first met you at Stanford, my whole life was about self-determination, self-empowerment, self-reliance." She ticked them off on her fingers. "And, don't get me wrong. I mean, I still believe it. Like, the Glitch hasn't made me religious—at least, not in, you know, a religious way. But it has definitely changed the way I see the world. Part of that is realizing that you can look out for yourself, and you *should* look out for yourself, because not many other people in this world are going to have your back, but also, you can't be entirely focused on yourself, because you need other people, too. And they need you."

She risked looking into Airin's eyes. They were paying attention now, completely focused on her. A ripple of warmth gushed through her chest, and she continued before those beautiful spotlights moved their focus again.

"Also, I guess, I realized that part of free will is understanding that. Understanding that you can't be free without also being constrained, you know? I mean, it's less about determining your fate in the cosmos, and more about recognizing that you're part of the cosmos. Just this little, tiny conscious fragment of totality, infinitesimally small, but infinitely important. And all that any of us can do with our lives is to be that little bit of everything as mindfully as we can, and to help other people be their little bits, and to recognize that, whether there's anyone in charge of it all or not, whether there's an afterlife or not, whether there's a fucking future or not, it's still on us to tend to, you know, our little piece of here and now. Because it's part of everywhere and always. You know what I mean?"

She looked up again. Airin was smiling at her over the upturned bottle. A real smile. Guarded, but genuine.

"Yeah. Yeah, I know what you mean, Nev." They sighed. "Look, it's getting late, and I'm beat. But, okay. I'm still in. I'll help you with your little bit of all this. For now. And now is all we have, right?"

Now it was Nev's turn to smile. "Right. Good. Okay. So where and when did we meet yesterday?"

Airin knit their brows together, just a bit. "We didn't. Sorry, I've had a busy weekend. We met on Friday. Uh...September 1st. Your place, around 9:30 in the morning."

Nev's stomach plummeted, and she had to brace herself on the table. Friday... that was three days from now. No Airin for three whole days. What the fuck was she going to do in the meantime? Her time left on Earth was growing short, but still, she wished she could just go to sleep and wake up when it was time to see them again.

Airin was standing up, smoothing the wrinkles from their shirt. "What about tomorrow? When and where?"

Nev sighed. "Oh, yeah... your place. 9:42am."

Now it was Airin's turn to be surprised. Their eyebrows quickly darted up, then lowered again in suspicion.

"My place? Heh, no, I think not. I'm sorry, Nev. It's nothing personal. I just... I don't really invite visitors to my place. Especially people I don't really know all that well. You know, security and all that."

"Yeah, Airin. I know. But I swear, we've been working, will be working, at your place for the next couple of weeks." They shook their head skeptically. "Oh, for God's sake. You have a dog, okay? A beautiful, sweet, Great Pyrenees named Ada Lovesnacks. And—"

Airin shushed her, looking around with alarm. Nev stood up next to them, and continued in an urgent whisper.

"—and boy, did you name her well, because that big old dog really does love her snacks. And you have, like, glass transformer thingies on your shelf, and a Defender game, and a secret room—"

"Ssssshhhhhut up! Okay! Okay!" Airin whispered fiercely, looking borderline angry and more than a little nervous. "Okay. I believe you, alright? Just, okay. So if you know where my place is, I don't need to give you the address or anything, right?"

"Right. So, see you there tomorrow morning."

"Fine. Okay. See you tomorrow. Jeez." Airin turned and walked out of the bar, a little stiffly, without looking back.

Nev had to stop herself from shouting after them, *Don't forget to buy coffee and cashew milk!*

QT.44.23.10.03.09.2045

HER USUAL EZ5 hadn't been in stock at the Luxurental, which made sense considering that the car had fewer than a hundred and fifty miles on it the morning she drove it to the Park Chalet for her first meeting with Airin. Just as well, since the day's mission called for something more discreet. Although it went against all her mechanic's-daughter instincts, Nev opted for a subdued beige two-door Newmobile. At least, coming from Luxurental, it was equipped with a supercharger and a tricked out sound system, which was blasting Pocoloco's 2033 hit track 'Autopista Baby' with the bass cranked to maximum. The song brought her right back to the last year of high school, waiting for the bus after the night shift at the Holiday Inn Express, streaming Top 40 through her old-fashioned cans, ecstatic to have finally escaped the tyranny of The Osmonds and dreaming of the day when she'd catch a bus that would get on the Autopista and keep driving until the wasteland of eastern Washington was no more than a distant memory.

Goddamn it, she had loved California when she first got there. The people! The diversity! For the first time in her life, her tan skin and tight curls didn't make her stand out. She was just

231

another shade in a beautiful rainbow of brown (at least when she left the hallowed Spanish arcades of campus). Nights out in San Francisco were like nothing she had ever dreamed possible. Warehouse raves. Designer drugs. People of all genders. She couldn't wait to move to the city when she finished her degree. Some of her classmates dreamed of cozy futures secured behind the gates of Los Altos or West Menlo Park, but Nev always had her heart set on the city. Until the Glitch, it had been her plan to keep living in her little SoMa apartment until she died or the sea rose up and forced her out.

A man's heart deviseth his way, but the Lord directs his steps, as Mama would say. This morning Nev had watched the city shrink to nothing in the rear camera of the Newmobile, the car's nav programmed to a set of coordinates in the California desert so remote that they didn't have a name. The route followed a backwards trajectory through her past, passing Palo Alto on its way to the empty lands. The last major outposts of civilization she'd passed were the high-fenced camps outside Hollister. (Everyone knew that the Carlson administration had built the fencing just for optics. Biometric surveillance already kept the agricultural labor under tight control.) Beyond that was nothing but dust sweeping off brown hills.

Ashes to ashes, dust to dust. Nev's own return to the dust seemed to be barreling down on her as quickly as the highway disappearing beneath the car's wheels. She still had no idea what to think about the future that lay on the other side of the Glitch: September 24th and beyond. If her consciousness was trapped in the days leading up to the Glitch, what had happened to her future flesh? Did she keep living forward, another Nev's consciousness taking over her physical form? Did that Nev know of her? Or when Nev had first executed the SavePoint 2.0 alpha, had her body collapsed to the floor like an empty husk, only to be found hours later by Security or Custodial Services? Nev hadn't updated her personnel files to change her contact info since her Grandma died. Once they (Security? The police? Special police?) tried to notify Grandma, the message would likely be autoforwarded to Mama and Daddy. They'd have to make arrangements. Mama would probably want to stick her dead body in the windswept cemetery on the south side of the Palouse river, where Grandma and Faith were both buried. *And to dust you shall return.* It wouldn't have been Nev's first choice, but then, it wouldn't matter to her anyway. She'd be dead. It was Mama and Daddy who'd be left behind for a second time—third time, if you counted Nev's defection as its own abandonment. If it made them feel better to have her bones buried nearby, so be it. There wasn't much else she could do to make them feel better.

"Voice call: Christina Bourne," Nev instructed her viz.

"No contact information for Bourne, Christina."

Time to program her mother's number into the device. Not that it was strictly necessary. Nev knew Christina's digital thumbprint by heart: her favorite chapter and verse from John, the number of a beloved Psalm, chapter and verse for a rare encouraging prophecy from Jeremiah, and a final chapter and verse from Philippians.

"Hello? Who's calling?"

Her mother's voice streamed through the car's surround speakers, as sharp and clear as if she were sitting next to Nev.

"Mama? It's Nevaeh. Sorry if I startled you."

Her stomach twisted into the familiar cramps that gripped her any time she had to speak to Christina. They'd had little communication during the past fourteen years. Nev had heard her mother's voice in nightmares more often than in real life.

"Nevaeh? Is that you?"

"Yes, Mama."

"Oh, Nevaeh. Your father and I just finished praying for you. We're sorry we missed you last Sunday. But what you said to us at the funeral, it's still with us. We feel so blessed to have you back in our lives."

What she'd said at the funeral? Nev scanned back to her grandmother's burial, the way she remembered it, in the old timeline. Her mother shouting at her, "We don't want you here!

Go back to Babylon, where you belong!" Nev turning away, to deprive her mother the satisfaction of seeing her tears, hopping into her rental, programming it for San Francisco, for *home*, vowing never to return to Albion until the end of her days.

Now, the end of her days had arrived, and it looked like she'd be back in Albion soon enough, whether she wanted to return or not.

The funeral had been so tense, so toxic. What could she possibly have said or done to avert the disaster that erupted on seeing her parents for the first time in over a decade? After the funeral, she'd repeatedly asked herself that very question, scanning her memories like code, looking for the bug, wishing for a fix. Her searches always came up empty. There was absolutely nothing she could have said or done to make things right. Her parents just wanted to hate her, wanted to blame her for leaving them in the dust. For everything bad that had ever happened to them in their miserable, ridiculous, little lives. For letting Faith die, when it should have been her.

Or so she'd told herself. But now, Christina was on the phone, love softening her voice, thanking her for saying... something. Something that somehow fixed the hurt, made things right between them for the first time since forever. It was too good to be true, too preposterous to believe.

Nev cleared her throat, as quietly as she could. "Wow, Mama, that's... it's wonderful to hear you say that. It was really great to reconnect with you, too, and I'm so glad, just so glad that we're in each other's lives again." In the moment she said it, she knew it was true. "If you don't mind my asking, which part of what I said to you at Grandma's funeral was the most important? I... I just feel so... so blessed"—she winced, thankful that it was just a voice call, and reached back into her bag of biblical aphorisms for exactly the right reference—"that, uh, my tongue was able to bring you healing."

There was a silence on the other end, and for a moment, Nev worried she'd overstepped, that she'd somehow undone the magic. But of course she hadn't, as the next few weeks of phone calls with her parents had already demonstrated.

Then Christina told her, and the utter simplicity of it was like a clean, cool glass of water after a trackless age spent wandering alone in the desert.

Forty minutes later, after the conversation had ended in tears and promises and Nev had added her mother's contact to her viz, the Newmobile rolled to a halt in a cloud of dust alongside a narrow dirt road. The car settled into solar mode with a contented bleep. An old-fashioned wooden sign posted next to an even smaller gravel drive leading in between some enormous, gnarly evergreen bushes read 'Thyme Springs.'

Nev stepped out into the baking hot sun. The black yoga pants that she'd slipped into that morning, after taking a look at the misty sky outside her apartment windows, now felt misjudged. They clung to her thighs uncomfortably, and by the time she'd made it down the gravel path from the entry sign to the wooden quonset hut that served as the resort's reception point, the stretchy material was hot to the touch. The handful of guests who milled around reception, helping themselves to glasses of water from the fruit and ice filled glass carboys along the side table, were all wearing tiny athleisure shorts and blousy tops in synthlinen.

Thyme Springs kept its digital presence minimal, and Nev had been unable to discover before setting out whether the resort had vacancies or was even open to walk-ins. Beyond the rear glass wall of the reception area, she could see more gravel pathways branching out to the stripped-down wooden cabins and open-air tiled soak tubs. Around the entire resort, a palisade of eucalyptus trees cleverly disguised the razor-wire perimeter fencing that kept nosy paparazzi from intruding on the business gurus like Kusuma who visited the Springs for their periodic detechs.

The only way in was through the reception area doors. But if she went to the front desk and asked for a room and there were no vacancies, then she'd be forced to turn right around and she'd be back on the highway in ten minutes with nothing gained.

Nev lingered at the entryway, watching the guests. A middle-aged man in an olive drab shirt came in through the rear door, scoping around reception before his eyes settled on Nev with a sharp look. The man made a bee-line to where she was standing. Nev panicked, wondering if she had been made by security already, and considered turning around and fleeing by the front door, but the man was standing two feet in front of her before she had the chance to act.

"We need fresh towels in the yurt."

Nev knew that voice. She recognized it from her years working at the reception desk at the Holiday Inn Express. And she'd heard it on occasion since, when she was somewhere that a person who looked like her wasn't expected to be, and someone (typically an older white person) mistook her for 'the help.' She'd perfected her response over the years, a withering stare and icy polite recommendation that they go get whatever they needed (a napkin, a drink, keys to the dressing room) their own damn selves. This time, she bit her tongue.

"Well?" the man said expectantly. "You are the new girl the agency sent, are you not?"

"Sorry," Nev said, "Yes. Yes, sir. I just arrived. I haven't had a chance yet to—"

"Don't worry about that," the man cut her off. "We'll take care of the paperwork at the end of your shift. I need you now. Follow me."

With an imperious turn on the heel, the man strode towards the inner doors leading to the resort, expecting Nev (or whoever he thought she was) to follow.

As he led her along a series of winding flagstone paths, squeezing between 3D printed mud composite structures that looked like giant, yellow Hershey's Kisses (the treatment huts, the man explained with a wave), Nev reconstructed her mental map of the property. It was difficult, both because of the camp's impressive dedication to nonlinear design, but also because, as she realized early in the journey, she was getting the maid's-eye view, rather than the guest's view she'd gotten the first time. The paths she and her guide were traversing were negative space, the little niches hidden from the clientele, unmanicured and littered with spray bottles, service carts, and garden hoses.

They arrived at the foot of a short flight of stairs, where a uniformed woman in the same olive drab top and khaki pants sat against a closed door, eating a delicious-smelling fast food chicken sandwich out of a recycled paper wrapper. The man called to the woman in a crisp voice.

"Esme, please get our new SpringKeeper outfitted and show her where to find the towels to restock the yurt."

He turned and walked back towards the reception area without looking back or waiting for a response. The woman sighed, swallowed the rest of the sandwich in one massive bite, and stood up, brushing crumbs from her uniform. Nev could see the name 'Esmeralda' embroidered over her left breast. She looked Nev over quickly and sighed again, then opened the door and walked through it, first issuing a brusque "c'mon" over her shoulder.

Nev climbed the stairs and followed her through the door, finding herself in a dim, cool room surrounded by shelves full of towels, soaps, and other supplies. Esme looked her over again, pulled out a shirt and pair of pants that matched her own, as well as a visored cap with *Thyme Springs* embroidered across its front, and handed them to her with profound indifference.

"I think these'll fit. Put them on, then grab that towel cart in the corner and meet me back outside in ten."

Esme walked back out the door they'd entered through, leaving Nev alone in the room holding her new clothes. She stripped down to her underwear, relieved to peel the sweat-soaked yoga pants off her legs, stuffed the dirty clothes into her shoulder bag, and pulled on the uniform. It may have been ugly, but it was surprisingly light and comfortable, and Nev had to give it to Esme—she'd gotten her size just right. She examined herself in the mirror, pulling her curls back into a ponytail using a scrunchy from her bag and slipping the cap over her forehead. Yup, she looked like the help, alright. She wouldn't think twice about asking herself for an açaí foam infusion with taurine mist, accompanied by grilled meitaki on cricket flour crostini.

If there'd been any other door to leave by, Nev would have been happy to give Esme the slip. But the supply shed had only a single exit, so she grabbed the stainless steel towel cart, already piled high with folded towels and wash cloths, and wheeled it out into the bright sunlight, rolling it down the side ramp to ground level. Judging from Esme's lack of enthusiasm for mentorship, Nev felt sure it wouldn't be long before she was abandoned to her own resources and she could set to searching out Kusuma. In her new camouflage, she'd probably be able to access most of the grounds, while raising minimal suspicion from either the guests or the other SpringKeepers. The plan was to find Kusuma and then... well, confront him. She hadn't really thought much about what came next, but the urgency of her need for the Qbito founder's code had its own momentum, and she figured she'd know what to do and say when the time came.

Esme barely wasted an appraising glance at Nev's transformation before gesturing for her to follow along.

"I'll take you to the yurt. After that, you come back to the supply shed and restock the cart. Then take it around to the tubs, or wherever Mr. Pollock tells you to go, if he finds you first."

"Alright."

"It's not so bad here. The people are okay, but sometimes they act a little funny. Especially when they drink too much Ayahuasca. If they talk crazy, just ignore them. It's what I do. They don't remember later. And steer clear of the tea in the tea hut, less you want your eyes turning black."

"Got it."

Nev remembered the yurt from her visit to Thyme Springs with the Qbito team. She and Anissa had spent half an hour that night in the cabin just repeating the word *yurt* like a belch and laughing till the tears squeezed from their eyes. The canvas walls and roof, with a round chimney hole at its center, made for a serene space where guests could cool down on wooden benches after soaks in the outside tubs. As expected, Esme evaporated when Nev entered the yurt, leaving her free to scope out the guests while she slowly transferred the towels from her cart to the shelves by the doorway. Unfortunately, Kusuma was not among them. Abandoning her efforts at restocking, Nev pushed the half-full cart back out of the yurt and followed the short path to the tubs.

A tall woman with the figure of an Olympic beach volleyball competitor stood up in one of the tubs, buck naked and dripping, as Nev approached. Wordlessly, she reached out a hand to Nev, who stood gawking before remembering the cart in her grip. Nev handed the woman a towel, wondering what the appropriate thing was to say. But the woman showed no sign of expecting conversation, and merely climbed out of the tub, wrapping the towel around herself as she slipped her feet into flip-flops made from recycled tires, and padded off along the path back to the yurt.

Nev pushed the cart in a slow circuit around the stone tubs, awkwardly staring at the bodies, some clothed, others bare as the day they'd entered the world. She hoped that if she did spot Kusuma, she'd recognize him by the bald pate before she got an eyeful of his other parts.

Unfortunately, neither his head nor any other part of him was visible in this area, so Nev abandoned her cart and followed another winding foot path marked by a small wooden sign that read 'saunas and tea hut.' It led through some more of the scrubby evergreens she'd seen at the entrance to the property. As she rounded a particularly large bank of bushes, she was confronted by a tan, naked ass, which was attached to a wiry, triangular back, a neck with a small tattoo of a bee on it, and the back of a bald head.

"Noel!" The name escaped her lips as she thought it, like a blast of steam from a vent.

239

He turned around and stared at her, mouth set in a small, tight smile. A leathery white guy, tanned by prolonged sun exposure to nearly exactly Kusuma's shade and hue. Across his smooth chest, a couple dozen more bees swarmed around a polygonal wireframe of a rose. His eyes were wide, and his pupils were enormous.

"Not Noel, no." The man said. "Will you go walking with me?"

"Will I... what?" Nev was so embarrassed and confused, she couldn't gauge whether the guy was being weird, or friendly, or both. She tried to respond in a way that would allow her to exit the encounter gracefully. "I, um, have to..." Looking around for an excuse to leave, Nev realized that maybe it hadn't been a good idea to ditch the cart so soon.

"Nonsense." Was his smile turning into a leer? "We both know you're not who you seem to be. Come, I have something to show you." He bowed slightly and extended his hand down the path in the direction she'd already been walking. She could turn around and return to the baths, where Kusuma wasn't, or she could accept his offer and keep heading towards the saunas, where he might be. There was no clear third choice.

Nev followed the path at a brisk pace, hearing the man's bare feet flapping on the flagstones behind her. She considered breaking into a run, but realized that it would probably draw the attention of the real SpringKeepers, bringing an end to her escapade before she'd gotten a chance to grill Kusuma. After a minute or two, they came into a clearing, where five free-standing saunas huddled together, decorated in beautiful earth tone mosaics. Four of them had seasonal themes, while one looked like the night sky, sparkling with black and purple glass and stones. Off to the side, there was a small palapa with a wooden bar and some picnic style benches. The tea hut. The smell of genmai cha wafted in the air, making Nev thirsty for Airin. *What are they doing right this moment? Probably having a much better weekend than I am.* She was tempted to pour herself a cup of tea, but Esmeralda's warning scared her off.

With a wink and a beckoning nod of his head, the man entered the spring-themed sauna. The wooden door swung closed behind him. If Nev wanted to make her getaway, now was the time. But maybe Kusuma was in the sauna with the guy. Maybe they were part of some bald sweating cult. Maybe they were lovers. Who knew? The guy *had* said he wanted to show her something.

Nev overcame her trepidation and entered the sauna. The moment her eyes had adjusted to the pinkish light from the salt lamps, she realized her mistake. She was alone with the creepy guy, who was now lying flat on his back on a tatami mat, his erect penis pointing straight up at the dimpled minaret-style ceiling. She spun quickly around and headed back out the door, but not quickly enough to miss the bee tattoo that had been harder to spot when it was on flaccid skin, or to hear him chanting "Ommm kroom lingaya ommmm... ommm kroom lingaya ommmm..." in a husky undertone.

Fuck. What was the matter with rich people? Folks seemed to lose both their imaginations and their capacity for empathy the second they saw more than six zeroes in a row on their bank statements.

Back in the open air and sunlight, Nev took a couple of deep breaths to steady herself. *What next?* Kusuma had to be around somewhere. And, uniform or no, she was going to get caught eventually, and ejected as an unwelcome interloper. Or worse. She had to find him, had to get the code. *Suck it up, Nev. This is not about you. Do what needs to be done.*

She tried the summer sauna next. The floor was blanketed in a fine, pink sand. Two pairs of guests lay on tatami mats on opposite sides of the room. One pair had their eyes closed and looked asleep, or deep in meditation. The other pair—a man and a woman, naked of course—stopped their conversation and turned to look at her when she came in.

"Oh, good," the woman said. She had a beautiful jade necklace, and her jawline looked like it had been sculpted by Marin's finest plastic surgeon. "I was thinking it must be time for a hydration break. I'll have a lemon kombucha spritzer, and he'll have deionized water. Still." She made a 'cute' face. "Could we also have one of those wonderful soy cheese blondies? I know I shouldn't, but they're just so... Thank you, sweetie!" Nev bit back her bile, nodded, and backed out the door.

Two saunas down, three to go. It was entirely possible that Kusuma was somewhere else on the grounds, but best to be thorough and methodical.

The fall sauna was thankfully empty and silent, and cooler than the first two, pleasantly warming rather than cooking stone hot. Sunlight filtered in through stained glass illustrations of grapes on the vine ringing the ceiling, and decorative gourds hanging on the walls and piled on wooden boxes lent their earthy smell to the air. She took a deep breath, thanking her lucky stars to be free of the madness that seemed to grip all the clientele at Thyme Springs. Not so long ago, or not so long from now, she'd been like them, wanted to be more like them. To be a hammer in a world of nails, a shark in a tankful of minnows. But here, in this moment, in this quiet room, all she wanted was peace. Peace and Airin, and maybe a little more time to enjoy them.

A twinkle caught her eye. The vines on the windows seemed to be moving, writhing around one another like snakes in her peripheral vision. As soon as she looked directly at the glass, though, they reverted to their fixed positions. She squinted her eyes, trying to make out the reason for this peculiar optical illusion, then opened them wide as she felt a tug around her ankles. The vines had crawled down the walls and wrapped themselves around her like Kudzu, and now they were pulling her into the earth beneath her feet, down, down into the quicksand. She reached for a hanging tendril but her fingers were numb, and the purplish light turned indigo and then winked out altogether as her head was buried beneath the surface and she couldn't breathe and somehow she was falling, falling forever, through nothing, towards nothing, and blackness was all there was, all there ever had been, all there ever would be.

QT.55.47.20.03.09.2045

NEV'S EYES FLUTTERED open. The sauna was dark, and moonlight twinkled purply through the stained-glass windows, glinting off the stones embedded in the ceiling. Her head was pounding; and despite a lingering queasiness, her stomach growled loudly enough to scare the scorpions that came out at night in the desert. Another microglitch. Maybe the worst one yet. Airin was right, things were disintegrating quickly. Everything solid was turning to quicksand.

Nev stepped out into the clear night sky. The sun was fully descended, which put the time after eight o'clock, but clearly before 11:33. She checked her viz. 8:47. She needed to find Kusuma quickly. It didn't look like she'd be driving home that evening. In the futurepast, she would have to remember to program a bot to initiate a driverless return of the Newmobile the following day. Come to think of it, she'd better schedule a driverless return of the EZ-5 for the day following her impromptu trip to Esalen. She didn't need creditors hassling her pastfuture timeline.

Another sonorous growl. *Can't do this on an empty stomach.* Nev had to find something to eat. She checked the palapa, but even the table that held the tea service had been folded up and stowed away. She set off along the path leading from the saunas, dimly illuminated by blown glass solar lights spiked into the dirt every yard, and soon arrived at another signpost which pointed one way towards the guest huts and another way towards the cafetería. It did look classier with the accent, although as Nev recalled, the dining accommodations at Thyme Springs were as bare bones as the tubs and cabins.

First food, then an inspection of the guest cabins.

The screen door opened with a squeak, as Nev stepped inside the brightly lit dining hall. Only a few guests lingered at the long communal tables. A quick check turned up no bald heads. It was possible that Kusuma wasn't at Thyme Springs, that Nev had been too hasty to connect the dots, which were no more than disparate points in a patternless data field. But if so, she was only doing what humans did, making constellations out of stars in the night sky. This trip might turn out to be a bust, another false positive. Nev couldn't help wishing she was miles away, dining at the Park Chalet, while staring into the night sky of Airin's eyes.

Longing surged through her veins. Why couldn't Kusuma have invented a transporter instead of a rewind device, something that would let her beam herself to Airin, wherever they were? Without SavePoint she wouldn't be stranded in this god-forsaken desert trying to save the world. But if wishes were horses then beggars would ride, as Mama used to say (one of her few aphorisms that wasn't King James approved). Point of fact: Kusuma *had* unleashed SavePoint on the world—with Nev's vital assistance—and if she wanted Airin to enjoy the future that Nev had ratfucked herself out of, she needed to stay focused and hunt down Kusuma, wherever he was hiding. Nev had wasted so many years living just for herself. She only had a short time now to live for Airin, and she was going to try her damndest to make things right. But first, dinner.

Esme and another uniformed worker were hovering around the bowls and steam trays laid out along the buffet table at one end of the room, lifting the remains of the dinner service onto rolling carts like the one she'd used to distribute towels. Nev walked over to see whether there was any food left. She spied a trio of shriveled samosas in one of the steamer trays, wrapped two in a catering napkin, and popped the third into her mouth. Esme and the other worker continued their activities, ignoring Nev's sudden appearance, which was just as well since she wouldn't have been able to talk with her mouth so full. She was halfway out the door when she saw Mr. Pollock walking up.

"New girl! Where've you been? Toilet's clogged at Cabin 12."

Nev swallowed back five different responses, none of which would have been very helpful.

"On my way," she said, hastily stepping onto the path to the cabins and escaping into the darkness before the manager reached her.

Popping another samosa into her mouth, Nev made a mental note to save Cabin 12 for last in her hunt for Kusuma.

If he was here at Thyme Springs, was he more likely to stay in a bare bones eco-cabin like the one she'd shared with Anissa at the retreat? Or would he lodge in one of the two chrome-clad Airstreams that served as the resort's luxury accommodations? Money was limitless for Kusuma, and she knew for a fact that he'd sprung for the 'full package.' Nev had no doubt he could buy the whole damn resort if he chose. It was merely a question of taste. Judging from his office, and his grooming standards, Kusuma's preference for a clean aesthetic verged on filling the clinical criteria for a sensory-integration disorder. Nev thought of the smooth surface of his obsidian desk, his tight fitting tagless tee-shirts, his clean shaven head.

The cabins, as Nev recalled, had rough, splintery walls, and deep divots between the planed floorboards. The Airstreams, then.

Nev snuck up behind the first of the two trailers. On one side, the trailer opened onto a semi-circular wooden half deck, shielded by a canopy that stretched out from the roof.

An electric faux fire pit and a couple of wooden benches made for a pleasant place to sit outside on a warm night. The other side of the trailer was nothing but dirt and rocks. No one was sitting outside this evening; the dim illumination coming through the curtained windows overlooking the patio suggested that whoever was staying there had already retired inside. Nev snuck closer to the back side of the trailer. There were two long windows above head height, close to the roofline, that were not curtained. Just standing on her tiptoes didn't give Nev enough of a vantage point to see inside. She looked around the ground behind her, found a small boulder, and—praying to the scorpion gods to leave her be—began pushing it closer to the trailer. She gave up after ten feet, but that was close enough so that when she climbed on top of it, she could just peer inside.

Two middle-aged women were sitting on the floor. One was heavy, with wavy, bleached blonde hair hanging limply along the sides of her face. The other one was almost anorexically thin and dark skinned, with close-cropped hair and winking, multicolored LED earrings running up the sides of each ear. Both were completely naked. They sat cross-legged on faded woven mats, facing one another, knees nearly touching, moving their lips inaudibly. Nev strained to hear what they were saying, curious despite herself, but couldn't make out the words. As she watched them, however, she could tell two things: First, they were speaking in complete unison, lips and tongues moving simultaneously as though choreographed. Second, they weren't repeating a phrase; either they were reciting something very long, or somehow extemporizing in perfect synchronicity.

Suddenly and without warning, both women swiveled their heads to face Nev through the window, without breaking their stream of vocalization or moving a muscle below their necks. At first, she was so transfixed by their perfectly matched lips that she didn't notice anything else, but then something tugged at her attention, and she saw their eyes. They were almost entirely black, as though the pupils had expanded and swallowed up the iris, whites, and capillaries. She stumbled and slipped off her boulder, twisting an ankle as she landed on the dusty ground beside the Airstream. She could no longer see or hear the women inside, but somehow she could still feel their void eyes fixed on her, the apian buzz of their song tickling her inner ear.

Nev's heart was in her chest. She felt a rising panic she hadn't known since long-ago games of hide-and-seek with Faith after dark in the junkyard. Without thinking, she dashed up the steps to the second Airstream, pulled open its spring-hinged door, and flung herself inside, wedging the door shut behind her and willing her breath to slow as she leaned hard against it.

She was alone, wonderfully alone. No sound of footsteps outside, no zombie scratches at the door from the hideous yin yang twins and their empty stares. No SpringKeepers come to eject her from the property, no Mr. Pollock telling her to deal with a vomit situation in the Silent Temple. She flopped over to the sofa, which was surprisingly comfortable, and gulped for air, trying to scrub her visual memory of the horror show she'd just witnessed.

After a minute or two, she was sufficiently calm to look around and get her bearings. She was in a small living room area lit by warm, yellowish string lights surrounding the curvilinear contours of the Airstream's ceiling. In addition to the couch, there was a small table with a beautiful blue and brown batik cloth draped over it, and a wooden bench lined with some similarly decorated cushions. To her left was a kitchenette, with a pleasant combination of classic fixtures and ultramodern appliances. Beyond that was a short hallway with two doors, presumably a bathroom and bedroom. It was spotless and empty; if anyone had stayed here recently, the SpringKeepers had done a great job of tidying up afterwards.

Since there was no chance of returning home that night, Nev figured the Airstream was as good a place as anywhere to blip out. She wouldn't be spotted, would leave no trace either yestermorrow or futurepast. It was a shame she hadn't found

Kusuma, but it wasn't like she hadn't tried. One way or another, she'd get the founder's code. The alternative was too confusing to contemplate. For now, the only thing that would make the final hour or two of September 3rd even cozier would be a proper drink. No kombucha, no deionized water. Just alcohol, and maybe a dash of something sweet. She stood up and headed over to the kitchenette. There must be a bottle stowed somewhere.

"Saya senang perjalanan Anda telah membawa Anda ke tempat dan waktu ini."

The shock of hearing a familiar voice so close at hand, saying something so totally incomprehensible, was more than Nev could handle. She leapt up with a shriek and dashed behind the small kitchen island, hoping against hope that he hadn't seen her. The room was silent. After a minute, she risked a peek over the counter, sure that Kusuma was looming over her with a knife, ready to sacrifice her to some ancient god she'd never heard of. Instead, he was sitting on the couch, legs crossed, dressed—thankfully—in his customary canvas pants and form-fitting black tee. He extended a hand to the cushioned bench across from him.

"Come on over and have a seat." Shades of the naked sauna creep made Nev hesitate, but she bit back her fear in the interest of killing the Glitch, and headed over to join him. She quickly checked the time: 11:07. Close to reset, she had to work fast. She sat gingerly on the batik cushion, waiting to be snapped up like a fly in a pitcher plant.

In the dim, pleasant glow from the string lights, Kusuma looked almost normal. Almost. Like so many of the other patrons she'd encountered at Thyme Springs, his pupils were so wide she almost couldn't make out his irises. The memory of the two women in the next Airstream over sent an aftershock of panic through her veins, but she felt surprisingly safe in Kusuma's presence, and managed to quell her tremors before speaking.

"It's... nice to see you, Mr. Kusuma. I bet you're wondering—"

"Nev." He raised a hand, gently. "I told you to call me Noel."

She scanned her mind back quickly over both versions of the timeline. She'd always called Kusuma by his last name, and he'd never invited her to do otherwise. At least, not until the day before the Glitch, when she'd tried and failed to warn him. But that was almost three weeks in his future.

"Noel, then. I don't... when did you...?"

"Do you know what I'm doing here, Nev? At Thyme Springs?"

Fucking around with other rich people in the desert.

"You're on a retreat, right? Harmono-temporal Industries?"

He smiled, a little too indulgently. "Quite the opposite. I'm not retreating, I'm plunging in. Plunging into the allness of once, the singularity of ever." Nev sighed. "And, no, it's not Harmono-temporal. It's Temporoharmine. Temporo meaning—"

"Time. Yeah, I know that."

"Yes." He gave her a curious look. "Yes, you do. And harmine, also known as telepathine, a naturally-occurring substance in a plant native to this region called ayahuasca. It inhibits certain enzymes in the body, which in turn are responsible for deanimating specific neurotransmitters, such as dopamine and serotonin."

He watched placidly as she processed the information.

"So... you're high off your ass on ayahuasca and living in a trailer?"

He laughed, seemingly delighted by her précis.

"Yes, yes that's it. Precisely. I am high. Off my ass. And I have been for over a week, and I will be for almost three weeks. Until shortly after the equinox. When we are scheduled to launch the SavePoint 2.0 alpha. But those specificities..." he waved away invisible gnats. "They don't mean anything, Nev. As I believe you know."

Okay. Cards on the table, then. She was never one to be coy.

"So, *Noel*, you remember our meeting in your office? Three weeks from now?"

"When you will try to warn me about the SavePoint catastrophe, and I will remind you not to neglect the details. Yes, I 'remember.'" He put the final word in scare quotes. "But words like that mean nothing to you and me. We are no longer fettered by the evolutionary mechanism that constrains us within an artificially linear temporality. It's nothing more than a vestigial artifact, as useless as the webbing between our toes, or faith in gods. Time is not directional. The difference between past and future does not exist in the elementary equations of the world; its orientation is merely a contingent aspect that appears when we look at things and neglect the details. Rovelli, 91. Amirite?"

Nev wasn't sure where he was going with this, but she only had a few minutes left to get the code, so she did her best to keep him talking.

"Yes, right, I guess, but that's not true of everyone. Not yet. Amirite, Noel?"

"'Yet'… you are so bound by the tyranny of grammar, Nevaeh. I implore you, free yourself of expectation, of regret. Be the sum total of yourself, no more and no less."

"Okay, yes, I hear you, Noel. I do. I really do." He smiled and nodded. She tried to slow her heart, slow the pace of her speech. *Eyes on the prize, Nev. Get the code.* "But… but Noel, I'm worried about what will happen if we upgrade SavePoint without warning everyone. I mean, what's happening to me, what's happening to us… Don't you think it's unethical to force millions of people into the Glitch, which is what I call the—"

"Yes."

"—the situation that… wait… you mean yes, you know that's what I call it, or…"

"Yes, I agree. It's unethical. It would be disastrous, for all of those people, and for Qbito. It can't continue. The alpha must not launch. But it would also be unethical for me to betray my own company, to destroy my own creation. And that is why I put you in charge. As I will tell you at our next meeting, I have absolute trust in you to handle these challenges."

Mingled confusion and relief swirled into knots in Nev's stomach, exhausting and exhilarating her. She checked the time on her viz. 11:32. *Shit.*

"Okay, then, Noel. Listen carefully. I really need you to give me the founder's code, because without that, I can't—"

"Nev. You really don't understand, do you? I have already given you everything you need. And you have already accomplished your task. From a certain perspective."

"From a 'certain perspective?' From *what* perspective? Noel, give me the fucking code. I don't have time for mystical bullshit zen koans right now. This is serious. The future of the world—"

Series complete. LoopID?QT.43.33.23.03.09.2045

QT.41.03.09.01.09.2045

RAINDROPS ON THE windows. Nev remembered this morning from the first time around: her sense of relief at the coming of the first fall rain after two months of summer drought and skies pink-orange from the smoke of wildfires. It was the first day of September, and the change of the calendar along with the season had filled her with a renewed sense of purpose, as she'd resolved to put away the pain and grief of her grandmother's loss and throw herself into the programming homestretch for the SavePoint 2.0 alpha.

Nev patted the bedside table for her viz and snugged it into place above her ear before opening the calendar app. Sure enough, her memory was spot on. 9:03 a.m., Friday, September 1st.

Jerking up in panic, Nev stared wildly around her apartment. 9:03 am? Airin was going to be here in less than half an hour! The place was a disaster. Whatever she'd been doing in the final days of August, it didn't involve cleaning up after herself. *Fuck fuck fuck fuck*. Twenty-five minutes to wash, dress, and shove the mess in the closet before the love of her (short, vanishing) life arrived.

She raced to the bathroom to brush her teeth. At least her mouth didn't taste like old bong water, which it should have, if time had been working the way she was raised to expect. She'd resumed consciousness on Saturday morning back in her own apartment, drowning in the memory of her failure to get any usable information out of Kusuma on Sunday. Sure, she'd learned that the bastard knew what was happening all along (had always known? would always know?). But after listening to him bloviate on the meaningless of time for what felt like an actual eternity, the hard temporal limits of her own vanishing existence had come crashing down, sending her back another 38 hours to the previous morning. Nothing gained but time. Nothing lost but time.

Giving in to full-blown self-pity, she'd spent all of Saturday in her old sweats, smoking her way through the magically replenished stash of cannabiz freebies, and watching season 30 of "90-Day Fiancé" in its entirety, taking a break only to order in one of everything from PanAsiaExpress—considering which, it was amazing she'd had the initiative on the Sunday to drag herself out of bed and drive to Thyme Springs. She wished she could tell herself it was the effort that counted. But the rapidly impending englitchment of 150 million SavePoint-enhanced lives dispelled any sense of accomplishment.

Clean underwear. *Thank the time lords!* Jeans. Sports bra. Tee-shirt. Hair finger-combed and thrown back into a messy poof. Electric kettle turned on. Was that a tin of genmai cha on her kitchen counter? *Why, thank you, futurepast-Nev.* It hadn't been there over the weekend; Nev figured she'd send it home with Airin later, after their session. She grabbed two polycycled shopping bags from under the sink and raced through the apartment, stuffing them with the assorted junk that littered every flat surface before throwing both bags under her bed just as her viz chimed to signal a request for access at the front door. Nev buzzed Airin in and took a deep breath.

She had just enough time to steep the genmai cha and power

up the auto-Chemex before their steady knock sounded at the door.

"Welcome, welcome," she said, opening the door a little too swiftly.

Airin took a second to scope the interior, before stepping inside.

"Wow, you've cleaned up," they said.

"Oh, have I?" Nev blushed. "I, uh, had some free time." *Fuck.* Still bound by the tyranny of grammar, she could hear Kusuma scolding. Of course if it had been a mess, and Airin had already been coming by, they would have already seen that mess, and now instead of impressing them with her neatness, she was probably freaking them out by trying too hard.

There was an awkward pause.

"Is that genmai cha I smell?"

Nev was tempted to say no, and go spill the tea down the sink so that she wouldn't come off as desperate. But then, was it so bad to show Airin that she cared? Hadn't Airin shown her the same thing by countless small gestures when they first started collaborating? Deep breath.

"Yes. I just poured the water. Hopefully it's not overbrewed. Why don't you take a seat," she glanced around the small apartment, "wherever we've set up before, and I'll bring it to you."

Nev disappeared into the kitchen, happy to have a solitary moment to regroup. She strained Airin's tea and fixed her own coffee, then carried both drinks back out into the apartment's main room. Airin had taken a seat on the couch, placing a tiny data box on the coffee table by their knees. It projected a bright screen, nearly thirty-five inches high, at a better resolution than Nev had ever seen.

"That looks amazing, it's so sharp!" she said, setting down the tea by Airin's right hand.

"Meh, it's okay. I've got better at home, but this will have to do for us."

Nev stopped herself from commenting on Airin's coding dungeon. She wasn't sure where things stood, but they weren't there yet.

"So, we don't see each other again for a while—not until Monday night, 9:00, at Jimmy's. I'll send you the address. I've kind of lost track of where we're at in the program. Did we meet up August 31? Where did we leave off?"

"No we didn't meet yesterday. Our last meeting was the 30th. Here at your place. I got here around 10:30, I think."

"Oh, okay. Great. Did we... you know what, never mind."

Airin gave her a curious look. Not a cute, I'm-curious-about-you look, but a skeptical, I'm-curious-whether-this-woman-is-insane look.

"So, where are we at?" Nev anxiously flipped the mystery stone in her hands. *Past, future. Future, past.*

"What's the deal with that rock, Nev? You were messing with it the other day, too. Does it have something to do with the Glitch?"

"No. At least, I don't think so. Maybe it does. Hard to say. It just kind of travels with me. It... comforts me when I'm nervous."

"Are you nervous now?"

Nev cleared her throat. "I think we should concentrate on what we're doing here, since we have so little time. So, what are we doing today?"

"Uhh... I was hoping you'd tell me. We've really only started sketching out the basic groundwork, and I'm not exactly sure what we're supposed to be doing?"

"Oh, well, okay. Two things, really. The main thing is, we're building a version of the alpha that's engineered to fail. Basically, a stack smashing vulnerability. I can walk you through that process, no problem. But the other thing—the essential part, if any of this is going to matter—is we need for it to cascade all the way back down the stack and actually poison the Qbito root code. To fry the quantum mainframe, if possible."

Airin whistled. "That's a tall order." They sipped their tea contemplatively. "But you're from the future, right? So you already know whether we've pulled it off or not. And, if we did, you know how we did it." They knit their brows together. Nev loved the tiny crinkles between them like she loved the Pacific Ocean. "So what do you need me for, again?"

Nev shook her head. "It's not that simple. We've been working in parallel, kind of, but from opposite directions. Like, when I started this project, you were the expert and it was all new to me. And, sure, the SavePoint alpha is my baby, but nobody knows their way around an exploit like you do, Airin."

They nodded. "That's true."

"And, to be honest, there are a few things that I haven't figured out yet. I mean, I think that we do figure them out, because I'm in the Glitch, which means that we did, or will, but that doesn't mean that we can just let it go, because the timeline depends on us doing it." Airin was looking at Nev like she was spouting nonsense. "But it's like, I've explored every goddamned avenue and it's all just dead end after dead end and I'm just so fucking tired. Airin. I just can't…"

Nev folded over, elbows on knees and hands covering eyes, fighting hyperventilation. She could hear Airin across from her, breathing deeply. *God, they must think I'm crazy. Don't blow this, Nev. Get it together.* She steadied her breathing, taking her time before daring to look up again. Airin was watching her, a look of mild concern and pity on their face. But also a ghost of impatience, a desire to get to work, to get this all over with. Or maybe Nev was projecting.

"I'm sorry," Airin said. "I can tell this is really tough for you. Let's talk this through. You said you've been running into dead ends?"

"Yes." Nev took a deep breath, and tried to focus. "We can't fry the mainframe unless we install your rootkit in the Qbito base code, and that requires Kusuma's passcode. And I've confronted him twice about it, once this weekend, and once right before the

Glitch happens, and both times he just comes at me with this cosmic mumbo jumbo. I mean, he pretty much told me he *wants* us to do it. Some kind of honor thing. He knows the 2.0 alpha has problems, but he's duty bound to see it through, so it's our job to stop him. Real supervillain shit. But instead of giving me the key, he just starts talking about quantum time and metaphysical, existential blah blah blah."

Airin took another sip.

"Blah blah blah is what good crypto is based on. Misdirection. Make a signal look like noise."

"What?"

"Nev. Just because what he said made no sense to you doesn't mean it's meaningless."

She shook her head, not understanding.

"Think about it. He wants you—us—to succeed, right? That's what you said."

"Uh huh. I mean, I think so. Who knows what he really wants? Did I mention he was tripping balls on ayahuasca?"

"Well, it sounds to me like he gave you the key, and you just didn't get the message. What exactly did he say? Will he say? I'm not sure how to phrase it."

"Yeah, neither am I, welcome to the club." Nev scoured her memory. "Um, he mentioned Rovelli."

"Carlo Rovelli? The loop quantum gravity guy?"

"Yeah, he's like a patron saint to Kusuma. I think they even met each other back in the day or something. He kept quoting a line from one of his old popular science books."

"Hmm. What was the line?"

"Oh, I don't know. Something about the elementary equations of the world. It was weird, actually. The way he memorized and quoted Rovelli was creepily religious. It was like my mom with scripture. You know, always chapter and verse, chapter and verse."

Chapter and verse. Of course.

"What religion does your mom... Nev? Nev, are you laughing or crying? I can't tell. Hey! Are you okay?"

"Oh my god oh my god oh my god. That bald fucking bastard. Oh ho ho ho," Nev wheezed hysterically.

"Nev, are you alright? Do I need to…?"

Nev shook her head. "No, I'm great. And you, Airin, you are a genius!"

They nodded their head modestly, accepting the compliment.

"You're right. He did give me the key. It's just been sitting there the whole time, and I've been too stupid to pick it up."

She sprang to her feet and paced around the room, almost dancing with joy.

"'Don't neglect the details.' Okay, Noel, I won't. Not anymore."

QT.38.17.12.31.08.2045

NEV WOULD HAVE started the day earlier, if she'd had a say in the matter. The earlier she made it to Llanada, the fewer people would probably be hanging around the mainframe facility. But the Glitch ruled the timeline, and Nev had blipped into consciousness at 8:31 a.m., presumably the time she had awoken on the first go round. She did not feel great. A low throbbing behind her right orbital cavity suggested that her next night would involve the ingestion of more alcohol than was strictly wise. Hopefully that wasn't a bad omen for today's mission.

Yestermorrow, talking with Airin, she'd felt so certain that she'd figured out Kusuma's key. She'd been positively jubilant when she arrived at Qbito later that afternoon to put in the required face time and input the first tranche of doctored code. Her good mood hadn't gone unnoticed by the brogrammers on her team, who assumed she had some hot plans for the long weekend and flooded her viz with 'Finna Git It' memes. Their assfoolery didn't even get her down. She'd just programmed a bot to auto-reply every meme with personalized ads for erectile dysfunction counseling.

But the closer the Newmobile crawled through the sluggish

traffic to Llanada, the less certain Nev now felt. A week of fires in the central valley had reduced the visibility index to below fifteen feet. She could hear the car's filtration system straining to separate the particles from the air inside. Even so, she could taste ash in her mouth, mixing with the coffee she'd picked up at Abdul's on her way to the Luxurental lot. At least the traffic gave her time to think. She needed to find a way to persuade the mainframe security guards to let her in.

On her only previous visit, Kusuma had led the way like a slapcore star backstage at GoChella. Security had simply fallen to the side as he walked through the front door. Nev had no idea what to expect from the ordinary security procedures when Kusuma wasn't playing tour guide. How many ID checks were there between the turn-off from the highway and the programming terminal at the base of the underground facility? Would it be enough to flash her kappa six Qbito ID? Or did she need to be clearance level kappa nine? (Who even was kappa nine? Was that reserved for the big bald man alone?) It seemed unlikely that professional security would fall for the easy money she'd dangled in front of Hong-Mei. There must be some other way to get around them. Unless there wasn't. In which case, today was going to be a flop. And then she'd spend the next day polluting herself into oblivion, which would explain the hangover remnants still rattling around between her temples. No wonder Airin had seemed so distant at her apartment on September 1st. What if Nev was already drunk or high when they showed up on the 30th?

Nev chased the thought away like she was waving off an overly persistent pick-up artist.

She had two choices, neither of which sounded particularly promising. She could go in guns blazing, flashing her badge, wearing her best Maddy face, and insisting that Noel wanted her to inspect the Qbito mainframe code in advance of the alpha launch. The upside was, they wouldn't be able to check with him because he was on another plane of existence (though only ten miles or so down the road, as the crow flew). The downside was, they'd probably call the cops on her and charge her with corporate espionage.

Her second choice was to repeat her success at Thyme Springs and sneak in as 'the help.' The downside was that it was demeaning as hell. The upside was that it had a marginally better chance of working than the guns blazing approach. And that settled it.

Nev reached Hollister shortly after twelve thirty, stopped at a dot.mart to pee and refuel, and searched the maps app. *Bingo.* Yuna's Uniforms, 2.3 miles away. She programmed the location and arrived five minutes later at a low-roofed warehouse adjacent to a giant fertilizer plant. The air was so thick with nitrogen and sulfur that her eyes started burning before she'd even gotten out of the car. By the time she made it to the front door, she felt like she'd been gassed in the Third Gulf War.

She staggered inside, blinked the blear out of her eyes, and took stock of the situation: rows and rows of industrial shelving, stacked with plastic-wrapped bundles of clothes and gear. Aisles were conveniently demarcated by profession: Medical, Hospitality, Security. There were even exotic categories like Paramilitary and Clown/Entertainer. Nev imagined herself showing up to the Qbito Security booth in a polka-dotted muumuu, floppy shoes, and red nose, holding a bouquet of rainbow-colored balloons. She guffawed out loud, drawing a strange look from the only other person in sight: a very bored-looking middle aged woman in a Yuna's tunic, probably custom-made on the premises.

In the end, Nev opted for practicality over so-crazy-it-just-might-work. She grabbed three sets of 'standard food service' togs in brown, pink, and blue, as well as two 'janitorial/custodial' outfits in gray and black. It was good to have options. Then she paid, held her breath as she got back in the car, slipped into the pink togs in the back seat, and reprogrammed the nav for Llanada.

About forty-five minutes later, she pulled up to the security checkpoint outside the Qbito mainframe building—an old-fashioned tollbooth manned by a steroidal white guy with a buzz cut and a semper fi tattoo on his left forearm. Based on the memory of her previous visit, as well as the little online reconnaissance she'd been able to do, it was the only entrance or exit along the entire perimeter of the property; the rest was ringed with a high fence topped with concertina wire and studded with security cameras.

The security guy didn't say a word. He barely glanced at Nev and her nondescript Newmobile before hitting the button that opened the gate. As she entered the parking lot, she uttered a silent prayer of thanks to the anonymous grandfather who was responsible for her melanin and curls.

Nev parked in the shade of a spreading palm, on the opposite side of the spacious lot from the mainframe building, and put the car in idle/AC mode. It was over ninety degrees outside, according to the dashboard display, and there wasn't a hint of wind, or a wisp of cloud in the sky. The building itself—the aboveground part, at least—was just a tan box, so nondescript that a passing motorist could be forgiven for wondering why an abandoned fast food restaurant was so well protected from unwelcome intruders. Not that there were any passing motorists, of course. This land was too dry for farming, too remote for tourism, too hilly for development. About the only good use for it was burying a gazillion dollar computer a quarter mile beneath its surface.

Where the magic happens.

Nev kept her eyes on the doors to the facility. It was still lunchtime, so a gaggle of techs were standing around the front and side of the building in small clumps, eating, vaping, and chatting. Most of them were dressed like central casting nerds, short-sleeved button downs and khakis, badges on their waists or shirt pockets. They were almost all men, mostly white and a few South Asians, from the looks of it. Then the side door swung open, and a man and a woman exited. They were both wearing gray custodial one-pieces, pretty similar to the one in Nev's back seat.

Looking around to make sure nobody was watching, Nev ducked behind the car, ditched her pink food service outfit, and slipped into her own gray custodial uniform. When her two 'colleagues' headed back inside, she caught the door and followed them in, using her real digital Qbito credentials at the security desk scanner and walking quickly into the waiting elevator before either of the guards could stop to wonder why a janitor showed up as a managerial-level coder on their screen.

The two other custodians got off the elevator at Level -9 and held the door for her to follow, but she waved them to go on without her.

"Big spill by the clean room," she said, resisting the urge to jab repeatedly at the 'door close' dummy button as they looked at her with confusion and growing curiosity. "Don't worry. I got it. See you later." She cringed inwardly as the doors finally shut, and the elevator headed down to Level -22, which was the lowest this particular bank went. That was the level with the control rooms, she recalled, where she'd be able to input Kusuma's password (if her intuition was right) and install the rootkit Airin had cooked up. But she knew from her last visit that there was another set of elevator banks, only accessible from the building's C-suite, that went down to the very bottom of the facility, another forty floors or so deeper beneath the Earth, and gave you physical access to the mainframe itself. It would be a wonder to behold, if she could somehow see through its titanium shell: A pinnacle of human engineering, cascades of qubits shimmering in superpositional splendor, calculating causality faster than reality could keep up. Even despite all the grief the Glitch had caused her, some part of Nev still loved computer science, loved the sheer audacity of wet, sloppy, slow-witted humanity teasing the code of the cosmos out through brute force, prying the secrets of the gods loose from their greedy fingers.

Nev held her breath as the elevator doors opened onto the 22nd floor, waiting to see what gauntlet of Security would greet her on the other side. But nobody was there. The long hallway leading from the elevator bank was dim, barely illuminated by runner lights resembling the ones outside Airin's coding cave. Nev stepped out cautiously and then recoiled as the hallway instantly brightened under the illumination of glaring fluorescent track lights embedded in the ceiling.

"Helloooooooo?" she called out, the word echoing off the hard hallway walls.

No one answered back.

Come on, Nev. You can do this.

She strode purposefully down the hallway, sneakers squeaking on the polished concrete floors, hoping that if anyone did step out from the other direction they would think she had a reason to be there. She did have a reason, of course. Just not one she cared to disclose. Every fifteen feet or so, the hallway behind her darkened and the next stretch in front of her brightened, producing an unpleasant strobe effect. Nev would have pitied the poor suckers who had to work down here, except, weirdly, there was no one around to pity.

At its end, the hallway opened into a rectangular room with a window of thick shatterproof glass that looked over the stacked metal casings of the mainframe climbing upwards and downwards as far as the eye could see. The reception room that Nev had visited on Kusuma's tour was probably several stories higher. That room had been empty of any furniture. This room had a built-in desk that projected out from beneath the window, its surface embedded with twin control panels. Nev pulled a chair out from the desk and sat down at the left panel. She held her hands over the keyboard and a command screen illuminated the window in front of her.

The UI looked the same as the one at Qbito's main office.

<<USER ID>>

That part was easy. The company issued singular identity tags to all its employees. Your user ID was the same as your contact ID for the intranet. She typed Kusuma's twenty times on the average day.

timelord

Now for the tricky part.

<<PASSCODE>>

If she got it wrong, what would happen? Would sirens go off? Maybe there were sirens already blaring on some other floor, where there were actual people—Security people—monitoring mainframe activity. Surely they'd have access to Kusuma's schedule and they would know that he wasn't on site. For all she knew, they were hurtling down the elevator now, racing to drag her from the terminal before she caused any damage. No time to dither.

She entered the eight-digit number Kusuma had told her without telling her: *20180591.*

Rovelli 2018, Chapter 5, Page 91. Of course he knew she'd remember. A childhood spent memorizing Bible verses had its uses.

And she was in. The screen populated with code. Heart soaring in victory, Nev's fingers flew over the keyboard, scanning through lines and layers until she found the place she needed and opened the back door. *Hot damn, I'm good!* For once, Nev's internal monologue served up nothing but praise.

The hallway was as empty on her way out as it had been on her way in. The strobe of the ceiling lights made her feel like a character in one of the old paper flipbooks her father collected in the trailer he used for an office. They were the only books he owned, beside scripture and technical manuals. Or maybe she was a character in one of the old silent films that Jared tried to make her watch sometimes, jumping awkwardly from one pixelated frame to another. Maybe there was a director, just offscreen, calling the shots. Nev couldn't decide whether she found the idea creepy or comforting.

The elevator whizzed back up to main floor, releasing Nev into the small atrium by the front entrance. The two Security guards were huddled together in conversation. They didn't even look up as Nev walked by. She didn't register.

Nev was out the door and into the burning hot sun in a flash. She strode through the parking lot to her car until, at the last moment, like Lot's wife, she looked back over her shoulder.

She couldn't be sure, but Nev thought she saw the bright lights of the lobby reflecting off a bald head behind the shaded glass doors.

QT.29.26.09.30.08.2045

THE APARTMENT WAS a mess again. Of course. Nev beat back the urge to tidy, afraid to cause a glitch that would leave her mired in quicksand, unable to open the door when Airin arrived at 10:30. She poured her energies into getting herself primped and primed instead. After the past couple days spent largely in custodial togs and sweatpants, it felt good to glam up in a form-fitting summer dress she'd initially bought for a date night with Jared. If she wasn't mistaken, she'd worn it out to their evening at the sub-molecular gastropub. Today, it would be put to better use.

In the kitchen, Nev found a lotto ticket attached to the refrigerator door with a souvenir magnet celebrating King William's coronation, which Grandma had bought her as a Christmas present. It came in a set of ten, along with magnets of Buckingham Palace; the Queen Consort, Kate; the princes and princesses, George, Charlotte, and Louis; the royal family's two pet English cocker spaniels, Lido and Delia; and the King's brother, the royal formerly known as Prince Harry, along with his son, Archie, and daughter Lilibet. Grandma was disappointed that Meghan Markle wasn't included ('you look just like she did when she was your age, dear, like a princess,') but Megs had been persona non grata with the royals since the paparazzified breakup scandal and subsequent divorce.

Nev scanned the ticket with her viz, and was unsurprised to discover that she was the 'lucky' winner of a lotto Max jackpot. A notice of new funds in her savings account popped into the alerts field. Lots of zeroes. *Thanks again, futurepast-Nev*, she thought, making a note of the winning numbers. She'd need to remember to buy herself the ticket in the days to come. Although she couldn't imagine why she'd thought she needed the money. She would be spending quite a lot in September on rental cars and bribing Hong-Mei, but she had saved more than enough to cover the costs. What were the extra funds for? Time would reveal all, she supposed.

The doorbell notification appeared in her viz at 10:30 on the dot. Nev buzzed Airin in and ran to the bathroom to reapply her lipstick before opening her front door.

It was clear at first glance that Airin had not put the same attention into their appearance as Nev had. They were wearing a shabby hoodie, its front lip pulled low over their forehead, shielding their bloodshot (but still beautiful!) eyes. Their hands were jammed into the pockets of a pair of wrinkled track pants that looked like they'd been slept in the night before.

"Good morning!" Nev said, instantly wincing at her own chipper tone. She longed to use her SavePoint to redo the moment and dial back her all too evident excitement. After years of prolific undoing, she'd almost forgotten what it felt like to suffer through awkward moments in daily life. SavePoint was the best thing that had ever happened to the silent legions of the socially maladroit. Until it wasn't.

"Uh, hello?" Airin sounded confused. Their gaze flickered between Nev's figure in the front door and the chaotic apartment behind her, finally resting on Nev. "I, um, I'm sorry I didn't dress more professionally. I wasn't thinking too clearly this morning. I had a long night—needed to wrap up work on another project."

"Oh! No! Don't worry about it. Come in, come in. I mean—I

just have to dress this way for when I go to work after we're done, you know? It's nothing special. I mean, look at the place..." Nev made a sweeping gesture around the small apartment as Airin stepped in. "No need to dress up in this mess."

Airin laughed, sounding relieved.

"Cool. Right. Yeah, your place looks about as good as I feel." They paused a beat. "Oh, wait! Sorry—that sounds really insulting."

Nev watched in horror as Airin flicked all five fingers on their left hand in what was clearly their custom SavePoint gesture. Had the technology been working properly, she would never have seen Airin's fingers fly, or heard what they said in the five seconds beforehand. But the tech was not working right; *functions its disrupting was Glitch the of power the maybe.*

"Insulting really sounds that—Sorry wait, Oh!"

Nev's mind reeled as she watched Airin flick their fingers in the opposite direction from before, then take half a step backwards, oddly off balance. Something was wrong with her ears. The construction noise that had been going on outside her window, a constant soundtrack of hammering, drilling and pounding that she'd learned to ignore weeks ago, sounded like echoey suction, a mecha version of the milking machine they had at the Perkins dairy farm down the road in Albion.

Airin was still talking, but it didn't even sound like English any more, just a gush of glottal air with its own little sucking sounds in between the recognizable phonemes: "puprawutduhneentinegghholadaggghhheye..."

She panicked, trying to run, or apologize, or just shut the door and get some time to think, but she'd lost control over her body. Now her own mouth was moving and she could feel her cheeks and eyes straining with the force of a fake smile as she sucked in carbon monoxide and said "Gggninrom dugh," then exhaled oxygen into Airin's face and her vision filled with a million pointy stars, all zooming from her periphery to the black holes at the center, sucking up those twin galaxies swirling in Airin's tired, cautious face, sucking up their beautiful cheeks and chin, their ugly hoodie, and the whole dismal hallway until there was just blackness streaked with smears of light, redshifting and fading to the sucking sound of the pneumatic drill and the darkness finally receded and Airin was standing over her, saying, "Are you okay?"

Nev blinked her eyes. She was on the floor next to the door, sprawled over a pile of shoes and coats she thought she'd crammed into the tiny foyer closet. Airin looked concerned, but also a little annoyed, with more than a dollop of what-have-I-gotten-myself-into. They glanced back at the hallway, still visible through the open door.

"Should I come back another time?" Airin half turned, hand on the knob.

"No!" Nev didn't exactly spring to her feet, but she managed to stand a lot quicker than she would have thought possible. She shook her head to clear the cobwebs, and tried to take Airin's hand. Bad idea—they pulled back reflexively, burying their long fingers in their hoodie pockets. Nev noticed that their nails were no longer lacquered in iridescent colors, just a few flaking patches of black or dark blue. "Sorry. No, I was just... that happens sometimes. It's, it's nothing to worry about. Seriously. Please, come in." She indicated the same seat in the living room that Airin had occupied last time.

They hesitated, then shrugged, closed the door behind them, and followed Nev into the apartment. It was clear they had never been to her place before. *Well, I guess that's that, then... over before it began.* Nev followed their appraising eyes around the room, cringing with disappointment when she contrasted it in her mind's eye with the vibrant, immaculate quality of Airin's light-filled loft.

Once they'd presumably decided that Nev wasn't a serial killer, Airin took a seat on the edge of the couch and looked at Nev expectantly.

"Um, do you want a cup of tea, or should we...?"

"Let's just get started." They watched Nev's face as she struggled to maintain composure, then sighed a little. "On second thought, tea does sound nice, thanks."

"Great, I've got some genmai cha in the kitchen."

Airin raised their eyebrows a micron. Not impressed, but intrigued.

"I'll be right back."

QT.12.27.19.30.08.2045

"Hump Day Happy Houuurrrr! You coming with us, boss?"

A sweaty hand clamped down on the exposed skin of Nev's shoulder, laid bare by the thin straps of her slinky summer dress. After working with Airin for three hours to establish the protocols for their collaboration, Nev hadn't had time to change into her usual work uniform of jeans and tee-shirt before running out the door to Qbito's weekly Wednesday after-lunch all-staff meeting. Eyebrows went up when she walked in the door of the large conference room, but the brogrammers had just enough social grace—or fear of getting fired—to refrain from wolf whistles.

"Get your hand off before I cut it off," Nev said to Dorfman, the junior developer hovering over her Memeron.

He snatched back his hand with a mumbled apology and a look of terror that filled her with instant regret. The more senior guys had probably put him up to it.

"Sorry for snapping. It's been a day. But for future reference: no touching."

A 'day' didn't begin to describe Nev's feelings since parting with Airin. She'd spent the whole afternoon trying to dislodge

275

their awkward non-goodbye by losing herself in code. The tactic had been remarkably productive on the work front, but not at all effective on the emotional front. Work had lost the power to overwrite her feelings.

"Come on, Nev. Stop terrorizing the kid and have a drink with us." It was Theo, one of the veteran brogrammers—he had to be almost thirty.

Nev stared forlornly at the lines of code hovering in front of her. She'd reached the point where she remembered picking up Friday morning. There was nothing more to do for the day. And how many more opportunities would there be to drink with the boys? Plus, she already knew she'd say yes. It explained the hangover she'd woken up with on Thursday. If work couldn't sandblast away her blues, she was pretty sure that alcohol would still do the trick.

"Fine. Fine. Just, give me a moment."

Nev bought the first round. She was flush. She chose the most expensive shot on the happy hour menu at Dirty Diablo's, an ersatz Tijuana-style bar around the corner from the Qbito offices. The super-añejo Mezcal burned in her stomach like the oil drum fires they used for cooking in the ceegee camps. Then, to repay her generosity and advertise his own, Todd, the most senior dude on her team, bought another round of the same. He'd probably be the one who'd replace her when she went poof, Nev thought hazily. That is, if she and Airin didn't manage to bring down the mainframe first.

All of a sudden, she was ravenously hungry. She hadn't eaten a bite since the buttered toast she'd scarfed down before Airin came over that morning. She decided to stick around for the platters of nachos they'd ordered for the long table. The nachos, in turn, made her thirsty for the tall, cold, light-gold cervezas that followed. Which made her hungrier. Then thirstier. *A loop within a loop within...*

By the time Nev stumbled through her apartment door, she was feeling good. She was feeling right. She was feeling tight.

She was feeling loose. She was feeling flush. She was feeling lush. She hovered over Airin's icon in her viz. Should she? Would she? Could she? Just because they had no past and no future didn't mean they couldn't have right now. She'd seen Airin's eyes linger on her when she'd opened the door that morning. Maybe Airin was just waiting for her to call. Maybe they'd gotten together tonight and Airin was too much of a gentle-person to mention it in the days since.

She stumbled to the bathroom, peeling her dress from her sweaty summer body as she crossed the apartment, eyes lingering on Airin's icon. After she peed, she washed her hands in warm water and looked into the mirror over the sink. Perspiration beaded her hairline and dripped down the crevice between her breasts, barely concealed behind a thin lacy bra. She took a selfie on her viz, and let it hover over Airin's icon. If they saw it, would they come over? She imagined all the things they might get up to, down to, round to. If Nev had her way she would make Airin cry her name for hours, until the break of dawn.

Fuuuccckkkkkk

Nev flicked her selfie into the trash.

Fuck Fuck Fuck Fuck

She checked the time. 10:36 pm. She'd barely be able to buzz Airin through the door before she blinked out. Let alone...

Nev turned on the cold water tap and splashed her face, willing her thumping heart to slow down. All that bottled up energy and no place to spend it. Spend it. Thinking of which, what was she going to do with all that cash burning a hole in her pocket? She could have bought a thousand rounds of Mezcal for the doodz without making a dent in the string of zeros cluttering her bank balance. Nev stumbled back into the living room, flopped down on her couch, and closed her eyes.

A vision appeared before her. A thing of beauty. A gleaming tangerine orange 1973 Porsche 911 Carrera RS electrofit, with Airin looking fine behind the wheel. Happier days, sunshine, the smell of high tide.

She switched on her screen and began typing. She had an hour to find the needle in the haystack, track down this rarest of car models, make the purchase, and arrange for delivery in ten days. It was going to cost a pretty penny—more like 50 million pretty pennies—but she would have paid every cent in Kusuma's bank account just to make Airin smile.

Desire and grief battled inside of Nev, thrilling and exhausting her, squeezing her into ribbons, twisting her into knots. The memory of their parting conversation in Nev's condo had been briefly silenced by the loud voices competing to be heard over the electro mariachi at Dirty Diablo's. Now that she was alone at home, the memory resumed its ceaseless echo in Nev's mind.

"We're going to meet next on September 1st, 9:30 a.m, my place. When did we meet last?" Nev had used the past and future tense in ways that Airin would understand, trying to make the conversation easy on them. It had all seemed very new to Airin. Nev just didn't understand how new until Airin answered.

"Why do you need me to tell you where we met? You're the one who has this all planned out. You're the one who tracked me down yesterday, out of the blue, despite the fact that we haven't spoken since Stanford."

"I did? We haven't?" Nev barely squeaked out the words. "Can you tell me where and when?"

The weirdest feeling had swept over her. A fierce desire to tell Airin what had just happened. But not the stranger Airin, sitting in front of her that morning with a skeptical expression. Rather, yestermorrow's Airin, who had bought her hot chocolate and listened to her cry, warning away the waiter with their eyes to give Nev the space to find her breath again. The Airin who had protected her from the knowledge of what was to come, as she now had to protect this Airin in turn. The one person in the world who could understand the terror and pain she was going through didn't yet exist, and by the time they did exist, Nev wouldn't know the full terror of what was to come.

Airin. Oh, Airin. She would never know the taste of Airin's mouth, the smell of their sweat, the joy of their body grinding against hers. And Airin would never know the sweetness inside of her, the wide oceans of herself, the places she'd never allowed Jared, never allowed anyone. But at least... at least they would know she loved them.

This one's for you, Airin, Nev thought, as her finger hit <<purchase>>.

Series complete. LoopID?QT.43.33.23.30.08.2045

QT.15.22.08.29.08.2045

"Mmmmm. Morning, sunshine."

Nev opened her eyes to see Jared's face on the pillow opposite. He was almost cute, with the puppy-dog look he got sometimes and the early morning light slanting through the window across his stubbly jaw. But Nev knew far too well what came next. The line from puppy eyes to doggy style was straight and well-traveled.

She leapt out of bed, thankfully wearing a tee-shirt and pair of black leggings that could easily pass for either pajamas or casual outdoor clothes. Her viz was right in her pocket, alongside the mystery stone. Too bad it was all coming to an end so quickly, because Nev was starting to get the hang of this retrograde lifestyle.

"Wait…" There was a whiny edge to his voice, a palpable tang of neediness that dispelled any lingering cuteness like a whiff of smoke. "It's still early. We've got time to hang out before you have to go, right?"

Nev had no interest in hanging out, in, over, or under Jared. Not if he was the last man on Earth, which, for all intents and purposes, he was.

"No time this morning, J," she said and headed to the bathroom, where she took a quick, refreshing shower, deodorized, moisturized, and donned the leggings, shirt, and viz. Then she came out, gave Jared a brisk kiss on the cheek, dodged his grasping hands, and slipped out, closing the apartment door behind her softly.

Nev didn't stop at Abdul's to buy her winning lotto ticket on her way home to change her clothes. He hadn't mentioned anything about her big jackpot since the Glitch, which must have meant that she hadn't bought the numbers at his dot.mart. If she had, he would've gotten a cut from the multistate authority that ran the lottery. It felt shitty to cut Abdul out of the proceeds in fealty to preserving a timeline that she had no power over. But she was getting so close to the end. One wrong step now, and she'd lose everything she and Airin had been working for. Besides, he'd be getting a cut from Anissa's ticket in a few weeks, and if he sold more than one winning ticket in a month, the authorities would probably come sniffing. Maybe she should write a will. Leave a bequest for Abdul to make up for the missing revenue from the winning ticket that she bought, instead, at the dot.mart two blocks further from her apartment.

Once she'd changed and grabbed a quick snack from her pantry, it was only about a five-minute walk to her destination. The first and last meeting place in her absurdly short, incredibly productive, life-changing, world-shaking, heart-breaking collaboration with the Infamous Hacker Airin Myx.

Airin might have done their best work solo, in the secret code dungeon behind the false wall of their Dogpatch loft, but they often said it takes a village to raise hell, and even the most reclusive hacker had to roll with a posse sometimes. In blockbuster movies and games, hacker collectives always met in their high-tech clubhouses, surrounded by bleeping, blooping gadgetry, steamy vents, and ultraviolet lighting. It made for a good screenshot, Airin said, but in reality, elite hackers did about 99.9% of their collaborating online, and when they did meet, they tended to do it in public, where there was a lower chance of assassination and better snacks.

The Bay Area hackers club informally known as LastTuesday had been meeting monthly in the same public area since 2031, and Airin had been a regular member for over a decade. They were sitting right where they promised Nev she'd find them, at a wobbly table outside of Monsieur Macaron's on the fifth floor of the AMZ San Francisco Centre.

The building was a holdover from the previous century, a massive block of brick-and-mortar in one of the priciest square miles of real estate on the planet, stuffed to the rafters with high-end chain stores, immersive experiential marketing pop-ups, and consumer tech demo stations advertising futuristic devices and services that would raise a ton of investment capital and never get off the ground. Collectively, the retailers in the building probably would have lost fifty million dollars per year if their landlord and silent partner hadn't subsidized their rent by purchasing every byte of consumer data generated by transactions and foot traffic, as well as running the payment platforms, loyalty programs, inventory management solutions, local networking systems, and entertainment feeds for every store from a giant server in the sub-basement. It was, in other words, the world's greatest hacker playground.

Airin was talking to a young woman—a college student, by the looks of it—when Nev approached from the escalator. She felt an unexpected rush of jealousy flare behind her ribs. Who was this pert, pretty young thing, and what was she to Airin? Then, before she could regain equilibrium, they looked up and met her eyes, and Nev knew two things instantly: first, that Airin recognized her, beyond a shadow of a doubt. And second, that the gravitational pull of those twin galaxies was always and forever, and that they felt the attraction every bit as much as she did.

Airin murmured something to the girl, and she slipped away from the table, disappearing around a corner. Nev took it as an invitation, and sat down opposite them. There was a long, unnerving silence as Airin scanned Nev from head to fingertips.

"I thought I saw you last night at Jimmy's. It's been a long time, Nevaeh."

Nev smiled. "For you, maybe."

Airin arched their eyebrows, but didn't say anything. Another unspoken invitation.

How to begin?

"So, first of all," Nev said, speaking lowly and slowly, "I'm not stalking you. And I'm not crazy, though what's happening to me is pretty crazy, and you're a part of it. Or, rather, you're going to be."

Now Airin smiled. "Oh, am I?"

"Yes. You are. There's no simple way to put this, so I'll just lay it on the table. You know I work for Qbito, right?"

Airin nodded, never breaking eye contact.

"So, about a month from now," Nev lowered her voice to a whisper, "as I'm launching a new alpha rollout, something happens to me. Something bad. I get stuck in a kind of time Glitch, and, um…" Now that she had to say it aloud to Airin for the first time, it sounded so absurd she wouldn't have believed it herself. "Well, I start living backwards."

Airin blinked. "Backwards?"

"Yes. I mean, I'm living this conversation forwards, but each day I wake up a day earlier than the previous day. And you and I…"

Airin's eyebrows climbed even further.

"…You and I have been working on a, uh, a fix. A solution. A way to break the Glitch. By rooting the Qbito mainframe."

They were silent a moment, checking something on their viz. Then they looked around the mall, inspecting every pedestrian, shopkeeper, and security camera in turn. Finally, they turned back to Nev.

"I can't tell whether you're putting me on, or setting me up. What is this, some kind of a gag? Or maybe the worst sting operation in history?"

Nev shook her head, giving Airin what she hoped was a trustworthy look. "Neither, I swear. And I can prove it. I know you pretty well at this point, Airin. Even though," she had to fight not to choke up. "Even though you don't know me. Yet."

"Oh, you know me pretty well, huh? After how long? You said about a month?"

"Yes. Actually, it's only been about three weeks since we started, uh, collaborating. But Airin, I can prove it. You told me your deadname."

Airin stood up.

"Okay, sorry, this isn't funny anymore. I've wasted enough time on—"

"Adam." Nev whispered it so softly she couldn't even hear herself.

"WHAT?!" All of their suavity had evaporated, and they looked like they were trying to decide which piece of Nev to tear apart with their long fingers.

A woman guiding an e-stroller between a viz accessories stand and a Ben & Jerry's storefront was staring at them. She looked like she might be weighing a call to the cops. Airin stared levelly at the woman, who shrugged and continued on her way. Then they turned back to Nev, ferocity blazing in their eyes.

"Who told you that? Are you having me investigated? I haven't done anything. Why is Kusuma trying to fuck with me?"

"I'm sorry, but that's what you said to me, when we first met. Last met. 'You don't know me from Adam.'"

They shook their head.

"No. I don't believe you."

"It's the truth, Airin. I'll tell you one thing more. After you learned about silent letters, one of your first names for yourself was Ada." Nev smiled at the thought of the big, doofy dog she'd never see again.

Airin opened their mouth to protest.

"Just stop. I know you believe me. I know it because I've already lived it. Because I saw you tomorrow."

"You mean yesterday. At Jimmy's." The fire was gone, replaced by stony skepticism, but Nev could see the door had opened just a crack.

"No, Airin. Tomorrow morning. At 10:30. At my house. Here's the address."

Nev shared her viz contact, then got up and walked away. This time, she managed to avoid looking back.

QT.00.30.07.28.08.2045

YOU'VE GOT TO *be fucking kidding me.*

Nev awoke to the sound of Joni Mitchell's warble filling her small apartment like helium in a foil balloon. She listened long enough to recognize the lyrics to 'The Circle Game', and silenced her viz with a firm shake.

If this were really just a game, she'd be having a lot more fun. Whatever trip Joni had been on when she wrote the song clearly didn't involve the sensation of free-falling through cement in five dimensions at once.

Nev knew every word and every warble of the track. It was included in a wholesome 'Golden Age of Folk Rock' collection that had been on the short list of approved albums in the Bourne household. Faith used to love it, singing Mitchellesque harmonies in her sweet, pure soprano. Nev hadn't heard it since the day she left home. Eighty-year-old classics didn't turn up frequently on the soundtrack of daily life. She was glad for that. Hearing it now made her want to weep. If she ever met the insane rando who had designed this alarm app, she would give them a piece of her mind.

Nev let her eyes close again. No meeting with Airin to look forward to. No reason to drag herself out of bed. Except, except,

except. She was captive on a carousel of time. Her Memeron beckoned. Her code called. Her fingers needed to input the syntax that would bring her to the point where she had picked up the thread tomorrow. She had to go through the paces, whether she liked it or not. The past owes a debt to the future.

Nev caught the door to Qbito just before it swung shut, stepping into the lobby right after Madison Barnett. She really did have perfect timing.

"Morning, Nev," Maddy said.

There was something odd about the greeting. It lacked… Nev tried to put her finger on it… animosity. The greeting lacked animosity. Her mind traveled over all of the future month's interactions with Maddy, trying to isolate the exact moment when their relationship shifted from indifference to open warfare. Despite everything, Maddy and Nev had always managed a functional working relationship, until Nev began hacking the SavePoint 2.0 alpha.

"Morning, Madison," Nev replied, watching the CMO for a reaction.

Nothing there. Like, nothing at all. It dawned on Nev that Maddy's feelings about her, and about the job, were completely impersonal. Nev was willing to bet that everything in Maddy's life was impersonal. Success was the end all be all. It had been the same for Nev. And now? Now everything felt raw, like she'd been skinned. Grief, regret, fear. Her feelings were all so close to the surface. But also desire, joy, and love. And compassion.

"You know, it doesn't have to be this way," Nev said to Maddy as they stepped together into the elevator.

"What?" Maddy looked mystified.

"You're allowed to have feelings. It would be totally natural if you felt bad when you saw me, because I remind you of Anissa, who you forced out for raising totally valid concerns about product safety."

The first hint of the dislike that had become familiar to Nev during the future weeks appeared in Maddy's eyes.

"Speak for yourself, Nev. You might feel bad about throwing

your 'bestie' under the bus, but I don't. This isn't high school. I made the right decision for Qbito. And so did you. Get over it."

"You're right! I do feel bad about it! That's exactly what I'm trying to say. I didn't feel bad at first because I was all business. Just like you. But I've been going through some things, and I'm not all business any more. I've realized I should have felt bad at the time, and it's okay to feel bad now. I mean, it's alright having feelings. I've been feeling love too, and that's—that's…" Nev trailed off, unable to confine her feelings with words.

Maddy's eyes narrowed. "I don't know why you're telling me this. And I really don't care what you're going through. I'm sorry you're having second thoughts about your life decisions or whatever, but that's no excuse for you to fall off a cliff, especially this close to the alpha launch. If Kusuma were here, I'd tell him to refer you for a psych eval. But since he's off on his own quest for meaning, here's some free life advice: get your work done right and on schedule, and stay the fuck out of my way."

The door opened at Nev's floor. Maddy stared straight ahead impatiently, waiting for Nev to leave the elevator. Nev stepped to the threshold, reached out a hand to hold the door from shutting, and turned back to Maddy.

"I know for a fact that telling you this is going to cause me nothing but grief, but I'm saying it for your sake Maddy. Hopefully, you have a long life ahead of you. Don't waste your time being a cold-hearted bitch."

Nev let the door go behind her. *Well, that conversation explained a lot.*

The familiar cascade of notifications flooded Nev's viz as she crossed the threshold to the programming pit. She hadn't poured the cashew milk in her double espresso before Todd tracked her down.

"About time you're back, Nev. It's been a total shit show while you've been away. Dorfman broke the rx-identifier subroutine and I've had the whole team working to undo the damage. He's gotta go. Maybe we can pawn him off on temporal."

She had vague memories of this conversation from the first time around. Nev looked out, over Todd's shoulder, to see Najib Khan, junior coder on the temporal team, leading Darian Wilson past the open doorway of the break pod on his orientation tour. Naj picked up his pace when he caught Nev's eye, hurrying Darian to his next destination. No wonder he'd skipped the instructions for the La Pavoni.

"I think temporal may have filled their empty slot," Nev said, turning back to Todd. She poured her cashew milk and returned it to the fridge. "Looks like we're keeping the Dorf Man. Tell Theo to do some one-on-one with him this week. Train him up. Let's go back to my desk and you can walk me through the breakage."

Her Memeron sighed its familiar greeting. Her screen illuminated in welcome. She felt an echo of the relief she'd experienced her first time through this day, the Monday after Grandma's funeral. Not that she'd told her team her reasons for being gone Thursday and Friday. She was the boss, after all. And she'd accrued enough sick days to take a whole damned month off if she wanted to. They didn't know where she'd been, that her grandmother had died, or even that she'd had a grandmother to begin with. There was no signed card waiting on her desk. No dinky flower arrangement from HR. No awkward questions from the brogrammers. It was how she'd wanted it. That way, she could return to work as though the funeral had never happened. As though Albion had never happened. As though her entire goddamned childhood had never happened. She had simply sprung into existence one day, a full-grown programmer.

"How was your weekend, Todd?" Nev asked her second-in-command as he pulled a chair up to her console.

Todd tilted his head and stared at her.

"Unh—my weekend? I spent half my time here trying to fix Dorfman's fuck-up, and the other half at home, trying to drink away my anxiety. Why? How was yours?"

"It was sad. My grandmother died. I went to her funeral."

"Oh." The look of surprise on Todd's face shifted swiftly to discomfort. "I'm sorry, Nev. I didn't know. I, I don't know what to say. How was the funeral?"

"I don't know yet," Nev said. "I need some time to figure it out. Do me a favor till then, please don't mention this to anyone else, okay?"

"Yeah, sure." He nodded. "Mum's the word."

It was past sundown when Nev left the building. The hours had flown by as Nev burrowed into the code, excising Dorfman's errors, laying the foundations for the hacks she and Airin would be adding in the weeks to come. Jim Bone was curled up in the front doorway, looking older and more ragged than Nev had seen him for a while. She reached into her bag and fished out her wallet, hoping she had cash. She found a thick stack of hundred dollar bills tucked into the central pocket.

"Evening, Jim Bone. I think this is for you."

Nev handed him most of the cash, which swiftly disappeared into the inside pocket of his grease stained windbreaker.

"Put it away, Jim Bone," he croaked. "Don't know when I'll see this again. Here one day, gone the next. Take the money from the poor lady when you see her. Here one day, gone the next. Gone most of the time."

Nev paused, considering what Jim Bone was saying.

"When was the last time you saw me?"

"Don't see you, most of the time. Maybe one out of ten days. You're gone gone gone more than you're here."

What did it mean that Nev was just an erratic blip in Jim Bones' timeline? Could it be that her traveling companion wasn't merely sliding backwards like she was, but bouncing through life like a ping pong ball inside a perspex sphere, randomly striking a different spot in his timeline at every ricochet? If February 9th, 2057, the date he got his implant, marked one terminus of his timeline, and maybe December 26th, 2039, the day that the Qbito mainframe went online, marked the other, then he had a little more than sixteen years to bounce around, or—Nev did the math in her head—6,255 days. If Nev were present one out of ten of those days, that meant their timeline overlapped by six hundred and twenty-six days, give or take, a little bit less than two years, or about the time from when Nev was hired at Qbito in January 2043, to September 22, 2045, when she executed the hacked SavePoint 2.0 alpha. Unwelcome, but compelling, evidence that after the launch day, her timeline would end. It was no surprise, but still a bitter pill to swallow. Maybe, just maybe she would wake up on September 23rd and simply walk away from this life. Maybe she had a future, but not at Qbito? Or, maybe not.

She sat down heavily on the doorstep beside the grizzled ceegee.

"I think this might be it for me, Jim Bone. I don't know if I'm coming back to Qbito again."

"Not the end for Jim Bone. Not the beginning."

Nev had no words to comfort him. Nothing she could say would change anything.

"I'm so sorry, Jim Bone. I wish that—if only I could do something for you, I promise I would, but I can't. The timeline won't hold. It would put so many other people at risk, and I—"

"What about you?"

She sighed. "I'm fucked too."

Jim Bone reached into the shadowy depths of his windbreaker and pulled out a pint of Evan Williams. He took a swig from the bottle and handed it to Nev. She didn't bother to wipe the rim before she took a drink.

"Not about us," he said.

"True enough."

"I got time. Maybe someone else can help."

"Fucking hell, I hope someone else can help you. Ideally, someone who's got a better grasp on temporal anomalies than I do." Insight flashed in Nev's mind, beating back the morbid shadows. "Jim Bone, you're brilliant," she said. "Pass me back that bottle!"

Nev took another drink and returned the pint to Jim Bone. She called up the icon for Anissa's voice mail.

"Anissa. Don't hang up on this message. I'm sorry. I really am. I fucked up. You're amazing and brilliant and a true friend and I should have listened to you from the beginning. There's nothing you can do for me and when I come asking in person in a few weeks you should definitely kick me to the curb. Someone's got to teach me a lesson. But there's something you can do for someone else. Remember that ceegee who hangs around Qbito, Jim Bone? He's gonna need your help. A month from now, after you see Jim Bone again, you should get in touch with Airin Myx. You can find them at the San Francisco Centre on the last Tuesday of the month—uh, September 26th—outside Monsieur Macaron's. Tell them I said Jim Bone needs your help. He's out of temporal sequence, but there's nothing I could do, not in this short time. And, whatever you do, don't come talk to me about any of this. It won't help, it'll make things worse. Trust me. I know it's a lot to ask, but I swear I'm not asking for myself. Love you, babe. Sorry I didn't stand up for you when I had the chance."

Nev got up, brushing the dust off her jeans.

"I've got to take off now, Jim Bone. I wish I could spend more time, but my night is short, and I've got miles to go before I blink out."

She took off at a quick clip for Jimmy's Bar.

QT.11.56.20.28.08.2045

JIMMY'S WAS AS Jimmy's always was. Monday night happy hour was winding down, and Nev spotted a few familiar faces at the bar, cheeks red and eyes glazed from one too many five-dollar CBDaiquiris. Levi was tending bar, and he smiled at her blandly as she walked through the door. Not a hint of recognition, of course; going by the calendar, this was the first time they'd laid eyes on one another.

Nev ordered a fancy, top-shelf liqueur, pointing randomly at one of the oddly-shaped bottles she'd always seen more as decoration than as a legitimate beverage option. It had an Italian name, written in gold script on a deep magenta label. Levi shrugged, climbed up on a stool to reach the bottle, dropped two ice cubes into a rocks glass, rubbed the rim with an orange peel, and added a splash of bitters before pouring two fingers of the syrupy, amber liquid and placing it daintily before her on its cardboard coaster. He watched with detached interest as she raised the glass to her lips. *What the hell. Nothing ventured, nothing gained.*

It tasted like old socks steeped in sugar water.

"So," Nev said, trying not to gag. "This is how the other half lives."

Levi smirked. "How about a beer? On the house."

"Thanks, that sounds wonderful."

"Don't think I've seen you here before."

"That's because you haven't."

"Well, I hope you'll be back." He placed a frothy pint in front of her, and knocked back her liqueur in one gulp. "Waste not..."

Now it was Nev's turn to smirk. She laid a twenty on the bar and swiveled around on her stool to scan the room. No sign of Airin yet. She opened the juke app on her viz and spent $47.50 buying out the next half hour of music on the Jimmy's speakers; if she was going to be waiting a while, she didn't want to hear any more of that algo garbage. A few people looked up quizzically when Stevie Wonder's shimmering piano replaced the synthetic, thumping dance beat, but nobody complained. Maybe everyone needed a little Sunshine tonight.

Nev examined the thirty-odd people in the bar, one by one, wondering how many of them had SavePoints. Given the locale, probably the majority of them. Another reason to keep her distance; she didn't want to glitch out if one of them knocked over a drink next to her and then tried to undo it. She wasn't sure what the radius of damage was, but best not to find out the hard way.

So. Fifteen, maybe twenty SavePoints in this room alone. Twenty lives that would fracture into temporal shards, twenty souls doomed to their own, private hells, only a month from now, without Nev's and Airin's intervention. And another hundred and fifty million plus beyond Jimmy's oak-paneled walls. *Each one of them is someone. Each one matters.*

It was hard to wrap her head around. Up til now, the idea of the Glitch To End All Glitches had been an abstraction, a Doomsday scenario written in shorthand on her mental ledger. It might as well have been an asteroid, or a plague, like the one that killed Faith. But now that her work with Airin had ended, now that she was so close to the edge of oblivion that the world almost seemed translucent to her, the details suddenly mattered more than they ever had before.

That woman over there. The one with the shaved head and the low-slung jeans, playing pool. Nev watched as she sank three solids in a row, then took a gulp of her well drink and a pull from a vape. Professional sports had banned SavePoints, for obvious reasons, but nobody seemed to miss their shot at a playground hoop or a dive bar table any more. Nev watched closely as the woman sank another two, then aimed for the eight ball. There was no indication that she'd undone or redone a moment of it, but of course that was the point. Another woman with long, silky hair and a pouffy blouse watched, an unguarded smile of adoration on her face. Wife? Lover? Or just a friend hoping to become more than just a friend? It didn't matter. They'd have time to figure it out.

That guy with the mustache. He was bopping his head to 'Sir Duke,' staring out the window and tapping a skull-ringed finger on the coaster at his table. He looked uncomfortable in a slim-fit shirt with vertical white and lavender stripes. Definitely a hookup outfit, selected to show off his gym-crafted torso. Not a hair out of place, not a fleck of dust on him. His date hadn't showed up yet, maybe never would. If they did, Nev hoped they'd appreciate how much work he'd clearly put into his appearance. If they didn't... well, he'd have plenty of other romantic opportunities.

That person with the beautiful eyes. It was Airin, of course. Sitting at a table near the door, chatting with the same pretty young thing Nev had seen outside of Monsieur Macron's. As if they felt her eyes scorching their skin, Airin looked up and stared back at Nev. A flash of recognition in their starry depths. Was it more than recognition? Nev turned back to the bar, downed her beer, and beat a hasty retreat. The timeline had to follow its course.

She went home and quickly changed into the leggings and tee-shirt combination she remembered waking up in the previous morning. As she stepped back out into the cool San Francisco summer evening, a notification from Jared illuminated her viz.

J: 🐱📞?
N: OMW

Dryverless dropped Nev outside Jared's Marina loft at five past eleven. He opened the door wearing only a trucker cap, striped tube socks, and a boner. Nev burst into laughter, tears leaking out the corners of her eyes. Jared's puppy dog eyes drooped, and the angle of his manhood dipped below the meridian.

"Wait! Wait!" she said, "Don't SavePoint! It's not safe. There's been some trouble at work... it's really been a hell of a day. Sorry that I laughed at you, but I really needed that release."

She stood on her tiptoes, and gave him a chaste peck on the cheek. She could see the struggle in his eyes, as he made the effort to rein in his expectations.

"Would you mind if we just, I don't know, smoked some weed and watched something stupid? Maybe later I'll be in the mood."

With any luck, she'd reset long before she had to pay the piper.

QT.43.31.08.27.08.2045

WAKING UP TO the sight of the bare walls of her own apartment filled Nev with inexpressible relief. Consciously, she knew better than to expect to wake up in the same place where she'd fallen asleep, but at a vestigial level, her body had been primed to reject Jared's morning advances.

Nev wondered whether anything had happened between them after her consciousness blipped out. Did she even exist anymore in the mysterious world beyond 11:33pm? The question was impossible for her to answer, but she'd never been able to let it go.

The last thing she recalled, they were lying together in Jared's bed, pleasantly stoned, watching season fifty-seven of *The Simpsons*. Judging from the fact that she had woken up fully dressed the following calendar morning, it seemed likely that the evening ended that way. She was surprised to feel a little regret mingle with her relief. Had that been her last opportunity to get laid? The funeral was in T-minus two days. In the futurepast, she'd be on the road. It seemed unlikely she was going to meet anyone between here and Albion. No more orgasms for eternity? *Don't be stupid, Nev.* She was perfectly capable of handling herself. She got to handling.

It was strangely quiet in the apartment when she emerged from the shower. Though why the quiet should be strange, she didn't know. She'd lived alone ever since leaving home. What—or who—did she expect to hear? There was no chance of Airin appearing magically in the kitchen to fix her morning coffee. Maybe in another life. Not this one.

In this life, her mornings typically began with the most jumbled mix of meditations, affirmations, and music that a badly-designed algorithm could select. Only, this morning, nothing was playing. Her viz was silent. Again, Nev was surprised to feel regret mingle with her relief at the reprieve. As awful as waking up to Donny Osmond and the serenity prayer had been, each morning's selections were oddly well-matched to the day that followed. Sometimes even helpful. What did this morning's radio silence mean for the day to come? It couldn't bode well.

Unless…

She clicked her viz into place and searched through her app folder for the alarm. The holographic icon of bronze charms with Sanskrit engraving was nowhere to be found. The app had been deleted. Or rather, Nev corrected herself, it hadn't yet been installed. Whoever was going to hack her viz to implant the malware was going to do that today.

And, the other shoe dropped, that 'hacker' had to be her.

Reconstructing the next four weeks of daily alarm settings from memory took all morning. It was a painstaking process, but not without its pleasures, sort of like coding. She began with the dates and alarms that haunted her. The *namaste* that woke her the first day she heard it. The Sunday morning that began with church bells. The Sunday that began with the Osmonds. Then she moved forward and backward from each landmark, yipping in triumph when she grasped hold of a forgotten detail. The application failure alert that woke her the morning she was at her lowest, worrying whether she'd ever figure out Kusuma's passcode. The crowd chants of 'No God, No Masters,' the day she spear-phished Hong-Mei. When she was done, with a final frisson of evil pleasure, she chose a deactivation code that she was one hundred percent sure she would never be able to think of when she first found the app: A1r1n&N3v4fR!

The apartment still felt too quiet. There was something unnerving about the spare walls and uncluttered floors. It had taken years for Nev to acquire what little furniture she did have: the bed, the couch, the coffee table, the kitchen table. Once she'd graduated Stanford and entered the workforce, lack of money hadn't been an issue. She'd just never had the time or inclination to 'decorate.' What did it matter whether she had a bed? She spent all day and night in her Memeron. When she got home, she would collapse on the couch, watch a few viz vids, and pass out. She hadn't bothered to buy a coffee table until Anissa came over and made fun of her for using a packing box. She'd bought the bed after she started hooking up with Jared, to replace the lumpy futon she'd lugged from Palo Alto. Now she possessed all the necessary components of a home, even if she'd never have the skills (or the opportunity) for the curatorial decoration that made Airin's loft so perfect. So what was the problem? What was missing? The place was relatively clean and tidy. "Let all things be done decently and in order," her mother used to say. Mama would be pleased, Nev thought. Everything was tucked neatly into place.

Too neatly! Her place would be a mess by the time Airin came.

Sorry, Mama! Nev cranked up the dance hits audio stream to full volume and set to work trashing her own apartment. She pulled clothes from her dresser drawers, propelling tee-shirts and underwear in sails of color over her shoulder. She swept her arm across her kitchen table, sending small stacks of unsorted junk mail down to the floor. She scattered the books on her night table onto the black and white spiral rug around her bed. It was hard work making a mess out of her minimal possessions, but she did her best. Finally she stood back, hands on hips, and surveyed the destruction with satisfaction. It looked just right—which was a funny thing to say about an exercise in futility. She was only making the mess in the first place because she remembered it existing later, and because Airin had noticed the mess, and noticed her later efforts to clean up the mess, which meant that the mess had entered into the chain of causality and couldn't be eliminated without threatening the timeline. But where did the chain begin and end? Did she clean up the mess because she had made it? Or did she make the mess because she had cleaned it up?

Yes.

She could hear Kusuma's voice in her head: "Remember Rovelli." *The difference between past and future does not exist in the elementary equations of the world. In the elementary grammar of things, there is no distinction between "cause" and "effect."*

It didn't matter whether time moved forward or backwards. She was trapped in a web of interconnected events, and she couldn't disrupt one without imperiling the existence of all the others to which it was connected. Or, rather, she wasn't trapped in the web, so much as she *was* the web. Sever a critical point of connection, and the entire scaffolding of her life would collapse in on itself. The web was frayed, hanging on by its last threads. She could feel it. She had to maintain structural integrity long enough to get home and say goodbye.

Not long now.

Whatever. Time to go buy some genmai cha for Airin.

QT.42.21.07.26.08.2045

BEIGE WALLS. BROWN curtains. Geometric-patterned low pile carpeting. Dark veneer dresser. An old-fashioned vid-screen attached to the wall in the corner of the room. The familiar setting filled Nev with nostalgia. She was back in the Pullman, Washington Holiday Inn Express. The site of her first job (not counting the years of unpaid labor in Daddy's junkyard). Departure point for her independent future. And many years later, departure point the morning after Grandma's funeral.

Nev snuggled deeper into the starchy white sheets of the king-sized bed. She'd woken up before sunrise to the screech of her viz alarm, mystery stone clenched tightly against her chest. She told the viz to fuck off, pulled one of the hotel's big downy pillows over her head, and drifted back to dreamland for another three hours. Naps were the only chance she ever got to dream any more. And she'd taken so few since the Glitch began.

First time around, she'd been desperate to get back to California ASAP. She'd been feeling pretty damned ungodly after her blowout with Mama over Grandma's grave, and had swapped her 9am flight to Portland for a 5:45am to Seattle. The sooner she wiped the eastern Washington clay off her designer

303

sandals, the better. She'd spent her five-hour layover in the SeaTac wine bar, which opened at 6am to serve passengers arriving on transpacific flights and waiting for domestic connections. By the time she'd made it home, the combination of missed sleep and daybreak drinking had brought on a monster of a migraine. She'd downed a mix of painkillers and REMaidz, climbed into her own bed, and didn't get up again until Sunday morning.

It was a lost day, one she didn't see any need to repeat.

Life didn't give you many second chances. And Nev didn't have much life left to live. But she did have a whole day to herself, far from Qbito, and far enough from Albion to have options.

She rolled her neck and stretched her shoulders. Her body felt supple and well rested. Her mind was clear. But her eyes ached a bit, the tear ducts sore and the lids scratchy. Had she been crying? Last time through this day, she'd stayed up half the night bawling in her hotel room, replaying her mother's parting words over and over in her head. This time, she hoped to do better. So why did she still feel like she'd binge watched Miley Cyrus tearjerkers all night long? *There are two hypotheses,* her scientific mind answered. *And you're not going to like either one.*

Hypothesis one: She'd try, and fail, to fix things in the futurepast, repeating the devastating events of her history and ending up back in her room in a pool of her own tears.

Hypothesis two: She'd succeed in patching things up with her parents, but then glitch out for good, crashing like an app that was more patch than base code. The Nev she'd once been wouldn't even recognize the woman she was today, and now, she barely remembered what it had felt like to be that resentful, solitary soul. But if futurepast Nev somehow managed to make things right with Mama and Daddy, she'd probably evaporate on the spot, and then the original Nev would take over the rest of the day and cry her eyes out regardless.

You're right, I don't like either one. But let's hope it's number two.

Either way, she had to get out of this cramped, little room or she was going to lose what was left of her marbles. Should she get in her rental car and drive out to Albion to visit her parents? But what if the strain on the timeline caused the web to collapse, and she glitched out permanently before she even made it to the funeral? She'd never get the chance to make amends with Mama and Daddy, then, and they'd never call her in San Francisco, and maybe she'd never get closer to Airin, and the cascade of possible ramifications was too dizzying to consider.

No, visiting her parents was not an option. Instead, she'd spend the day exploring the landscape of her youth, interacting with as few people as possible. Don't strain the web. Just walk gently with light spider feet along the strands of memory and time. Put away childish things. Wipe the dark glass clear. Know, and be known, for once.

She ordered breakfast up to the room. The Lumberjack Plate. Eggs, bacon, breakfast links, sausage patty, potatoes, toast, and pancakes. Enough calories to fuel a day.

There was an old, out-of-commission train track that ran alongside the south fork of the Palouse River, from Pullman north to Albion, passing through copses of hawthorne shrubs and wild roses, skirting the occasional farmhouse and barn, but keeping well clear of planted fields, before it passed by the cemetery on the outskirts of town where Grandma was now freshly buried. Back when Nev had worked reception at the motel, she'd scheduled birdwatching tours along the tracks for guests. Lots of hawks and herons and woodpeckers took refuge in the shady groves.

In Albion, kids used to get high down by the tracks. Nev had longed to join them before she left home, but Mama and Daddy kept too sharp an eye on her, and she never got the chance. Later, she made up for lost time. Crothers dorm, where she spent her first year away from home, was basically opaque with vape plumes and bong smoke from 5pm to midnight. Yet, she still felt as though she'd missed out on something important, something formative. She wondered if the local kids still hung out by the tracks. There still wasn't a damned thing to do in Albion, so they probably did.

Why not find out for herself? Nev imagined walking up to a kid half her age and asking for a puff of whatever backyard ganja they were passing around between them. Or maybe it would be the kids she'd gone to school with, now pushing thirty like she was, still spending their Saturdays scrawling graffiti and goofing off together. In Albion, it was almost believable. Time never seemed to pass here. At least not as fast as it did on the coast, further from her center of gravity.

But of course, time was passing. Had passed. Would pass. And maybe Albion was the same as it ever was, but she herself had changed, even since the last time she'd woken up at the motel—so recently, and so long ago. Last time, she was alone, proudly and fiercely independent, glad to be making the final, definitive break from her family and past. This time, she felt as tender and needy as a newborn. And oh, so lonely. But that loneliness was a gift she'd earned, and her sacrifice would be her gift in return. She wouldn't switch back, even if such a thing were possible. She'd become capable of loving, and worthy of being loved. Seen herself reflected like a gorgeous supernova in the twin galaxies of Airin's eyes, and surrendered herself completely to their gravity.

Nev found herself wishing, as she had every day for weeks, that she could remember their lost night together. Wishing that she'd gotten to kiss Airin's beautiful mouth before the first megaglitch had struck, making it hideously clear to them both that they were living in a tragedy, not a love story. But what if they had kissed that night, and just didn't remember it? Or what if the megaglitch had happened an hour later, or not at all? Would that really change anything? Would it change Nev's feelings, or Airin's? Would it change her pastfuture, or change what she needed to do in the dwindling futurepast, before it all ended and began?

Of course not. Their love was real. It had happened. Would

happen. And nothing would change that now. Besides, Nev realized, as fucked up as her timeline with Airin might be, their story wasn't really so different than that of any other lovers. Nobody except for an unlucky few had perfect recall of their entire lives. How many kisses did 'normal' couples forget over the course of their lives together? How many forgettable nights had she shared with Jared, during their long and shallow romance? What did it matter whether her lips and Airin's had ever touched, when she still carried them in her heart?

It would probably take Nev two and a half hours to reach the cemetery on foot. She could go visit Faith's and Grandma's graves, and still return in time for a late afternoon swim in the Holiday Inn pool. The weather was sunny and dry, but there was a pleasant breeze coming off the river, and there wasn't a thing in the world Nev would rather do with her day. Well, maybe one, but that door was closed for now. Or hadn't opened yet.

She bought a bottle of water in the lobby gift shop then stepped out into the warm Albion morning.

QT.59.11.08.25.08.2045

THE SUN SLANTED through the crack between the room's brown curtains, laying a bright beam right across Nev's eyes. She opened them just enough to see miniature rainbows nestled between her lashes like snowflakes, then shut them again and pulled the sheets up over her head. She cinched them tight, looking through the sunlit linen tunnel at her feet, flexing and pointing each in turn.

I should have spent the whole Glitch at a hotel.

Something about this place made it easier. Maybe it was the timeless furnishings; the room looked exactly as it had when she'd worked here, back in the early '30s. Maybe it was the fact that everything reset each day, whichever direction you were moving in: New soap, new shampoo, spotless floor, freshly made bed. Maybe it was just that rooms like this were designed to be temporary stopping points, a place for goodbyes.

The funeral was scheduled for 10:30am, with a lunch afterwards at Grandma's, where a dozen families would bring two dozen covered casseroles. Last time through today, the funeral had ended in a screaming match, and Nev hadn't stuck around long enough to see whether Mrs. Waltheim's banana candle salad still had a cherry on the top.

Today would be different. There would be no screaming match, she hoped. Though Nev still probably wouldn't make it to lunch.

Last time through, Nev had done her best to look the part Christina had cast her in: A cosmopolitan stranger from Babylon on the Bay, wearing a little black dress and designer shades, sticking out like an alien beacon plunked down in the dust and grit of the little country cemetery. The outfit was calculated to offend, to enrage. A declaration of independence from Albion and everything it represented.

Fortunately, she'd packed a few different options, and today Nev chose to wear an unassuming indigo sundress, with a pair of plain black leather sandals and no sunglasses. Muted, respectful, down-to-Earth. She hoped. Before leaving the room, she made a quick search for her mystery stone, but couldn't find it in any of the familiar places. Not on the dresser next to her hair-ties. Not in the bed, under her pillow. Not in her pockets. Why did it have to vanish at the precise moment when she most needed something solid to hold on to?

The Holiday Inn still had its make-your-own waffle bar, with a limitless supply of crispy bacon, concentrated orange juice, drip coffee, and styrofoamy scrambled eggs. Nev ate downstairs today, helping herself to a giant portion of each. Not what she would have chosen for her last meal, but somehow more appropriate than omakase from Sushi Fukuoka or the King Henry VIII Cut from The House of Prime Rib. When she was done, she went back upstairs to her room and freshened up, emptying her wallet to leave all the cash for the maids (who she knew for a fact were criminally underpaid), then headed out to the rental car and drove to the cemetery.

The scene was exactly as she remembered it, two months ago, ten minutes from now. Always and never. Christina was standing next to the casket, stony faced and clear-eyed, lower lip quivering minutely with the effort of keeping her emotions in check. Daddy was next to her, arms hanging limply at his sides, looking like he wished he had a tool in his hands so he'd know what to do with them. Various members of her mother's flock and friends of Grandma's milled about, offering condolences and prayers and speaking softly to one another. There was no preacher; Christina would serve as both grieving daughter and placating pastor.

Nev wanted desperately to walk over and give her a hug. Maybe the assembled well-wishers couldn't see past Christina's resolute facade, but Nev knew her mother's pain when she saw it. She couldn't risk it, though. Couldn't risk the chance of a pre-funeral blowout, couldn't risk glitching out by messing with the timeline. Not yet. Instead, she did as she had done the first time through: Stood by the side of a nearby mausoleum, close enough to be in Christina's line of sight, but out of easy earshot.

It happened exactly the same as the first time. Christina looked up from a parishioner's face and saw her. Her reddish gray brows lowered like storm clouds as they locked eyes, and Daddy turned to follow her gaze. His face was a mix of joy, sorrow, and mute frustration. He looked sober, Nev realized. She wasn't sure whether she'd registered that the first time through. Despite herself, she gave them a tight smile and waved. Daddy started to raise his hand to wave back, but lowered it again when he saw Christina's storm clouds darken.

After what felt like an hour but was probably all of two seconds, Christina broke eye contact, turning to greet another mourner with a put-on smile that said 'Christ shouldered his burden, so I can shoulder mine.' She didn't look back over at Nev throughout the rest of the service, though Matthew frequently snuck a glance.

Christina's eulogy was beautiful. The last time through, Nev had been so caught up in her own rage and remorse that she hadn't noticed. It just sounded like blah blah blah bible bible bible to her ears. But her mother wasn't simply parroting scripture. Nev could hear how she spoke through it, cut and pasted selected lines and verses into what she now realized was a graceful rhapsody, a lament to loss and joyous declaration of hope that was simultaneously personal and universal. It was like hearing a great vocalist freestyling, or watching a dancer improvise. Nev found herself wondering who Christina could have been if she'd been the one to escape to the coast. If she'd had a chance to be an artist. Then again, she seemed to find her congregation and her life in Albion fulfilling. Who was Nev to judge?

Four or five mourners, mostly old friends of Grandma's, offered their memories and prayers. Nev knew she'd heard them, probably word for word, the last time she'd lived through this day, but she didn't remember any of it, except for a story Mrs. Elwood told about the time Grandma had sat by her bedside after an operation. The stories were sweet, but after Christina's eulogy, they sounded plain, shallow even. Finally, the well-wishers began to get into their cars and drive off to the reception. Christina and Matthew remained alone at the gravesite, speaking quietly to one another.

Now. This is the moment.

Nev walked over. All this time, and she still didn't know where to begin.

"How dare you show your face here? In this sacred place?" Christina fired her first salvo before Nev had even reached the grave.

"Hi, Daddy. Hi, Mama."

Matthew put his hands gingerly on her upper arms and gave her a quick kiss before his wife could intercede. His grip felt weak, his fingers stiff.

"No! No, you cannot suddenly"—for a change, Christina seemed to be at a loss for the right words—"*appear* before us, like some, like some, I don't know, *ghost* out of the past and, and, think that... Where *were* you, Neveah?"

"Mama, I..."

"Where were you when your grandmother, God rest her, who took you in when you were a lost soul, who gave you shelter and comfort, and more love than she had to spare, was *dying in her bed?!*"

Christina was screaming now, so loud Matthew had to cover his ears. It felt like a blast of desert wind in Nev's face, and she could feel her blood approaching boiling point. She instinctually started to trigger her SavePoint, then stopped herself.

Not yet.

But why hadn't she done it the first time? Why had Nev allowed things to get so bad between her and her mother before the Glitch ever happened? Why hadn't she hit the undo button the moment her mother had screamed at her, or at least the moment she'd screamed back? Situations like this were exactly what SavePoint was designed to fix, as Nev knew better than almost anyone. A chance to start over, try something new.

The answer was obvious, and terrible: she hadn't wanted to. Once Grandma was dead, Nev wanted nothing more to do with Albion, with her parents, with her past. She *wanted* to fight with Christina at the funeral. It was a validation, a final rite of passage. A definitive break that could not be unbroken. No wonder her mother had given up.

"We don't need you here. We don't want you here! Go back—"

God, I've been so selfish!

"What?" Christina was staring at her, gaping. She actually looked like she'd seen a ghost.

Nev hadn't meant to say it aloud, but somehow she had. And now that the words were hanging in the heavy summer air between them, she was glad.

"I said, I've been selfish, Mama. You're right. And I'm so sorry. I should have been here for Grandma. I should have been here for you." She turned to face her father. "For both of you. And there's nothing I can do about it. I can't—I can't go back and fix the past.

"But I can apologize. If it's not too late. And I can tell you both that, even though I'll never be a believer in your Church, I have found something to believe in. A meaning, and a purpose. Love.

And I can't save everyone. I couldn't save Jim Bone. I couldn't even save myself. But I've saved a lot of people, I think. From something horrible. I don't expect you to understand, but that's okay. What's important is that you know I love you. And—and I forgive you."

"What?" It seemed to be the only word Christina Bourne still possessed.

"I said, I forgive you, Mama. And you too, Daddy. For letting Faith die. I was so angry. For so long. But I'm not angry any more. I know you did what you thought was right, and I didn't understand. But now I do. I couldn't save her, either, any more than I could save myself. When I took off all those years ago, it didn't bring her back, it just cost you another daughter, and it cost me my family. I should have shared in your grief, not added to it. I was thoughtless and cruel, and I am so very sorry and ashamed. I wish I could go back and do it all over, but I can't fix that now. The past is past. But, for what it's worth, I forgive you. And I hope you'll forgive me, too."

These are the words my mother told me I'd say. These words are true.

Then, the three of them were embracing, for the first time Nev could remember. It lasted forever. It was over before she knew it. Christina backed away, brushing her dress off absently and looking at Nev with a tenderness she'd missed more than she knew.

"We should get back to Grandma's. Will we see you there?"

"I'm sorry, Mama, Daddy. I... I don't think I can join you for the reception. There's something I need to do. But I'll talk to you real soon, okay? I promise. I'll call you next week."

Christina looked like she had something to say, then seemed to think better of it.

"Ok, Nevaeh, we'll talk to you soon."

Goodbye Mama, goodbye Daddy. Nev whispered to herself the words she couldn't say out loud, as Matthew and Christina walked away, leaning on each other for strength.

She lingered at her grandmother's grave for an extra breath, gathering herself for what came next. A glint of sunlight from the fresh-turned dirt of her grandmother's grave caught Nev's eye. A smooth, flat, round, grey pebble. She leaned over and picked it up, clenching the stone close against her heart as she walked back in the direction of the parking lot. She passed behind the mausoleum and stopped, leaning against its cool marble in the shade of some water birches. The thought of Grandma and Faith buried nearby gave her strength. They were gone, but not gone. They existed as she existed, in moments of time that were neither before nor after. They were all together in those moments where they were all together. A slight breeze had started, and she heard her parents' prayers on it, wafting over like music.

This is the moment.

As she triggered her SavePoint, she could just barely hear their words:

"...and we thank you for the return of our beloved Nevaeh."

Acknowledgments

WHEN WE WERE little, we used to put on plays together, making up stories to perform for our suffering families. To recapture that collaborative creative energy by writing this story together during the height of COVID social isolation was an incredible gift and kept us sane.

So much of our lives together as siblings, then and now, has been shared through the medium of stories, and we are deeply indebted to the thousands of authors who conjured their characters, plots, settings, and perspectives into existence, and in so doing, created spaces for us to play and places to explore. Nothing could make us happier than to expand the terrain a little further, making room for others to dream their dreams, live their lives, and tell their stories too.

Of course we'd like to thank our parents, Masha Zager, Jonathan Sinnreich, and Emily Pines, for reading our fiction from the very beginning. And we mean the very beginning: from "Max the Detective" (Rachel's third-grade novella about a detective dog) and Aram's second-grade story about traveling the world on a water-gun with wheels, onwards.

Rachel thanks her husband Tim and her kids Eli and Maya for reading drafts and giving great feedback and for taking walks with her and talking about her ideas for stories and giving her their ideas (many of which make it to the page). She also thanks Solace Cooper for being so attached to Nev and Airin (sorry about that).

Aram thanks his wife Dunia, the best romantic and creative partner an artist could hope for, and our children, Simon, and Asha, who seem to take it for granted that their dad can write and publish books—an article of faith that has helped me to believe in myself.

Two people who owed us nothing and stood to gain nothing except helping to usher another book into the world gave us the gift of reading the draft manuscript in its entirety, and offering us concrete, actionable feedback. Virginia Scharff and Stephanie Grant: thank you. This book is far better for having your eyes on it, and we promise to pay your kindness forward. Along similar lines, thank you to all the authors who took the time and care to read the finished manuscript before publication and offer their endorsements on our cover. We are honored to be welcomed into your company.

Finally, we'd like to thank the people who helped us bring this book out of our heads and into the world: Our tireless, dedicated, and supportive agent Jennie Goloboy; acquiring editor Jim Killen at Rebellion who said YES after we'd heard so much no; and our editor Amy Borsuk and copy editor Charlotte Bond, who read this book more closely than anyone else probably ever will, unsnarled more than a few temporal paradoxes, and helped us bare Nev's heart for all to see. We learned so much from working with you, and we are profoundly grateful.

FIND US ONLINE!

www.rebellionpublishing.com

/solarisbooks   /solarisbks   /solarisbooks

SIGN UP TO OUR NEWSLETTER!

rebellionpublishing.com/newsletter

YOUR REVIEWS MATTER!

Enjoy this book? Got something to say?

Leave a review on Amazon, Goodreads or with your
favourite bookseller and let the world know!